ACCORDING TO CHEKHOV

Thoughts on the Writing of *Uncle Vanya*

By Motti Lerner

Translated from Hebrew by Lior Yatsiv

Edited by Michael Posnick

NoPassport Press

According to Chekhov by Motti Lerner
© 2014, 2011 by Motti Lerner

This text was originally published in Hebrew by
Mofet Institute, Tel Aviv 2011.

NoPassport Press
PO Box 1786, South Gate, CA 90280 USA
www.nopassport.org, NoPassportPress@aol.com

First Edition.
ISBN: 978-1-312-75667-0

ACCORDING TO CHEKHOV

By

Motti Lerner

Motti Lerner – About the Author

Playwright and screenwriter, born in Israel in 1949, teaches playwriting at the Kibbutz College in Tel Aviv. Most of his plays and films deal with political issues. Among his plays are: **"Kastner**", **"Pangs of the Messiah**", **"Paula**", and **"Pollard**", all produced by the Cameri Theatre of Tel Aviv; **"Exile in Jerusalem**" and **"Passing The Love of Women**" at Habima National Theatre, **"Autumn**" at the Beit Lessin Theatre, Tel Aviv, **"Hard Love**" at the Municipal Theatre in Haifa, and **"The Hastening of The End**" in the Khan Theatre in Jerusalem. His play **"The Murder of Isaac**" was produced at Heilbron Theatre in Germany (1999) in Centerstage Theatre in Baltimore (2006), and at Tel Aviv University Theatre (2013), **"Benedictus**" was produced by Golden Thread Theatre in San Francisaco (2007) and Theater J (2009), **"In the Dark**" by Chingari Theatre in Delhi (2011) , **"Paulus**" by Silk Road Rising theater in Chicago (2013), and **"The Admission**" in Theater J in Washington DC (2014). He wrote the screenplays for the films: **"Loves in Betania**", **"The Kastner Trial**", **"Bus Number 300**", **"Egoz**", the 12 episodes of the TV drama series **"The Institute**", **"A Battle in Jerusalem**", **"The Silence of the Sirens**", **Altalena**, **"Spring 1941**" and **"Kapo in Jerusaelm**". He is a recipient of the best play award (1985), and the Israeli Motion Picture Academy award for the best TV drama in 1995 and in 2004. He won the Prime Minister's of Israel Award for his creative work (1994) and the Landau prize for the performing arts

(2014). His plays have been produced in the US, Germany, Switzerland, Italy, Austria, South Africa, Australia, Canada and India. His book **According To Chekhov** - on Chekhov's writing method - was published in 2011. His book **"The Playwright's Purpose"** will be published in 2015. He taught playwriting at Duke University, North Carolina 1997, Knox College, Illinois 2005, 2007, 2012 and was a fellow at the Institute of Advanced Studies at Jawaharlal Nehru University, New Delhi 2010.

Table of Contents

Introduction

Introduction

This book is an act of love — a belated love, yet one that has grown over many years. I first read *Uncle Vanya* in 1975 during my undergraduate studies and found it artificial and boring. The characters seemed distant, the plot static, the dialogue banal. However, in 1989, while preparing to teach a course in playwriting at the Drama School of the Kibbutzim College of Education in Israel, I returned to the play and my eyes were opened. I had just turned forty and it seemed to me that only then was I mature enough to appreciate this complex, seasoned play. As a playwright and teacher of theatre, I have read hundreds of plays over the years and can say with confidence that *Uncle Vanya* holds a unique position. I study it with my students nearly every year and continue to discover depth and complexity previously unknown -- hidden character motivations and precise, sophisticated dramaturgy, which attest to the playwright's exceptional skill.

As with any book written out of love, this work cannot be viewed purely as an academic or scholarly text. It makes no attempt to analyze the play according to the tools of traditional dramatic scholarship nor from the current rubrics of literary or theatre criticism. This is a personal book, offering a personal interpretation rooted in the writer's naïve trust in his own instincts – and in his love of the material. I thus urge my readers not to consider what I have written as a definitive interpretation, but rather as a starting point for discussion.

This book is not only an interpretation of the play *Uncle Vanya*, but also an attempt to decode Chekhov's thought process as a playwright. While we can never know what the master was thinking while writing this play, I hope that I have managed to identify certain recurring dramatic patterns that attest to the existence of a method.

The terminology used in this book grew out of the need to define a discursive language to explore certain questions regarding the writing of a play. This book does not offer a comprehensive playwriting language; however, it does attempt to outline the grammatical foundations for such a language. I hope that in time, playwrights and scholars will find this language useful and will continue to enhance and improve upon its clarity and efficacy. The terminology was initiated in a series of meetings for theater professionals, directors, actors, playwrights and scholars, hosted by Professor Yossi Yizraeli, in Tel Aviv between 1990 and 1993. However, the vocabulary matured in subsequent years while I was teaching playwriting at the Kibbutzim College and at Tel Aviv University. I am grateful to Professor Yizraeli and the participants of the forum he hosted, and also to the hundreds of students, who have had to listen to me deliberate and ponder these terms, altering them each year, until they were found to reflect my understanding of playwriting.

While I hope this book will be of use to all theater practitioners, it is primarily intended for playwrights, in an attempt to share some thoughts about the art of playwriting through the analysis of Chekhov's method, as I imagine it. It is not a playwriting manual, nor does it offer instruction on how to write a play. It does, however, provide precise terminology and a vocabulary, which I hope will enhance discussion of the principles of playwriting and inspire the process of play development. For all other theater practitioners – actors, directors, dramaturges and students of theatre - whose work involves the search for keys to decipher this challenging art in order to hone their own professional theatrical skills, the book can offer direction and guidance. And for those theatre artists fortunate enough to be engaged in productions of Chekhov's plays, especially *Uncle Vanya*, reading this book might well create new understanding of character and plot, and provide tools for creative discussion throughout rehearsal process.

Last but not least, I believe this book will be helpful for teachers of playwriting. Since the publication of the Hebrew edition in 2011, it has become an invaluable resource in structuring my courses in advanced playwriting.

The book contains five chapters and a glossary. The first four chapters deal with the characters, their relationships and the plot as it unfolds over the course of the four acts of the play. Chapter five analyzes the ways in which Chekhov creates the dramatic structure for his play: exposition, plot development, catharsis, etc. The short glossary at the end is intended to assist the reader in navigating the dramaturgical language and terminology. Since the book contains many references to passages in the play, I recommend having *Uncle Vanya*[1] handy while reading.

This book could not have been written without the generous support of the Mofet Institute - Research, Curriculum, and Program Development for Teacher Educators in Tel Aviv, which allowed me the time to write; nor would it have been possible without Dr. Judith Shteiman, Chief Editor and Publication Manager of the Mofet Institute, who demonstrated the understanding and sensitivity necessary for such a comprehensive endeavor. I would like to give special thanks to Professors Gad Kaynar and Harai Golomb of Tel Aviv University for overseeing the writing process from the start, and for being involved in the many deliberations throughout. Without their wisdom, scholarly judgment and advice, I would not have been able to complete this process. Last but not least, many thanks Lior Yatziv for her careful translation and to Professor Michael Posnick, whose editing skills made this book accessible to the English reader.

---

[1] Translated by Marina Brodskaya, published by Stanford University Press, 2010

That being said, the responsibility for all that is written in these pages is mine alone.

Motti Lerner
Tel Aviv, Spring 2014

Chapter 1: Act 1

External Actions

The garden of a country estate. In the courtyard, under an old poplar, a table is set for tea and next to it, garden seats and chairs. A guitar rests on one of the chairs and a swing is nearby. It is three o'clock on a cloudy afternoon. Marina, the old nurse, sits next to the samovar knitting a stocking. Astrov, a doctor who has been called to treat Professor Serebryakov, the owner of the estate, paces nearby.[2] The garden is very peaceful. Marina pours Astrov a glass of tea. He takes it reluctantly but does not drink. A moment later, she offers him some vodka. Astrov refuses, adding, "I don't drink vodka every day" (p. 116). Marina, who knows him well, is aware that he is lying and probably chuckles to herself. He senses this, avoids reacting and instead complains about the sultry weather. We later learn that these two characters are awaiting the return of Serebryakov, Yelena Andreyevna, Sonya, Marya Vassilyevna and Telegin, all of whom have gone for a walk around the estate.

These are the *external actions* of the two characters, which reveal to the spectator initial information regarding the events unfolding on stage. The external actions of the characters are those actions

---

[2] This description is based on Chekhov's opening stage directions for *Uncle Vanya*, *Chekhov:Five Plays*, Marina Brodskaya trans., 2010

that are visible to the spectator. This term will be discussed in further detail below.

The spectator has just been introduced to the two characters and information about them is still very limited. However, as we examine the scene in light of events to follow, we will see that Chekhov, prior to writing a single word, possessed a deep familiarity with these characters and invested great effort in their formation and in the roles they will play. The abundance of detail about the characters and their integration into a coherent picture reveal that they populated his mind long before coming to life in the play.[3]

What did Chekhov know about Marina's internal process before writing this scene?

Let us look at Marina's response to Vanya's entrance[4] a few minutes later in the scene:

---

[3] Some of the main characters in the play appear in Chekhov's earlier work, *The Wood Demon*, written in 1889, about seven years before *Uncle Vanya*, first mentioned by Chekhov in 1896. However, a comparison of the two plays reveals that Chekhov saw *Uncle Vanya* as a new play, for which he reconceived the plot, the characters and their relationships. The discussion in this book also relies on the assumption that *Uncle Vanya* is, indeed, a new play written by a more experienced playwright, with stronger and more solid dramaturgical insights, which deserves a separate discussion.

[4] Vanya is the nickname of Ivan Petrovitch Voynitsky.

"Some customs! The professor gets up at noon, and the samovar's been boiling all morning, just waiting for him. Before they got here, we used to sit down to eat at noon, like everybody, but now it's after six. At night, the professor reads and writes, and then, around one in the morning, out of the blue, there goes the bell... Heavens, what is it? Tea! Wake everyone up for him, start the samovar... Some customs!" (P. 117)

Marina is complaining. This is her *external* action. She is frustrated and angry at the new 'customs' on the estate. Because of her age, she finds it difficult to adjust to this new order. Similar concerns are echoed in the characters of Anfisa in *Three Sisters* and Firs in *The Cherry Orchard*. Chekhov stresses in his stage directions that Marina is "a pudgy, slow-moving old peasant woman" (p. 116). She has been concerned about her physical decline long before Serebryakov and his wife settled on the estate.[5] Her worries certainly have worsened in the two hours preceding the start of the play, while she was sitting impatiently by the samovar awaiting the return of Serebryakov and his entourage. Although Marina does not speak directly about her age, it is reasonable to surmise her concerns from the nature of her complaints. Chekhov must have known this while he was writing the stage directions for the opening of the play. Otherwise, he wouldn't have

---

[5] According to Vanya (p. 117).

15

known what led her to voice her complaints so vociferously later on (p. 116).

The necessity to define the internal action of a character

Let us look at Marina at the beginning of the scene. Marina's *physical actions* are: waiting, sitting, knitting, offering a cup of tea. Her *external action* is to appease and calm Astrov. When she offers him vodka – another physical action – her external action remains the same - to appease and calm him. Later, when Vanya enters, she complains. That is her external action, which she carries out by the physical action of speaking. In other words, the *external* action is the meaning of the *physical* actions.

But there is a huge gap between Marina's physical and external actions and the storm that rages inside her. Chekhov does not settle for an examination of the characters' external actions, but rather explores an inner level of activity, which is not visible to the viewer, but which penetrates the viewer's consciousness and emotions while he is watching the characters' external actions. This internal process is always the more meaningful one for Chekhov. We must therefore define a term that will help us understand it.

Chekhov's development as a playwright grew primarily through his collaboration with theater director, Constantin Stanislavski, who emphasized the idea that the actor's craft is based on action. In turn, Chekhov, himself, realized that action is also the basis of the playwright's craft. Thus we observe that Chekhov planned the events of his plays to reveal both external and internal levels via actions.[6]

At the beginning of the play, Marina's external actions are very clear: she sits waiting for the return of Serebryakov and his entourage, she tries to appease Astrov with a cup of tea, while he paces impatiently near her. When he rejects her offer, she offers him vodka.

How can we understand Marina's *internal process* as an action, as well? It is clear that Marina feels anger and frustration because of the deviations from routine on the estate and her concern that she may not be able to adapt to these changes. Her complaints attest to the fact that she yearns for the restoration of the old order and, more important, that the perceived threat to her well-being be removed. She yearns to be relieved of the fear that, useless and unwanted in old age, she might be cast away. This yearning is **her internal action**. Despite its 'invisibility', this action is powerful, important and can be clearly felt. If the actress playing Marina manages to realize this internal action, she will consequently experience and express the same emotions experienced by Marina - the aforementioned anger, frustration and concern.

---

[6] See Stanislavski, 1963, pp 62-68

17

The essential examination of action as the basis for the playwright's and the actor's craft is not surprising. In *The Poetics*, Aristotle writes:<u>*"the objects the imitator represents are actions"*</u> (Chapter 2). And later, leaving no room for doubt, *"Tragedy is essentially an imitation not of persons but of action and life, of happiness and misery. All human happiness and/or misery takes the form of action; the end for which we live is a certain kind of activity, not a quality. Characters give us qualities, but it is in our actions we are happy or the reverse"* (Chapter 6).

Aristotle doesn't distinguish between external and internal actions; rather he uses the term *praxis*, meaning "the motivation that drives the character to act, and the deeds that stem from this motivation" (Halperin, 1977). It may be that Aristotle preferred using a term that unified the external and internal actions because the gap between these two kinds of action was not evident in the plays available to him. In Chekhov's plays, on the other hand, these gaps are highly meaningful. In fact, the essential dramatic life of his plays depends on them.

It is important to note that a character's internal action is different from the widely used term **subtext.** An internal action is the character's primary motivating force. Subtext is the unspoken meaning of a spoken text, which the character chooses not to spell out, in hopes that the listener will recognize it beneath the text. Thus, subtext is the means by which an **external** action, rather than

18

an internal action, is carried out. The connection between the subtext and the internal action is indirect.

Let us review the way in which we identified Marina's internal action. At first, we observed her external actions and then tried to understand the source of her distress. Recognizing her anger, frustration and concern, we discerned that her internal action was the yearning to break free of her emotional anguish. That would be possible, of course, if the routine of the estate were to be reinstated. In general, a character's internal action usually involves the yearning for internal distress to be dissipated.

Did Chekhov consider these terms while constructing Marina's character? We cannot say for sure. He may have built his characters intuitively, but we must keep in mind that in his collaboration with Stanislavski, a methodical and highly opinionated director, terms such as these may have been discussed and even defined. Either way, as we analyze Chekhov's plays in order to learn about his writing processes, these terms will be useful in order to understand his thinking, intuitive as it may have been.

Did Marina exist in Chekhov's mind as a whole character with a full biography? This, too, is difficult to say. It is clear that he held a few basic assumptions about her, which are expressed from the first moments of the play. For example, during the conversation between Marina and Astrov at the start of the play, Astrov says, *"I don't love anybody… Well, with the exception of you, of course.* [He kisses her on the head.] *When I was little, I had a nanny like you"* (pp. 116-117). Both Astrov's words and the kiss indicate a closeness between himself and Marina, despite their differences in age and social status. Marina's amazing ability to calm Serebryakov in Act 2 (pp. 128-129) and Sonya at the end of Act 3 (p. 150), reflects the trust in which she is held by the family - trust that she has earned through decades of devoted work and complete selflessness. I tend to assume that the lack of concrete biographical information about Marina illustrates the fact that Chekhov did not need more detail in order to justify her actions.[7] Marina's character was a part of him, an archetype, so well-known to Chekhov, his actors and his audience, that there was no need to drawn her in detail. We, on the other hand, who are unfamiliar with late 19th century Russian culture, need to make an extra effort to construct Marina's character more fully than Chekhov did. Later we will see that Telegin and Marya Vassilyevna, both minor characters like Marina, lack the fully developed biographies Chekhov provides for his main characters.

---

[7] We will later discuss the connection between a character's biography and its actions.

What did Chekhov know about Astrov's internal process before writing this scene?

Since Astrov affects the plot more than Marina does, Chekhov clearly knew much more about him. We begin by observing Astrov's external actions at the beginning of Act 1. He has been called to the estate to tend to Professor Serebryakov and, when he arrives, he discovers that his patient has gone for a walk. Despite being a busy doctor, working from sunrise to sunset and sometimes into the night - he tells us that he lies under the bedclothes in continual terror of being dragged out to a patient (p. 116), - he continues to wait, in a seemingly idle state. We later discover that, in truth, he is waiting because he wants to feast his eyes on Serebryakov's wife, Yelena, with whom he had fallen in love during his last three visits (p. 133). However, this is only a partial description. Astrov admits to Marina that he is tired and, despite the fact that according to Yelena, he is only thirty-six or thirty-seven years old (p. 137), he bemoans his premature aging. He speaks about his boredom, his disappointment in himself for being odd and the dullness of his emotions. Later, he also painfully confesses that three months earlier, during the third week of the Lenten fast,[8] a signalman from the railroad died on the operating table after he had sedated him with chloroform. This event haunts him and he says that his conscience tortures him as though he had killed

---

[8] The play itself opens in mid-summer, while the incident described by Astrov occurred about three months earlier during the Lenten season.

the man on purpose, (Note the similarity to Dr. Chebutykin's feelings about the woman who dies in his care in *Three Sisters* (p. 198)).

Waiting for Yelena is Astrov's external action, but it is secondary to the action of confession, on which he is focused and around which his thoughts revolve.[9] However, despite the weight of his confession, which is also an external action, we will soon see that the internal process happening within him is far more profound.

What is the underlying source or motivation for his confession? We can assume that Astrov confesses because his feelings of failure, lack of fulfillment, boredom and disappointment weigh heavily on him, and have done so long before the day on which the play opens. The death of the signalman exacerbates his feeling of failure and accelerates his attempts at soul-searching. Now, while waiting with Marina, Astrov has time to engage in the process of self-examination more intensely. Here we have a powerful example of an internal action – the yearning to relieve his feelings of distress and to alleviate his guilt over the accidental death of the signal-man, which signals his failure as a doctor. It is for this reason that he so desperately needs Marina's encouragement. He asks her, *"Have I changed much since then?"* (p. 116), fully expecting

---

[9] The use of the word "thoughts" is intentional. Simply put, the external action takes place in the mind whereas the internal action takes place inside the heart.

her to answer that he has not changed since they had met. However, she doesn't make things easier for him and tells him the truth: *"Very much. You were young and handsome then and you've grown old now. Your looks aren't what they used to be. And you drink vodka now, too"* (p. 116). Astrov longs for comfort and receives none. He admits that he loves nobody but confides to Marina that, in fact, he may only love her. He needs her love and especially her compassion. Though this is not obvious in the text, it can be intuited. His yearning can also be seen in his final words to Marina, when he asks, *"Those who'll live a hundred or two hundred years after us and for whom we're now paving the way, will they remember us kindly?"* (p. 117). Astrov may be concerned about how he will be perceived by the next generations,[10] but it seems as though he is far more interested in his own opinions of himself. According to the standards he has set for himself at this point in his life, he has apparently earned a very low score in self-esteem

Dramatic Compression

It is useful to note that Chekhov does not create Astrov's internal action in this first scene, but makes it clear that it has existed long before the beginning of the play. When the scene opens, the internal action is already working powerfully within him, as though it were compressed by a

---

[10] It is for this reason that he is involved in protecting the forests (pp. 123-124). We later see that he is a man of deep social responsibility.

piston in the limited space of his heart. The principal of **compression**,[11] by which each character enters a scene with a powerful motivating internal action, is essential to Chekhov. This is not only important for his main characters, in whom the processes of compression have begun long before their first entrance, but it also applies to secondary characters such as Marina. Since Chekhov takes such care to present the internal actions of his characters at the beginning of each scene, this group of actions can be defined as **the compression of a scene**.[12]

As we have previously observed in the dialogue between Marina and Astrov in the opening of the scene, Chekhov also meticulously defines the characters' **external actions**. We will call this grouping of external actions **the convergence of a**

---

[11] The principal of **compression was developed** by my teacher and friend, Prof. Yossi Yizraeli, whose insight regarding dramatic mechanisms has been an inspiration to me. However, Prof. Yizraeli uses the term to describe the compression of the events of a "whole world" condensed into a two-hour theatrical event. It is possible that the term "expositional saturation of a character" that he uses is closer to the term **compression** that I use in this book. (See Prof. Yizraeli's definitions in an interview with Prof. Gad Kaynar in "Teatron" (June 2000), 2, 64-65)

[12] I use the term compression in three different ways: a *compressed action* describes an action that intensifies over the course of the play; a *compressed character* is one who contains or is driven by a compressed internal action; and the *compression of a scene*, which refers to the assemblage of internal actions held in the characters at the beginning of a scene.

scene because it describes how and why the characters assemble for the scene.

In order to define Astrov's internal action at the beginning of the play, we must first become familiar with his biography, which is the source of this internal action. The biography of a character refers to his history and includes many details about his family, childhood, youth, etc. However, not all of these biographical details are relevant to the playwright. Only those elements that contribute to and generate the compressed internal actions of the character are included. We will call this carefully selected collection of details **the dramatic biography of a character.**[13] A close examination of the characters in *Uncle Vanya* reveals that Chekhov uses their dramatic biographies as a powerful tool to justify their actions within the play.

What dramatic biography did Chekhov provide for Astrov ?

We do not learn much about Astrov's childhood from the play. We don't know where he was born. Marina mentions that he arrived in the region about eleven years previously (p. 116). We have no clear information about his family life, but we can surmise some sort of early dynamic when he later says to Marina, *"I don't love anybody" (p. 116)*. Even if Astrov's parents and/or siblings are alive, he clearly has no contact with them. The one detail

---

[13] I also learned this term from Prof. Yossi Yizraeli.

relevant to the immediate scene comes when he says to Marina, *"...when I was little, I had a nanny like you" (p. 117)*, an indication that his sole source of love and affection came from his nurse, not his mother, whom he never mentions.

Astrov was probably not born to a family of peasants. His medical education attests to the socio-economic standing of his family and to his intellectual capabilities. He also apparently visited the theater when he lived in the city. He recalls *"a character in a play by Ostrovsky, a man with a long moustache and short wits" (pp. 122-123)*. Astrov, himself, sports a big moustache, which he calls *"a stupid moustache" (p. 116)*. In the fashion of late 19th century Russia, Astrov has grown a particularly flamboyant moustache to which he attaches great meaning. He considers himself *an oddball* because of his moustache (p. 116). Chekhov gives us the impression that Astrov cultivates his moustache in order to laugh at his own strangeness. It reminds him not to become arrogant or proud, since, in his view of himself, he is no better than the "short witted" character in Ostrovsky's play. His over-sized, 'stupid' moustache defines his identity in much the same way as Salvador Dali or Groucho Marx made use of theirs. This small but important biographical detail illustrates Chekhov's insistence on constructing Astrov's character without excess sentimentality or self-pity, providing, instead, a dose of irony and self-awareness to neutralize these elements.

Astrov lives in great loneliness, by choice, not by fate. However, he demonstrates great devotion to his patients. At the end of the first act (p. 122), he decides to leave Serebryakov's estate in order to take care of a patient, a factory-worker. He makes this decision only a few moments after being invited by Sonya to spend the night at the estate, *and* despite his desire to enjoy the company of Yelena. Could this dedication to his patients be an attempt to assuage his guilt over his failure to construct meaningful family relationships? Is his obsessive preoccupation with the forest also a byproduct of this guilt? It seems so.

In most of the scenes where Astrov appears, he is very talkative, eloquent and charming. He enjoys the sound of his own voice. Chekhov uses Astrov's verbal abilities to mask his frequent embarrassment, especially when in the presence of women. Examples of this can be seen in the first and third acts in Astrov's conversations with Yelena (pp. 124; 142), and in the second act in his conversation with Sonya (pp. 133-134). By this choice, the playwright widens the gap between the visible and the hidden, creating many layers of complexity and contradiction in the character.

Astrov's ownership of an estate tells us something about his current financial status. The estate may not be large, but it is well kept, in fact, it boasts the finest garden and nursery in the county (p. 123), a great source of pride for the doctor. The government forest that lies beside the estate is only partly cared for by an elderly, sick forester, so Astrov maintains the forest himself. Sonya says that he plants new trees every year and has even won a medal for this (p. 123). Astrov explains his concern for the forests as a means of caring for both the landscape and the future of humanity.

Forest maintenance is certainly of great ecological importance to Astrov, but it seems as though there are additional reasons for his enthusiasm. In Act 2 (pp. 131-132), he explains the reasons for his drinking to Vanya. He says that he only gets drunk once a month, but all indications point to more frequent episodes. Astrov admits that when he drinks, life seems easier to him. This statement reveals that he finds his life very difficult. Only when he drinks does he not feel odd and is able to believe that he is of immense service to humanity. Later in the play, Astrov describes the depths of his despair, blaming his provincial life and the people who surround him: *"I suffer unbearably sometimes, but I have no light in the distance. I don't expect anything for myself"* (p. 134). In light of this surprisingly honest revelation, we can now surmise that one of the reasons Astrov looks after the forest is to sublimate or overcome this terrible despair. Perhaps he clings to this activity to give meaning to his life. Astrov repeatedly confesses that he loves no one and that he never will. The absence of love in his life pains him deeply and it is highly probable that Astrov's obsessive interest in forestry serves as a substitute for human love.

It is important to emphasize these descriptions of Astrov's misery. Chekhov knew of this misery before he started to write *Uncle Vanya* and even before starting to write *The Wood Demon*, an earlier version of the play as previously mentioned.

He knew that Astrov's drinking was not merely a habit or a means of creating a friendly, social atmosphere. His drinking was the result of a conscious decision to avoid his despair. He says, *"I don't think of myself as an oddball then"*, referring to the times in which he is drunk. He continues, *"...I believe that I am bringing enormous benefit to humanity...enormous!"* (pp. 131-132). Fortunately for himself, Astrov doesn't seek relief from despair in religion. He does say to Yelena, *"God alone knows what our true calling is"* (p. 123). However, this statement sounds less a testament of faith than an ironic declaration that the mere idea that it is possible to have a purpose in life is ridiculous. Very likely, had he seen the possibility of hope in religion, he would have been quick to examine it. On the other hand, despite the fact that Chekhov may ridicule faith through Astrov, he does not deride the religious characters in the play, namely Marina, Sonya and Telegin, who remains faithful to his wife in keeping with the vows they exchanged in church (p. 120).

Despite his despair and the sense of meaninglessness in his life, Astrov is an attractive, charismatic and fascinating man. Sonya says to him, *"...you're so fine, your voice is so tender... More than that, you are, unlike anyone else I know - beautiful"* (p. 134). And Yelena says, *"sometimes he shows up, so unlike the rest — handsome, interesting, captivating, like a bright moon rising in the dark... Give in to his charm, forget yourself..."* (p. 141). These expressions of admiration by two women raise a fundamental question: why at the age of thirty-seven, has Astrov never married? He never mentions any real relationships with women throughout the play, yet, he fancies himself very experienced with the opposite sex (p. 144). The manner in which he dares to embrace Yelena and ask her to meet him the next day (p. 144) shows that he has had relationships with women in his life and yearns for more. Chekhov may be telling us that, while Astrov has had some experience with women, the relationships must have been casual, lacking intimacy and commitment. Why, despite his yearning and his need for love, has he never managed to develop any mature relationships with women? The main reason might stem from his enormous inner despair. Astrov may have often tried to develop real relationships, but his internal anguish, which he is unable to hide, engulfs the intimacy he craves. Lacking intimacy, he probably quickly grew tired of these relationships and distanced himself from the women involved. Realizing that the relationship was doomed, the woman, too, would feel the need to withdraw. Thus, an unbearably vicious cycle was created: as Astrov's despair intensified his need for love, it simultaneously distanced him from meaningful relationship.

At the start of the discussion, we determined that Chekhov built a detailed biography of Astrov in order to justify and shed light on his internal actions, particularly his terrible despair. It is useful to note that the theatrical tradition preceding Chekhov did not much consider dramatic biography an important tool. Shakespeare did not take the time to reveal the biographical details of his main characters. We know almost nothing about the biographies of Macbeth or King Lear, and we know very little about Hamlet's early life. For Chekhov, on the other hand, while the essence of character is defined by his actions, even a clearly and accurately defined character must be justified through biographical details. This approach was adopted by many playwrights at the start of the 20th century. In *Miss Julie*, Strindberg provided many important biographical details about Julie and her relationship with her parents, which, in the playwright's opinion, were the motivating force for her actions. This phenomenon was a byproduct of the development of psychology in the early 20th century. It gave playwrights, most notably, Henrik Ibsen, August Strindberg, Eugene O'Neill, Tennessee Williams and Arthur Miller, powerful tools for the examination and understanding of their characters.

How, then, does Astrov's biography explain his despair? Chekhov offers a biographical outline as follows: Astrov did not feel hopeless as a youth; on the contrary, the simple facts that he decided to become a doctor and to work in a rural area reveal that he felt great hope. He believed that people could be made happier. However, as soon as he moved to the country and attempted to realize his ideals, he faced a difficult reality, and in the decade that followed, he discovered that, while the body may sometimes return to health, society's ills cannot be cured. He stresses this on many occasions. At the start of the play, he says to Marina, *"life itself is boring, stupid, and filthy…"* (p. 116). He later tells her about the typhus epidemic in Malitskoe:

> *"In the huts, peasants are side-by-side, all in a row… The filth, the stench, the smoke, the calves are on the floor next to the sick… And the pigs are there, too…"* (P. 117).

In Act 2, he says the following to Sonya:

> *"I love life, in general, but I can't stand our Russian provincial, narrow-minded life and despise it with every fiber of my soul"* (p. 133).

In Act 3, he says the following to Yelena:

> *"I understand if the cut-down forests were being replaced by new roads, railways, plants, factories, and schools – the people would be healthier, richer, more intelligent – but there's nothing of the sort! The same swamps and mosquitoes exist in the district, the same impassable roads, abject poverty, typhus, diphtheria, fires… Here we're dealing with*

extinction as a result of a back-breaking struggle for survival" (p. 142)

Astrov came to the country with the zeal of a social revolutionary, only to discover that social revolution cannot be achieved by man. He then becomes deeply discouraged, telling Vanya in Act 4:

> *"We have but one hope. The hope that when we're sleeping in our coffins, visions, maybe even pleasant ones, will visit us"* (p. 154).

And later:

> *"Oh, well, my friend. In the whole district there used to be only two decent intelligent people: you and me. But in a mere ten years, this narrow-minded, despicable life has sucked us in; it has poisoned our blood with its rotten fumes…"* (p. 154).

These well-chosen elements of Astrov's dramatic biography by the playwright provide an accurate understanding of the causes of the doctor's despair – straight from the horse's mouth.

The External and Internal Processes in the Scene

Now that we have intuited some of what Chekhov knew about Marina and Astrov before starting to write the opening scene, let us consider the events of the scene itself. As previously noted, the two characters await the return of Serebryakov and his entourage from their walk around the estate. Marina sits by the samovar and knits, but she contains compressed bitter complaints. Astrov, who has been waiting with her for a long time, confesses his frustration. We have already discovered in these two characters meaningful internal actions: Marina yearns for relief from the anxiety that she is worthless and useless; whereas Astrov yearns to free himself of his disappointment in himself and his despair about his life. What is the relationship between these two internal actions? It is clear that Chekhov does not allow Astrov and Marina to assist each other in realizing[14] their internal actions. However, there is more here than merely lack of co-operation. In fact, the two internal actions stand in stark contrast to each other. If Astrov successfully overcomes his despair, regains hope and takes action to begin a relationship with Yelena, as he secretly desires, an even greater disorder would overtake the estate. Conversely, if Marina manages to regain her status by re-establishing the old order on the estate, the current deviations would be corrected. Astrov wouldn't dare flirt with the married Yelena and she, in turn, would remain true to her husband until the end of his days. In short, the realization of Marina's internal action would necessarily prevent Astrov from realizing his own internal action, and vice versa.

---

[14] The realization of a character's internal action is the **fulfillment of the character's desire**.

We have now come to the all-important term "conflict", well known to us from various facets of our lives. Defined as a theatrical term, a **conflict between two characters is the contradiction between their internal actions**. This contradiction means that the realization of the internal action of one character will not allow for the realization of the other, and vice versa. It is important to note that the contradiction between the **external actions** of the characters alone is insufficient to create a genuine conflict. As we see in the opening scene of *Uncle Vanya*, the contradiction between the two external actions of the characters does not reflect the essential contradiction between them, which is revealed in the depth of their internal actions.

This definition of conflict, whether by conscious or instinctive design, is a very significant structural element of Chekhov's dramaturgy. In fact, the playwright places conflict at the heart of every scene. Conflict is the centre of attention and effort for the characters and, in turn, becomes the centre of attention for the spectator, as well. Thus, the basic structure of the Chekhovian scene is clearly demonstrated in the first scene of the play: highly compressed characters with accurate convergence strive to realize their opposing internal actions via their external actions. With the precision and meticulousness of an architect designing a house, Chekhov makes a conscious effort to delineate the external actions of the characters, their internal actions and the conflict between them, aware that without these components, the actors would be unable to act out the scene.

With this in mind, it is important to note that structure is not Chekhov's goal, but rather his means. He uses conflict in order to provide the actors with the tools necessary to deepen the emotional dynamics of the characters. In other words, rather than describing the emotional processes that the characters undergo, Chekhov defines the internal actions that create these processes. The actor must also do the same. By following the actions set out for him by the playwright, he creates the precise deep emotional progress of his character.

Re-examining the characters' actions from the perspective of their underlying emotional dynamics, we can see the following: Marina, sitting and knitting, yearns to dispel her fears rising from the disruption of order on the estate. Her inability to do so is the source of her frustration, anger and anxiety. Astrov paces near her and appears upset. She offers him tea; he refuses. She then offers him vodka. He refuses this, too, claiming falsely that it is because of the heat. Why does he lie? Very likely because he wishes to conduct his self-examination in sobriety. She knows that he is lying. The nature of their conversation indicates that it had started before the scene began. Chekhov gives no indication of the content of their previous interaction, but these can be determined by Astrov's first question. *"Nanny, how long have we known each other?"* (p. 116). Why does he ask? He certainly knows the date of his arrival there. We must assume that he asks because he wants **her** to remember. He wants her to imagine him as he was then, to describe the changes that have taken place in him. We can therefore discern that prior to this scene he was talking about himself, which is not surprising since this is Astrov's usual pre-occupation. What was he saying this time? We can guess by studying his actions. Astrov is engaged in the act of self-examination. He does not wish to reveal this to Marina, so he probably diverted her attention to some other irrelevant or banal topic – maybe the tea, maybe the weather. It is only when he can no longer conceal the fact that he is engaged in self-examination that Astrov asks Marina how long she has known him. Chekhov has cleverly omitted the parts containing the irrelevant conversation, although he hints that such conversation took place with the lines about the tea. (p. 116)

Marina responds by stating the number of years that have passed, but lingers on the premature death of Vera Petrovna, Sonya's mother and Vanya's sister. In her eyes, compared to the death of her wonderful landlady, Astrov's arrival is a meaningless event. Moreover, Vera Petrovna's death signaled the start of the chaos on the estate. When, after some contemplation, she adds that Astrov might have even arrived before then, it becomes even clearer that she is far more concerned about Vera Petrovna and her own troubles than about the doctor.

Astrov immediately responds by shifting the conversation to himself; he asks about the changes that have occurred in him since his arrival. He, of course, is seeking consolation for his inner despair, but Marina answers cruelly:

> *"You were young and handsome then and you've grown old now. Your looks aren't what they used to be. And you drink vodka now, too."* (P. 116).

Why does Marina answer so cruelly? Clearly, because she is caught up in her own anger, frustration and worry as to her future on the estate. Astrov is painfully surprised by her answer. Marina, the only person he admits that he loves (p.117), has hurt him deeply. He is well aware of the changes that have occurred in him, but still, he hopes to hear that not everything is lost, that he still has a chance to find a wife, that perhaps even beautiful Yelena may fall in love with him, and that maybe, with her help, he could escape from the trap in which he lives.

Astrov does not deny Marina's observations, but he blames the changes on the hard work that was forced on him: *"Well... In ten years I've become a different person. And why is that? I'm overworked, Nanny"* (p. 116). First, he blames the patients who bother him day and night, then he blames his life,

38

which he sees as boring, stupid and filthy, then the people around him, who are all odd in his eyes and the cause of his own strangeness. The fact that Astrov rejects the possibility that he, himself, may bear responsibility for his deterioration is surprising. He is not stupid. He knows that he is fully responsible, but clearly is not ready to admit this, neither to himself nor to Marina. However, the process of realization has, in fact, definitely begun. After admitting his strangeness in the ironic 'stupid moustache' speech, a harsh and painful statement follows: *"I don't want anything, I don't need anything, I don't love anybody" (p. 116)*. This confession reveals enormous anguish, but Astrov is not ready yet to examine it and is quick to repress and deny it with humor: *"Well, with the exception of you, of course"* (p. 117), and kisses Marina on the head. This action is also surprising. Marina hasn't done anything to warrant a kiss. It is possible that the kiss expresses Astrov's need for affection, which rises from his profound loneliness, which we will observe again and again. He quickly apologizes, and explains: *"When I was little, I had a nanny like you"* (p. 117). The memory of the nurse who loved him more than his mother did and is long since gone, only compounds his pain.

Marina's response to Astrov's confession gives rise to a purely Chekhovian comic moment. A tortured man bares his soul to another, only to be asked, *"you want something to eat, maybe?"* (p. 117). Marina hears the confession and very likely understands Astrov's distress; yet, at that moment, she is self-involved and her banal comment reveals an apparent lack of concern. On the other hand, Marina's reaction can be interpreted in the opposite way: she is sympathetic to Astrov and shares his pain, but knows she cannot help him. As a consolation, she offers food, something she *can* do. I tend towards this interpretation, because later in the play, Marina shows her capacity for deep empathy for Serebryakov (p. 128), for Sonya (p. 150) and even for Telegin (p. 152). The first interpretation may create a comical moment, but also diminishes Astrov's powerful confession and Marina's response. The second interpretation affirms the profundity of the confession and gives depth to Marina as a character.

Astrov hears Marina's offer and knows it cannot console him, but he can no longer contain the flow of despair rising inside. Seeking empathy, reassurance and encouragement, he tells Marina about a traumatic experience that has been haunting him for the past three months. During Lent, a spotted typhus epidemic broke out in Malitskoe. Bodies lay in heaps in the huts. The sick lay among calves and pigs in filth, stench and smoke. He attends to them all day without rest or food and, on returning home, exhausted, a wounded signalman was brought to him from the train station. He laid him on the operating table, anesthetized him with chloroform and soon discovered that the man was dead.

This confession teaches us a great deal about

Astrov. He mourns the death of the signalman just as he had mourned the typhus victims in Malitskoe. However, he is particularly tortured by the thought that because of his exhaustion, his dissatisfaction with his work and even his contempt for the wretchedness of his patients, he may have purposefully killed the signalman. Could Astrov's despair have caused him to resort to murder? Has he not only become an 'oddball', but also emotionally blunted and cruel? Could his frustration have caused him to fail in his mission to save the lives of his patients? Has he become their angel of death? Astrov observes himself and can't believe this to be true. Similarly, in *Three Sisters*, Dr. Chebutykin also painfully remembers a woman who died while in his care:

> *"And the woman I killed on Wednesday, it all came back to me…everything came back, and everything twisted up inside, and it felt so vile and sickening… I went and started drinking…"*
> (p. 199)

It is important to note that not only does Astrov mourn his failure as a doctor, he also wonders whether he has failed as a human being. The self-examination regarding the death of the signalman occurs in conjunction with Astrov's ongoing self-examination regarding the meaning of his life, as he says to Sonya in Act 2: *"I love life, in general, but I can't stand our Russian provincial, narrow-minded life and despise it with every fiber of my soul"* (p. 133). As previously noted, when Astrov argues that coming generations will not think of him fondly, he is actually confirming their opinion, since he sees his own life as unworthy of remembrance.

In her reply, Marina says that she doesn't care what *others* think about her life, rather she is concerned how God values her. There are two possible and opposing interpretations for this statement. Either she is worried and self-absorbed, paying only partial attention to Astrov's words, and simply repeats words she has heard in church, *or* Marina has heard his words, feels empathy for his suffering and suggests that he take comfort in God. Either way, Astrov is disappointed in her answer and replies, ironically: *"Thank you for that. Well said"* (p. 117).

At this point, there is a long silence. Neither has been comforted by their conversation; in fact, the dialogue has widened the gap between them. Marina's irritation continues to grow due to the fact that Serebryakov and his entourage have not yet returned; and Astrov's despair with himself and his life intensifies. Examining the structure of action at work here, we see that since neither has managed to fulfill their internal actions, the conflict between them has only worsened. What does Astrov think about during this silence? He certainly doesn't seem very concerned about the professor's health. He does seem to wonder whether to stay and meet with Yelena or to mount his horse, return to his estate and avoid the meeting, which is doomed to fail. At the end of the silence, he probably has decided to leave. But he doesn't have the chance to take his bag, say goodbye to Marina and set out for home before Vanya enters the garden.

Vanya's Entrance

Vanya's entrance is an excellent example of Chekhov's shrewd writing skill. At first glance, it appears as though he has just awakened from his mid-morning nap. In the stage directions, Chekhov even makes a point of illustrating Vanya's satisfying slumber following breakfast[15] (p. 117). Vanya yawns and appears disheveled. While straightening his fashionable tie, he says only, *"well... (a pause). Well..."* (p. 117). Later on his words also sound like silly complaints: *"...all I do is sleep, eat, drink... That's not good"* (p. 117). After Astrov's stories about the typhus epidemic, Vanya sounds like a spoiled, bored ne'er-do-well, living a pointless life - sleeping, eating and drinking. He doesn't seem to mind that Sonya, his niece, keeps working on the estate without him. Vanya is aware of his situation and jokes about it, saying, *"that's not good"* (p. 117). He might even laugh while saying this. However, this initial description, which could easily portray a comic character, is a trap. Vanya, as we will soon see, is a tragic character in every sense of the word.

---

[15] In Brodskaya's translation Vanya had his nap after lunch. In the original he had his nap after breakfast.

What did Chekhov know about Vanya's internal process before writing this scene?

Vanya is the lead character in this eponymous play.[16] This follows a long, classical tradition of naming tragedies after their main character, their **protagonist**. The protagonist[17] is characterized by his immense, highly compressed internal action, which is the cause of most of his internal dynamics long before the start of the play. We will refer to this internal action as **a character's primary internal action**. It differs slightly from Stanislavski's term *super objective*, as Stanislavski does not insist that the super objective be the goal of the **internal** action of the character. The meaning of this term will become clear as we discuss the character of Vanya.

Let us take a closer look at this yawning, complaining man. Chekhov, having planned the main events of his play, already knows that Vanya is deeply in love with Yelena. He is persistent and stubborn in his attempts to woo her; and with unexpected surprise, Vanya pursues her publicly. At the end of the first act, he begs her, *"just let me look at you, hear your voice… Just let me speak of my love for you, don't shoo me away"* (p. 125). This is said

---

[16] Shakespeare named his tragedies after the lead characters. Chekhov named this play *Uncle Vanya* after Ivan Voynitsky's nickname, adding the title Uncle. He thus creates a personal, even familial connection between the viewer and the main character of the play.

[17] We will review the other prerequisite characteristics of a protagonist in Chapter 5.

in front of Marya Vassilyevna and Telegin, who are sitting near them in the garden and listening. Even Astrov hints to Vanya that he knows about his love for the professor's wife (p. 119) and Sonya says to Yelena, *"Look: Uncle Vanya doesn't do anything, and only trails you like a shadow"* (p. 139). Does Serebryakov, Yelena's husband, know about this? It appears so. Chekhov doesn't stipulate this directly, but in Act 2, Yelena tells Vanya that the professor fears him (p. 129), very likely because of the threat of his amorous advances. Later, in Act 3, the professor will announce intention to sell the estate in order to keep Vanya away from his wife.[18]

Vanya's bold, impetuous advances toward Yelena are strange. No sensible person would attempt to woo his sister-in-law openly with no effort to conceal his intentions from her husband. This behavior violates the basic norms of almost every society. Vanya's willingness to break these societal rules can be attributed to his deep despair. He seems to have initially expressed interest in Yelena a decade before, when she married Serebryakov. His advances probably went unnoticed at that time, perhaps even by Yelena. Over time, however, he became more open and insistent, and by the time she moved onto the estate, Vanya's had no qualms about public display. Vanya's respect for the professor ceased, his anger grew and he no longer feared the professor would discover about his

---

[18] See chapter 3.

intentions. Vanya's lack of self-restraint attests to the compression of his internal action: he yearns with all his heart to alleviate his despair. His need is so great that he is willing to do anything to find some relief, even to the point of transgressing a taboo and turning his social circle against himself.

Chekhov presaged this internal action before writing the stage directions depicting Vanya's lazy entry. The profusion of biographical details about Vanya strewn throughout the play reveals the methodical construction of this character and his past. Chekhov knew that a phenomenon as fundamental as Vanya's terrible despair must be justified by his dramatic biography.

Vanya is forty-seven. His father was a senator.[19] His mother was a lover of literature. But his older sister, Vera Petrovna, was perhaps the most important person in his life. He loved and admired her and very likely lived in her shadow. Vanya is an educated man who had, at one time, far-reaching intellectual goals. He says about himself: *"I'm talented, clever and brave... If I lived a normal life, I could become another Schopenhauer or Dostoyevsky"* (p. 149). Though he wishes that he had a more richly fulfilling life, it is unlikely that Vanya has the potential to become a great philosopher or writer. Chekhov doesn't substantiate Vanya's skills at any point in the play in order to play up the gap

---

[19] A senator is a high-ranking public official.

between Vanya's aspirations and his abilities. This gap may create a comic effect in the eyes of the viewer, but that is not to say that Chekhov ridicules Vanya. On the contrary, Chekhov is highly empathetic toward characters with these kinds of gaps. Many of his characters dwell in the uneasy disparity between their actions and their aspirations.[20] Examples of this can be seen in Treplev and Nina of *The Seagull*, the three sisters and their brother in *Three Sisters* and in Trofimov in *The Cherry Orchard*. Using the terms we have established, we can say that Chekhov creates characters who are driven by powerful internal actions, but fail to carry out their desires though their external actions.

Vanya is constructed in the same way. He had a high school or possibly even a university education and aspired to become a great philosopher or writer. However, instead of working to achieve his goals, at twenty-two[21] he chose to work on the estate bought for his now deceased sister, Vera Petrovna, from Telegin's uncle. A decade went by before he managed to repay his father's debt of 25,000 rubles for the purchase of the estate. During this time he continued working hard on the estate, transferring his income to Serebryakov and keeping only 500 rubles a year for himself. He

---

[20] Prof. Harai Golomb taught me this important distinction.
[21] On page 149 Vanya says that he had been managing the estate for twenty-five years.

spent years supporting the dreams of the professor and giving up his own:

> *"Twenty-five years, cooped up with this mother, like a mole, in these four walls… All our thoughts and feelings were about you alone. During the day we talked about you, about your work, we were proud of you, uttered your name in awe"* (p. 149).

Vanya didn't pursue his education, nor did he learn a profession. He didn't marry or have children and he didn't save any money. His stuttering advances toward Yelena reveal that he has had very few relationships with women. In fact, in his youth, Vanya's complete selflessness with regard to Serebryakov and his sister caused him to fall into a trap from which he could not escape. How did this happen?

It could, of course, be argued that Vanya is weak and defeatist by nature and thus gave up his dreams. However, this argument portrays him as a shallow character; if Vanya is weak, his defeat is neither surprising nor of dramatic interest. On the contrary, the defeat of a *strong* person, who has fought to achieve his goals, catches our interest and obliges us to explore the causes of this reversal.

Let us first consider Vanya's adulation of his sister, Vera Petrovna, whom he describes as follows:

"His first wife, my sister, a beautiful and gentle creature, pure as this blue sky, honorable, generous soul, who had more suitors than he ever had students - she loved him as only the purest of angels can love others as pure and fine as themselves" (p. 119).

This description in part explains Vanya's willingness to act to ensure Vera's happiness twenty-five years earlier. Of course, he didn't know at the time that this would entail giving up his own dreams but as the years went by, the financial burdens increased. It took ten years for Vanya to fulfill his promise to repay the debt for the purchase of the estate. During this decade, Vanya and his mother, Marya Vassilyevna, supported Serebryakov's career. Sonya attests to this fact when she says to Serebryakov:

"Do you remember, when you were younger, Uncle Vanya and Grandmother at night would translate books for you and copy your papers... every night, every night!" (P. 150).

Vanya worked relentlessly on behalf of the professor because he believed that his sister's happiness depended on her husband's success. His sister's love for the professor caused Vanya to view him as "a higher being" (p. 149). As much as Vanya admired his sister, he also depended on her. In a moment of crisis in Act 2, he tearfully says to Sonya, "my sister - my dearest sister - where is she now? If she knew! If only she knew" (p. 132). Vanya's need for his sister long after her death is an indication of how much he depended on her while she was still alive.

Chekhov was personally familiar with a similar sibling relationship - that of himself and his sister, Marya. This relationship is described beautifully in Henri Troyat's biography. However, Vanya's relationship with his sister is a symmetrical opposite to that of Chekhov and his sister, who devoted her life to him. Chekhov was well aware that his sister lived a life of self-sacrifice, putting his needs before her own. He probably also understood the dynamics that created this selflessness: she was younger than he and since childhood she felt that she was worthless compared to her brother. She repressed this feeling, rationalizing that her brother was the greatest writer in Russia and that it was her duty to support and protect him. Chekhov uses this mechanism in reverse with Vanya. He assumes that from childhood, Vanya felt worthless compared to his sister. He suppressed this feeling with a similar rationalization: *"my sister, a beautiful and gentle creature, pure as this blue sky, honorable, generous soul"* (p. 119), thus making her worthy of dedicating his life to her. Vanya consciously developed this rationale into a worldview, which dictates that a decent human being puts others before himself. He adhered to this worldview even after the death of Vera Petrovna, never imagining that *he* should demand his share of the estate, but rather that Sonya, his niece, should inherit it. He also never considered asking Serebryakov for a raise in pay (p. 148). Selflessly, he made do with little for the sake of the happiness of his sister and her husband. Vanya's generosity is the mechanism that allowed him to repress his feelings of worthlessness. And it was this deep-rooted feeling of worthlessness that prevented him from fighting for himself and ensuring his own happiness. As with many of Chekhov's characters, Vanya is unaware of this fault. In his own eyes he is a generous man who cares for others, which is the reason for his extreme distress when he discovers that Serebryakov has taken advantage of his selflessness, leaving him penniless, dissatisfied and unhappy.

It can be assumed that following the death of his beloved sister, Vanya began to see things more clearly. The feeling of loss exposed his emptiness and he understood that in order to overcome it, he must finally attend to his own needs. This would naturally include initiating an intimate relationship with a woman other than his sister, through whom he could regain his youthful vitality and enjoy some years of happiness. Vanya believes in the power of his love. When he says to Yelena, *"I know, my chances for reciprocity are measly, equal to zero, but I don't need anything, just let me look at you, hear your voice"* (p. 125), he doesn't forego reciprocity; he simply expresses a willingness to compromise for a time, in hopes that his love might soften her resistance and that he could eventually win her heart.

Chekhov purposely chose to place the death of Vera Petrovna a decade before the beginning of the play and that her death would spark Vanya's reawakening. Chekhov is aware that the development of the protagonist's primary internal action begins long before the play starts. The primary internal action requires a period of gestation in order to become compressed enough for the character to begin a journey. The protagonist's struggle to realize his primary internal action is the mechanism by which the plot advances. The protagonist's deep yearning for the realization of his desires forces him to confront the characters around him who obstruct his path to self-actualization, thereby entering into conflicts with them. These conflicts are the key to the characters' external actions, which when assembled, create the plot. Without the powerful compression of the protagonist's primary action, he would not have the energy to continue fighting through these conflicts. He would give up his desired self-realization and return to his routine. Chekhov has created a very effective dramatic biography, which so compresses Vanya's primary internal action that he can neither deny nor suppress it.

We do not know if Chekhov, himself, defined Vanya's primary internal action in as many words. More than likely, he did not, and I am not sure if it was necessary. A character's primary internal action is a complicated matter and its definition in a sentence or two might reduce its essence.

However, Chekhov himself certainly felt Vanya's deep need in all its complexity. His ability to design the man's actions so precisely throughout the play shows that he understood the primary internal action clearly, felt it acutely, and that it resonated with his own soft spots. As we know, Chekhov was a bachelor for most of his life and did not engage in long-term relationships with women. He was thus well acquainted with the feelings of loneliness and missed opportunities experienced by Vanya. Just three years before his death, at the age of forty-one, Chekhov married the actress Olga Knipper. Chapters 13 and 14 of Troyat's biography record the extent to which Chekhov, like Vanya, yearned to transcend his loneliness through love.

Was Chekhov aware when he began the play that in the end Vanya would try to commit suicide? We could, of course, surmise that he did know because the Vanya of *The Wood Demon* does successfully commit suicide. However, regardless of *The Wood Demon*, the answer seems to be the same, as we see in Vanya's unforgettable line at the beginning of the first act: *"It's good weather to hang yourself"* (p. 122). While it is possible that this line was added late in the writing process, we know that Chekhov was well aware of Vanya's despair from the start and would likely have considered his suicidal tendencies at a very early stage.

That being said, it is important to note that despite his sporadic despair and suicidal thoughts, Vanya, overall, is not a depressive type. Depression and despair appear only sporadically in him. Astrov states this explicitly (p. 133). Vanya is primarily a man who has a great lust for life - *he is in love.* He wants to turn over a new leaf. He wants to live with Yelena, to fulfill his passions and desires. In his mind, the possibility of having Yelena as his wife is very real:

> *"...the thunderstorm would wake us up; she would be frightened by the thunder, and I would hold her in my arms and whisper: 'Don't be afraid! I'm right here.'"* (p. 130).

His descriptions of love are poetic and touching. His mourning at the failure to fulfill that love shows how deep it is:

> *"It will stop raining, and everything in nature will be refreshed and will breathe easier. I alone won't be refreshed by the thunderstorm...*
> *Here's my life and my love: how and what am I going to do with them? My feeling is perishing in vain, like a ray of sunlight caught in a pit..."*
> (P. 129).

In other moments, Vanya is filled with humor and self-irony. Some of his lines are very funny. He can also be bitingly sarcastic, as in these lines about Serebryakov:

> *"Not everyone can be a writing* perpetuum mobile *like your Herr Professor"* (p. 122).

He also says to his mother: *"For fifty years we've been talking and talking and reading pamphlets. It's time to be done with it."* (p. 121).

And when he drinks, his emotions take over; his lust for life increases and he is capable of uttering the startling confession that when he is drunk, *"at least it feels like life"* (p. 130). In Act 4, he describes to Astrov his desperate desire for change:

> *"...you see, if you could only spend the rest of your life in a new way. To wake up on a clear, quiet morning feeling that you have begun a new life, and that the past is all forgotten, diffused like smoke. [Crying] To begin a new life... Tell me how to begin...what to begin it with..."* (p. 153).

In Vanya, Chekhov has successfully created a multi–layered character of depth and intelligence, a well-educated, sensitive, amusing and fascinating man, whose life turns to tragedy because he has chosen to be too kind and too fair.

The External and Internal Processes in this Scene

Vanya enters from the house after waking from his nap. In the stage directions, Chekhov emphasizes that he appears "rumpled" (p. 117). He *"straightens his stylish tie"* (p. 117). We could assume that Vanya is a careless person who pays no attention to his appearance. However, we could also assume that Vanya generally takes pride in his appearance, but that this day, upon awakening, he was in such a rush to go outside that he didn't take time to arrange his clothes or his tie. This assumption is supported by the fact that Chekhov describes the tie as 'fashionable'. Why does he hurry outside? Probably to look for Yelena. He sees Astrov and Marina sitting in the garden. Astrov's presence is not a surprise to Vanya, since the doctor had been summoned to tend to Serebryakov, who has not been well. Does Vanya suspect that Astrov is in love with Yelena? It seems unlikely at this point in the play. Unlike himself, Astrov hides his emotions and, in addition, Vanya is not a suspicious type; he could hardly imagine that his dearest friend would take his love from him. And even if he did suspect a relationship between Astrov and Yelena, this assumption is not plausible at this point in the play, since it would undermine the dramatic process that occurs later between the second and third acts, and especially in the third act, where Vanya discovers the awful truth: not only is Astrov in love with Yelena, *she* is in love with *him*.

Vanya sits down, looks around and says, "*well… (a pause). Well…*" (p. 117). It is difficult to tell what he means. I tend to interpret his terseness based on a hint given by Yelena at the end of the act, when she says to Vanya, "*…and today at breakfast you argued with Alexander again. This is all so petty!*" (p. 124). It seems that earlier in the day, Vanya managed to enrage Serebryakov and, in order to separate the two, Sonya and Yelena suggested to Serebryakov that they go for a walk. When they left, Vanya took a nap and now that he is up, he wishes to know if

Yelena has returned and if she is still angry with him. He comes into the garden looking for her but she is not there. The first *"well"* is actually a question: Well, where is she? Since he doesn't ask explicitly, he doesn't receive an answer. He waits, observes Astrov and Marina and tacitly understands that nothing substantial has changed. If, for a moment, he had feared that Yelena and the professor had left the estate because of the argument, it is now clear that he can lay his fears to rest. This is the meaning of the second *"well"*. Of course, this is not the only viable interpretation. A typical Chekhovian *"well... (a pause). Well..."* can be interpreted in many ways that suggest other actions.

Astrov, who, as we remember, wanted to leave the estate, decides to delay his departure. Why? First of all, he wants to share his deep despair with Vanya. Secondly, his desire to see Yelena has not subsided and a conversation with Vanya would allow him to remain a while longer. And so, he cautiously asks, *"Did you sleep well?"* (p. 117), and tries to find out where he can lead the conversation.

Vanya answers favorably and yawns, then launches into a long monologue. At face value, his external action includes several complaints concerning the changes in the running of the estate. However, we should avoid jumping to conclusions. A more meticulous read reveals that Vanya's complaints are made jokingly and ironically. Examples of this can be seen in the complaint, *"that's not good"* (p. 117) and later, in *"all I do is sleep, eat, drink... That's not good!"* (p. 117).[22] This is a humorous, ironic complaint, illustrating the fact that Vanya knows what pathetic a state he is in, and attempts to use irony in order to diminish his self-contempt.

Marina is shocked at Vanya's jokes and his laughter. *She* sees the changes in the old order of the estate as a catastrophe. It would be a mistake to accept her words only as a detailed description of the changes. Marina demands that Vanya put an end to the uncontrolled chaos and that he re-establish order on the estate. After all, he is the manager of the estate and is responsible for its orderly affairs. Marina knows, of course, that Vanya is in love with Yelena and this seems almost incestuous to her, though she wouldn't dare even to hint at such a thing. She secretly hopes that the restoration of the order on the estate will include Vanya's recovery from this madness.

Astrov probes Marina's complaints in order to find out how long the professor and his wife are planning to live on the estate. This question is puzzling. After all, Astrov has visited the estate a number of times since Serebryakov and Yelena moved there and he knows that they plan on living there indefinitely. Yet, his heart must be telling him

---

[22] In *Three Sisters*, Andrei mentions that one's existential state is inferior if one "only eats, drinks, sleeps and then dies" (p. 217).

that they are having trouble adjusting to their new life, and he imagines that they will not stay there forever. Vanya does not agree with him. He whistles in order to express shock at the idea that the professor might live on the estate for the rest of his days. In his answer, *"a hundred years"* (p. 118), he emphasizes the fact that every moment with the professor, whom he hates, feels like an eternity to him. The settling down of the professor and his wife on the estate would be a disaster to Marina as well. Though she would never say so explicitly, her anger and frustration are growing, as evidenced by her complaint about the samovar, which has been ready and waiting for hours while the professor and his entourage amble around the estate. Vanya, concerned that her excitement might be injurious to her health, tries to calm her, saying, *"Here they come... Don't you worry"* (p. 118). Indeed, voices are heard as Serebryakov, Yelena, Sonya and Telegin return.

What did Chekhov know about Serebryakov before writing this scene?

Chekhov does not state Serebryakov's exact age. We do learn, however, that he is retired and is subject to growing frustration and rage because his health and his status have deteriorated and because everybody around him sees him as a bothersome, useless, old man, and because his life has become as empty as a crypt (p. 127). He is probably about sixty-five, perhaps closer to seventy. He is obviously sickly and suffers from gout, a chronic joint illness that causes acute pain in the hands and feet. Though he takes a lot of medication, the pain is not eased. The cold worsens this pain, so Serebryakov wears an overcoat, gloves and galoshes even on warm days. Vanya describes Serebryakov's biography in detail, as follows:

> *"A son of a simple deacon, a seminarian, attains academic degrees, lands a professor's chair, and becomes His Excellency, a son-in-law of a senator, etc. etc." (P. 119).*

After the death of his wife, at fifty-five, Serebryakov married Yelena, his seventeen-year-old student. This shocked many people, but the marriage has survived for a decade. Serebryakov's financial condition is also not healthy. Vanya tells us that the old man lives on his first wife's estate *"because he can't afford to live in the city"* (p. 119). The professor himself explains his financial troubles in a speech in Act 3: *"To live in the city on the income that we receive from the estate is also impossible"* (p. 147). Serebryakov continues to work in his study, writing and reading from morning until night, periodically requesting books from the library, which Yelena brings to him. He would like to continue in this way until the end of his life. In Vanya's eyes, this is useless. He claims that Serebryakov's career is nothing but a soap bubble (p. 131).

On the other hand, the facts of this biography can be read in a different light. Serebryakov was indeed born to a humble deacon and studied to become a minister. Despite this traditional training, he gathered up his courage and took his destiny into his own hands. He left the church, and in doing so, very likely left behind his God. He then began to study art. This dramatic change describes a man who possesses great inner strength. We must also be skeptical of Vanya's description of the professor's failed life. Had Serebryakov not succeeded in his academic research, he would not have achieved his post. We should also be skeptical about Vanya's views regarding Serebryakov's publications and fame. Vanya accuses Serebryakov of *"chewing other people's thoughts on realism, naturalism, and other such nonsense"* (p. 119). Although this description is meant as ridicule, in fact, it attests to Serebryakov's familiarity with the latest artistic developments of the 19th century. This also reveals Vanya's ignorance and his attitude toward the cultural and artistic discourse of his time. Serebryakov, himself, bemoans his reduced status since his retirement. Rather than admit to failure, however, he claims that he is surrounded by foolish people and nonsensical conversation (p. 127). This phenomenon is familiar to us nowadays, where life expectancy is prolonged and people often must retire at their peak.

Vanya refuses to see in Serebryakov a talented man who is unwilling to surrender his career despite his advanced age. Blinded by anger and jealousy, he cannot see Serebryakov's lust for life, for accomplishment and fame. Vanya himself states that his sister, Vera Petrovna, loved Serebryakov "as only the purest of angels can love others as pure and fine as themselves" (p. 119). Vanya's mother continues to admire Serebryakov, her son-in-law, certain that "he knows better what's good and what isn't" (p. 147). This is so despite Serebryakov's contempt for her; behind her back he calls her "that old idiot" (p. 127). And Sonya says, "he had, I heard, great success with women, and the ladies spoiled him" (p. 133). Serebryakov resembles Dr. Dorn in The Seagull and Chekhov, himself, both of whom were popular with women. Describing her initial acquaintance with Serebryakov, Yelena remarks: "I married your father for love. I fell for him" (p. 136). The attraction of these three women to Serebryakov attests to the fact that he is not as monstrous as Vanya thinks.

Old age has certainly ravaged Serebryakov. However, Yelena eventually chooses to stay with him despite his age and despite being wooed by Astrov and Vanya. This can, of course, be explained by her own personal character flaws – her low self image and fear of her own sexuality, which we'll discuss later; but these flaws alone aren't enough to justify her decision. It seems that in her eyes, Serebryakov has not lost all of his magic. Many theater directors tend to view Serebryakov as a sickly and bothersome Harpagon or Pantalone, at the expense of the play's depth[23]. It

---

[23] In 1963, with the direction of Laurence Olivier, Max Adrian famously portrayed Serebryakov as an old, troublesome

is important to examine other possibilities that could balance the power play between the three men competing for Yelena's love.

What did Chekhov know about Sonya before writing this scene?

Chekhov doesn't stipulate Sonya's age, but she may well be younger than Yelena, who says to her, *"you're still a little girl"* (p. 136). Yelena even tries to treat her as a responsible adult in her attempts to pair Sonya and Astrov. Marina hints that when Vera Petrovna passed away a decade before, Sonya was still young and hadn't yet matured. Hence, we can assume that Sonya is about twenty when the play begins. Sonya is not beautiful. She is mournfully aware of this:

> *"Oh, it's so awful that I am not pretty! So awful! I know that I'm not pretty, I kow, I know... Last Sunday, when walking out of church, I overheard them talking about me and one woman said: 'She's good-hearted, generous, but it's a pity that she's so plain'... So plain..."* (p. 135).

Later, she admits to Yelena: *"No! When a woman is plain, they always tell her: 'You have beautiful eyes or you have beautiful hair'"* (p. 140). Yelena, too, says, *"she isn't pretty"* (p. 141). However, in the same line, she says *"but for a country doctor, at his age, she would*

---

character in London's National Theatre. This established a tradition that has affected many subsequent productions.

make a wonderful wife. She's such a good girl, generous, pure" (p. 141).

Sonya is industrious. Despite her youth, she is as responsible for maintaining the estate as her uncle Vanya. She puts all her effort and devotion into her work, even when Vanya stops working because of his love for Yelena. For Sonya, work is a saving grace, especially after her hopes for Astrov's love are shattered. She is also not afraid to speak up to her father. She scolds him when he behaves capriciously: *"Please, don't act up! Maybe there are those who like it, but spare me, please!"* (p. 128)

Sonya seems to have spent her whole life on a provincial country estate. Chekhov doesn't hint at an urban upbringing or education. She is not an academic. Her sole occupation is the management of the estate and the supervision of its employees. Serebryakov's selfishness and imperiousness never allowed his daughter the opportunity to study. Instead, he took advantage of her loyalty and was content to live off of her work. Sonya appears to be aware of this and begrudges her father for it. Her lack of education is obvious when she unhesitatingly states her opinion regarding Astrov's forestry, citing his words in a way that shows that she has completely misunderstood his point:

> *"In countries where climate is milder, people struggle with nature less, and that's why man is milder and gentler there; there, the people are*

beautiful, adaptable, passionate, their speech is
elegant and their gestures are graceful. The arts
and sciences flourish there, their philosophy isn't
dark, and women are treated there with elegant
dignity…" (p. 123).

Sonya is unaware that such a generalization is
absolutely wrong. Though Vanya ridicules her
ignorance, it is obvious that he loves her very much
and even gives up his part of the estate for her
sake.

Sonya enjoys a very special relationship with
Vanya. After the death of her mother and in her
father's absence, Vanya was the adult closest to her
and served as a father figure. However, over the
course of the play, the tables turn and twenty-year-
old Sonya takes on the role of mother to forty-
seven-year-old Vanya, whose mother is still alive
and is even sitting right next to him. Sonya doesn't
hesitate to reproach him when he talks about the
life he never had, saying that he is boring her (p.
122). She silences him when he provokes
Serebryakov (p. 128), is angry with him when he
gets drunk with Astrov, saying, *"it doesn't suit you*
at your age" (p. 132), and even chides him for his
laziness (p. 132). However, when Serebryakov
directs his anger at Vanya, Sonya comes to his aid,
pleading for mercy on his behalf:

> *"You have to show mercy, Papa! Uncle Vanya*
> *and I are so unhappy! [controlling her despair]*
> *You have to show mercy! (…) Uncle Vanya and*

I worked without rest, were afraid to spend a kopeck on ourselves, and sent everything to you..." (p. 150).

Perhaps the early maturity that was forced on her and the considerable responsibility she has assumed have robbed her of her youthful joy and turned her into the unattractive woman she seems to be.

Sonya is religious and attends church on Sundays (p. 135). When she is tortured by her doubts about Astrov's love for her, she prays all night (p. 135). Her revelatory words at the end of Act 4 sound much like a passage from a sermon:

> *"and when our time comes, we'll die calmly, and there, within the veil, we'll say how we suffered and cried, and how bitter we felt, and God will take pity on us, and Uncle, dear Uncle, we will see a bright, beautiful, and fine life"* (p. 160).

The primary internal action that Chekhov provides for Sonya is her yearning to be worthy of Astrov's love. This yearning began when she was fourteen and grew with time, as she confesses to Yelena:

> *"I've loved him for six years; I love him more than my own mother, and I hear him every waking moment, I feel his handshake [...] I don't have any pride left, and I can't control myself... I couldn't help it and confessed to Uncle Vanya yesterday that I love him... And all the servants*

know that I love him. Everybody knows" (p. 140).

Sonya wants to believe that Astrov will recognize her virtues and love her even though she is not beautiful. The use of the word "love" to describe her external action requires some explanation and clarification: Sonya openly showers Astrov with love, but her internal action is her yearning to be *worthy* of his love. After having spent most of her life without her mother and being ignored by her father, she yearns for Astrov's love in order to realize her femininity, to be a wife and mother to his children and to free herself from the loneliness of a provincial estate.

What did Chekhov know about Yelena before the writing of this scene?

Yelena is the only character whose age Chekhov stipulates in the list of characters. She is twenty-seven, from Saint Petersburg and a former student at the music conservatory (p. 141), where she studied piano.[24] At the age of seventeen, Yelena met Serebryakov and his wife Vera Petrovna, who lived in Saint Petersburg at that time. Yelena may even have been Serebryakov's student, since she herself testifies that she fell in love with him

---

[24] According to Prof. Harai Golomb, Chekhov doesn't state in his original version of the play in Russian that Yelena plays the piano. Prof. Golomb posits that Chekhov did not mention a specific instrument because any other instrument seemed illogical to him.

because of his education and fame (p. 136). She also met Vanya there when he visited his sister (p. 130). A year later, Vera Petrovna passed away, and before Vanya could overcome his grief, a relationship had formed between Yelena and Serebryakov and they were married. Yelena insists that she loved the professor, but at the same time she admits that this love was false and unreal (p. 136). She states that she was always a minor character. She displayed no real talent for the piano and functions mainly as nurse and secretary to her husband. Like the others in this play, she never took the initiative or made use of the opportunities presented to her (p. 137). Today, she admits to being miserable and complains: *"there's no happiness for me in this world"* (p. 137). She also claims that idleness is one of the reasons for her misery: *"I'm bored to death and I don't know what to do"* (p. 138). When Sonya offers her the opportunity to work on the estate, to teach or to care for the sick, Yelena answers, *"I don't know how. And it doesn't interest me"* (p. 139). We must avoid taking her words literally. She is not lazy. The tasks Sonya offers her are at some distance from her self-image. Yelena says that she is bored mainly in order to conceal her profound identity crisis. She sees that her marriage to Serebryakov was a mistake, but she lacks the necessary courage to follow her instincts and free herself, as Vanya encourages her to do. She has *"the blood of a water nymph"*[25] (p. 139),

---

[25] The *Rusalka* is a mythical creature, a water nymph who symbolizes a magical, seductive woman. The poet, Pushkin,

according to Vanya, who senses that she is hot-blooded and finds it difficult to cool down. Yelena knows that she is caught in a death trap, but because of her anxieties, she cannot break free.

What is this trap? The characters surrounding her try to decipher her mysterious personality. Vanya says to her, *"You're too lazy to live! Oh, this laziness!"* (p. 125). However, as previously mentioned, this description fails to reflect her internal life. Vanya defines her tragedy far more accurately when he says: *"...next to me, in the same house, another life is perishing – yours!"* (p. 130). Later, he says, *"...be a good girl! The blood of a water nymph flows in your veins... Let yourself go..."* (p. 139). Astrov calls her a *"beautiful, bushy polecat"* (p. 144), insinuating that she is a lustful woman who hunts men. She rejects this description outright and claims not to understand his words, even though she clearly does. Later, he brutally demands that she admit:

> *"...there's nothing for you to do in this world; no goal in life, nothing to occupy your mind, and sooner or later you'll give in to feelings – it's inevitable."*
> (p. 155).

When she doesn't surrender, he continues:

---

wrote a play entitled *Rusalka*, which was made into an opera in 1885 and was well-known in Russia at the time *Uncle Vanya* was written.

*"You seem good and sensible, and yet there's
something strange about your whole being...no
matter where you and your husband set foot,
you bring destruction everywhere..."* (p. 156).

These observations reveal that both Vanya and
Astrov have observed powerful impulses in
Yelena. She is not a spoiled, self-indulgent girl, but
a woman capable of changing the lives of others.
All her talk of boredom is nothing but a front
intended to mask her complex and difficult internal
dynamics. Chekhov was aware of this before he
started writing the play. Yelena's words to Vanya
at the end of Act 1 serve as decisive proof of this:

*"It's what Astrov just said: you all are blindly
destroying the forests, and soon there'll be
nothing left on earth. The same way you are
blindly destroying people, and soon, thanks to
you, there will be no loyalty, no purity, no
capacity for self-sacrifice. Why can't you look
with equanimity at a woman who is not yours?
Because – and the doctor's right there – the
demon of destruction is inside all of you. You've
no pity for forests, or birds, or women, or one
another"* (p. 125).

These are very powerful words. Yelena blames
men for destroying humanity with their arrogance
and irresponsibility. She says that they have no
mercy for the birds, for women or for each other. A
woman who blames men so brutally and so
comprehensively surely must have been hurt by

men. She even describes *how* she has been hurt. Ever since coming of age, men have been leering at her. They cannot look at her indifferently without trying to claim her or, in other words, sleep with her. Chekhov doesn't detail the history of sexual intimidation suffered by Yelena, but the advances of Vanya and Astrov are clearly meant as examples. Yelena's beauty has been an obstacle to her and the lust of men has always felt like a nightmare. Her marriage to Serebryakov provided a means of escape and protection. She assumed that once the men who lusted after her learned of her marriage, they would leave her alone. She also assumed that because of his age (Serebryakov was fifty-five when they married), he wouldn't pose the same lascivious threat. In planning these moves, she did not consider that she, too, like the men who pursued her, was a lustful being, that she, too, needed love.

A definitive example of her fear of men can be seen in her panicked rejection of Astrov's protestations of love. She says, *"Oh, I'm higher and better than you think. I swear to you"* (p. 144). She even tries to leave the room, and all this despite her love for him. In her fear, she rejects Astrov, claiming that she is a decent woman, although he never suggests otherwise. Taking the high ground with moralistic fervor, she defends herself by claiming that extra-marital love is adultery -- a ploy used by cowards throughout history.

A discussion of Yelena's biography always raises the question of the possible reasons for her childlessness, and why, throughout the entire play, she never even hints at the subject of motherhood,[26] even though she is twenty-seven. It is, of course, possible that Serebryakov, because of his age and self-centeredness, could not or did not want to have children. His relationship with his daughter, Sonya, is a clear indication that the experience of fatherhood was never very important to him. However, is it only for these reasons that Yelena forgoes motherhood? Possible, but such a choice would flatten her character. It is more preferable to find an internal reason for her failure to consider divorce from Serebryakov or the possibility of bearing of a child with Vanya or Astrov.[27] Given the emotional trap she is in, she very likely fears that her distress and her doubts would not allow her to raise a child properly. As a 'secondary character' all her life, Yelena does not feel ready to fulfill the primary role of mother.

---

[26] Chekhov himself didn't have any children, although Olga Knipper did become pregnant but unfortunately suffered a miscarriage. A description of this episode can be found in the Troyat's work (1989), pp. 272-273. Troyat posits that "the loss of the baby was less important to Chekhov than his wife's physical and mental balance".

[27] It is interesting to note that neither Vanya nor Astrov, both of whom are childless, think of Yelena as mother to their children.

What did Chekhov know about Telegin before the writng of the scene?

Telegin is a bankrupt estate owner currently living on Serebryakov's estate. The estate was bought by Vanya's father from Telegin's uncle as dowry for the marriage of his daughter, Vera Petrovna, to Serebryakov. Telegin is a close family friend and was even chosen as godfather to Sonya (p. 121). Though he appears to work on the estate, he is lazy by nature and tries to evade any task given to him. He says as much to Marina in Act 4 (p. 152). In this act, Astrov instructs Telegin to arrange for his carriage, which he does. However, in Act 2, he tells Serebryakov that he has been suffering from a headache for two days, clearly an excuse after Serebryakov has chastised him for his laziness. That he was made godfather to Sonya twenty years before indicates that he is not a young man. However, the play requires him not to be too old or too weak to work. Here we have a middle-aged man, let us assume around fifty, still capable of physical labor, but odd and chronically lazy. He plays polkas on the guitar, which seems to be his main contribution to the estate. Astrov has no qualms about waking Telegin after midnight to entertain at a party the doctor has arranged so he could see Yelena (p. 131).

Because of his pockmarked face, likely the result of a skin disease he contracted in his youth, Telegin is known among the country folk by the humiliatingly graphic nickname, 'Waffles'. He was once married, but his wife ran away from him the day after the wedding. He claims it was because of his unpleasant appearance (p. 120), but this explanation is unsatisfactory, since his wife surely must have seen him before the wedding. More than likely, on the wedding night, she must have been confronted with other characteristics previously unknown to her -- possibly a suggestion that he was impotent. However, he claims that he still loves her and remains faithful out of moral principle. It is possible that his fidelity may also be due to his inability to please other women. His wife subsequently married her lover and raised a family, all of whom Telegin supported. He claims to have given them all of his possessions (p. 120). However, the in the cast of characters preceding the play, Chekhov stipulates that the man is bankrupt. Telegin may be lying to Vanya when he says that he gave his fortune to his ex-wife and her children. The truth may be that he simply lost it. As with all of the developed characters in Chekhov's plays, Telegin suffers the painful gap between his self-image and his actions. He, himself, says that the villagers see him as a freeloader (p. 152) and he knows that if he is sent away from the estate, he will have to work - otherwise he will starve. Therefore, from the beginning of the play, he constantly ingratiates himself with Serebryakov, the owner of the estate, and tries to reconcile Serebryakov and Vanya in order to ward off a crisis that might jeopardize his current life of laziness.

The Entrance of Serebryakov, Yelena, Sonya and Telegin

Marina, Vanya and Astrov are in the garden. Marina has announced that the samovar has been ready on the table for two hours. This means that Serebryakov, Yelena, Sonya and Telegin left the house more than two hours before, since Marina would have set the samovar on the table in time for their return. Marina has mentioned that the professor wakes up at noon, so the breakfast table argument between Serebryakov and Vanya probably took place between noon and 12:30, after which, Serebryakov and his entourage went for their walk. The walk, then, would have been about two and a half hours long. This is a very long walk for old Serebryakov, who must have been reluctant to return and see Vanya. Who initiated the walk? Probably Sonya, who says that the walk is not over and that there is still much to see: *"Tomorrow, we'll go to the forest preserve, Papa."* (p. 118). Why do they return? Very likely due to Serebryakov's fatigue. This interpretation is confirmed when the four of them enter the garden. Vanya welcomes them and offers tea. Unwilling to spend another moment in Vanya's company, Serebryakov requests that his tea be brought to his study. Yelena and Sonya assist him inside. He is exhausted from the long walk in the noonday heat, especially so, since he is dressed in his usual overcoat, galoshes and gloves – and carrying an umbrella (p. 118). Even a younger, stronger man would be worn out after such a trip.

What was the reason for the argument at breakfast? Chekhov doesn't stipulate, but we may learn about it from the conversation between Vanya and Astrov in the garden. Vanya's accusations against Serebryakov were probably a continuation of their ongoing conflict. Vanya claims the following:

> *"... the man's been writing about art for twenty-five years and he doesn't understand a thing about it. For twenty-five years, he's been chewing other people's thoughts on realism, naturalism, and other such nonsense; for twenty-five years, he's been reading and writing things that any intelligent person has known for ages, and the stupid ones couldn't care less about..." (p. 119).*

The topic of the argument was art, but its roots lay in Vanya's jealousy of the professor.

Both Vanya and Astrov wait impatiently for Yelena's return and are stunned when she ignores them as she escorts her husband inside. Vanya offers her tea, but she ignores him. He vents his frustration by ridiculing the professor: *"It's hot and stuffy, but our famous scholar is wearing a coat, galoshes, gloves, and carrying an umbrella."* (p. 118). Astrov answers, *"that means he's taking care of himself"* (p. 118). At face value, this is a neutral statement about Serebryakov's health, but Astrov's subtext is clear – the old professor is not planning to leave this world and let other men flirt with his wife. Vanya understands the hint but cannot hide his feelings for Yelena: *"How beautiful she is! So beautiful! Never in my life have I seen a more beautiful woman"* (p. 118). In fact, had Telegin not intervened, Vanya would have continued hyperbolizing about his love for Yelena. Telegin, fearing another eruption that would send the estate into further disorder, interrupts with a tedious statement about the wonderful weather and the peace and harmony it brings, which, of course, will be ruined if Vanya doesn't control his impulses. Vanya, as though hallucinating, carries on: *"Her eyes... A marvelous woman!"* (p. 118). At this point, aware that he may have overexposed his feelings, he falls silent.

Vanya's silence goes on for quite a while until Astrov prods him to speak. What happens during that silence? Vanya stews in his anguish about having missed the opportunity to have tea with Yelena. He fears that she is still upset with him about the argument at breakfast. And Astrov wonders whether he should stay or go; but the prospect of a few moments with Yelena is too tempting. In the pause, Astrov not only decides to stay, but also to learn more about Yelena's relationship with Serebryakov. At the end of his conversation with Vanya, he explicitly asks, *"Is she faithful to the professor?"* (p. 120). What are Astrov's intentions? Is he contemplating an affair with Yelena? Unlikely. The good doctor is not looking for sex; he is looking for salvation -- for freedom from his chronic despair. A man like Astrov could hardly be satisfied with anything less than a profound and utter change in his existential state. Proof of this is that later in the play he will neglect his estate and abandon his patients, all to make daily pilgrimages to Yelena. Astrov's desperation drives him to follow an illusion, a fantasy that a beautiful woman in the form of an angel will save him. Later in the play, he confesses to Sonya:*"The only thing that still fascinates me is beauty. I'm partial to that. I think that if Yelena Andreyevna only wanted to, she could turn my head in a day..."* (p. 134-135). And so, having decided to stay, the doctor turns to Vanya and says, *"...come, tell us something, Ivan Petrovich,"* (p. 118). Of course, Astrov wants to talk about Yelena, but Vanya can't bear to do so. When Astrov insists, he begins to rant about himself and his mother: *"I've become lazy, I don't do anything, and grumble like an old fart. The old chatterbox, Maman, is still blathering about the emancipation of women"* (p. 118). When Astrov persists and asks a question about the professor, the levee breaks and even if he tried, he could not stop Vanya's surge of complaints.

How does Chekhov utilize Vanya's complaints? This is certainly a good opportunity to reveal more of Serebryakov's biography to the audience. However, this long monologue contains much more than mere exposition. Vanya's external action is clear: he tries to prove to Astrov that Serebryakov is full of hot air, that the professor only pretends to work, that the work he produces is worthless and that he sits all day in his study ruminating over dead ideas. According to Vanya, the professor has been writing and lecturing about art for twenty-five years without understanding any of it (p. 119). The monologue also reveals a fascinating internal action. In truth, there is no reason for Vanya to prove to Astrov that the professor is a failure. He needs to prove it to *himself*. If he succeeds, then his advances toward Yelena would not be considered immoral, despite the fact that she is married. In Vanya's opinion, if she is married to a person who pretends to be what he isn't, who takes advantage of her innocence and promises love he can't deliver, the marriage should end. At the end of the monologue, Vanya openly confesses the moral paradox that enrages him: *"Cheating on an elderly husband whom you can't stand – that's immoral; trying, on the other hand, to repress in yourself your poor youth and natural feelings – that's not immoral."* (p. 120). In this expression of his internal action, Vanya shows that he is aware that his open advances toward Yelena are morally problematic; yet he seeks to justify his behavior in order to continue seeing himself as a moral man. As the play proceeds, Vanya's paradox wanes and in Act 3, it will disappear completely. Vanya will put aside his scruples and attempt to murder Serebryakov (p. 151)!

In response to Vanya's moral dissertation, Telegin protests: *"Those who cheat on their wives or husbands are by definition disloyal; they could betray a country as well!"* (p. 120). Vanya dismisses him, but Telegin persists. He tries to persuade Vanya with an example from real life and tells him about his own

wife's betrayal one day after their wedding. He
says that his wife was punished for her perfidy and
was left with nothing. He, on the contrary, got to
keep his pride. It is not difficult to imagine Vanya's
opinion of Telegin's pride. But before he can
answer, Sonya and Yelena enter followed by Marya
Vassilyevna, Vanya's mother.

Now let us review the scene between Vanya and
Astrov from the perspective of dramatic *conflict*.
Both men seek salvation through the ministrations
of Yelena. Vanya's internal action is his yearning to
see himself as a decent person, thus allowing him
to justify his amorous pursuit. Similarly, Astrov's
internal action is his yearning to be set free from his
loneliness. The conflict between these two internal
actions is clear: if Astrov achieves salvation
through Yelena, Vanya will fail -- and vice versa.
At this point in the play, the conflict is mostly
hidden. We can only discern hints of its existence.
Astrov has still not openly revealed his desire for
Yelena. Thus far, Vanya is not yet aware of
Astrov's intentions, and even if does suspect a
threat, he has not yet acted on his suspicions.
Chekhov presents these faint hints to create
suspense both for the characters and the viewer,
drawing our attention to what is to come.

What Does Chekhov Know About Marya Vassilyevna?

Marya Vassilyevna is about seventy years old. She
is the widow of a senior public officer, who earned
the title of senator for his contributions to the czar's

regime. The family's financial situation was poor and she was left bankrupt after the senator's death. She is forced to live on Serebryakov's estate, which was bought for her daughter, Vera Petrovna. Vanya emphasizes this when he asks Serebryakov what he proposes to "do" with him, his mother and Sonya after the estate is sold (p. 147). Despite her age, Marya Vassilyevna supports women's rights and follows their struggle in books and articles. She greatly admires Serebryakov. Vanya says, *"my mother, his mother-in-law, still adores him and he still inspires sacred awe in her"* (p. 119). She has followed Serebryakov's career as Vanya testifies to Serebryakov: *"Twenty-five years, cooped up with this mother, like a mole, in these four walls... All our thoughts and feelings were about you alone"* (p. 149). Sonya reminds her father that when he was younger, Uncle Vanya and her Grandmother spent nights translating books for him and copying his manuscripts (p. 150). Along with these positive qualities, Chekhov also includes some eccentricities. With each of her entrances, he notes that she is holding a book, reading, even writing comments in various publications, but her external action would be much more interesting if we assume that she is only pretending to do so. Chekhov also gives her the odd habit of using a French accent in order to sound more cultured. She calls Vanya *'Jean'* (p. 121) and Serebryakov *Alexandre* (p. 121), with appropriate French inflection. [28]

Marya Vassilyevna's blatant flattery of Serebryakov is apparent throughout the play. She updates him with the latest news (p. 121). Without even considering her own fate if the estate were to be sold, she urges Vanya not to question Serebryakov's decision. (p. 147). She also requests a photograph of the professor before he and Yelena leave the estate. Is Marya Vassilyevna aware that Serebryakov considers her to be a foolish old woman, as he tells Yelena at the beginning of Act 2 (p. 127)? Although there is no evidence in the text, I think that the internal action of the actress playing Marya Vassilyevna would be far more interesting and complex if she *were* aware of Serebryakov's disdain and yet continued with her flattery.

That said, a too simplistic view of Marya Vassilyevna would be a mistake. Her flattery of Serebryakov is a means of preserving a wonderful past, when the professor was a famous, respected academic and she served as his faithful research assistant, contributing to the important cultural developments of the time. She absolutely refuses to agree with Vanya's description of Serebryakov as full of hot air. To do so would mean that she had wasted her life. Her avid reading of books and journals can be seen as an attempt to maintain her

---

[28] In the London production staged by Laurence Olivier (1963), she spoke with a pronounced French accent, as though she were indeed French.

lucidity in her old age and preserve her self-respect in the face of Vanya's contempt for her. Is she aware of Vanya's intentions concerning Yelena? She witnesses them with her own eyes at the end of Act 1 (p. 125), but she knows that she is incapable of stopping her son and chooses to ignore them in the same way that she ignores the pronounced decline in the professor's status.

The relationship between Marya Vassilyevna and Vanya is complex. Even though her speech is minimal, he chastises her for her babbling and demands that she be silent. On the other hand, at one of his most difficult moments in the play, at the end of Act 3, when he realizes that his life has been ruined, Vanya begs for her help: *"Mama, I'm so miserable! Oh, Matushka!"* (p. 149). A moment later he leaves her. She is not aware that he intends to shoot the professor. She is similarly unaware that he may have left the room in order to shoot himself. She sees his misery and follows him in order to console him. Despite her age and their obvious differences, Marya Vassilyevna's maternal feelings are undimmed. Chekhov doesn't state that she follows him back onstage after the first shot at the professor. Perhaps she realizes that she cannot prevent him from shooting again and prefers not to witness this horror.

The Entrance of Sonya, Yelena and Marya Vassilyevna
Sonya enters, rushes to Marina and asks her to talk to the peasants who have come to the estate. The

83

peasants arrived a few hours earlier to discuss farming the uncultivated land around the estate and have been waiting for someone to respond to their request. Vanya, consumed by his love for Yelena, fails to even ask the peasants why they have come. Sonya noticed them on the way back to the house, but intent on Astrov's company, sends Marina to speak to them. On a normal day, Sonya would have attended to the peasants, but today she prefers not to miss an opportunity to serve tea to Astrov and to engage him in conversation. Marina exits and Sonya pours tea. Yelena sits, child-like, on the swing. Marya Vassilyevna enters with a book, takes tea, sits down and reads.

Let us examine the relationship between the external actions of these three women and what they wish to accomplish. Sonya's first action is to attend to the tea, which would provide an opportunity to converse with Astrov. Marya Vassilyevna enters with her book, takes tea, sits and reads. Her physical actions are meant to show the rest of the family that she is filling her time with constructive activity and that she is not yet senile. What is Yelena's external action? She, too, may wish to engage Astrov in conversation, but there is also another possible interpretation: she may have come out intending to chastise Vanya after the quarrel at breakfast. We can surmise this because, immediately following the exit of Astrov and Sonya (p. 124), Yelena turns to Vanya and confronts him: "...*and today at breakfast you argued with Alexander again. This is all so petty!*"(p. 124).

84

Very likely she wanted to address the issue when she entered the garden, but refrained because of Astrov's presence. This interpretation allows for another advantage: Yelena's relationship with Vanya is important to her. She doesn't disrespect him; on the contrary, she recognizes his unique qualities and also is touched by his despair. The relationship is not as one-sided as one might assume. She may not desire his love, but she wants to maintain a close relationship with him. That is why she wants him to improve his relationship with her husband. Later in their conversation at the beginning of Act 2 (p. 126), she tries to persuade him to stop his petty fights with the people that surround him. Clearly, a peaceful atmosphere in the house is important to her. Yelena's trust in Vanya is apparent in these conversations. At this stage of the play, it would be unwise to assume that Yelena has decided to forego her relationship with Vanya and begin a relationship with Astrov. Chekhov saves all this for later in the play.

Astrov immediately turns to Yelena and asks about Serebryakov. He has been summoned to tend to the professor and the patient is nowhere to be found. He is, of course, far more interested Yelena's well-being than in the health of her husband. Missing the point, she continues with some embarrassment, *"He was under the weather yesterday evening, complained of leg pains, but today he seems alright"* (p. 120). At this point, Astrov makes his move and announces that he has decided to stay for the night. This is particularly surprising, because, since

85

Yelena and Serebryakov moved to the estate, Astrov has visited three times (p. 120), but has never stayed the night. Explaining his decision, he says that he simply wants to get a good night's sleep. Sonya, of course, responds with joy and interprets his decision according to her heart's desire. She invites Astrov to lunch and he accepts. He is well aware of Sonya's feelings for him. In fact, the whole estate knows, including Yelena, who will discuss the matter with Vanya momentarily (p. 125). Astrov enjoys a close relationship with Sonya (we will discuss their relationship in Chapter 2), but he clearly stays in order to woo Yelena. Propriety is hardly the name of the game here. Astrov must save his life.

When Astrov accepts Sonya's lunch invitation, she makes sure to mention that they eat at six o'clock (p. 121). At face value, it is only natural that she should mention this, since it is already past three and she is noting that they had not had lunch at the usual hour. However, Yelena's presence opens another perspective. We later discover that Sonya and Yelena have not been speaking in recent weeks (p. 135). Yelena assumes that this is because of her marriage to Sonya's father. However, they have been married for ten years! This could hardly be the reason. Moreover, at this point in the play, Sonya is probably unaware that Yelena is falling in love with Astrov. What, then, has caused the rift between the two women? Sonya is quite irritated by Yelena's laziness, which is rubbing off on Vanya. At the beginning of Act 3, She scolds her with surprising vehemence: *"You're bored, don't know what to do with yourself, but being bored and idle is contagious."* (p. 139*)*. Like Marina, Sonya is upset by the disruption of the routine of the estate. She emphasizes that lunch will be served at six o'clock in order to clarify to Yelena, who is responsible for the disruption, that she must obey the rules. Even her complaint, *"the tea's cold"* (p. 121), is indirectly meant for Yelena. Here Chekhov, never missing an opportunity for a joke at his characters' expense, has Telegin also complain about the temperature of the tea. However in Telegin's considered opinion, it is because the samovar, itself, has cooled. Sharp-witted Yelena catches Sonya's attempt to scold her, but since they are not speaking to each other, she replies through Telyegin, saying, *"it doesn't matter, Ivan Ivanych, We'll drink it cold"* (p. 121). Yelena mistakenly calls him by the wrong name even though they have been eating lunch together for three weeks. Telyegin defends his honor and reminds her of his real name and his nickname – Waffles. And, to reaffirm his position in the estate where he has resided since he became bankrupt, he reminds Yelena that he is Sonya's godfather. Sonya jumps at the opportunity to announce that, unlike her stepmother, she respects Telyegin and she pours him another cup of tea.

Let us review the main plot developments in this scene. Astrov's wishes are fulfilled. He decides to stay, announces this to Yelena, convinced that he will manage to talk to her over the course of the evening. And so he enjoys his tea and has time to think about his plan. Vanya, on the other hand, has failed to achieve his goals. He waited for Yelena to placate her about the breakfast argument, but he becomes impatient with the conversation, which he sees as trivial. When his mother, Marya Vassilyevna, talks about the letter she received from Kharkov, he becomes even more impatient and tells her to be quiet. She becomes angry and chastises him: *"…in the last year you've changed so much that I don't recognize you at all… You used to be a man of convictions, an enlightened individual…"* (p. 121). This enrages Vanya, who says, *"Oh, yes. I was an enlightened individual who shed light on no one"* (p. 121). His rage explodes even further when he admits in front of everyone: *"I lie awake at night, frustrated and angry that I've so stupidly wasted the chance to enjoy all those things that my old age denies me now!"* (p. 121-122). The level of suffering contained in this statement is startling and attests to Vanya's long held misery and frustration. Sonya, who can't deal with her uncle's misery, shields herself with the claim that he is boring. And for once, Marya Vassilyevna, who usually restrains her own opinions in favor Serebryakov's, speaks sensibly. She tells Vanya that he has only himself to blame for his situation, that he should return to his old views and that instead of talking, he should go to work. Vanya answers mockingly that, unlike her respected professor, he is incapable of writing *ad infinitum* like an automatic machine. Marya Vassilyevna protests her son's scorn of the professor whom she so admires, but Sonya interferes and asks then to stop arguing. Vanya apologizes and promises to be quiet.

Now follows another silence. Yelena breaks in this time: *"The weather is very good today... It's not hot..."* (p. 122). Yelena's comments about the weather appear to provide very little **dramatic yield**.[29] However, much can be gleaned if we take a closer look at her experience since she entered and sat on the swing. She has come to the garden to speak with Vanya about the morning's disruption. She is still angry with him. She is also angry with Serebryakov, who stubbornly refuses to reconcile with Vanya. All morning she has felt trapped and hasn't had the courage to escape. In other words, she is having a very bad day! Therefore, her statement, *"the weather is very good today"* (p. 122) could easily be heard as an ironic comment on her own situation: even the weather ignores me; I am rotting away and it is improving. Vanya's response is tinged with a darker irony: *"It's good weather to hang yourself"* (p. 122). At this point, they look at each other and understand one another very well, but they are clearly unable to offer succor, and certainly not salvation.

Vanya's harsh, sarcastic observation elicits no appropriate response. Those who hear it might even laugh, each for his own individual reason. At that moment, Marina enters and grounds everyone in reality. She is seeking a lost chicken calling

---

[29] See definition in the Glossary.

"chicka, chicka, chicka" (pg 122). As he often does, Chekhov uses this interruption to avoid the excessive sentimentality inherent in the complex internal actions of Vanya and Yelena. For Chekhov, excessive sentimentality is a doubly dangerous trap: As a writer, he himself doesn't feel close to the characters if they display excessive emotion and he assumes that these characters might appear disagreeable to the viewers as well. While he leads his characters to places of emotional density, Chekhov inevitably balances their emotional excesses with the introduction of simple, commonplace events, usually incorporating a dash of humor. We witness such a moment at the opening of the play when Astrov says to Marina:

> *"But then, life itself is boring, stupid, and filthy... This life... it sucks you in. You're surrounded by oddballs, nothing but oddballs; and after living with them two or three years, you, too, unbeknownst to yourself, little by little, become an oddball yourself. It's your inescapable lot in life."* (P. 116).

When Astrov becomes too overwhelmed with despair, Chekhov brings him back to the ridiculous, simple reality: *"...look at this long moustache... A stupid moustache"* (p. 116). At the beginning of Act 2, when Vanya is drunk and alone on stage, feeling bitter and rejected because his own naïveté has failed him, Chekhov silences him with Telyegin's guitar. (p. 131). And again, later in Act 3, during the climax of the play, as Vanya pursues Serebryakov to shoot him, Sonya breaks down in alarm in Marina's arms. Marina offers her *"...a little linden tea, raspberry jam, and it'll go away"* (p. 150). These examples, among many others in Chekhov's plays, indicate that the escape from excessive sentimentality is not an accidental, but a fundamental, artistic choice. The effect of this choice is evident in 20th century film and theater. Woody Allen, one of Chekhov's best students, employs this strategy in dozens of scenes to a great comic effect.[30] For example, in *Annie Hall* (1977), at a critical point in their relationship, Annie calls Alvy and asks him to help her kill a cockroach in her kitchen sink.

It is important to note that when Chekhov brings a character into a scene in order to undo excessive sentimentality, the entrance is always justified with a clear action. In this scene, as well, Marina's entrance isn't arbitrary. Sonya had sent her to deal with the farmers (p. 120) so that she, herself, could serve tea and be alone with Astrov. Of course, Marina is aware of this and is unwilling to give up her duty. So she enters the garden, pretending to look for the lost chicken, in order to discern whether it's time to resume her duties. Did Marina talk to the farmers? Probably not. She spontaneously makes up an answer for Sonya. Marina, sensing the tension between Vanya and his mother and between Vanya and Yelena, decides

---

[30] In *Interiors* (1978), echoes of *Three Sisters* are most evident.

not to get involved and leaves. Telyegin, also intuiting the ill feeling, picks up his guitar and plays a polka.

Once again, the silence is broken by a laborer who has come to summon Astrov to tend to a worker at the factory near-by. This is an unexpected entrance, containing a problematic coincidence left over from the 'well-made play'. Chekhov brings the man into the scene at the precise moment when it is convenient to remove Astrov and leave Vanya and Yelena alone. This is not a successful dramatic decision. Had Astrov decided *not* to spend the night on the estate because of the family tensions, Chekhov could have used the laborer's illness as an excuse and devised a much more meaningful exit.

What do we learn from Astrov's exit? Why does he decide to leave the estate only a few moments after his decision to stay? Firstly, he feels deeply obligated to his patients. When he is called, he is immediately available. Secondly, it appears as though he only *pretends* to find it difficult to leave the estate, and he is using the laborer's call as a means of changing his mind. This is a reasonable assumption because Astrov could easily treat the patient at the factory and return to the estate for the night. A plausible reason for his decision to go can be inferred when, later in the scene, he invites Yelena to visit his estate. The doctor would certainly prefer to meet with Yelena without the frustrating, cumbersome presence of Vanya, the professor, *et. alia.*

Further support for this assumption comes when Astrov once again compares himself to the character in Ostrovsky's play, the man with the large mustache and little wit. What little wit is he hinting at? Surely not his medical skills of which he is sure. Rather, he is referring to his lack of competence in his quest for Yelena. He probably feels that the conditions on the estate minimize his chances of winning her, so he invites her to his estate in order to pursue her in more comfortable circumstances. He also invites Sonya -- as an alibi. Astrov uses her formal name here - Sofya Alexandrovna - on purpose; thereby subtly expressing to Yelena that his relationship with Sonya isn't as intimate as she might think. Does Sonya suspect that he has invited Yelena to his estate to play out his romantic intentions? It doesn't seem so. Had Sonya seen Yelena as a competitor, she would not have revealed her feelings for Astrov to her stepmother with such honesty in Act 2.

Astrov's invitation to Yelena creates an important twist in the plot. This could be the moment when Yelena realizes for the first time that she has an opportunity not to be missed. She doesn't accept Astrov's invitation, but instead uses the occasion to hint at her interest in him. She does this clumsily because she is somewhat embarrassed. She grasps at the first silly thought that comes into her head and asks if his interest in forestry is an obstacle to his medical goals. Her other questions sound equally artificial, yet Astrov is obliged to answer them: *"God alone knows what our true calling is."* (p. 123). Vanya also recognizes the irrelevance of her questions and maintains his ironic pose as he comments on them. Only Sonya, unaware of these underlying currents, flatters Astrov, compliments him on his hobbies and even praises him in a way that reveals her naiveté:

> *"..He says that trees adorn the earth, and that they teach people to understand beauty and instill a sense of pride in them. Forests help temper harsh climates. In countries where climate Is milder, people struggle with nature less, and that's why man is milder and tender there"* (p. 123)

Vanya laughs at her and turns to Astrov: *"allow me..., my friend, to continue to use firewood in the stove and build sheds out of wood."* (p. 123).

Astrov is hurt by Vanya's words. Had Yelena not been present, he may not have ordinarily responded, but she is, and the competition between himself and Vanya has begun. Astrov begins a monologue intended mainly for Yelena's ears. His arguments for the conservation of the endangered forests are valid, but their importance now lies in the impression he is trying to make on the woman he desires. Indeed, he presents himself as a broad-minded idealist, aware of man's self-destructive instincts and working to protect the future of humankind. This passionate description of his life's purpose surely impresses Yelena, but Astrov himself quickly realizes how pompous and ridiculous he sounds and ends his monologue with a typical deflation: *"But all this may just be too odd after all."* (p. 124). Finally, Astrov is ready to leave. He drinks a glass of vodka, offers a vague response to Sonya's question regarding his next visit and enters the house with her.

We have now reached the climax of the first act. Vanya and Yelena have been left almost completely alone together. They move to the veranda overlooking the garden. Marya Vassilyevna and Telyegin remain seated around the tea table. He plays the guitar and she makes notes on the margins of her texts. The meeting of Vanya and Yelena serves as the climax of the act because they have been planning to discuss their deteriorating relationship throughout the entire act. Yelena chastises Vanya for making Marya Vassilyevna angry, for calling Serebryakov a writing machine and most pointedly, for his quarrel with Serebryakov at breakfast, which has unsettled her all day. Vanya, ignoring her words, says what he has been wanting to say to her for a long time: *"If you could only see your face, your movements..."* (p. 125). She reacts scornfully and he turns his excessive emotion into irony: *"You're too lazy to live! Oh, this laziness!"* (p. 125). Yelena loses her temper. She is not lazy; she is in severe crisis. However, she dares not speak about it openly. Instead, she blames the men who destroy the forests and reproaches all of humanity, saying that soon, there

will be no fidelity, purity or selflessness. (p. 125).
On the surface, these are the three central values in
Yelena's life. She is faithful to her aging husband
and pure and selfless in her care of him. However,
as we have seen, her insistence on adhering to these
values is clearly not a result of their general import,
but rather of her lifelong fear of the lustful men
who want to take advantage of her innocence.

> "Why can't you look with equanimity at a
> woman who is not yours? ...the demon of
> destruction is inside all of you. You've no pity
> for forests, or birds, or women, or one another."
> (p. 125)

Vanya doesn't know how to interpret her words
because he is unaware of the painful traumas she
experienced in her youth. He very likely thinks she
is inventing this illogical "philosophy" in order to
reject him, so he dismisses it: *"I don't like this
philosophy!"* (p. 125). Yelena falls silent. She feels
that Vanya has not understood what she was trying
to say. We could also speculate that she senses that
had she spoken these words to Astrov, he would
have understood. However, she immediately feels
guilty about her desire to continue her relationship
with Astrov and reminds herself that Sonya loves
the doctor, so she must not even think about him.
She adds that, because of her shyness, she has
never properly addressed Astrov during his visits
or developed a fondness for him. She even suspects
that Astrov may think she resents him.

What are Yelena's actions in this monologue regarding her relationship with Astrov? Her external action is to conceal from Vanya her attraction to Astrov. Her internal action is to alleviate the guilt that has arisen from this forbidden attraction.

Vanya listens to Yelena's monologue with bewilderment. Could he have heard the echo of Astrov's words in hers and fears that the doctor has her heart? It doesn't seem so. It is more likely that she fears that Vanya suspects her. That is why she dismisses herself and Vanya as *"tedious and boring people"* (p. 125). Vanya's bewilderment deepens. Why is she speaking this way? After all, in his eyes, she is the epitome of beauty and of femininity. Yelena is keenly aware of Vanya's lovesick looks and cannot bear them: *"Don't look at me like that, I don't like it"* (p. 125). But Vanya is unable to suppress his love any longer:

> *"How can I look at you any other way if I love you? You're my happiness, my life, and my youth! I know, my chances for reciprocity are measly, equal to zero, but I don't need anything, just let me look at you, hear your voice..."* (p. 125).

Vanya speaks with great optimism, hoping that the expression of his love for Yelena might convince her to reciprocate. However, she rejects him forcefully: *"Sshhh, they might overhear you!"* (p. 125). Vanya persists, begging: *"Just let me speak of my love *for you… this alone will be the greatest happiness for me"* (p. 125). Yelena cannot handle his protestations and enters the house. Vanya's openness in declaring his love painfully reminds her how afraid she is to openly admit her own.

Chapter 2: Act 2

The dining room in Serebryakov's house. It's twenty minutes past midnight. Serebryakov sits in an armchair next to the open window, dozing. Yelena sits beside him, also dozing. The watchman's tapping in the garden is heard from outside.[1] A storm is approaching and will soon slam the window shut. No one is asleep, nor does anyone allow the others to sleep. The inhabitants of the house and their guests are so exhausted and frustrated that their defense mechanisms have gone awry. In this stormy midnight hour they will no longer hide what they managed to conceal in Act 1.
[2]

Chekhov doesn't explicitly state how much time has passed since the end of Act 1. However, at the beginning of the act, Yelena tells Vanya that Sonya hasn't spoken to her for two weeks (p. 129). Since Sonya spoke to Yelena in Act 1, passionately defending Astrov's obsession for his forest preservation (p. 123), we may assume that at least that much time has passed, perhaps even more - since at the end of Act 2, Yelena says to Sonya, "*we don't talk to each other for weeks*" (p. 136). Chekhov offers further hints that his characters have

---

[1] The watchman would tap his stick on a tree trunk to signify the end of his rounds.
[2] In *Three Sisters*, Act 3 opens late in the night with the characters also on edge.

undergone more changes between the acts. Serebryakov's health has deteriorated; he is impatient and exhausted and has not slept in two nights (p. 126). Yelena is likewise exhausted and uses very harsh language when talking to her ailing husband: *"Keep quiet! You've exhausted me!"* (p. 127). Sonya also loses patience with her father and dares to reprimand him: *"Please, don't act up"* (p. 128). And Vanya, having just entered the room, says that he, too, has not slept for two nights owing to his growing frustration and despair (p. 128). However, in spite of these hints the exact time since Act 1 cannot be determined. We have to make do with a general estimate of three to four weeks.

The discussion of the time between acts is not academic; it is fundamental to Chekhov's dramatic strategy. Many playwrights compress important preparatory actions between acts or scenes. Chekhov does so in most of his plays. For example, in *The Seagull*, during the few short days between Acts 1 and 2, the relationship between Nina and Treplev cools down substantially, while Nina, Arkadina and Trigorin grow closer. During the week between Acts 2 and 3, a highly traumatic event occurs – Treplev attempts suicide. Chekhov chooses not to portray this event on stage, but uses it to maximize the compression in Act 3. The event illustrates the increase in Treplev's suffering after discovering Nina's love for Trigorin. It also reveals to Arkadina that Trigorin is in love with Nina.

100

What other events, then, have occurred between acts 1 and 2 in *Uncle Vanya*?

On the surface, it seems that aside from Serebryakov's deteriorating health, no important dramatic events have taken place. Astrov is invited to examine him but Serebryakov refuses to see him, stating that he lacks medical skill. (p. 127). This does not make much sense. Serebryakov knows that Astrov is an excellent doctor. Is it possible that his refusal to be treated stems from his desire to keep Astrov off the estate and away from his wife? Serebryakov is not blind. He is keenly aware of Yelena's beauty and of her magical affect on men, especially Vanya and Astrov. When he calls Astrov a *"holy fool"* (p. 128), his anger is hardly due to a concern about the doctor's diagnostic skills! As time has passed, not only has Serebryakov's health deteriorated, but his fears about the future of his marriage have increased. Indeed, he says to Yelena, *"Disgusting you must find me first"* (p. 126). Yelena's harsh words, *"Keep quiet! You've exhausted me"* (p. 127), reveal that her doubts about their relationship have, in fact, increased. Moreover, upon entering, her first question is, *"Where is the doctor?"* (p. 135). While her interest may be with her husband's medical condition, her overarching concern is to speak with Astrov about her feelings for him, which she no longer denies.

Although the relationship between Serebryakov and Yelena has much deteriorated, it is important to reiterate that for a long time the marriage was satisfying and good. Serebryakov fell in love with Yelena's youth. In the eyes of those close to him, as well as in his own, the marriage was proof of his full sexual potency, despite his age. It proved that he was not ready to give up his emotional or erotic life. The marriage was rewarding for Yelena, as well. She loved her husband's intellect and abundant charm, which had long garnered the adoration of women. She admired his maturity and enjoyed the stability he offered; she appreciated the intellectual dialog they shared and was grateful to him for protecting her from the lust of other men. During their decade-long marriage a real sense of intimacy grew between them. The depth of their intimacy is painfully present in their mutual feelings of anger at the beginning of the act. It is important to emphasize this intimacy because the deterioration of an alienated relationship holds far less dramatic impact than the disintegration of a deeply intimate union.

And what has happened to Astrov? Chekhov gives no indication that he has visited the estate since the end of Act 1. On being called to examine Serebryakov, he rushed to the estate, leaving all his other engagements, so he could meet Yelena. Despite Serebryakov's objections to the examination, Astrov stays the night on the estate, awaiting the opportunity for a private meeting with Yelena. Indeed, as he leaves his room, he immediately asks Vanya: *"Are you here by yourself? No ladies?"* (p. 131). Astrov's attraction for Yelena has grown between the acts and he now hangs all his hopes on her.

And what has happened to Vanya? Though Chekhov does not offer any concrete information, he does stress the growing intensity of his actions. His advances toward Yelena are more impulsive than they were in Act 1; when the two are alone, he kisses her hand and says, *"here's my life and my love"* (p. 129). Vanya persists even when she flatly rejects him: *"I'm sorry, I can't say anything to you."* (p. 130). He also becomes more and more aware that life is passing him by: *"Day and night I'm haunted by the thought that my life is lost irretrievably."* (p. 129). We can assume that between the acts Vanya has kept up his desperate pursuit with less and less effort to conceal his feelings. His gestures are public and overt and he has lost his fear of appearing ridiculous. Though Yelena is increasingly uncomfortable with Vanya's advances, she does find relief in his willingness to listen to her as she describes her sufferings. (p. 129). Vanya is aware of this and knows that Yelena has chosen him above all others to bare her heart. He is proud that she trusts him as her intimate confidante. And all the while Vanya does not suspect that Astrov is in love with Yelena, since Astrov refrained from revealing any of his feelings during his last visit in Act 1, and has not visited the estate since then. In Vanya's mind, he is certain that his only competitor is Serebryakov.

What has happened to Sonya? Chekhov stresses the fact that Sonya is still hard at work. The hay harvest has begun[36] and unfortunately, there have been heavy rains and she must make sure that the workers harvest and store the hay before it rots. She is frustrated with Vanya's unwillingness to assist her and blames him openly: *"The hay's all cut, it's been raining every day, everything's rotting, and you're busy with mirages!"* (p. 132). In Act 3 she will also blame Yelena for not helping her with the business of the estate (p. 139). Despite her frustration, or perhaps because of it, she keeps thinking about Astrov. When he visits, she stays up to talk to him until 1:00 a.m., even though she is tired and has to get up early in the morning to work. Like Vanya, Sonya is still unaware that Astrov comes to the estate only to meet Yelena, and she perceives his visits as an opportunity to reveal her feelings for him - and to discover his feelings for her.

Chekhov planned the beginning of Act 2 meticulously. He informs us what has happened to the characters since the end of Act 1, though the events do not occur on stage. Chekhov's goal is to ensure that the **convergence** (the collection of the characters' external actions at the start of an act) and the **compression** (the collection of the characters' internal actions) are effectively in place.

---

[36] Hay is used as animal feed. After it is cut, it must be stored and dried to protect it from the rain.

To ensure that both the **convergence** and **compression** are effective, Chekhov chooses the dining room of the estate as the setting for the act. This is an obvious choice since the dining room is a common area in the house, allowing all the characters to enter and exit with ease. On the other hand, had Chekhov situated the act in a space that did not allow easy entrance, he might have provided more interesting obstacles for the characters, leading to more complex interactions. For instance, had he chosen Serebryakov and Yelena's bedroom, the entrance of another character would have been intrusive, requiring justification by extreme actions and appropriate changes of behavior. Cunning Chekhov, however, employs an opposite strategy. Instead of a setting that requires the characters to intrude upon one another's territory, he chooses a public place, but at a very late hour of night – twenty minutes past midnight. The hour raises an equally interesting question: what are these characters doing in a public space so late at night and why are they not asleep in their rooms?

Why are Serebryakov and Yelena in the dining room? Why are they sleeping there and not in their bedroom? Who was the first to move from the bedroom to the dining room and who followed? Chekhov keeps these details to himself, but it is more likely that Yelena left the bedroom in order to avoid the advances of her husband. Despite his age and illness, Serebryakov refuses to surrender his conjugal pleasures and desires some moments of intimacy with his young, beautiful wife. When they both retired to their bedroom an hour or two earlier, Serebryakov attempted to become intimate with Yelena, if not for sexual intercourse, then at least for some close conversation and affectionate physical contact. Yelena has no desire for intimacy with Serebryakov, not only because of his old age and hypochondria, but because of his tiresome behavior over the last weeks in response to the threatening overtures of Vanya and Astrov. She even harshly demands, *"Keep quiet! You've exhausted me"* (p. 127). It may also be possible that Astrov's presence in the next room makes it difficult for Yelena to become intimate with her husband. She may secretly hope to meet Astrov in the dining room when he goes for a nightcap.

These assumptions allow us to guess the events on the estate prior to the beginning of the act: after being rejected, Serebryakov followed Yelena to the dining room and persisted in his advances. She continued to reject his attempts until they both became exhausted and fell asleep, despite the powerful internal actions compressed inside them.

What is Serebryakov's internal action? What is his distress? Serebryakov is very anxious about Vanya's advances towards his wife; in addition, in his heart he senses that Astrov also desires her. He is also keenly aware that the growing distance between himself and his wife is a warning sign. His illness and pain exacerbate his concerns, making him less desirable to her. He even explicitly says:

106

"Disgusting you must find me first" (p. 126). If this is indeed Serebryakov's distress, his internal action must be to alleviate this distress. He yearns to feel alive, young and healthy, attractive and loved, first and foremost by Yelena.

What is Yelena's internal action? Her distress is clear. She can no longer bear her husband's attempts at intimacy. She is disgusted by him and painfully aware of the terrible trap she is in. It is no accident that she says to Serebryakov: *"Wait, have patience: in five or six years I'll be old, too"* (p. 127). Thus, her internal action is her longing to break free of this trap. She, too, longs to live, to fulfill her emotions and dreams, to be young and passionate, loved and desired by men as passionate as she. She might even play the piano again. Indeed, at the end of the act, she says to Sonya: *"I'd play something… I'd play something now"* (p. 137).

These internal actions define the conflict between Serebryakov and Yelena. The more he wishes to be loved and desired by her, the more his anxieties weigh on her and the more she longs to be free of him. Similarly, the more Yelena longs to fulfill her passionate dream of being loved by some young lustful man, the greater Serebreyakov's longing and the greater his fear that she will abandon him.

The External and Internal Processes in the Scene
As described above, Serebryakov is sleeping in the armchair next to the open window. Yelena, also asleep, sits next to him. Serebryakov suddenly

107

awakens and asks, *"Who is that? Sonya, is that you?"* (p. 126). Why does he ask this question? Doesn't he recognize Yelena, who is beside him? We could assume that Serebryakov was suddenly awakened by his painful rheumatism, as he says, and in a state of confusion, failed to recognize his wife. The dramatic impact of this assumption is minimal, since it attributes Serebryakov's awakening to a random pain. Let us explore another possibility. Perhaps Serebryakov awoke because of the dream he speaks about: *"...I had a dream that my left leg belonged to someone else."* (p. 126). The dream describes the loss of a crucial body part, which could certainly reflect his fear of losing Yelena, a crucial part of his life. [37] Thus, as he wakes up, he may well believe that he has already lost her and mistakes her for Sonya.

When he hears Yelena's calming voice, he relaxes. Realizing that in his anxiety he woke her up, Serebryakov apologizes and says he was awakened by his rheumatic pain. Yelena forgives him and does not complain. On the contrary, she attempts to calm him, suggesting that the pain he feels is due to the chill in his legs. She covers them with a blanket and closes the window.

---

[37] An actor cannot dream and cannot differentiate between a thought that arose in a dream and a daydream. Thus, from the point of view of the actor in the part of Serebryakov, he must see the dream as a daydream.

Serebryakov's health has, in fact, deteriorated. He struggles to breathe and asks Yelena to leave the window open. Then he tells her of the dream, which could be seen as the annoying complaint of a self-absorbed old man. However, the dramatic impact of such an interpretation would be minimal since it reduces Serebryakov to a stereotypical old tyrant, conceited and arrogant, insensitive to the needs of others. It would be better to see the dream as an attempt to regain connection with Yelena by sharing his deepest thoughts and feelings. Serebryakov may also want to entertain Yelena with a surreal image of his left leg belonging to someone else, and that the pains he just described to her are phantom pains that he felt in his dream.

Yelena does not find this image entertaining. Serebryakov refuses to give up, returns to reality and tells her that it is not gout, but rheumatism. Perhaps he wishes to calm Yelena by stating that his illness is less serious - rheumatism and not gout, and that he would soon recover. Yelena does not respond; she remains distant and cold. Serebryakov has failed. This is not surprising, since Serebryakov's attempts at closeness often involve 'old people's' jokes, which she hates. Then he explores another route to her heart and asks her the time. Why is he suddenly interested in the time? This is probably because he wishes to discuss Batyushkov's poetry.[38] Perhaps he knows that she

---

[38] A Russian poet who influenced Pushkin.

likes these poems. However, when she answers that it is twenty minutes past midnight, he realizes that it is too late to send her to the library to fetch the book, and postpones the reading to the next day. Yelena is stunned by his late night request and responds with an incredulous, *"What?"* (p. 126). She has heard him alright, but lets him know that she considers his request rude and inconsiderate. She is exhausted. Serebryakov fails again. Then he asks, *"but why is it so hard for me to breathe?"* (p. 126). This question can be interpreted as a complaint, but also as an apology for the trouble he causes her because of his breathing difficulties.

Yelena rejects his apology and reminds him indifferently that he has not slept in two nights and his breathing difficulties are caused by exhaustion. She would like him to go to sleep, and be free of his advances, but Serebryakov does not stop. He continues to talk about his illness, comparing himself to famous writer Turgenev. This, of course, can also be seen as a complaint: as if my situation were not bad enough, it will get worse, in the same way that Turgenev's gout was the precursor to his angina pectoris. However, this can also be seen as yet another humorous statement: Turgenev and I are similar. Both of us have gout and both of us will have had angina pectoris.

Chekhov doesn't judge his characters by giving them negative, one-dimensional characteristics. Many of his characters are selfishly motivated, e.g. Arkadina in *The Seagull* or Liubov Andreyevna in

The Cherry Orchard, yet they are portrayed fully and examined empathically. Chekhov is well aware that to judge a complex character is counterproductive. A prejudicial view prevents the playwright and the spectator from seeing the character respond differently in different situations, thus limiting the character's diverse and complex actions. The following quote by Leah Goldberg is particularly appropriate in this case (1968, 223): *"Chekhov is capable of loving people who are objectively incorrect, not clever, nor even good."*

And so Chekhov constructs Serebryakov empathically, as a complex and multi-layered character. He is an old man struggling to accept the loss of his youth, yet who is still charming, confident and attractive to women. If Chekhov had designed Serebryakov only as an annoying, complaining old man, Yelena would simply run away with the first man to offer his love. The playwright knows that he must create a certain balance among the three men in Yelena's life in order to make her choice more difficult. An easier choice would exempt her from deliberation and would have flattened her as a character. This assumption is further justified at the end of the play: early in the process of writing, Chekhov knew that Yelena would remain with Serebryakov. If Serebryakov were presented only as a tyrannical, selfish old man, Yelena's decision to remain with him would be impossible to justify.

The miserable marriage of Serebryakov and Yelena is hardly a unique example of an unsuccessful romantic pairing in Chekhov's plays. In fact, all the couples in his three major plays live in misery: Arkadina and Trigorin in *The Seagull*, Masha and Kulygin in *Three Sisters* and Liubov Andreyevna and her lover in *The Cherry Orchard*. Chekhov clearly was a skeptic regarding man's ability to maintain happy romantic relationships over time. However, all the abovementioned couples continue to live together despite their misery. Even Liubov Andreyevna returns to her lover in Paris at the end of the play. For Chekhov, it seems that a life apart is far more frightening than a wretched union.

Returning to the scene, let us assume that Serebryakov's initial statements about his illness are said in jest, in order to relieve Yelena and to regain some closeness with her. Unfortunately for him though, his joking comparison to Turgenev is scornfully rejected, without the slightest hint of a smile. At this point, Serebryakov loses patience and curses the wretched old age that clings to him through no fault of his own. He also blames those around him for judging him: *"This damn disgusting old age! To hell with it. Having gotten old, I find myself disgusting. And, all of you, most likely, find me disgusting, too"* (p. 126). Serebryakov's anger about the injustices he endures in old age clearly demonstrates his lust for life, his desire to continue working and being active, as well as his desire to continue loving and being loved. The Chekhovian gap between a character's self image and his actions is discernible once again. Serebryakov must have forgotten that he is not only an old man battling to maintain his life, but also a grumbling, egocentric narcissist, who makes it very difficult for people to like him.

However, Yelena is a young twenty-seven years old and she cannot empathize with her husband's tragic view of himself. In her mind, she fantasizes about younger, more attractive men. She rejects Serebryakov's self-revelations: *"You speak about your old age as if we're to blame that you're old,"* (p. 126). She is now discovering, in this late midnight hour, when all of her defenses are down, the magnitude of the price that she has paid for marrying Serebryakov. She is not angry with him for being old, but with herself for failing to foresee this. Serebryakov is surprised and devastated by Yelena's attack. After baring his soul, her cold response reveals how substantial the distance between them has become. Serebryakov, in pain, can no longer ignore it and attempts to provoke her, saying, *"disgusting you must find me first"* (p. 126). He hopes that she will deny this, maybe even apologize or attempt to calm him with an embrace, a touch, or a kiss. Instead, she gets up and walks away.

Serebryakov sees that he has been mistaken and once again Yelena fails to respond to his pleas. However, he persists, trying to ease the sting of his harsh words. He uses irony and tries to appease Yelena by extolling her youth. He even jokes about his own age: *"And, of course, it's stupid that I'm still alive."* (p. 126). And with dark humor, he also promises, *"but wait, I'll set you all free. I don't have much longer"* (p. 126). Again, Yelena rejects his attempts to mollify her. Why does she behave this way? Yelena, too, should not be judged too quickly. This scene can only be dramatically potent if the end is not determined at the start, i.e., if Serebryakov still has a chance to appease her and regain her heart. What would bring this young woman back to the bedroom? Had Serebryakov stopped his romantic overtures and let her return to her bed, she probably would have felt less agitated, forgiven him and fallen asleep. However, Serebryakov makes a doubly serious mistake: not only does he persist with his demands, he also jokes about his old age. He fails to take into account that his age and illness are sensitive issues for Yelena. Each time he mentions his age, he forces Yelena to admit to the horrible mistake she made by marrying him, a mistake that she has managed to suppress until now. Therefore, when he says, *"and I'm an old man, practically a corpse"* (p. 126), Yelena's anger and frustration worsen and she responds, *"I can't take this anymore... For God's sake, be quiet"* (p. 126). Has Serebryakov ever heard such harsh words from her before? We don't know. However, the actor portraying Serebryakov would do well to decide that this is, indeed, the first time that Yelena has told him to be quiet. This way his wound would be deeper, and he would leap to find a response to conceal his pain. Serebryakov chooses sarcasm: *"It turns out that, thanks to me, nobody can*

*take it anymore, they are all bored, wasting their youth,
all thanks to me; and I'm the only one content and
enjoying life"* (p. 127). Again, in his misery,
Serebryakov repeats the same mistake and Yelena
responds even more desperately than before: *"Keep
quiet! You've exhausted me!"* (p. 127); and then,
*"that's unbearable! Tell me, what is it you want from
me?"* (p. 127). At last Serebryakov understands. He
realizes how painful his jokes are to Yelena. Yet his
own pain is so great that he cannot keep quiet. He
changes his tactics, stops joking and talks honestly
about himself, displaying impressive self-
awareness. He asks not for mercy, but for justice.
Justice for a man who has aged through no fault of
his own, who was exiled from his work, his status
and from the attention of those close to him. The
injustice he suffers is too great for him to bear
because, in his opinion, a man of his achievements
and status deserves better treatment than what he
receives from Vanya or his old idiotic mother-in-
law, Marya Vasilyevna. Surprisingly, Serebryakov
admits: *"Well, let's suppose I'm disgusting, an egoist, a
despot, but don't I, in my old age, have a certain right to
be an egoist?"* (p. 127).

Serebryakov does not ask for mercy; he demands
what he rightfully deserves. Perhaps he even thinks
that he did Yelena a favor when he married her.
She probably was his student. It was he who
granted her the status of professor's wife. Aside
from her beauty, she had no exceptional qualities,
as she later confesses: *"I was always a minor
character"* (p. 137). From his perspective, should

she abandon him now, it would be shameful exploitation on her part. Without naming names, Serebryakov rants about the treatment he receives from "everybody", but it is clear that he is referring to treatment he suffers at Yelena's hands. When he says, *"everybody starts feeling miserable"* (p. 127), he is really begging for Yelena's consideration. Yelena answers, *"No one's impugning your rights"* (p. 127). This reply could be interpreted as a way to stop his ranting, but Chekhov has her say it twice. Have Serebryakov's words possibly touched a nerve? Does she think that his claims are correct? She might. However, it is also possible that she stops short of telling him that love is not driven by justice and that she cannot love him despite the validity of his claim. Either way, Serebryakov senses that she has heard him, and continues his pleas for consolation for the injustices he has suffered since his retirement:

> *"To devote my whole life to scholarship, get used to my study, an audience, my venerable colleagues – and, suddenly, to find myself in this crypt, look at stupid people here every day and listen to their inane conversations… I want to live, I love success, I love fame, excitement, but here – I'm in exile. To long every minute for the past, follow the success of others, and fear death… I can't! I do not have the strength! And now they don't want to forgive me my old age!"*
> (p. 127)

This illustrates once again the difference between Vanya's appreciation for Serebryakov and Serebryakov's appreciation for himself. Serebryakov does not give up despite his old age and deteriorating health. He wants to live, to succeed, to publish his work and to remain a respected scholar. He rails against his fate, his exile, his lost past, his pain at witnessing the success of others and, entwined in all, the fear of death. He ends his speech with a clear intimation that, along with the others, Yelena has failed to forgive him for his old age. Picking up the hint, Yelena responds: *"Wait, have patience: in five or six years I'll be old, too"* (p. 127). As mentioned above, her response reflects bitter recognition of the trap she finds herself in, as well as a measure of empathy for Serebryakov - you are not alone in your old age; I will soon join you.

Plot and Shifts
Let us continue to explore this scene to help define some additional dramaturgical terms. **Plot** is a very common term in the language of theatre. In light of the definition of **external action** it would only be natural to define the plot of a scene or a play as the series of external actions it contains. This definition does not differ fundamentally from Aristotle's definition in *The Poetics*: *the Plot is the imitation of the action - for by plot I here mean the arrangement of the incidents.*[3]

---

[3] *Poetics* by Aristotle, Chapter 6, S. H. Butcher, trans., Dover Publications, New York, 1951.

Although Aristotle does not differentiate between external and internal actions as we have done for the purposes of this study, this distinction is useful because it allows us to define the plot as a series of actions that are visible to us, and to use a different term to define the series of hidden, internal actions. This generates an inspiring, productive discussion of the dialectic between the visible and the invisible forces.

When we define the plot as a series of external actions, we assume that each character must have at least one external action in every scene. Otherwise the character would not have a role to play and would be superfluous. However, if each character were given only one external action and engaged in that same action throughout, the scene would be static, which in theatre jargon would mean that "nothing was going on". Let us examine the ways in which Chekhov deals with the demand for "something going on" by reviewing Serebryakov's words:

> "I heard that Turgenev's gout developed into crushing chest pain. I worry it might happen to me. This damn disgusting old age! To hell with it. Having gotten old, I find myself disgusting. And, all of you, most likely, find me disgusting, too." (p. 126).

At the beginning the speech, Serebryakov's external action is to appease Yelena with banter comparing himself to Turgenev. His internal action, however, is his longing to feel wanted and loved by Yelena. When he fails to achieve his internal action with the Turgenev comparison, he turns to a new external action. He condemns his old age, which makes his life bitter and accuses everyone of hating him because of it. This external action is, indeed, different from its failed predecessor, and thus Chekhov reveals the dramatic structure necessary for every scene: when a character fails at one external action, he or she resorts to a different strategy and employs a different external action in order to achieve the same internal action, or sometimes even a new one. The change in external action will be defined as a **shift**.

Yelena responds to Serebryakov's new external action and says, *"You speak about your old age as if we're to blame that you're old"* (p. 126). Her external action is to reject his accusation. At this point, Serebryakov does not change his external action; he intensifies it, accusing Yelena of hating him more than anybody else. This time, Yelena does not respond verbally; she chooses a physical action instead – she gets up and moves away from him. This is a meaningful, albeit not a textual **shift**. Serebryakov interprets her action correctly and changes his strategy yet again. Regretting his accusations, he flatters and validates her, then jokes again about his impending death. The scene becomes more and more dynamic, with 'more going on' as the shifts increase. Moreover, as the shifts increase in an effort to realize a single

internal action, the fundamental nature of the
internal action becomes increasingly evident,
otherwise why would struggle so hard to carry it
out.

Clearly, Chekhov was intuitively and consciously
aware of this dynamic as he carefully constructed
his plays.

Sonya's Entrance

Where does Sonya come from? Why is she awake
at such an hour of the night? As previously
mentioned, this evening is of great importance to
her because she is planning to explore her chances
of marrying Astrov. He probably arrived at the
estate during the evening and, since Serebryakov
refused his medical services, the doctor decided to
spend the night on the estate for his own reasons.
Sonya has not yet managed to be alone with him,
but she does not abandon her plan, even after he
retires to his room. At this stage, she does not dare
knock on his door and enter his room to talk with
him. The rules of courtship forbid this for Sonya,
who is religious, uneducated and conservative.
And so, she sits in her room, angry and frustrated,
hoping Astrov will knock on her door but knowing
for certain that he will not. She is aware of the fact
that if she goes to sleep, she will miss her
opportunity. And while she is genuinely concerned
about her father's health, she now uses it as an
excuse to wander around the house, lying in wait
for the doctor. After long deliberation, she finds a
solution: she will convince her father to allow

Astrov to examine him. Once he agrees, she will call Astrov, who will come out of his room, examine her father, send him to bed and stay for a drink with *her*. Her plan does not raise any suspicions because her father, overwhelmed by illness and anxiety, is indeed struggling to fall asleep.

So Sonya enters the dining room and demands that her father agree to the examination. Serebryakov refuses. He will not allow his rival the pleasure of seeing him old and sick, and he certainly will not allow the doctor an opportunity to meet Yelena. He rejects Sonya's demand, claiming that Astrov is incompetent. Sonya persists, saying that it doesn't take much skill to treat gout. Serebryakov answers, *"I won't even talk to that holy fool"* (p. 128). Sonya's plan has failed, but she doesn't give up. She decides to stay in the dining room and wait on the off chance that Astrov will appear.

Sonya's presence in the dining room interferes with Serebryakov's private conversation with his wife, so he tries to persuade his daughter to leave. At first, he asks her the time to remind her that it is late and that she should go to sleep. Yelena says it is past midnight, but Sonya does not move. Then Serebryakov attempts to make things more difficult for Sonya and asks her to bring him his medicine from the table. Sonya does so, but Serebryakov reproaches her angrily, claiming that he asked for a different medicine. Sonya is hurt by his anger and demands that he stop abusing her. She is not happy with this situation. Time is running out and she needs to wake up early to tend to the haymaking. Nevertheless, she remains in the room, determined to meet Astrov. Yelena follows the conflict between her husband and her stepdaughter without becoming involved. In fact, she is silent for a long time. This raises the suspicion that her silence is intentional, a means to defy her husband: *I will not become involved nor will I help you. Our conversation is over. Go to bed. I will not join you there.* Poor Serebryakov is left to sit helplessly in his chair. Yelena and Sonya remain seated. Nobody moves.

Vanya's Entrance

We have already described the intensification of Vanya's actions since the end of Act 1. In order to define the convergence more accurately, we will now try to interpret his external actions as he enters the dining room. While Vanya is clearly aware of Serebryakov's deteriorating health, Serebryakov is his enemy and he sees him as an annoying hypochondriac. Vanya knows that Astrov has come to examine Serebryakov, but is unaware of the real motive for his arrival. How is it possible that Serebryakov knows the reason for Astrov's arrival and Vanya does not? The explanation seems to lie in Serebryakov's paranoid suspicion that any younger man is a threat. Vanya, on the other hand, does not even imagine that Astrov, his only friend on earth, would dare lay eyes on the woman he loves. We can even assume that Vanya is happy about Astrov's visit. In recent years, Vanya's only source of entertainment has been drinking with his educated and charismatic friend. The two may have even enjoyed a drink together before retiring to their room – unaware that two hours later, Serebryakov and Yelena would return to the dining room, followed by the rest of the residents of the house.

Vanya had retired to his room following the early drink with Astrov. Did he want to sleep? He may have. Chekhov even stipulates that he is wearing a housecoat. Vanya hints at his fatigue and later tells Yelena that he has not slept in three nights, not because of Serebryakov's ill health, but because of his own concerns (p. 129). As sparse as this description may be, it allows us to understand what Vanya has endured over the past two sleepless nights. He knows that Serebryakov and Yelena have not slept either. They must have moved from their room to the dining room and from the dining room to the guest room, and then back to their own room. We can assume that sometime during the previous two nights, Vanya has tried to join them, pretending to offer his assistance, especially to Yelena, who has been caring for her husband. However, his real objective has been to spend private time in conversation with Yelena. Serebryakov is keenly aware of this fact. For this reason, he rejects Vanya angrily when he enters the dining room to offer his assistance: *"No, no! Don't leave me with him! Don't. He'll talk my head off!"* (p. 128). Yelena, on the other hand, does not reject Vanya's offer, knowing that while he is present, Serebryakov will stop harassing her.

Moreover, her conversations with Vanya bring her some respite, despite the fact that she is unsure of her feelings towards him.

Tonight again, Vanya has put on his housecoat, pretending to go to sleep. But he really has been waiting in his room for an opportunity to return to the dining room. He is aware of Serebryakov's illness and of his refusal to let Astrov examine him. He hears the couple whispering. He does not eavesdrop but is cognizant of the growing rift between them. He also hears Sonya leave her room and has heard her attempts to convince her father to let the doctor examine him. Vanya hears Serebryakov's objections and when the volume rises, he decides it is time to enter the dining room. In other words, Vanya's external action is to find a way to be alone with Yelena. To what end? We will soon understand. His internal action is expressed in detail, courageously and honestly in his conversation with Yelena. When she rejects his kiss, he says:

> *"Day and night I'm haunted by the thought that my life is lost irretrievably. There is no past; it was wasted stupidly on trifles, and the present is hideous in its absurdity. Here's my life and my love: how and what am I going to do with them? My feeling is perishing in vain, like a ray of sunlight caught in a pit, and I'm perishing, too."* (p. 129)

Vanya speaks of his distress in desperate terms: *"my life is lost"*; *"there is no past"*; *"the present is hideous"*; *"my feeling is perishing"*; *"I'm perishing"*. His internal action is to alleviate this distress. He longs to find a way to express the love that is raging inside him, a love that is not returned. His external action is, of course, evident in his attempts to convince Yelena to requite his love. This interpretation teaches us again that the internal action is autonomous; it is the urge to fulfill the character's innermost desires. Whereas, the external action is generally directed at the others characters with the goal of obtaining something from them.

The External and Internal Processes in the Scene

As he enters Vanya says, *"Helene[4] and Sonya, go to bed, I've come to relieve you"* (p. 128). This, of course, is an outright lie. Vanya wants Sonya and Serebryakov to return to their rooms so he can talk to Yelena privately. He hopes that his suggestion will direct any suspicion away from him. Serebryakov, however, is not naïve. He knows Vanya's intentions, but his pride will not allow him to admit that Vanya is pursuing his wife. He prefers to lie and ask not to be left alone with Vanya (p. 128). Vanya continues to lie: *"But you have to let them rest! They haven't slept for two nights"* (p. 128). Serebryakov agrees to let Yelena and

---

[4] Vanya uses the French version Helene and not its Russian version Yelena in order to hide the intimacy he feels for Yelena.

Sonya go to bed, on the condition that Vanya does so as well. With a touch of irony, he patronizes Vanya to conceal his real concerns: *"Thank you very much. I beg you. For the sake of our former friendship, don't object. We'll talk later"* (p. 128). As though Vanya wanted to talk to him! Vanya, too, is no stranger to irony and makes fun of Serebryakov: *"our former friendship... Former..."* (p. 128). He also angers Sonya, who has had enough of the battles between her father and uncle. Serebryakov turns to silent Yelena and asks for her help. He repeats, *"My dear, don't leave me with him! He'll talk my head off"* (p. 128), but Yelena does not respond. She knows that her husband fears that Vanya might win her heart; she says as much on the following page. Does Vanya stand a chance at this moment? The chances may be very slim, but the actress portraying Yelena would do well to refrain from deciding this before the ensuing conversation with Vanya. Vanya fails to get rid of Serebryakov, but dismisses his claims as ridiculous. The four characters in the dining room sit helplessly, unable to find a way out of the complicated situation they find themselves in. At this moment, Marina enters.

Why is Marina Awake at this Hour?
The answer to this question seems clear. Marina must tidy the dining room up after everyone else has gone to bed. While the house is awake, she must be, too. However, on rare occasions such as this, when the others have not yet retired, she would very likely have gone to bed before them. Note that tonight, however, she does not return to

the dining room to tidy up at the end of the act. This distinction allows us to assume that Marina may have already gone to bed, as Sonya tells her to do when she enters the dining room, but prefers to stay awake for reasons of her own. She may, of course, insist on tidying the dining room to demonstrate that she is still capable of fulfilling her duties. Yet, as we will soon see, her actions are so powerful and unselfish that concern about her position hardly comes into play. Is it possible that old Marina understands the tragedy of Serebryakov's aging better than anyone else? Is this why her empathy for him is more pronounced than the others? Has she come to relieve his agony? Is it possible that she was sitting in a nearby servants' room, listening to the conversations in the dining room and feeling worse and worse for Serebryakov? Has she finally reached a breaking point and come to the dining room to help him? This is very likely, since she addresses Serebryakov immediately, fully aware of his suffering.

She enters, holding a candle. Sonya, who is in charge of the routines on the estate, tells her to go to bed. She loves Marina, who has raised her since the death of her mother, and is also aware of her age and weakened condition. More than that, however, Sonya wishes to disperse the crowd that has gathered in the dining room so she can finally meet with Astrov. Marina does not immediately reveal the real reason for her presence; rather, she observes that the samovar must be removed from the table. However, she adds the blunt remark *"can't exactly go to bed"* (p. 128). According to our interpretation, this remark is not directed at Serebryakov, but at the other members of the household, namely Yelena, Vanya and Sonya, who fail to take his age into consideration, Serebryakov, however, thinking that she means to blame him, defends himself with his habitual sarcasm: *"No one can sleep, everyone's exhausted, and I alone am in a state of bliss"* (p. 128). Misunderstood, Marina turns to him and Chekhov emphasizes that she does so tenderly:

> *"What's the matter, dear? Is it hurting? Oh, my legs are throbbing, oh, so throbbing. [Arranges his blanket] It's an old illness of yours. The late Vera Petrovna, Sonechka's mother, may she rest in peace, used to stay up nights crying her eyes out with you... Oh, she loved you so...[A pause]The old are just like children, they so want someone to feel for them, but there's no one to feel sorry for us old people. [She kisses Serebryakov on the shoulder] Let's go to bed, sunshine, I'll make you linden tea and warm your feet for you... I'll pray to God for you..."*
> (p. 128-129)

Chekhov emphasizes that Serebryakov is touched by Marina's words. Indeed, her empathy enables her to recognize his distress and meet his needs. At first, she speaks about the pain he experiences as a result of his gout and says that her legs hurt too; she understands his suffering while others cannot. Then, by reminding him of his first wife, Vera

Petrovna, who loved him with all her heart, she attempts to alleviate his bitterness at being unwanted and unloved. She knows how much he needs compassion and acknowledges the tendency in human nature to neglect the feelings of old people. Thus, the lack of compassion he feels from the others is not due to his sins or to a personal flaw. Serebryokov is very precious to her. He is the light of her life and she promises to bring him linden tea, warm his feet and pray to God for him. With all this, Marina manages to relieve Serebryakov's misery, strengthen and encourage him, and he agrees to go to bed. Sonya joins her and they walk him to his room. On the way, Marina encourages Sonya, as well, recalling her mother, who loved Serebryakov so much that her heart broke at the sight of his suffering. Sonya, just a baby then, was unaware of this. In this way, Marina makes it known that Serebryakov deserves Sonya's compassion as well.

It is impossible to remain aloof from Marina's presence in this scene, despite the fact that she is a secondary character. We cannot say for certain when Chekhov discovered this power while writing the play. There is no indication of it in Act 1. However, once having displayed her strength in this scene, Chekhov develops it in Acts 3 and 4, creating a vital character capable of remaining sane and humane in the midst of the play's trials and tribulations.

Vanya's Love for Yelena and Yelena's Rejection

Vanya's plan has, at last, almost miraculously come into being. The moment he has been waiting for has arrived. Now that Marina, Serebryakov and Sonya have left the dining room, he and Yelena are alone. During the last two weeks, there have not been many opportunities for private conversation with Yelena, and he is aware of the rarity of this opportunity. Tonight he will do everything in his power to show Yelena how much he loves and needs her and how desperate he is without her. He knows that his salvation depends upon his ability to open Yelena's heart. Yelena, on the other hand, is exhausted. She says that she can barely stand up. Her exhaustion is more emotional than physical, and she herself says, referring to Serebryakov, "*I am utterly exhausted with him*" (p. 129). Her honesty is surprising and attests to the close relationship that has formed with Vanya over the last two weeks. The fact that she is in crisis and that Vanya is her only confidante, the only one who understands her, does not necessarily mean that she would share with him the details of her relationship with her husband and her stepdaughter, or expose her desolation. That she does so should not be taken for granted. The closeness between Yelena and Vanya is crucial to the play. It allows us to conclude that, despite her occasional harshness, her feelings for Vanya are not unequivocal. Maybe – and this would add to the complexity of the play - her decision to reject his advances is not final before the end of Act 3. In other words, she continues to consider the possibility of accepting his offer in each of their meetings and rejects him only because of what occurs in the meetings themselves.

This observation raises deeper questions: Why, despite her trust in him and the seriousness of his offers, does Yelena eventually decide to reject Vanya? After all, his love for her is deep, generous and mature. And if she desired children, he could still father them.

We could answer simply by saying that there is no logic in love and that one cannot just decide to fall in love. This, however, is a general response, insufficient for Yelena's unique personality. Moreover, it is difficult to believe that after ten years of marriage to a man forty years her senior, she would find the twenty-year age difference between herself and Vanya problematic. It would even be a bigger mistake to assume that Yelena is a stupid, shallow woman, selfish, spoiled and unable to distinguish between good and bad. Such an assumption would also flatten the characters of her three admirers, presenting them as fools pursuing her only because of her looks. As we observed at the start of the play, Yelena is a woman in crisis. She is well aware of this fact. Her self-awareness is developed enough even to label herself an 'episodic character' at the end of this act.

Yelena offers no explicit verbal explanation for her rejection of Vanya, but much can be gleaned from her actions. In Chapter 1, we discussed Yelena's anxieties about men and the damage they do to the world in general and to women in particular (p. 125). However, Yelena is not blind. She sees that Vanya is different than most men she has known. She recognizes his gentleness and his kindheartedness. She knows that he truly loves her and that she can trust and confide in him. Their closeness gives her strength and consolation. So why does she recoil from his love? And why does she not recoil from Astrov? Clearly, Yelena compares the two men in her mind. Examining this comparison, we may be able to discover one of the reasons why she rejects Vanya. He speaks of his love in existential terms: *"Here's my life and my love: how and what am I going to do with them?"* (p. 129). He tells Yelena that his life depends on her love for him and thus holds her responsible for his future happiness and even his sanity. But Yelena does not feel she can bear this responsibility; she fears that she may not be able to save Vanya's life. Her fear of this all consuming love is so great that she recoils each time Vanya speaks of it (p. 129) and her responses become opaque and laconic. In contrast, Astrov does not burden Yelena with such responsibility. His expectations are more in the realm of lust and conquest: *"I submit to you. Here, have me!"* (p. 144). After they both confess their love, Yelena says, *"How funny you are... I'll always remember you with fondness"* (p. 156). On the other hand, she closes her meetings with Vanya with: *"Leave me alone! This is so cruel!"* (p. 139). Although Astrov, too, expects Yelena to save him, his demand is not explicit as Vanya's, and therefore less threatening in her eyes. Yelena's response to the challenge of Vanya's love seems to be based in her low self-esteem. She fears that she will not be able to withstand this challenge. She sees herself as *"a tedious, minor character... In music, in my husband's house, in love – everywhere, I was always only a minor character"* [40] (p. 137), and a minor character is not capable of saving anyone. An additional and equally important explanation can be found in the following observation, which is also based on Yelena's low self-esteem. Yelena is certainly aware of the trap that she has fallen into by marrying Serebryakov. Vanya offers her an escape from this trap, but in his plan she must take responsibility for *his* life and not her own. Before she can leave with Vanya or anyone else, for that matter, Yelena must be able to make choices about her marriage and her relationships. She must accept her own capacities and responsibility for her destiny. However, her feelings of inferiority and inadequacy render her incapable of doing so. And so, she is unable to escape the trap despite the fact that she knows where the exit is. This is why she will later reject Astrov, who offers her another kind of escape. At the end of Act 2, Chekhov provides proof of Yelena's incapacity to follow her own desires. She longs to play the piano: *"I haven't played in a long time. I will play and cry, cry like a fool"*

---

[40] Note the irony in the term "minor character". The spectator's knowledge that Yelena is far from being a secondary, allows for a more profound sense of the difference between her self-image and her status in the play.

(p. 138). She longs to make her voice heard, to say: "Here I am! I'm alive! I'm playing the piano!" However, she needs Serebryakov's authorization for this. He forbids it and she complies.

The External and Internal Processes in the Scene

We can assume that following the exit of Serebryakov, Marina and Sonya, Vanya rubs his hands together in excitement, but remains cautious, taking his time to approach Yelena and speak his mind. What exactly does he want to say to her? He has already declared his love for her at the end of Act I, so what remains to be said? What action does Chekhov give to Vanya to move the plot forward? At the end of the scene when Yelena turns to leave the room, Vanya stops her and asks, *"What are you waiting for? What damned philosophy stands in your way?"* (p. 130). He urges her to stop vacillating. Vanya does not specifically address the nature of Yelena's struggle to reach a decision, but in his monologue following her exit (p. 130), he describes their hypothetical marriage and his suffering because of this missed opportunity. It seems highly likely that during the weeks in between Acts 1 and 2, Vanya spoke openly with Yelena about the possibility of her divorce from Serebryakov and their subsequent marriage, but with no positive response from her. In the present scene, he again seeks a clear answer. This is why he waited in his room; this is why he went to the dining room; and this is clearly why he is so nervous.

Interpreting the scene in this way, we can learn much about Chekhov's dramatic strategies. At the start of each scene he defines new external actions for the characters. To accelerate the plot, these newly established external actions must be uncharacteristic of the character's usual habits or routines. Here, Vanya's external actions must not be similar to those of the previous night, which included helping Yelena and Sonya with Serebryakov and pursuing Yelena. Vanya's newfound external action is to elicit a definite answer from Yelena – will she marry him or not! Chekhov does not specify this action in the text or stage directions, but as we observed above, this external action can be deduced from Vanya's questions to Yelena. Having examined the scene in detail and recognized this new external action, the actor is able to create a deeper, more focused portrayal of the character.

At the beginning of their meeting Vanya lingers for a moment and observes Yelena. She sighs with relief and then admits, *"I am utterly exhausted with him"* (p. 129). As we have seen, this confession reflects Yelena's closeness to Vanya, who is quick to use the moment to prepare Yelena for his proposal. Using her confession as a springboard, he says, *"you are [exhausted] with him, and I am with myself. I haven't slept for three nights"* (p. 129). However, before he can offer himself as an escape from her husband, she continues to recount her sufferings:

"Things are not well in this house. Your mother hates everything save her pamphlets and the professor; the professor is exasperated, afraid of you, and doesn't trust me; Sonya's angry with her father and me, and hasn't spoken to me for almost two weeks; you hate my husband and openly despise your mother; I'm exasperated and I must have been on the verge of tears twenty times today... Things are not well in this house." (p. 129)

Vanya is painfully aware of all this. He does not, however, respond to her intimation that Serebryakov is afraid that Vanya might successfully seduce her. He dismisses her words as unimportant, mocks them, calling them *"philosophy"* (p. 129). He is intent on returning to the action he has been preparing for all evening - winning Yelena's acceptance of his marriage proposal. Though all too aware of Vanya's intentions, Yelena is still unsure and does not respond. Instead, she changes the subject and demands that he be more sensitive to the conflicts in the house. She says, *"the world is perishing not because of some thieves or fires but because of hate, rivalry, and all these petty squabbles"* (p. 129). She demands that he create peace on the estate. Vanya, however, is fed up with his own altruism and, still intent on his quest, refuses to take on this responsibility: *"First, help me make peace with myself"* (p. 129). For further emphasis, he takes her hand and kisses it. Yelena responds sharply, *"Stop it!"* (p. 129), pulls her hand away and says, *"Go away!"* (p.

129). Deeply offended, Vanya realizes that if he persists in this way, he will receive a firm '*no*'! So he relents, waits a moment for Yelena to calm down, then continues to pour out his feelings for her in hopes that she will finally understand and relent:

> "*It will stop raining, and everything in nature will be refreshed and will breathe easier. I alone won't be refreshed by the thunderstorm. Day and night I'm haunted by the thought that my life is lost irretrievably. There is no past; it was wasted stupidly on trifles, and the present is hideous in its absurdity. Here's my life and my love: how and what am I going to do with them? My feeling is perishing in vain, like a ray of sunlight caught in a pit, and I'm perishing, too.*" (p. 129)

At the beginning of this chapter, we examined the ways in which Vanya's words express his internal action: he longs to realize the powerful, loving feelings inside him before he grows old and dies, but he has not yet found a suitable, willing recipient. Yelena can certainly not remain aloof in the face of this forceful action. To say that she is insensitive to Vanya's suffering would make her a shallow foil for him. It is far more poignant and dramatically viable to decide that Yelena, indeed, hears every word; her heart almost breaks at Vanya's honesty, his courage and the depth of his yearning. The possibility that she might surrender, embrace and kiss him and accept his offer cannot be rejected at the outset. This is a very difficult moment for the actress portraying Yelena because Chekhov does not provide her with words to express her feelings. However, a fascinating stage moment can be created through in-depth, concise and accurate attention paid to this moment of deliberation. Yelena's fears eventually overcome her hopes of being saved by Vanya and she uses all of her energy to desensitize herself to him. Her answer is laconic and opaque: *"When you talk to me about your love[41], I become stupid somehow and I don't know what to say. I'm sorry. I can't say anything to you."* (p. 130) She attempts a quick escape for fear that she might acquiesce, but Vanya blocks her way out. Vanya is a sensitive man and can see her panic. He also recognizes that her resistance is weakening and he knows that he must continue to urge her to respond. Now he talks not about himself, but about her: *"If you only knew how much I suffer knowing that next to me, in the same house, another life is perishing – yours!"* (p. 130).

This observation pains Yelena very much. She knows that Vanya is right. She realizes that he is offering her a real escape that will save her before she is totally lost. She looks at him, hesitates, but once more the idea of taking responsibility for her life frightens her and she rejects him: *"Ivan Petrovich, you're drunk!"* (p. 130) Vanya does not

---

[41] Masha in *Three Sisters* avoids Vershinin's declaration of love in a similar way: *"When you talk to me like this, it makes me laugh for some reason although I feel scared"* (p. 183).

deny this, but his drinking habits are hardly of interest at this moment. He needs to break down the walls she has built around herself. Changing the subject, she asks, *"Where's the doctor?"* (p. 130). Vanya answers, *"He's there… Spending the night in my room"* (p. 130). He tries to return to the marriage proposal, *"maybe, maybe… Anything may be"* (p. 130). Before he has an opportunity to explain what may be, she complains about his drinking again. He confesses that drinking allows him to feel some semblance of life, and again pursues his quest. Yelena refuses to listen and sends him to bed. In desperation, Vanya takes her hand again and kisses it. It is at this moment that Yelena finally decides to reject him. She responds cruelly, *"Leave me alone. It's disgusting, after all"* (p. 130). She exits and Vanya is left alone.

Vanya in Private

At this point, Chekhov breaks the fourth wall and allows Vanya to speak his mind before the audience. Later in the play, he will give the same opportunity to Sonya and Yelena. He uses this theatrical device to refine and purify Vanya's insight during a hopeless crisis where there is no one else to talk to. Chekhov is, of course, aware of the dramatic weakness of this device, which does not allow for challenge or confrontation with other characters. However, he also knows that confrontation with the other characters can be substituted by strong internal and external actions of the character in question, allowing depth even without confrontation. Firstly, let us examine the external actions at the core of Vanya's soliloquy. Initially, Vanya tries to understand why he did not propose marriage to Yelena a decade earlier while she was still single. He has no answer to this question at this point. He is still unable to admit the real reasons for his failure to propose before Serebryakov did. He still cannot utter the words, "I am a weak, cowardly, defeated man. I am not worthy of Yelena". He avoids this confession with a fantasy where he is married to Yelena and eases her fears during a raging storm. However, he quickly returns to reality and asks, *"Why am I old?"* (p. 130). Beneath this seemingly banal question is a subtext that asks, "How could I have missed the opportunity when I was young?" Later he asks, *"Why doesn't she understand me?"* (p. 130). This question, too, masks a more profound question: "What is so wrong with me that she cannot understand me?" Then, in a surprise move, Vanya's thinks: maybe it is *her* fault! She doesn't understand me because of *'her rhetoric, her lazy moralizing, ridiculous and lazy thoughts about the demise of the world – it's thoroughly hateful'* (p. 130). After blaming Yelena, he turns to the main reason for his failure, his great rival, Serebryakov, the man who cheated and used him, forced him to labor tirelessly, to *"live and breathe him"* (p. 130). Vanya claims that Serebryakov has not only cheated Sonya and him, but the whole world: *"He's retired, and his life's work is now for all to see: not a single page of his labor will survive him, he's completely unknown, he's a nonentity! A soap bubble!"* (pp. 130-131). What conclusions does Vanya reach at the end of this self-examination? *"And I've been deceived... I see... Stupidly deceived..."* (p. 131).

By blaming others for his failures, Vanya misses the opportunity for real self-examination and an honest appraisal of his responsibility for his own sad state. And why? Chekhov knows that a character can only engage in true self-examination when his precious illusions are totally shattered. As long as Vanya holds on to the fantasy that Yelena might accept his proposal, he will choose the illusion over honest soul-searching. Even though Yelena rejected him harshly, Vanya somehow does not feel that she has closed the door in his face. He saw the effect of his words on her and bore witness to her indecisiveness. He saw that she almost relented and so prefers to hope that she might finally change her mind.

These external actions whereby Vanya places the responsibility on others attest to the depth of his internal action: he is straining to deny his own responsibility for his misery. This internal action requires great effort because even Vanya cannot ignore the fact that he didn't propose to Yelena while she was single and that he has enslaved himself to the professor throughout his adult life. The strength of Vanya's internal action is again revealed momentarily after his conversations with Astrov and Sonya. He comes to the point where he is longer able to deny responsibility for his failure, and, on the verge of tears, he admits: *"It's painful, not good... Never mind... Later... Never mind..."* (p.

141

132). He hides his painful realization from Sonya
and hurries from the room.

Astrov's Entrance
Astrov enters wearing a jacket, but no waistcoat or
tie. He is tipsy. Telegin follows him into the room
with his guitar. Where has Astrov come from?
Probably from Vanya's room, as Vanya had
mentioned to Yelena earlier. This is Astrov's first
visit to the estate since Act 1. He has been called to
see Serebryakov, who refused to be examined by
him. We may also assume that Astrov's desire to
meet with Yelena has intensified. We have few
details about Astrov's activities in the hours
preceding the start of Act 2. He arrives on the estate
after everyone has had dinner and admits to Sonya
that he has not eaten anything all day (p. 133). Has
he already spoken to Yelena or to Sonya? We have
no indication of this and we may assume that he
has not had the opportunity to talk to either of
them privately. He was called to Serebryakov's
room immediately upon arriving, tried to examine
him and was refused despite the urging of Yelena
and Sonya. Astrov left the room, apparently in
anger, and decided to spend the night in Vanya's
room with the excuse that it was too late to return
to his own estate. Since Vanya comes out of his
room at the start of the act, we can assume that the
two men had been drinking together and had gone
to bed. However, both of them were yearning to
see Yelena. After midnight, Vanya leaves the room
saying that he wanted to help Sonya and Yelena
with Serebryakov. Astrov, now alone and awake,

waits for Vanya's return so that he can get up and find Yelena. Time passes and Vanya does not return. Astrov is convinced that Yelena and Vanya are still talking in the dining room. He may also fear that Yelena has acquiesced to Vanya. He drinks more and more vodka and when he can no longer bear the thought that he may have missed his opportunity, he decides to leave the room. He fears that he will enter the dining room and find Yelena in Vanya's arms. So he wakes Telegin, forces him to take his guitar and follow, hoping that if he suggests a "party" he won't have to suffer a painful embarrassment. Why does Chekhov stipulate that Astrov is dressed carelessly? This is probably done in order to emphasize both that Astrov is tipsy and that his decision to go to the dining room was impulsive.

Entering the dining room, Astrov is surprised to find Vanya alone. Now, he no longer needs Telegin's presence, but in order to hide the reason for bringing him, he tells him: *"Play!"* (p. 131). Telegin, who has been forced out of bed, hesitates, but Astrov adamantly repeats his instruction and Telegin starts to play his guitar softly. The first question Astrov asks Vanya is: *"Are you here by yourself? No ladies?"* (p. 131), thus indicating his true intentions. And since he is so relieved to see Vanya there alone, he puts his hands on his hips, perhaps even takes a few dance steps, and sings a cheerful folk song about a homeless master in search of a bed. Why has Chekhov chosen this song? Astrov is not, after all, a homeless person in search of a warm bed. We will soon see that this song was not a random choice. Astrov's painful loneliness will become more and more evident over the course of the play. Vanya, confused by this drunken behavior, may be looking at Astrov, as if to ask, "What is the meaning of this dancing? You were already in bed!", and Astrov 'explains': *"The thunderstorm woke me up"* (p. 131). Then Astrov again reveals his real motivation and says, *"I thought I heard Yelena Andreyevna's voice"* (p. 131). Does this arouse Vanya's suspicion that Astrov may have, in fact, come out of the bedroom to meet Yelena? No, it does not. Vanya does not suspect that his friend and 'room mate', would betray him. Then Astrov tries to find out what has just happened between Vanya and Yelena. In order to elicit a response from Vanya, he refers to her as *"a gorgeous woman"* (p. 131). Vanya does not respond. Astrov paces around the room, notices Serebryakov's medication and tries to start a conversation hoping to find out more information about Yelena. At first, he demeans the prescriptions that Serebryakov has collected in his travels. Then, he expresses doubt about the genuineness of Serebryakov's illness. Vanya, having refused to engage Astrov from the moment he entered the room, responds drily, *"he is ill"* (p. 131).

Astrov finally understands that Vanya is in a foul mood and is not eager for a conversation. He asks, *"Why are you so sad tonight?"* (p. 131). When Vanya does not answer, Astrov continues to mock, *"Feeling sorry for the professor?"* (p. 131). Vanya explicitly says, *"Leave me alone"* (p. 131), but Astrov makes a pointed comment aimed at Vanya's heart: *"Or, maybe, you're in love with the professor's wife?"* (p. 131). Judging from Vanya's mood, Astrov has probably figured out that something painful must have happened between Vanya and Yelena. Why, then, does he mock him? Doesn't he realize that he is hurting him, is that, perhaps, his intention? Astrov probably still believes that he might be able to meet Yelena but in order to have an honest conversation with her, he must first get rid of Vanya. Since the doctor cannot reveal his plan to Vanya, he tries to make him uncomfortable enough to leave the dining room. Even when Vanya insists that Yelena is his *"friend"* (p. 131), Astrov continues to mock him: *"A woman can be a friend to a man only after being first his acquaintance, then his lover, and only afterwards his friend"* (p. 131). Vanya immediately rejects this comment and responds in anger: *"A vulgar philosophy"* (p. 131). At this point, Astrov fully registers Vanya's anger and understands that he has gone beyond the bounds of reason. He stops mocking Vanya, admits that he has become a vulgar man and a drunk, and, without apology, he explains his monthly binges:

> *"...When I'm in this state, I become impudent and insolent in the extreme. Everything's a breeze then! I take on the most complex surgeries and I do them flawlessly; I draw the most sweeping plans for the future, and I don't think of myself as an oddball then, and I believe*

that I am bringing enormous benefit to humanity..." (pp. 131-132)

A new action can be seen in this confession. Astrov is no longer trying to get rid of Vanya, but to share with him his inner despair, his failures and his sense of meaninglessness. He knows that Vanya will understand him. Perhaps he even hopes to convince Vanya to drink so that they might cheer each other up. However, even at such an intimate moment, Astrov is still unable to surrender his irony and ends by mocking himself – and the others: *"And I have my own philosophy then, and all of you, my buddies, appear to me the tiniest of bugs... mere microbes"* (p. 132).

In hopes of lightening Vanya's mood, he tells Telegin to play. Telegin worries that this may awaken the household, but Astrov insists and Telegin begins to play. The music does not help; Vanya remains seated and mournful. Astrov feels for his friend and makes an offer he cannot refuse: *"A drink's in order. Come, I think there's still some cognac left. And as soon as it gets light out, we'll go to my place"* (p. 132). Astrov knows that in order to improve Vanya's mood, he must distance him from Yelena. Moreover, Vanya's suffering has made Astrov realize that he, too, must distance himself from Yelena, the sooner the better, before he, too, is disillusioned about his own salvation. Vanya does not respond to his offer. Continuing his attempts to lift Vanya's mood, Astrov tells another joke, but fails again. As he racks his brain for a solution,

Sonya enters. Astrov is embarrassed and leaves the room.

Why does Astrov exit? He tells Sonya that he must excuse himself because he is not wearing a tie, a lame excuse in light of the relationship Chekhov has prepared for them. Astrov is aware of Sonya's feelings for him and perhaps at this moment, he simply has no patience to hear more of her declarations of love. However, from the playwright's perspective, this choice would serve to weaken their relationship. If Astrov has decided in advance that he has no interest in Sonya, their relationship would be static, shallow and have nowhere to go. If, on the other hand, he is *un*decided, if in each of their meetings Sonya still has a chance, and if Astrov decides not to marry her only later in the play, from a dramatic point of view, the relationship becomes dynamic, intriguing and surprising both to the characters and to us, the audience. We might even assume that had Serebryakov and Yelena not come to the estate to live, and had Astrov not fallen in love with Yelena, he might well have acquiesced to Sonya and married her. This is not mere conjecture. In Act 3, Astrov himself explicitly says to Yelena: *"If you had told me (that Sonya wants to marry me) a month or two ago, I might have considered it"* (p. 143). Creating such closeness and complexity in their relationship allows Astrov and Sonya to develop as characters in the play and makes their relationship a much more succulent addition to the list of Yelena's victims. Seeing it from this perspective, Astrov leaves the room when Sonya enters because he cares about her opinion of him. He does not want her to see him when he is drunk and behaving foolishly. He is embarrassed and leaves immediately, followed by Telegin, in order not to embarrass Sonya.

Sonya's Entrance
Where has Sonya come from? When she last left the dining room, she was escorting her father to his room. She probably helped him into bed, gave him his medicine and a glass of water or tea. Chekhov does not detail these events, so it seems that nothing unusual has occurred. However, it is later revealed that Serebryakov could not sleep, left his room and spent the night in the living room. Sonya might well have been impatient with him because of her fatigue, the late hour and more to the point, her inability to talk to Astrov. Did she hear Astrov leave Vanya's room and join him in the dining room? Did she hear Telegin's music? Very likely. So she left her father and rushed to make the best of the opportunity. This clarifies Sonya's expectations as she enters the dining room. She is sure that she will finally have an opportunity to talk to Astrov. And so, she is surprised and disappointed when Astrov hurries out of the room with the ridiculous excuse that he is not wearing a tie. Sonya manages to swallow the insult. This is not the first time that Astrov has rejected her. Moreover, she has become accustomed to rejection by her father, since childhood. She immediately erupts in anger toward Vanya: *"Uncle Vanya, you*

got drunk with the doctor again. Birds of a feather. Well,
him, he's always like that, but what's gotten into you? It
doesn't suit you at your age" (p. 132).

Despite her love for Vanya and despite the age
difference between them, Sonya scolds him
harshly. She also carries great anger about Astrov
and his drinking problem. In her fury, she fails to
notice Vanya's depleted spirit and aims her darts at
his Achilles heel – his age. Vanya woefully
responds: *"Age has nothing to do with it. When you
don't have a real life, you make do with mirages. At least
it's better than nothing"* (p. 132). This statement is a
continuation of his earlier soliloquy. Vanya has
begun to see things more realistically. He has
begun to recognize his reliance on fantasy and on
alcohol to alleviate his loneliness. Sonya would
ordinarily have picked up on such a deep personal
crisis, but owing to the late hour, her frustration
and anger, she continues to complain about his
idleness:

> *"The hay's all cut, it's been raining every day,*
> *everything's rotting, and you're busy with*
> *mirages! You've completely neglected the*
> *estate... I've been working by myself, and I'm*
> *worn out"* (p. 132).

Sonya is surprised to see tears in Vanya's eyes.
Chekhov emphasizes that she is also frightened.
She has never seen him so unhappy. Moreover, she
herself is in crisis. She knows that should

149

something happen to Vanya, she would be left alone in the world. Does she know the reason for his tears? It seems so. She has just accused him of living in a fantasy - and his pursuit of Yelena is no secret. Is there anything she can do to help him? Not much. Vanya notices Sonya's panic and realizes that he must pull himself together. He denies having cried and says, *"What tears? There's nothing... It's nonsense"* (p. 132). Vanya looks at Sonya. The similarity between Sonya and her late mother is apparent to him and he is once again overwhelmed by sadness: *"My sister – my dearest sister – where is she now? If only she knew! Oh, if only she knew"* (p. 132). Sonya does not understand. What is the connection between her late mother and Vanya's tortured love for Yelena? Vanya answers in pain: *"It's painful, not good... Never mind... Later... Never mind"* (p. 132). To hide the depth of his sadness from Sonya, he leaves the room.

Chekhov does not allow Vanya to describe what would have taken place had Vera Petrovna known of his suffering. However, his desire reveals yet another aspect of the relationship between Vanya and his late sister. In Chapter 1, we discussed Vanya's adoration of her. He spoke about her as *"a beautiful and gentle creature, pure as this blue sky, honorable, generous soul"* (p. 118). He also gave up his portion of the inheritance for her benefit and even worked the land of her estate for many years to repay the loan taken for its purchase. Now, Chekhov allows us to realize how much Vanya depended on his sister. During times of crisis, he seeks her help as if she were the only one capable of helping him. She, and not his mother. How could Vera Petrovna have helped him? Though Vanya does not specify, we may assume that her love would have alleviated his loneliness and feelings of failure.

In all of these events beginning with Yelena's exit, Vanya has remained silent. From the moment Astrov enters, Vanya is seated, silent and mournful. Despite his silence, however, his presence dominates the room. The audience is undoubtedly watching him, not only because the other characters are trying to engage him in conversation, but because of the power of his internal actions - his struggle to admit that he has fallen into a trap, to understand why has he has done so and to escape its snares and begin to live. If the actor portraying Vanya can carry out these complex and difficult actions with depth, the spectators will sense its presence even without knowing the details. All of this would become visible to the spectator the moment before Vanya exits, struggling to hide his tears and confessing his pain to Sonya. Chekhov possesses the courage and the craft to expose a character through silence. He utilizes the silence to allow the internal workings of the character to gain momentum and power.

Where does Vanya go after his confession? Not to the room which he is sharing with Astrov. Nor to the living room, for we will soon discover that

Serebryakov and Yelena are there. He probably goes to the garden despite the storm. Chekhov uses these spaces to create a setting for the rising storm of emotions from which none of the characters can escape. Even Astrov, alone in Vanya's room, will be sucked into it momentarily.

The Planning of Sonya and Astrov's Meeting

After Vanya's exit, Sonya remains in the dining room alone. She is deliberating what to do next. At first she feels that she no longer has patience for the troubles of others and wants to return to her room to sleep. However, she cannot forget that Vanya is alone in the garden while a storm is raging. She considers trying to bring him back inside the house. She also considers checking in on her father, whom she left before he fell asleep. She is unaware of the fact that he, too, has left his room and is sitting in the living room quite upset. She would, of course, like to talk to Astrov, but cannot yet bring herself to knock on his door. She looks for a reasonable excuse, but can only come up with something weak and unbelievable. After all, Astrov is not naïve; he would see through her immediately. Finally, her desire to see Astrov overcomes her reason and she knocks on his door. As she waits for him to answer, she is prepared to have him call out that he is going to sleep and would like to be left alone; but to her surprise, he answers immediately, *"Coming!"* (p. 132). He opens the door, dressed in a waistcoat and tie. Sonya thinks that he has dressed up for her, but she will soon find out that he was planning to return home.

What was Astrov doing when Sonya knocked on his door? He was considering and reconsidering his options and finally concluded that he would not succeed in meeting Yelena. He was also disturbed by an unsettling doubt about his love for her. In his conversation with Sonya he will honestly say,

> *"but all she does is sleep, eat, walk, enchant us with her beauty – and nothing else. She has no responsibilities, others do the work for her... Isn't that right? But an idle life can't be pure"* (p. 133).

Later, he will add, *"That's not love, it's not attachment"* (p. 135). He is also very much aware of Sonya's desire to speak with him, but he is not at all delighted at the prospect of discussing their relationship on this of all nights. And so, he decides to return home. He packs his bag and puts on his suit and tie. He is very disappointed - with Yelena, but mostly with himself. And he is terribly frightened by the possibility that the rest of his life will be tormented by unbearable feelings of loneliness and regret over missed opportunities. Suddenly, he hears a knock on his door. For a moment, he hopes that it is Yelena, but, no, it is Sonya. Despite his hopes to see Yelena, later in the scene he will show that he is, in fact, very happy to see Sonya. He promises to fulfill her requests, tries to make conversation with her, to eat and drink with her and he even begins to reveal his deepest emotions to her. What has made him so happy?

Earlier, when we examined Astrov's exit from the dining room (p. 132), we observed that he does not rule out the possibility of marrying Sonya one day. At this moment, with Sonya knocking at his door, hoping to alleviate his loneliness, this possibility seems more feasible than ever.

Here is yet another example of Chekhov's impeccable planning. In this act he brings Sonya and Astrov together in a scene which could easily have a happy ending. She loves him deeply; he feels great loneliness and has doubts about his feelings for Yelena. Moreover, he is happy to see Sonya and desires her closeness and attention. At the end of the scene, it looks like they might finally decide to get married. Unfortunately unexpected events will create an unbridgeable gap between them.

Chekhov is aware that the **plot gap**, i.e. *the gap between the external actions at the beginning of the scene and the external actions at the end of the scene,* determines the pace of the scene. The deeper the plot gap, the faster the pace. In the scene at hand, Chekhov creates a huge plot gap. The two characters start the scene with feelings of great optimism, thinking that their relationship is headed for a positive change and that they may even get married. By the end of the scene, at least one of them will realize the futility of their desires.

The External and Internal Processes in this Scene

Astrov enters the dining room, happily asking Sonya, *"What can I do for you?"* (p. 132). Sonya almost swallows her tongue in surprise. His happiness at seeing her changes her plans, but she has no substitute for the excuse she has prepared and so she has to use it: *"You can drink if you don't think it's disgusting, but I entreat you, don't let my uncle drink. It's bad for him"* (p. 132). Now it is Astrov who is surprised. Is this why she knocked at his door so late at night? He looks at her, sees her embarrassment and decides to play along: *"All right. We won't drink any more"* (p. 132). Sonya hesitates. What now? Will she reveal her feelings? Will he reveal his? After a silence, he tells her that he has decided to go home, all the while hoping that she will ask him to stay. Indeed, she does: *"It's still raining. Wait till morning"* (p. 133). Astrov, looking for a stronger invitation, says:*"The thunderstorm is passing over, and I'll avoid most of it"* (p. 133). As much as he would like to go home, he still desires the warmth and heat of conversation, like the homeless man in the song he sang to Vanya earlier in the act (p. 131). And so he initiates a conversation about her father. Astrov is aware of Sonya's feelings toward her father and he is sure that their views about his illness, real or exaggerated, will correspond. Indeed, Sonya agrees that her father is spoiled. Then she feels that the moment she has been waiting for has arrived. She asks Astrov if he would like something to eat. Astrov eagerly accepts. Reinforcing the long-awaited sense of unity between them, she offers him some cheese and reveals that she, too, occasionally enjoys a midnight snack. Astrov is grateful for the food, since he has not eaten anything all day. At this point, breaking his promise not to drink, he takes a bottle of vodka from the sideboard and requests her permission to have a drink. Perhaps he thinks that the vodka will make it easier for him to broach the subject of marriage. She grants permission and he does. The atmosphere between them becomes much warmer and it is difficult not to be impressed with Astrov's honesty about his feelings toward Sonya. He embarks on a long monolog, which Sonya refrains from interrupting except for a few short questions. We can decode this monologue by deciphering the primary external action in it. As we've seen, in order to advance the plot, Chekhov operates methodically under the principal that the *convergence* of the scene must include external actions that are not initiated by habit or routine, but new actions that surprise and challenge the characters. And such is the case here. We must discover a new, profound, and powerful external action for Astrov. What could it be?

Let us return to the assumption that Astrov has considered proposing to Sonya on several occasions in the past, and consider the possibility that his primary external action during the monolog is, indeed, to finally do so. When did he decide? It must have happened sometime between the moment she knocked on his door and the moment she offered him the cheese. What made him decide? As we have noted, not only is Astrov increasingly disappointed with Yelena, but his loneliness and regret over missed opportunities have intensified. He is also deeply touched by Sonya's faithful love, which she offers generously and unconditionally with no desire for return. And now, at this late hour, Astrov wants to believe that Sonya could be his saving grace.

Still indecisive, Astrov struggles to propose directly. Despite his self-confidence and experience with women, this is his first proposal and he is nervous and confused. He beats around the bush, trying to prepare Sonya with cryptic suggestions and hints. Thus his long monolog, like so many in Chekhov's plays, rambles and seems inconsistent, unfocused and not aimed at any concrete goal.

In the first part of the monolog, Astrov tells Sonya how difficult it is for him in her home. He feels suffocated by her father's obsession with his gout and his books, by Vanya's moods, by her grandmother and especially by her stepmother (p.133). Beneath the complaints, Astrov's subtext is a veiled message to Sonya that if she moved to his estate, he would be much happier. Sonya is surprised to hear that her stepmother is a burden to him. In response, he says that Yelena may be physically beautiful, but, he insists that everything about a person should be beautiful -- one's clothes, one's thoughts and one's soul. Yelena, he observes, only eats, sleeps, walks around the estate and charms everybody and that such a life cannot be pure. When it seems that Sonya is struggling to understand him, Astrov apologizes: *"However, maybe I'm being too harsh. Like your Uncle Vanya, I'm not particularly satisfied with life, and we're both turning into grouches"* (p. 133). Here again, is another version of his veiled suggestion for Sonya: if we lived together, I would be happier with my life. He hesitates to say this, of course, and Sonya hesitates to affirm that she would do anything to make him happy. Instead, she asks him why he is unhappy. He provides a long-winded answer, describing his disappointment with the provincial life he has chosen in order to help farmers improve their social standing. He describes the emptiness of his personal life. He compares himself to a person in the woods at night with nothing to light his way. He finishes with, *"I don't expect anything for myself, I don't love people... I haven't loved anyone in a long time"* (p. 134). Another hint to prepare her for his next statement: if you lived with me, I could be different – I could love people.

How does Sonya interpret Astrov's words? Perhaps she thinks that they are meant to discourage her, i.e., if Astrov does not love people then he must not love her either. But the fact that she continues undeterred with the conversation indicates that she has not interpreted Astrov's statements negatively. In her eyes, he is describing the pain and hardship that keep him from loving humankind. She may even feel that he is crying out for help and asks empathetically, *"No one?"* (p. 134). Of course, she would love to hear, "no one but you," but Astrov is still not ready for *that* and continues to harp on his disappointment with the human race:

> *"The peasants are all alike; backward, living in filth, but the intelligentsia is hard to get along with. It fatigues you. All our good friends think shallow (…) – simply put, they're stupid. And those who are wiser and weightier are prone to hysteria (…). People no longer relate to nature directly in a pure and free way, and to other people, either."* (P. 134)

At this point, Astrov himself realizes that he has again digressed. He rises to have another drink in order to work up the courage to finally say what he has planned. Sonya quickly asks him not to drink any more, framing her request with a series of compliments, the likes of which he has never heard before:

> *"You're so fine, your voice is so tender… More than that, you are, unlike anyone else I know – beautiful. Why would you ever want to be like ordinary people who drink and play cards? Oh, I entreat you, don't do it! You always say that people don't create and only destroy what's been handed to them from above. Why, why do you then destroy yourself? Don't, I entreat you, I implore you, don't!"* (p. 134)

Sonya is sure that these compliments will demonstrate to Astrov how much she loves him,

159

and indeed, he takes her hand and promises not to drink any more. She asks him to give his word and he does. Then she squeezes his hand, as Chekhov stipulates in the stage directions, certain that she has won his love and maybe even saved him from himself. However, ironically and perhaps also tragically, at this very moment, poised on the edge of possibility, doubt creeps into Astrov's heart: Is this the woman I will spend my life with? A cloying, petty woman, who is blind to my faults? A self-righteous woman who will forbid me to drink and to play cards? A woman who will chase me and try to 'fix' me, change me to make me more like her? These questions terrify Astrov and all at once, a new realization is thrust upon him: *I must change my plans. I must not propose to her tonight.* With their hands still touching, he says, *"Basta! I've sobered up. See, I'm completely sober, and I'll stay sober for the rest of my life"* (p. 134). Sonya is convinced that he is referring to sobriety from alcohol; but Astrov is, in fact, referring to something else entirely – sobriety from the illusion that he might live happily ever after with Sonya. He looks at his watch, hoping that this will provide an excuse to end the conversation. However, his watch fails him. Astrov does not wish to hurt Sonya. He knows that he owes her an explanation for the change that has occurred in him so abruptly, so he says:

> *"…My time is over, it's too late for me… I've aged, I'm overworked, I've gotten vulgar, all my feelings have grown blunt, and I don't think I*

could ever become attached to someone. I don't
love anyone... and I never will." (p. 134)

Astrov tries to be as clear as possible as he explains
to Sonya why he cannot marry her, or any other
woman, for that matter. Having decided once and
for all against proposing to Sonya, he can now say
that he is unable to love even Yelena however
moved he may be by her beauty. He admits that
she could turn his head in a day, *"But that's not love,
it's not attachment"* (p. 135). Now he covers his eyes
with his hand and shudders in great agony. Sonya
asks, *"What's wrong with you?"* (p. 135). Astrov
answers, *"Never mind... During Lent, a patient died
under the chloroform"* (p. 135). Although he certainly
grieves the loss of his patient, this is not the truth.
He uses this event to mask his own pain; he knows
that he will find salvation neither with Yelena nor
with Sonya. He finally realizes that he will continue
to live the same miserable life he described to
Sonya with no hope of remedy.

Sonya feels the change in Astrov. She does not
understand it, but her heart tells her that it does not
bode well. So she takes the initiative and asks, *"If I
had a friend or a younger sister, and if you found out
that she... well, let's say, loved you, how would you
react to it?"* (p. 135). Astrov is, of course, aware of
the agenda behind Sonya's innocent question and
he answers directly, as if she were speaking about
herself: *"I don't know. Most likely I wouldn't. I'd let
her know that I wouldn't be able to love her... and that I
have other things on my mind"* (p. 135). Now that

Astrov has clearly said 'no', there is no hope for either of them and it is time to go. He shakes her hand, calls her *"my dear"* (p. 135) and leaves. Although he has been unaware that Yelena and Serebryakov are in the next room, he notices them on his way out, turns and leaves undetected through a side door.

Sonya in Private

After Astrov's hasty exit, Sonya is alone. Surprisingly, though that Astrov has clearly indicated that he could not marry her, she is filled with a strange feeling of euphoria: *"He didn't say anything to me... His heart and soul are still hidden from me, but why do I then feel so happy?"* (p. 135). While this blissful feeling courses through her, she is unable to acknowledge the painful truth. She chooses to hear Astrov's words as vague statements and even finds hope in them. The external action is revealed at the opening of her soliloquy: Sonya convinces herself that Astrov still has not rejected the possibility of marrying her. She is excited and proud of the caring, loving words she showered on him – probably for the first time. The idea that these very words ruined her chances with Astrov does not even cross her mind. Later, Sonya will deal with the consequences of her misinterpretation. She chooses to believe that Astrov simply failed to catch her meaning when she spoke about the *'friend or younger sister'*. His rejection could not possibly apply to her! It is far more difficult for her to take comfort in Astrov's statement that he cannot remain indifferent to beauty. She knows that she is not beautiful. She has felt the cruelty with which her personal traits have been overshadowed by her appearance. Even strangers have talked about it in church. However, Sonya does not give in to self-pity. Her words can be interpreted in this way: she does not deceive herself about her appearance; yet she is still determined to win Astrov's heart with her character. This interpretation is immediately substantiated in her conversation with Yelena, in which she is still euphoric.

Two profound internal actions can be detected in Sonya's soliloquy. In its first part, when she seeks a glimmer of hope in Astrov's words, her internal action is to suppress her fears that Astrov will not marry her. In the second part of the soliloquy, when Sonya admits she is not beautiful but is not discouraged by this fact, her action is much deeper and more fascinating. She puts all of her energy into believing in herself, in her positive qualities, in her future and in the knowledge that she is worthy of love. While she strengthens herself with this belief, Yelena enters.

Yelena's Entrance
Where did Yelena go after her escape from Vanya at the start of the act? She did not go to her bedroom; Serebryakov, Sonya and Marina were there. More likely she went into the empty living room. What did she do there? She sat and thought about herself and her life, her relationship with her husband, with Vanya and with Astrov. How and

where did she meet with Serebryakov? He probably left his room looking for her and found her there. They both remained in the living room until Yelena became impatient and went to the dining room, hoping finally to meet with Astrov, as is clear from her first question: *"Where is the doctor?"* (p. 135). Yelena's external action is to find Astrov and find out how he feels about her. However, when Sonya tells her that Astrov has returned home, her action changes and she now attempts to reconcile with Sonya. How did Yelena arrive at her new action? Let us examine the events of the night from her perspective: she has quarreled with her husband, she has deeply insulted Vanya and even missed her long desired chance to meet with Astrov. And now, in the late night, she feels very lonely. She has no one to confide in. She must find someone who will listen to her. Then she comes across Sonya, who is also unable to sleep. Yelena is, of course, aware that Sonya carries a long-held grudge against her, but her heart also tells her that this could be an opportunity to reconcile with her step-daughter. Indeed, after reaching this decision, Yelena speaks to her directly: *"How much longer are you going to pout at me? We haven't done each other any harm. Why should we be enemies then? Enough"* (p. 135).

Sonya, equally in need of a confidante, quickly agrees. She, too, has desired this reconciliation for some time, which she will later admit to. They embrace. Chekhov states that both of them are emotional and excited. After several weeks in

164

which not a word was exchanged between them, they are not sure how to begin. They start with 'small talk: Sonya asks Yelena about Serebryakov. He is in the living room and not yet asleep, Yelena sees the remnants of a late meal and Sonya tells her that it was Astrov's. Then Yelena sees the wine bottle and asks Sonya to join her in a toast to their friendship. Sonya agrees and they share a glass. The wine and the closeness encourage Sonya to make a confession: *"I've wanted to make peace for a long time, but I was a little embarrassed to"* (p. 136). She cries. Her tears soften Yelena's heart and she too begins to cry. But it will soon be clear that each of them is crying for a different reason.

For the first time, Yelena tells Sonya the reasons for her marriage to Serebryakov. She swears that she married him out of love and not for money. At the time, she thought the love she felt was real, but she has since realized that it is not. She pleads with Sonya, *"It's not my fault. And you, ever since our wedding, have looked at me accusingly with your intelligent and suspicious eyes"* (p. 136). This confession is, in fact, not meant for Sonya, but for Yelena herself. She is desperately trying to justify her marriage, to disprove the rumors that have spread through the estate and to alleviate her feelings of guilt because of the terrible mistake that she has made – unintentionally, she says, and not for improper reasons.

Admitting her mistake to Sonya, her stepdaughter, is so unexpected and irresponsible, that it can only be understood as a result of the tumultuous self-examination she has been conducting. When she says to Sonya, *"ever since our wedding, (you) have looked at me accusingly"* (p. 136), she is, in fact, accusing and tormenting herself. When Sonya tries to calm her saying, *"Well, peace, peace! Let's forget it"* (p. 136), Yelena cannot quiet down and says, *"Don't look like that"* (p. 136). Yelena is clearly trapped in her own accusatory glance. Moreover, when she cautions Sonya saying, *"You have to trust everyone, you can't live your life otherwise"* (p. 136), the subtext is clear: you have to believe me, *trust* me. I couldn't live if you didn't believe me. Yelena's confession is an excellent example of the technique that Chekhov uses to create depth in his characters. Depth of character is determined by the depth of action. The deeper the external and internal actions, the more profound is the exposure of the character's internal life. In the conversation with Sonya, Yelena's external action is to reconcile with her stepdaughter. While of importance, this action is not revelatory because, as we have seen, Yelena does not struggle to carry it out and Sonya willingly co-operates. Yelena's internal action, fired by her self-examination concerning her marriage to Serebryakov, is to alleviate her guilt. This is a potent, complex action that Chekhov uses as the primary tool for creating depth in Yelena's character, who because of her beauty on the one hand, and her weaknesses on the other, has fallen into a trap from which she cannot escape.

Sonya, we discern, is not interested in discussing her stepmother's hollow love for her father at this moment. In fact, she may not be listening to Yelena's confession at all. Sonya is still euphoric after her conversation with Astrov, when she spoke genuine, loving words that she has never spoken to anyone before. And therefore she believes that Astrov loves her. She wants to become closer to Yelena and to share her excitement with her. She asks, *"Tell me honestly, as a friend... Are you happy?"* (p. 136). Yelena answers honestly, *No*. While not surprising, this answer is intriguing. Sonya hears this answer in a narrow way, attributing Yelena's unhappiness to her marriage. She asks, *"Would you prefer to have a young husband?"* (p. 136). Yelena laughs and says yes. Then Sonya asks, *"Do you like the doctor?"* (p. 137). When Yelena answers, *"Yes, very much"* (p. 137), Sonya, in her naïve, ecstatic state, does not put two and two together. Sonya's naiveté reveals itself again at the beginning to Act 3, when she confesses to Yelena that she loves Astrov and even agrees to have Yelena find out if he would marry her. Being religious, Sonya does not even consider the possibility that a married woman would be interested in another man. At this late hour, Sonya takes Yelena's appreciation of Astrov as an indication that she, Sonya, has fallen in love with the right man.

Sonya becomes more and more excited. She fears that she may look silly in her euphoric state, but this does not bother her. She describes Astrov's voice and his footsteps echo in her mind, even after he has gone. She sees his face reflected in the darkened window. Yelena may wish to bring Sonya back to reality, but Sonya cannot hear her. She worries that her voice may be too loud and invites Yelena to her room where she can speak more about her love. Then, embarrassed by her honesty, she falls silent. Then she asks Yelena to say something about Astrov, to build her confidence so that she does not feel that her love is silly.

Two contradictory explanations can be given for Yelena's response to Sonya's confession: on one hand, her defamation of Astrov can be seen as manipulation and pretense, for example: *"He drinks, acts a little coarse sometimes"* (p. 137) or:

> *"Just think about the kind of life he has! Muddy and impassable roads, freezing cold, snow storms, huge distances, and the people are coarse, uncivilized, illness and destitution are all around him, and under these circumstances, it's hard for someone working and struggling day in and day out to remain squeaky clean and sober by the time he's forty"* (p. 137).

It could be that Yelena, who is in love with Astrov, herself, is trying to create doubt in the heart of her competitor by emphasizing Astrov's age and negative qualities. After all, Sonya is only twenty years old. On the other hand, a more generous interpretation would bear greater dramatic yield and enable us to avoid the trap of seeing Yelena

168

merely as a negative character, selfish, manipulative, bored and shallow. In order to view her as a more complex and well-rounded character, capable of overcoming her selfishness with genuine acts of kindness and sensitivity, it would be better to assume that Yelena is empathetic toward Sonya and wants to help her stepdaughter to find happiness, even though she, herself, is unhappy. In this way we can develop some compassion and empathy for Yelena and her tragedy, Thus, her description of Astrov can be interpreted as an attempt to convince Sonya that he is indeed a worthy partner for her, and that his shortcomings (his drinking and his coarse behavior, for example) are minor flaws.

However, this interpretation, which allows Sonya a chance at happiness, forces Yelena once again to confront her failure in every aspect in life:

> *"Me, I'm a tedious, minor character… In music, in my husband's house, in love – everywhere, I was always only a minor character. To tell you the truth, Sonya, come to think of it, I'm very, very unhappy! There's no happiness for me in this world. No!"* (P. 137)

This candid revelation exposes the roots of Yelena's suffering and reinforces the view that her comments about Astrov were not a manipulation, but rather an honest attempt to support Sonya's love for him.

But this is Chekhov; and Sonya, in her euphoria, cannot even hear Yelena's confession. She laughs and says, *"I'm happy... So happy!"* (p. 137). Sonya's insensitivity does not hurt Yelena – she understands her stepdaughter and may even be happy for her, despite her own frustration and pain. Perhaps Sonya's determination to be happy inspires Yelena to better her own life. She says she wants to play the piano. Sonya encourages her, but Yelena must first obtain her husband's permission, and sends Sonya to make the request. Now, Yelena is alone, longing to play the piano, to play and to mourn her life. She hears the watchman's tapping outside and asks him to stop lest he wake Serebryakov. The watchman leaves. Sonya returns, saying, *"You can't"* (p. 138). Why does Serebryakov refuse? He didn't object to Telegin's music earlier in the act. Serebryakov, anxious and irritable in his room, simply, cruelly, will not allow his wife to be happy without him.[43] Yelena surrenders her own struggle for happiness and accepts his decision in silence.

---

[43] Natasha in *Three Sisters* also does not allow her family or their guests to be happy without her. On entering the guest room (p. 179), she stops the celebration with the weak excuse that Bobik is ill, and cancels the invitation of the masked guests.

Chapter 3: Act 3

September. The living room. Twelve forty-five in the afternoon. Vanya and Sonya are seated. Yelena paces back and forth, absorbed in thought. They are waiting for Serebryakov, who has requested everyone to convene around one o'clock so that he may *"convey something to the world"* (p. 138), as Vanya puts it. No one is aware of Serebryakov's intentions. Even Yelena, his wife, knows nothing and assumes that it is *"for some business matter"* (p. 138). What is going on inside these three characters while they're waiting?

In the stage directions, Chekhov stipulates that Yelena is *"absorbed in thought and pacing the stage"* (p.138). Vanya interprets her pacing in the following way: *"Just look at her: she walks and sways from laziness. Very nice! Very!"* (p. 138) Yelena responds: *"I'm bored to death and I don't know what to do"* (p. 138). Is this an accurate description of what is going on inside of her? It doesn't seem so. In a moment, Yelena will reveal her thoughts: *"It's September already! How are we going to make it through the winter here!"* (p. 139). Over the course of the summer, her life has turned into a living hell. In a few moments, as the tension reaches its peak, she will scream, *"I'm leaving this hellhole right this minute!"* (p. 149). Even the presence of Astrov, who is in Vanya's room writing, weighs heavily on her. Her feelings toward him are clear to her at this point. Soon, when alone, she will admit to them (p. 141). Making decisions is difficult for Yelena. How will she escape the trap that she has fallen into? How can she undo her marriage to Serebryakov, who has not bothered to share his plans with her? How will she overcome her fears about her love for Astrov? There is no doubt that her remark about boredom is, in fact, intended to conceal her emotional turmoil.

What is going on in Sonya's heart? She claims to have left her work and come to the living room not in order to hear what her father has to say, but to talk to Yelena (p. 139). Astrov's daily visits to the estate have greatly increased her distress. By now, she is sure that his visits are not to see her, but rather to engage the charms of her stepmother. And so she waits impatiently to speak to Yelena. We later discover that her suffering is so great that she considers asking Astrov to stop visiting them.

And what is going on in Vanya's heart? His coarse statements about the meeting reveal his impatience. He also bitterly mocks Yelena, as we have seen: *"Just look at her: she walks and sways from laziness"* (p. 138). Yelena responds in kind: *"You drone all day long – drone, drone – how you don't get fed up with it!"* (p. 138). Why is she so aggressive with him? What has he repeatedly said to her during the morning that sounds like an incessant drone? They must have argued on the previous night because Vanya awoke early in order to gather a bouquet of autumn roses for her, *"As a symbol of peace and harmony"* (p. 139). Their quarrel must have been particularly acrimonious because Vanya has been trying unsuccessfully to appease her all morning. What were they arguing about? We can surmise something about it from Vanya's unexpected comment, which is unrelated to anything that has been said thus far:

> "Why languish? (Lively) Come on, my dear, my gorgeous, be a good girl! The blood of a water nymph flows in your veins, so then be a nymph! Let yourself go..." (p. 139)

Clearly, Vanya has returned to the uncomfortable subject of her sexual longings. He continues to appeal to her: "quickly fall head over heels in love with a water sprite, and plunge head-first straight into a deep, still water, leaving Herr Professor and all of us at a loss for words!" (p. 139). Even if we assume that this was indeed the main topic of their argument, we still have no idea how it played out. Later, we will try to guess. We must remember that Chekhov, the master craftsman, would not allow a character to open the act with a routine action. He would instead introduce a new action to advance the plot. Although Chekhov does not reveal its content, the argument of the previous night is worth examining because it may well be the **generating event** of the act.

What Is a Generating Event?
At the beginning of the previous two acts, we observed that Chekhov's characters harbored powerful compressed internal actions, which were present long before the act began. However,

although these internal actions were brewing within, the characters did not act overtly to carry them out. A **generating event** is an event that causes the characters to begin to act in order to fulfill their compressed internal actions. In Act 1, the generating event is the argument between Vanya and Serebryakov at breakfast. After the argument, Serebryakov, Yelena and Sonya go for a walk and purposely delay their return, forcing Astrov to wait in the garden. Vanya enters the garden also as a result of the argument, hoping to make up with Yelena. In Act 2, the generating event is the deterioration of Serebryakov's health, which leads to another visit from Astrov. Serebryakov's refusal to be examined leads to a series of arguments, first with his wife, then with his daughter and finally with Vanya and Astrov. That is the reason no one has been able to sleep and that is the cause of the conflict between Vanya and Yelena. Later we will see how their mysterious quarrel on the night preceding Act 3 drives the action throughout the act. These three examples show that the generating event does not necessarily have to be overt. Often it does not take place in front of the audience and is revealed only as the plot begins to unfold.

Unlike the audience, the playwright is well acquainted with the details of the generating event and so are the characters. This observation clarifies one of Chekhov's primary dramatic principles: *the characters almost always know more about their motives and actions than the audience does*. In this way,

Chekhov creates a **reverse dramatic irony**. In most plays the audience knows more about the characters than the characters themselves. In Chekhov's world, the characters very often conceal their motives from the audience and shroud themselves in mystery and uncertainty, thus creating tension and curiosity in the audience. It is important to note that Chekhov employs this principal in the development of the internal actions as well. As soon as a character reveals an internal action, the spectator realizes that beneath that revelation there lies hidden a deeper internal action, as yet unknown to the spectator and catching his interest. Unlike a 'whodunit' drama, which inspires our curiosity to know how the detective will catch the murderer, (i.e. the progression of the characters' *external* actions), the Chekhovian drama inspires us to discover the progression of the characters' *internal* actions: Will Vanya and Astrov achieve salvation through Yelena? Will Yelena overcome her fears and satisfy her desires? Will Sonya overcome Astrov's rejection? Despite their great importance, the external actions of the characters are but the means of revealing their internal actions, which is Chekhov's main interest.

Let us return to the characters' compression at the beginning of Act 3 and to the ways in which Chekhov utilizes the two months that have passed between the acts.

Astrov, has undergone a tremendous change during this time. He now makes daily visits to the estate. He may not stay the night, but he spends most of the day there, and Vanya's room has become Astrov's workroom, as well. (p. 142). Sonya says:

> "The Doctor, Mikhail Lvovich, used to come see us rarely, once a month maybe, it was impossible to get him to come over, and now he comes over every day, he's abandoned his forests and medicine" (p. 139).

Sonya is no fool; she knows he is there to see Yelena. Yelena is also aware of this fact: "He comes here every day now, I can guess why he's here, and I already feel guilty" (p. 141). Astrov himself says to her, "you know perfectly well why I come here every day. Why and for whose sake, you know perfectly well" (p. 144). He even invites her to meet him the next day in the forest. In Act 4, which takes place on the same day, he tells her outright;

> "I was taken with you, I didn't do anything the whole month; and during this time people were ill, and the peasants were bringing their cattle to graze on the seedlings that I am planting" (p. 156).

He is completely overcome by his desire for salvation. Sonya knows that Astrov has fallen in love with Yelena, but she as yet has no idea that Yelena feels the same way about him. Although she

176

is well aware of Yelena's misery in her marriage to Serebryakov, she is certain that her marriage vows would prevent a liaison between Yelena and the doctor. Over the past two months, Sonya has discussed Astrov with Yelena on several occasions: *"I keep coming to you to talk about him"* (p. 140). Yelena tries to empower Sonya, but despite her encouragement, an example of which was seen at the end of Act 2, Sonya fails to deepen her relationship with Astrov: *"Now he comes here every day, but he doesn't look at me, he doesn't see me... I'm suffering! I have no hope, none, none at all"* (p. 140). Her despair has deepened during the night and she prays to God for strength. In the morning, with Astrov again on the estate, she decides that the time has come to act. She must bring an end to her suffering.

The past two months have been difficult for Yelena. Her life has turned into a living hell and she admits this openly: *"I'm leaving this hellhole right this minute"* (p. 149). What has occurred in this hellhole? Her relationship with Serebryakov has deteriorated and she is increasingly more disgusted with his illnesses, his sexual advances and his despair. They fight and argue every night. In addition, Vanya has become much more compulsive. He constantly pressures her to leave her husband and marry him. The more insistent he becomes, the more fearful and irritable she becomes. As if these stressors were not enough, Astrov has also begun to make direct advances, which are all the more threatening because she is in love with him and has to struggle with all her might to resist. This is apparent when she twice submits to his embraces and kisses (pp. 144 & 156). These stressors intensify Yelena's feelings of helplessness and she, like Sonya, knows that the time has come to act. She also knows that she will not find happiness until she parts with Serebryakov and marries either Vanya or Astrov. Yet she is still very afraid to accept their love.

Over the past two months, Vanya has continued his incessant advances toward Yelena, and with each rejection his passion has grown. But now, with Astrov on the scene, Vanya is hardly oblivious to the doctor's intentions. Everyone else on the estate is aware of this sad triangle. Even though Vanya knows that his rival is gaining on him, he will not demean himself by asking Astrov to cease and desist. He is aware that his window of opportunity is fast closing. Like Sonya and Yelena, he knows that he must act and that failure to do so will mean that his chance for a new life will be gone forever. And so, it is very likely that on the night before Act 3, the argument between Vanya and Yelena was precipitated by his incessant pleas for her to leave Serebryakov. Although Vanya was painfully aware of Yelena's impatience with his advances, he persisted because if he were to fail to convince her that night, she would fall into Astrov's arms the next day like a ripe fruit. Driven by an uncontrollable urge to win her, Vanya may have acted with new fervor and intensity. He may have pleaded with her, cried, shouted or even tried to kiss her forcibly. And she may well have banished him and sworn never to speak to him again. All this is, of course, a hypothetical rendering of a quarrel we know nothing about. However, it is clear that Serebryakov is aware of their falling out and has therefore summoned the members of the household in order to put an end to this farce in which Vanya and Astrov openly pursue his wife.

The details of the quarrel, which is the generating event of Act 3, are never revealed anywhere in the play, but they are crucial to Chekhov's writing process. Without knowing what happened between Yelena and Vanya (and it is very likely that Chekhov imagined these details differently to the way we do), he couldn't have set down the actions of the characters at the beginning of the act nor could he have written the line; *"You drone all day long – drone, drone – how you don't get fed up with it"* (p. 138). Or this: *"As a symbol of peace and harmony, I'm going to bring you a bouquet of roses; I made it for you this morning"* (p. 139). With these lines, the aftermath of the falling out, Chekhov offers a very strong indication of what took place. Moreover, in order to clarify the actions for the actors in Act 3, they, too, must know the details of the argument and are bound to seek out any shred of information they can. If they are able to imagine what took place, they can proceed more precisely with their own actions. In this way, the meaning of the quarrel is clear to the audience despite our lack of detail. The actors' precision is the most important means of creating empathy with the characters. The deeper the empathy, the more the spectators may feel the emotions of the characters - which is what Chekhov wants.

How did Chekhov choose the setting for Act 3? Since Serebryakov called the meeting, Chekhov chooses the space which suits him best. Serebryakov prefers the living room because he needs a closed space where everyone will clearly understand his message. Chekhov also ingeniously uses this public area for private scenes, thereby creating one of the act's most climactic moments: when Astrov and Yelena embrace in the living room, Vanya, with no door to knock on, enters and sees them.

The External and Internal Processes of the Scene

Why have Vanya, Yelena and Sonya gathered in the living room? As mentioned above, Yelena was probably seeking refuge from Vanya, who has been harassing her since she left her room that morning. He followed her into the dining room and then out into the garden. She does not return to her room because her husband is there, so she eventually decides to enter the living room before the meeting, hoping that Vanya might refrain from hounding her in the presence of the others. They both enter the living room and find Sonya there. She has come to the living room before the meeting in order to talk to Yelena. As the act begins, the three characters have been in the living room for some time. Yelena paces, attempting to escape Vanya and balance her feelings of love and anxiety. Vanya and

Sonya are seated. Vanya slanders Serebryakov, hoping to convince Yelena to finally leave him. He is completely unaware of Serebryakov's reasons for calling the meeting and sees it as only an expression of the man's exaggerated self-importance. Yelena, who is also unaware of her husband's intentions, assumes that the meeting is about some business matter. Vanya continues to malign Serebryakov: *"He has no causes. He writes rubbish, grumbles, and feels jealous – nothing else"* (p. 138). What jealousy is Vanya referring to? After all, the professor's academic accomplishments are unrivaled by anyone on the estate. He is probably hinting at Serebryakov's feelings about Yelena's increasingly apparent relationships with Vanya and Astrov. In a few moments, when the meeting begins, we will bear witness to the consequences of this jealousy.

Sonya intervenes and angrily silences Vanya. What has angered her? Considering Chekhov's insistence on specific justification for the characters' actions, we may assume that she is not angry because of Vanya's general pestering, but because he accuses her father of being jealous. Like all the members of the household, Sonya is well aware of her father's jealousy over his wife. The advances of Vanya and Astrov are an open wound for her and mention of it angers her. This is partly due to the breach of her closely held religious and moral codes, but even more so because Astrov's pursuit of Yelena means that he is not interested in her.

Vanya apologizes for his dreadful comments, even though the entire household is aware of the situation, but then he ridicules Yelena's laziness (p. 138). If he wishes to appease her after last night's falling out, why does he ridicule her? He probably wants to continue the quarrel, accusing her of failing to satisfy her desires because of her laziness and a false air of calm while a fire burns inside her. Vanya will momentarily reaffirm this claim (p. 139).

Fed up with his constant pestering, Yelena catches his meaning and scolds him bitterly: *"You drone all day long – drone, drone – how you don't get fed up with it"* (p. 138). To avoid risking a conversation that might reveal her true thoughts, she says: *"I'm bored to death and I don't know what to do"* (p. 138). Vanya, who is perfectly familiar with Yelena's internal life, recognizes that this is a defense mechanism. Sonya, however, believes Yelena's claim of boredom but does not understand it: *"What to do? There's plenty to do if you only wanted to"* (p. 138). Yelena jumps at the chance to divert the conversation to conceal her painful dilemma, and Sonya responds: *"You could help with the house, teach, treat the sick"* (p. 138). These suggestions will hardly serve to relieve Yelena's distress. And so she rejects them, claiming that they, too, are boring and that they only exist in *"the novels of ideas"* (p. 139).

At this point, Sonya decides to take action. She ceases her accusations of Yelena and takes a more positive approach, hoping to reestablish their closeness and discuss her own difficult predicament. In the stage directions, Chekhov even stresses that she hugs and jokes with Yelena. These physical actions constitute her external action: to initiate a private conversation with Yelena in order to enlist her help with Astrov – and to drive Vanya out of the room. She later admits: *"I'm glad that Uncle Vanya went out, I need to talk to you"* (p. 139). Thus, Sonya forgives her stepmother's laziness, despite the fact that it is a contagious illness that has affected Vanya, Astrov and even herself. She flatters Yelena and calls her *"a sorceress"* (p. 139) because of her profound effect on Astrov. Interestingly, Sonya does not lament or even hint at the fact that Yelena's 'sorcery' is ruining her own chances with Astrov.

Vanya, however, does not give up so easily. He stubbornly persists in urging Yelena to acknowledge her own desires. In his desperation and despite Sonya's presence, he speaks loudly and boldly about her stepmother's sexual yearnings:

> *"Come on, my dear, my gorgeous, be a good girl! The blood of a water nymph flows in your veins, so then be a nymph! Let yourself go at least once in your life; quickly fall head over heels in love with a water sprite, and plunge head-first straight into a deep, still water..."* (P. 139)

It is difficult not to be astonished by the directness of his words. Vanya is exhorting the wife of his brother-in-law to cheat on her husband and fall in love with someone else in order to fulfill her desires -- and all of this in front of her stepdaughter! He is even prepared to give her up to another man so that she could satisfy her desires. This conversation transgresses all of the accepted behavioral codes. As we observed in Chapter 1, only a person whose despair has overcome his logic would behave in this way in public. Yelena, fed up with Vanya's overbearing behavior, accuses him of brutality and turns to leave. He blocks her way, apologizes and kisses her hand. Yelena's anger is so great that she cannot forgive him; *"You would try the patience of a saint"* (p. 139). Vanya senses her anger and realizes that she has not forgiven him. He says: *"As a symbol of peace and harmony, I'm going to bring you a bouquet of roses; I made it for you this morning"* (p. 139). Without waiting for a response, he leaves. Although Vanya keeps his word and will soon return with the roses, the reasons for his exit at this point are not so clear. In fact, the exit points to a deeper, more painful and embarrassing reality that Vanya cannot reveal.

An examination of the events of the two months preceding Act 3, and the previous night and morning in particular, reveals Vanya's journey towards self destruction. His desperate attempts to convince Yelena to marry him have failed and, despite his best efforts to appease her throughout the day, she does not forgive him and refuses to reconcile with him. In fact, she now makes it decisively clear that she has had enough of his advances and that she will not consent. This is a profound moment in their relationship and it must be fully emphasized. Until this point, Yelena has kept a narrow opening in her heart for Vanya, despite her repeated rejections. This opening has allowed him to continue to pursue her and allowed us as spectators to wonder about the outcome of their scenes. Now, however, we have arrived at a different stage. Yelena has shut and locked the door, forcing Vanya to realize that he has finally been defeated. His emotional response is devastating. Thus, while he indeed leaves the room to gather a bouquet of roses, the deeper, more painful reason for his departure is to conceal his heartbreak.

This is not an easy moment for Yelena, either. Her relationship with Vanya is important to her and with this final rejection, she must now give up his friendship, as well. Sonya intuits their suffering and, as an expression of empathy, she repeats Vanya's last line *"Autumn roses – delightful, mournful roses"* (p. 139). With these words, Sonya mourns her own suffering, as well.

Sonya and Yelena look out the window pensively. Suddenly, Yelena is struck by the terrible thought that she might be forced to remain on the estate for the coming winter. This would be endless torture for her. Sonya is silent. She also fears that she will live forever in her own hell. Then Yelena, considering the possibility that Astrov might save her from this suffering, asks, *"Where is the doctor?"*

(p. 139) Sonya, missing the point of Yelena's question, takes the opportunity to open a discussion about her own problem: *"I'm glad that Uncle Vanya went out, I need to talk to you"* (p. 139). Self-absorbed, Yelena does not catch Sonya's intention at first, but she will soon understand. Sonya rests her head on Yelena's chest. Now the stepmother ascends to the level of real mother. Sonya cries and Yelena, embarrassed by this display of emotion, tries to calms her: *"Well, there, there... (stroking her hair) There"* (p. 139). Having always thought of herself as "a secondary character", Yelena now finds herself fulfilling the meaningful, important role of mother. She feels some sense of consolation and treats Sonya with kindness and compassion as her stepdaughter bares her soul.

Sonya has entered the living room in order to share her suffering with her stepmother and to ask her advice. Indeed, she opens by saying *"I am so plain"* (p. 139). This admission would be difficult for any woman, not only because it reflects a painful and sobering insight into reality, but because for Sonya, it means that her chances of winning Astrov's love are slim. Astrov has already told her how important beauty is to him. With this admission, Sonya makes it clear that she has conducted a painfully thorough self-investigation and is no longer deluding herself with false hopes. Yelena responds, *"You have beautiful hair"* (p. 140). Sonya finds no consolation in Yelena's words: *"No! When a woman is plain, they always tell her: 'You have beautiful eyes or beautiful hair'"* (p. 140). Rejecting consolation, she demands that Yelena accept reality, however difficult, and for once, continues with determination and precision:

> *"I've loved him for six years; I love him more than my own mother, and I hear him every waking moment, I feel his handshake, and I look at the door, waiting, and thinking that he might just walk in. And see, I keep coming to you to talk about him. Now he comes here every day, but he doesn't look at me, he doesn't see me... I'm suffering! I have no hope, none, none at all!"*
> (P. 140)

Sonya speaks bluntly. She does not spare her emotions, nor does she ask for mercy. She presents reality as she sees it, with eyes wide open. Without embellishment, she demands that Yelena help her cope with her situation. These powerful words make a strong impact on Yelena. While she does not respond verbally, she must be amazed at the courage of this young, provincial, uneducated girl to confront the trap that she has fallen into. In contrast, with all her maturity, education and experience, Yelena fears any honest confrontation or clear assessment of her own life. Sonya continues:

> *"Oh, God, give me strength... I was praying all night... I often walk up to him, myself start the conversation with him, I look into his eyes... I don't have any pride left, and can't control*

187

*myself... I couldn't help it and confessed to
Uncle Vanya yesterday that I love him... And
all the servants know that I love him. Everybody
knows."* (P. 140)

What strength does Sonya pray for? She does not
pray for beauty. Nor, does it seem that she prays
that Astrov's heart will open to her. She made it
clear earlier that there was no hope of that. What is
most painful for her is that she has lost her sense of
pride and self- control. She may well be praying for
the return of these, so as not to appear foolish in the
eyes of others and her own. Sonya is all too aware
of the inner contradiction that tears at her heart. On
one hand, she knows that she has no chance of
winning Astrov's love and, on the other, she knows
that she will never stop loving him. She presents
this contradiction to Yelena, but does not ask for a
solution. She knows there is no solution. Her only
request is that Yelena help relieve her pain, so that
she can reclaim her honor as a person and as a
woman.

Yelena offers a complicated response. She knows
now that Astrov will not marry Sonya. Is this a sign
that she will now surrender to his advances? In a
moment she will say: *"I think I'm taken with him a
little myself... here I'm smiling just thinking about
him"* (p. 141). However, she immediately feels
guilty for thinking such selfish thoughts and says,
*"I already feel guilty and ready to fall to my knees before
Sonya to apologize"* (p. 141). After a long
contemplation, she regains her self-confidence and

decides that Sonya's well-being is more important than her own. Out of empathy for the suffering of her stepdaughter and a genuine desire to help her, she suggests a practical solution: she will talk to Astrov: *"I'll be discreet and only drop a hint"* (p. 140). She will question Astrov about his intentions and thereby hopefully end Sonya's suffering. For Yelena, as we have seen, uncertainty is unbearable. Sonya nods in agreement. Yelena expands her offer: *"All we need to find out is: yes or no? (A pause). If it's no, then he shouldn't come here anymore. Yes?"* (p. 140). Sonya nods again. Knowing that her state of uncertainty will soon come to an end, she feels a bittersweet sense of relief. But the idea that she may lose Astrov for good is very difficult. Yelena senses Sonya's dismay and her maternal feelings grow stronger. Eager to play a key role in Sonya's life, she continues to encourage her: *"It's easier when you don't see him"* (p. 140). And to accelerate the process, she says that she will talk to Astrov immediately. Excited by the prospect, Sonya agrees, but pleads with her stepmother to tell her the whole truth, no matter how Astrov responds. Yelena promises to do so and calms her again: *"I think the truth, no matter how bad, can't be worse than uncertainty"* (p. 140). Not quite convinced, Sonya agrees and turns toward Astrov's door. Then, at the last minute, she changes her mind and stops: *"No, uncertainty is better… There's hope at least"* (p. 141). Perhaps Yelena either does not hear her or fails to understand her. It is also possible that Yelena does not agree. Sonya changes her mind again and exits.

Yelena's eagerness to talk to Astrov raises a suspicion that is difficult to ignore. Is she responding to her natural maternal feelings for Sonya and thus play a more meaningful role in the household? Or is she interested in talking to Astrov for her own reasons? At this moment, the latter does not seem likely. If she were interested in finally solidifying her relationship with Astrov, she would not have offered to bar him from the estate. Moreover, there is no need to create a special opportunity to see Astrov, who comes to the estate to woo her on a daily basis. However, in order to dispel these suspicions, Chekhov leaves Yelena alone on stage to reveal her intentions in a soliloquy in the same way that Vanya and Sonya bare their motives in Act 2.

Yelena's Soliloquy

Left alone, Yelena suddenly realizes the weight of the responsibility she has taken on. This is not a game, but a serious involvement in the fate of others. Familiar doubts arise regarding her ability to handle this responsibility and assume a greater role in the household: *"There's nothing worse than when you know someone's secret and are unable to help"* (p. 141). Yelena, for once, decides not to surrender to her doubts and continues to consider Sonya's chances:

> *"He's not in love with her – that much is clear, but why shouldn't he marry her? She isn't pretty, but for a country doctor, at his age, she*

190

would make a wonderful wife. She's such a good girl, generous, pure[45]" (p. 141).

Clearly, Yelena wishes to be positive and to assist Sonya unselfishly. Then a new thought suddenly crosses her mind: *"No, no, but that's not it"* (p. 141). She realizes that a man like Astrov would not marry a woman simply because she is good, generous and pure. He would require something more. Though she does not specify what this other quality might be, we may assume that it is passion, the same passion that she carries inside her but is unable to release. Later, she will admit this openly: *"Uncle Vanya says that a water nymph's blood flows in my veins"* (p. 141). These thoughts frighten Yelena. She falls silent, regains her composure and continues to examine Sonya's needs:

> *"I understand this poor girl. In the midst of this excruciating boredom, when instead of people, grey smudges surround you, and when you hear nothing but vulgar things, when all they do is eat, drink, sleep, sometimes he shows up, so unlike the rest – handsome, interesting, captivating, like a bright moon rising in the dark..."* (p. 141)

She may be talking about Sonya, but there is no doubt that she is thinking about herself and her own life. She feels that *"instead of people, grey*

---

[45] In "The Cherry Orchard", Liubov Andreyevna tries to persuade Varya and Lopakhin to marry for similar reasons.

smudges surround you, and... you hear nothing but vulgar things" (p. 141). Indeed, she realizes this in the next breath: *"I think I'm taken with him a little myself. Yes, I'm bored without him, and here I'm smiling just thinking about him"* (p. 141). At this moment, Yelena's action changes. Through her initial concern with Sonya's needs, she discovers her own. Astrov is not only Sonya's hope, but her own, as well. She loves him just as Sonya does. She starts to think about herself and recalls Vanya's entreaty : *"Let yourself go at least once in your life"* (p. 141). Indeed, she has heard every word Vanya has said from the start of the act, and finally, she is willing to admit that he is right:

> *"Well? Maybe I should... Oh, if only I could fly as a free bird away from all of you, from your sleepy faces and conversations, forget that you even exist in this world"* (p. 141).

For the first time, Yelena dares to consider the possibility of escaping the trap that she has fallen into, to set her desires free and fly away. However, these thoughts frighten her and force a second change. She takes back her words, retreats into her low self-image and to the moral code that hems in her desires: *"But I'm timid and a little shy... My conscience would bother me"* (p. 141). She then returns to Sonya's needs: *"He comes here every day now, I can guess why he's here, and I already feel guilty and ready to fall to my knees before Sonya to apologize, cry..."* (p. 141). At the end of the soliloquy, after two significant changes, she returns to the starting point.

An examination of the *external* actions in Yelena's soliloquy reveals a circular motion with no plot development. Yelena considers her needs, but immediately surrenders to her deep anxieties, which act as an impenetrable obstacle. This pattern is typical of Yelena throughout the play: Her desires stimulate her to action, but her anxieties prevent her from acting. Chekhov is aware of the problems inherent in this circular structure, which does not allow for the advancement of the plot. Therefore, he empowers the circular structure with significant progress in the internal action. Internally, Yelena deliberates whether to fulfill Sonya's needs or her own. This deliberation reflects a strong internal action: the suppression of her desire and love for Astrov. During the soliloquy, it seems for a moment that her suppression has failed and that her feelings for Astrov rise to the surface and demand to be satisfied. However, Yelena, proceeds to fight off these feelings and suppresses them with an equally powerful wave of guilt. This suppression, painful as it is, is the meaningful development in Yelena's inner action, which strengthens the soliloquy despite its circular structure. However, we will soon see that this strong internal action is only temporary. Very soon Yelena will surrender to her desires and give in to Astrov, though only for a moment.

Astrov's Entrance

At the beginning of the chapter, we observed that in the two months between the acts, Astrov's desire for Yelena has so escalated that he visits the estate every day. We hear little more about his actions between the acts or immediately before his entrance into the living room. When they meet, Yelena says to him: *"Yesterday you promised to show me your work"* (p. 141). On his previous visit he promised to show her his topographical sketches of the province. That morning, Astrov arrived on the estate as usual, intending to fulfill his promise. We do not know whom he met or spoke to, but there is no doubt that he sensed the estate was in chaos. Though he may not have been aware of the falling out between Vanya and Yelena on the previous night, he certainly witnessed Vanya's frantic attempts to appease Yelena and sensed the tension between them. He had also heard about the meeting Serebryakov had called and intuited an impending storm. Did Astrov mean to attend the meeting? Though he probably would not have missed the opportunity to meet with Yelena, for obvious reasons, he will not attend. In the meanwhile, Astrov stays in Vanya's room, waiting for the opportunity to show Yelena his sketches.

Astrov's decision to remain in Vanya's room does not mean that he is aloof from the events on the estate. He is all too aware of his competition with Vanya for Yelena's heart. And though he thinks his chances are better, he acknowledges Vanya's strengths and worries that, in desperation, Vanya might act impulsively and persuade Yelena to leave her husband and marry him. Like Vanya, he also fears that time is running out. Therefore, while he pretends to work on his sketches in Vanya's room, he is listening closely to events as they unfold. He is waiting for the right moment to meet Yelena, not to show her the sketches, but to convince her to surrender to him.

Waiting for his moment, he hears a knock at the door. It is Sonya, who has come to inform him that her stepmother wishes to see his sketches. What happens during this conversation and why has Chekhov chosen not to show it to the audience?

Sonya knocks at Astrov's door after deciding to leave her fate in the hands of her stepmother. She does her best to relay the message without revealing her feelings, which, as she confessed to Yelena, have already shaken her self-confidence. Astrov is probably very surprised to see Sonya so reserved, but upon hearing the message he had hoped for, he hastily collects his sketches and heads for the living room. Where does Sonya go? Probably to the dining room to join Marina and Telegin, who are awaiting the meeting. Chekhov decided not to write this scene because nothing unexpected happens. Here, we bear witness to another principal in Chekhov's writing: he chooses to portray an event on stage only if it includes the unexpected and unobvious.

The External and Internal Processes in the Scene

Astrov enters carrying his sketches of the land around the estate. He wishes Yelena a good morning even though it is nearly noon, and remarks that neither of them is working. Then he shakes her hand. The formality of their conversation is surprising. After all, they have met every day for two months. It seems as though Astrov's self-confidence is not as high as we expected. Despite his frequent visits, he seems to have failed to create any real closeness between himself and Yelena, and he fears that she may reject his advances. Yelena is doubly afraid. First of all, she has taken on the impossible task of finding out Astrov's feelings for Sonya. Secondly, she fears that she will be unable to prevent herself from admitting her own feelings to him. Embarrassed, Astrov asks if she wanted to see his sketches. She reminds him that he promised to show them to her the day before. He lays out one of the sketches on the table and asks her where she was born and where she studied. She answers that she was born in Saint Petersburg and studied at the conservatory. Doesn't he know these details? Of course he does. Then why does he ask? He does so in order to caution her that the subject may be foreign to her. She has spent most of her days in the city and may not understand the ecological crisis that is happening in the country -- and she may be bored. Yelena is quick to reassure him: while she does not know the countryside well, she has read about it and is curious to know more. Astrov is not sure she is telling the truth and proceeds to deliver

196

little preface intended to demonstrate to her that, despite his occupation as a doctor, he is very serious about the country's ecological problems. In fact, this ecological avocation offers him an escape from taking care of the farmers, which he finds extremely tedious. When he is overcome with tedium, he puts medicine aside and hurries to Serebryakov's estate, where he has a desk of his own and can sit with Vanya and Sonya, absorbed in his sketches. He does not admit what Yelena already knows – in the last two months he has been coming to the estate not to avoid caring for the farmers, but to meet her. He adds, *"and I feel warm, peaceful, a cricket is chirping"* (p. 142). With these words, Astrov reveals his profound loneliness in his own house and confesses that his frequent visits are his way of finding warmth and homelike comfort. Does Yelena catch his meaning? It seems so. She may have even understood his statement as an invitation to build a warm and comfortable home with him. She fails to respond to the offer because she is still determined to fulfill her promise to Sonya. Astrov, however, thinks she does not respond because she lacks interest. But he does not give up and begins to explain the meaning of the maps he has drawn.

His description of the environmental damage caused by civilization is detailed and convincing. He shows her three sketches: the first depicts the flora and fauna of fifty years prior; the second, of twenty-five years prior; and the third, in the present time. His conclusions are clear:

*"I understand if the cut-down forests were being
replaced by new roads, railways, plants,
factories, and schools – the people would be
healthier, richer, more intelligent – but there's
nothing of the sort! The same swamps and
mosquitoes exist in the district, the same
impassable roads, abject poverty, typhus,
diphtheria, fires… Here we're dealing with
extinction as a result of a back-breaking struggle
for survival; this extinction is due to laziness
and ignorance and a total lack of awareness –
when a cold, hungry, and sick person, in order
to save his children and whatever is left of his
life, instinctively, without thinking, clutches at
anything that can provide warmth and satisfy
his hunger and destroys everything, not
thinking about tomorrow…"* (pp. 142-143)

What is Astrov's external action during this long
monolog? He is explaining the ecological and
social deterioration in the province in which he
resides. However, this explanation is only an
excuse that stems from his basic insecurity. His
more fundamental and pressing action is to come
closer to Yelena in order to show her how much he
loves and desires her. Throughout the monologue,
his focus is on Yelena. Overly concerned that she
may not be listening or, worse, that she may be
bored, he watches her, follows her every glance
and reaction. He does everything that he can to
fascinate her in hopes that she will eventually fall
at his feet and admit her love for him. But is Yelena

listening? It seems so. Does she imagine the destruction of the forests, the starving farmers and animals he describes? Probably not. She is focused on him, his gestures and glances, the sound of his voice and the emotions that have been stirred inside him. Perhaps she is secretly waiting for him to stop talking, to take her in his arms and embrace her. And at the same time, her heart is trembling with fear that he may do just that.

Much can be learned about Astrov from the way he uses his environmental and socio-political ideologies to court Yelena. Astrov is indeed a man of socio-political awareness. As we discussed in Chapter 1, he moved to the country in order to help the farmers improve their living conditions. He is aware of the challenge and is also painfully aware of the fact that he has not accomplished very much in the past decade. In declaring the necessity for a social revolution, he could well be hinting at a revolution in their relationship. While expounding his deep-seated connection to nature, he could, in the same breath, be appealing to Yelena to connect to her own nature. And in his desire for a more beautiful world, which he also expressed to Sonya in Act 2, he may be revealing his own heart's desire for Yelena's beauty.

Astrov's internal action is unrelated to the *content* of his words, but rather to this heartrending action of courtship. His internal action is clearly to overcome his fears. How does he do this? By masking his efforts at courtship with a presentation of his environmental and social vision. As can be expected, Yelena's internal action is also related to her relationship with Astrov. While she longs to realize her love for him, her fear of this realization is greater than her longing. Like Astrov, the fear dominates her internal action: she fights to alleviate the fear of acting on her love for Astrov by adhering to the promise she made to Sonya.

Still, Astrov continues with determination. He gets carried away with his ecological concerns, but at the monolog's climax, at the culmination of his decisive insights about the environmental crisis, he discovers that his words have been in vain. Yelena's facial expression indicates that she is not particularly impressed by his enthusiasm nor does his ecological rant reveal to her the extent of his desire. And so he stops speaking and coldly says, *"I can tell by looking at you that you are not interested"* (p. 143). While he is afraid that he is boring her, he has no idea that at that very moment, she is consumed by her fear that he might embrace her. Yelena is quick to apologize and says: *"But I understand so little about these things"* (p. 143). Again, she conceals her real feelings for him and makes him think that she is not interested in him. At this point, Astrov gives up. He says decisively, *"There is nothing to understand here really; you are just not interested"* (p. 143). Intending to leave, he starts to put away his maps. Yelena realizes it is now or never. Retreating to her promise to Sonya, she tells Astrov that, though embarrassed, she must subject him to an interrogation. But she is not sure how to begin. Astrov hesitates in hopes that the interrogation is related to their relationship. Sensing his hope, Yelena feels even more embarrassed and her words are ambiguous and confusing to Astrov: *"It concerns a certain young person"* (p. 143). Now Astrov is certain that she is talking about herself and that she will soon confess that she loves him. Yelena also realizes that her ambiguity has revealed her feelings for Astrov. Her embarrassment increases and in order to escape it, she suggests that they now speak openly, without artifice, and that they forget the confusion that has just occurred. Astrov happily agrees, thinking that she will now say what he has been longing to hear. At this point, Yelena's irresolution reaches its climax. Will she fulfill her promise to Sonya, or will she reveal her own feelings to Astrov? Her fears worsen at this critical moment and instead of sharing her own feelings, she talks openly about Sonya, although she promised to address the topic indirectly: *"It's about my stepdaughter Sonya"* (p. 143). To put it mildly, Astrov is stunned. Why is she is talking about Sonya? His expectations have been dashed, leaving in their wake profound disappointment. When Yelena asks if Sonya appeals to him, he answers drily: *"Yes, I respect her"* (p. 143). When she adds, *"Do you like her as a woman?"* (p. 143), he answers cruelly, *"No"* (p. 143).

This is a turning point for Yelena. She says explicitly: *"You don't love her; I see it in your eyes"* (p. 143). With these words, she convinces herself that the way is now clear and that she would feel no

201

guilt in taking Astrov from Sonya. In the stage directions, Chekhov emphasizes that she takes Astrov's hand. This gesture is very significant. It attests to the great closeness that Yelena feels toward Astrov. Is this finally the long-awaited moment of confession, of liberation? Not quite! Her lips cannot utter the words and she returns to the subject of Sonya: *"She's suffering... Try to understand that and... don't come here anymore"* (p. 143). These fragmented words show the extent of her vacillation, her difficulty in speaking her own truth, and her hope that he will respond by saying: 'I won't come for Sonya. I'll come for you.' On hearing this cruel request, Astrov struggles to understand her real intentions. Overcome by disappointment and frustration, he stands, searching for the words to ease his pain. Stung by this heartless decree of banishment, he responds with vague fragments: *"My time has passed... And I have no time... (Shrugging his shoulders) When could I? (He is embarrassed)* (p. 143). [46]

Astrov's response only makes matters worse. At face value, Yelena seems to be glad that the conversation is over: *"Well, thank God we are finished! Let's forget about it, as if we've never even had this conversation..."* (p. 143). And yet she does not lose hope and hints at other intentions: *"You're an*

---

[46] Professor Golomb suggests a clarification for the translation: "My time has passed... And there is no opportunity... (Shrugging his shoulders) And when would it even be possible... (He is embarrassed)

intelligent man, you'll understand" (p. 143). Astrov
lingers, wondering what she means and what he
should understand. Confused, he stands and looks
at her. As if her secret has been revealed, she is
embarrassed and apologizes: *"I'm all blushing even"*
(p. 143). Astrov, hoping that her blushing is due to
her desire to tell him what he longs to hear, tries to
lead the conversation with more hints and half-
sentences:

> *"If you had told me a month or two ago, I might
> have considered it* [i.e., marrying Sonya], *but
> now* [after falling in love with you, I cannot
> even think about it]... *If she's suffering, then,
> of course* [I will not worsen her suffering]...
> *Only I don't understand one thing: why did you
> need this interrogation?" (pp. 143- 144).*

Finally, Astrov realizes Yelena's true intentions: all
her talk about Sonya was, in fact, her way of
revealing her desire for him. All at once, his self-
confidence returns and, like an experienced doctor,
sure of his diagnosis, he looks into her eyes, points
at her and says: *"You are very cunning!"* (p. 144).
Yelena is embarrassed and asks: *"What do you
mean?"* (p. 144). Astrov laughs with relief. All of his
worries have dissipated:

> *"Very cunning! Suppose Sonya is suffering, I'm
> willing to accept that, but why this
> interrogation of yours? (Preventing her from
> speaking, and continuing quickly) Please don't
> give me that surprised look; you know perfectly*

well why I come here every day. Why and for
whose sake, you know perfectly well. My sweet
vixen, don't look at me like that, I'm a wise old
bird..." (p. 144)

Yelena is astonished. Of course, she knows he is
right, but she cannot admit it and claims she
doesn't understand. The levee has broken. Astrov
removes his mask and admits: *"I haven't done*
anything in a month, abandoned everything, all I do is
seek you out greedily..." (p. 144). In the same
moment, he also removes Yelena's mask: *"...and*
you like it terribly... terribly" (p. 144). He offers her a
new game in which she is a hunter and he is her
prey. Yelena is stunned. The walls have crumbled;
her secret has been exposed. Her only option is to
accuse him of madness. Astrov easily dismisses this
conjecture: *"A little shy"* (p. 144). He insinuates that
he is well aware with how women often use
reticence to mask their desires. Yelena then retreats
to the good old moral code that has always
protected her and claims she is a faithful wife: *"Oh,*
I'm higher and better than you think. I swear to you!"
(p. 144). She tries to leave, but Astrov will not have
it. He blocks her way and passionately asks her to
continue seeing him in secret:

> *"I will leave here today and won't come back,*
> *but... (Takes her by the hand and looks around)*
> *Where are we going to see each other? Tell me*
> *quickly, where? At any moment someone could*
> *walk in here, tell me quickly. (With passion) So*

beautiful, gorgeous... One kiss... Just to kiss
your sweet-smelling hair..." (p. 144)

Again, Yelena swears that she is a good and faithful wife, but for Astrov the time for talk has passed. Though he knows that at any moment someone could walk into the living room and despite his confidence in her desire for him, he demands proof. He needs the touch of her hand, the softness of her lips, the warmth of her body. He takes her hand and she pulls away. He insists and grabs her waist: *"You see, it's inevitable, we have to see each other"* (p. 144). He kisses her and she succumbs.

At this very moment, Vanya enters with the bouquet of roses. Not seeing him, Yelena begs Astrov to have mercy and not to put her to the test, since she will surely fail. Despite her protestations, she lays her head on his chest, submitting for a moment - and then she panics and tries to escape. Astrov will not let her go until she promises to meet him in the woods at two o'clock on the following day. Before she can reply -- and her intention is certainly to reply favorably -- she catches sight of Vanya, who has observed it all. Filled with shame and embarrassment, Yelena pulls away from Astrov and goes to the window. Then Astrov sees Vanya, as well.

This scene between Yelena and Astrov is one of Chekhov's best. He manages, with sophistication and sensitivity, he manages to create a complex set of actions that expose other actions, which, in turn, expose further actions when they are carried out. This structure of "concealment and disclosure" allows Chekhov to investigate his characters with intricacy and to uncover their deepest secrets. Let us attempt to sketch the skeleton of this complex structure:

a. The two characters enter the scene with powerful compressed internal actions that have developed over the course of two months. He longs to redeem himself through her love but is afraid she might reject him. She longs, through his love to escape from the trap that she is in, but is afraid of her own desires.

b. Both characters are uncertain about the other's internal action, leading them both to hide their own internal actions.

c. Both characters enter the scene armed with an indirect, masking strategy: he plans to tell her about the ecological crisis of the area, and she plans to question him about his relationship with Sonya.

d. He uses his indirect strategy, hoping to show Yelena that he loves her. Thus, a misunderstanding is created: she interprets his strategy literally, failing to see it as an expression of his love.

e. She employs her indirect strategy, hoping to show him that she loves him. But due to the ambiguity of her words, he fails to register her intentions. Thus, he concludes that she does not love him.

f. Despite her desire to have him know of her love, she fears this, and resorts again to her indirect strategy in order to conceal her feelings, this time speaking clearly and unambiguously. Subsequently, another misunderstanding is created: he interprets her indirect strategy literally, feels hurt and sees that he must leave the estate.

g. She tries to show him that she does not wish to distance him from *her*, but rather from Sonya. Again, she is unable to say this clearly and gives him only a hint.

h. He senses that she is trying to relay a message, but he cannot understand her oblique response. As he tries to elicit a clear statement from her, he realizes that she does indeed love him, but wants to conceal it.

i. In her anxiety, she denies what she would like him to know most of all.

j. He regains his self-confidence and is now sure that she desires him as much as he does her.

k. In another change of direction, she insists that she is a good wife and attempts to leave the room.

l. He rejects the moral argument, prevents her from leaving, holds her and kisses her.

m. She acquiesces then begs him to let her go.

n. He claims that now that their love is revealed, they cannot escape it and they must continue to meet.

o. She is on the verge of saying yes, but before she can respond, Vanya enters, ending their private moment.

Writing as a Dialectic Process Between the Planned and the Spontaneous

How is such a complex and sophisticated structure created? It is difficult to imagine that Chekhov preplanned it, although he was certainly aware of the efficacy of concealment and disclosure as dramatic mechanisms. In addition, he certainly knew that indirect strategy is a far more effective measure than direct strategy in the development of the plot; that misunderstanding is more effective than understanding; and that failure in achieving a goal is more effective than success. These principles are present in all of his plays, and they were an essential part of his creative process despite the fact that they were not written, formulated or developed as a method. In this scene too, while we do not know for certain that Chekhov preplanned each stage in the development of the plot, he surely set the opening conditions, i.e., the compression and convergence; and from that moment, it seems as though he was led by the abovementioned principles and by his characters. How can Chekhov allow his characters to lead him this way? Probably because they already exist within him. He contains their recent and distant past, their secret motives, their compression and convergence. Thus, he is able to reveal their actions in the present with such accuracy and depth.

In fact, we might say that Chekhov writes his plays by granting his characters autonomy. Once having carefully established the conditions for the scene – the compression and the convergence - he allows the characters to act according to their instincts. The highly articulated mapping of the characters' dramatic biographies before writing is what allows autonomy to his characters. He relies on the characters' independent decisions about their actions, knowing that they are right for the play. We can assume that one of the constant questions in Chekhov's mind during the writing process is, 'What do the characters want to do right now?' It is important to stress again: he does not ask what he would like them to do, but rather what they would like to do. He listens to them. All of this allows for the unplanned and spontaneous formation of the complex structure of action detailed above. Chekhov is not the only writer who grants his characters autonomy. A relevant anecdote regarding this phenomenon is included in Leah Goldberg's essay *"Chekhov's Comedy"* in her book *The Russian Literature of the 19th Century* (p. 261): "Can't you understand", wrote Pushkin to one of his friends during the writing of Eugene Onegin, 'my Tatyana has run away, to my utter surprise she ran away.'"

Chekhov's dialectic perspective is based on the harmony between careful planning of the convergence and compression of each scene and the great spontaneity that stems from the independence granted to his characters.

Furthermore, this dialectic means that the basic conditions in each scene affect the characters' spontaneous actions, while their spontaneous actions interpret, deepen and alter the scene's basic conditions.

This dialectical perspective teaches us about the similarity between Chekhov's method as a writer and the actor's method. The actor, in order to determine his actions in a particular scene, gathers basic information from the text and from the director's comments. During rehearsal, he performs these actions spontaneously in order to examine their meaning, and to become intimate with them in all their complexity. Chekhov may well have followed a similar method in his writing process. After establishing the compression and convergence of a scene, he lets his imagination and his emotions run free, allowing the actions of the characters to take place inside him. It is his experience of these actions that creates the words that he writes on paper.

Vanya's Entrance

In interpreting Vanya's earlier exit, we came to the conclusion that the bouquet of roses he wished to give Yelena was nothing but an excuse. His real desire was to distance himself from her so that he might conceal his heartbreak. He gathers the bouquet, of course, but then he sits on one of the garden benches, thinking about his life and about Yelena. Eventually, he gets hold of himself, decides not to give in and to returns to Yelena in hopes that she will reconsider and forgive him. Vanya is not naïve; he does not expect Yelena to fall at his feet and immediately run away with him the moment he enters with the roses. Yet, despite knowing about Astrov's love for Yelena, he was hardly expecting to enter the living room and find Yelena in Astrov's arms. His pain is unbearable. He puts the bouquet on a chair. He is sweating and dabs his forehead and neck with a handkerchief, mumbling: *"It's all right... Well... It's all right"* (p. 145). What does he mean? It seems as though he means to say, "Never mind. I knew anyway. I am not surprised. I should have known a long time ago."

Astrov is furious with Vanya for this devastating interruption. Surprisingly, however, he does not apologize or express any grief for the pain he is causing his friend. Instead, he talks about the weather! It is difficult to imagine that Astrov could be so insensitive to Vanya's feelings. He must be so confused that he is somehow at a loss for words. He gathers his maps, utters a cliché and quickly exits. It is Yelena who understands that this entanglement has to end. She quickly approaches Vanya and demands that he do everything in his power to ensure that she and her husband leave the estate that same day. Vanya is still in shock. He has probably not heard her correctly or fails to understand her intentions, so he dabs his face again, this time to wipe away tears rather than perspiration and says: *"Huh? Well, yes... all right...*

Helene[47], I saw everything, everything" (p. 145). He is
not only referring to the fact that he saw her in the
arms of Astrov, but also to the fact that he has now
seen his life in all its emptiness and understands
that he has been left with nothing. Yelena fears that
he has not heard her request and stubbornly
repeats it: *"Do you hear me? I must leave this place this
very day"* (p. 145). Before Vanya can respond,
Serebryakov, Sonya, Telegin and Marina enter the
living room.

The Entrance of Serebryakov, Telegin, Marina, Marya Vasilyevna and Sonya

We do not know much about the activities of
Telegin and Marina during that day. Both are
aware of the general tension in the household and
probably also of the quarrel between Vanya and
Yelena on the previous night. However, like the
others, they do not see the connection between that
event and the meeting Serebryakov has called.
They fear that Serebryakov might announce the
worst. Telegin is convinced that Serebryakov has
had enough of his laziness and that he will be
banished from the estate. Therefore he makes a
point to apologize and excuse his laziness saying
that he has been suffering from a headache for the
last two days. Marina, too, has feared for a long
time that she might be fired, as we witnessed in Act

---

[47] Vanya uses the French name "Helene" rather than the
Russian name "Yelena" due to the abyss that has opened
between them at that moment, an abyss that prevents him from
feeling the closeness expressed in the use of the Russian name.

1. However, upon entering, she does not express
her worries verbally. Sonya's thoughts are
completely unrelated to the meeting. She is
anxiously awaiting Yelena's report on her
conversation with Astrov. She has taken care not to
interrupt their conversation and has probably
remained in the dining room. With her father on
his way to the living room, she knows that the
conversation between Yelena and Astrov has ended
and she now joins her father. Marya Vasilyevna
enters late, as usual. She is aware of the hatred
between Vanya and Serebryakov, but she does not
imagine how grave it truly is. As a great fan of
Serebryakov, she is happy to hear him speak.

Serebryakov's entrance is the most meaningful of
all. What has he experienced over the last two
months? His relationship with Yelena has
completely fallen apart. It seems as though they
hardly speak to one another. Evidence for this is
that Yelena is completely unaware of the purpose
of the meeting. Serebryakov has been aware of
Vanya's desperate advances toward Yelena for
some time and is feeling angry, betrayed and
humiliated. Then, when Astrov began his pursuit
of Yelena, life on the estate became unbearable for
him. He is wild with jealousy. He feels helpless in
the face of this competition, but he will not dare
expose his feelings of humiliation by confronting
them. He has probably also stopped pleading with
Yelena for her attentions. He spends most of his
time in the library, thinking of ways to separate
Yelena from her suitors. He is also aware that this

pressure cooker is about to explode and destroy the house.

Indeed, as we have already hinted at the beginning of the chapter, Serebryakov knows about the falling out between Vanya and Yelena. Whether he witnessed it himself, heard its echoes or just assumed what happened by observing the results, he understands that a catastrophe is about to happen and that unless he acts quickly, he will lose his wife, to either Vanya or to Astrov. Serebryakov has decided to put an end to the farce that is being played out before his very eyes and to reclaim his wife whether she likes it or not.

Serebryakov has very likely contemplated selling the estate because he is so miserable there. In the three months since his arrival, he has checked with the banks and found that his profits from the sale of estate would be greater than the profits from its produce. However, economic considerations were relinquished in favor of the human consequences. Marya Vasilyevna, Vanya and Sonya make their home on the estate. Sonya is her mother's natural heiress and Vanya also has many rights of ownership. Serebryakov knows that he cannot expel them. Therefore, despite his financial difficulties, he decided to limit his expenses and to allow his mother-in-law, his brother-in-law and his daughter to continue to live there. All of this was relevant until the previous night. After learning about what had happened between Vanya and Yelena, his anger became so great that he decided to use the doomsday weapon. He will now take vengeance on Vanya, even if Sonya and Marya Vasilyevna have to pay heavily for it. He only has one goal in mind, and that is to distance Yelena from her two suitors and to show these two men their proper place. They must know that despite his age, he still sees himself in his prime and will not allow anyone to seduce his wife. Thus, he has called the meeting for the following afternoon. Having found solace in thoughts of revenge, he went to bed.

Upon awakening in the morning, Serebryakov's anger has subsided but his plans remain intact. However, he now realizes that if he were to expose the reasons for his actions, his jealousy would also be exposed. In order to avoid any further humiliation, he decides to hide his true motives and to present his plan as a means of improving his financial standing.[48] In this way, he would catch two birds with one stone: he would have his revenge while keeping his pride. Therefore, he decides to conceal his rage and to pretend that everything is normal. And so, with feigned cheerfulness, he enters the living room slightly late, expecting to see all the members of the household waiting for the meeting to begin. The significance of this decision lies in the complexity it offers the actor portraying Serebryakov as he prepares for

---

[48] In *The Seagull*, Nina's father also leaves his entire will, which he himself inherited from his late wife, to Nina's stepmother.

this scene: he will pretend that everything is normal and that his decision is purely financial. However, from time to time, there will need to be some visible signs that his true desire is for revenge.

Where is Astrov at this time? He returned his sketches to Vanya's room but could not stay there[49]. He went into the garden, pacing in irritation, awaiting the end of the meeting. He has no interest in the goings-on in the living room. All he wants is to meet Yelena again and have her agree to meet him in the forest on the next day. Despite the day's tumultuous events, he is not planning to give up on her. Later in the day (p. 155), he will even ask her to stay with him. He does not think much about Sonya and probably feels no guilt about the pain he caused his friend, Vanya. When they meet after the meeting, he will not even apologize, a topic that we will discuss later.

The Meeting
Serebryakov enters the living room accompanied by Sonya, Telegin and Marina. To his surprise, he sees only Vanya. Yelena, who just a moment ago begged Vanya to help her leave the estate that same day, heard her jealous husband approach and went to the corner of the room so he would not see her in the company of her suitor. Disappointed, Serebryakov rings a bell and asks that Marya

---

[49] We know that Astrov did not stay in Vanya's room because he was not there when Vanya entered in order to fetch the gun.

216

Vasilyevna and Yelena be summoned immediately. Yelena draws his attention to her presence. Serebryakov asks those present to sit down. He decides to wait for Marya Vasilyevna because he knows that his decision will have important consequences for her. Sonya approaches Yelena and impatiently asks her for news of Astrov. Yelena answers, *"later"* (p. 145). She is still shaken after her meeting with Astrov and the interruption by Vanya. Sonya sees that she is trembling and assumes that Astrov has rejected her marriage proposal. She also understands that he will no longer visit the estate. Yelena does not confirm this and Sonya insists on receiving a clear answer from her. She wants to cease living in fantasy. Yelena shakes her head, no. Despite the fact that she anticipated this answer, Sonya finds it difficult to bear. She remains standing with her head hung down (p. 146), oblivious to the surrounding conversation.

Serebryakov continues his charade. He engages Telegin, the sycophant, and tells him how he hates the country life. He says, *"I have a feeling as if I fell off the face of the earth and landed on another planet"* (p. 146). He is, of course, hinting at his reasons for leaving the estate. Even if these reasons do contain a grain of truth, they are nothing but a subterfuge. He sees that Sonya is standing, frozen, and asks her to sit down. She does not hear him and he repeats his request. Again, she does not hear him. In all his anticipation of the meeting, he does not bother to inquire about her state and asks Marina to sit down. She obeys and begins to knit. Serebryakov decides not to wait for Marya Vasilyevna and begins the meeting. Attempting to hide his motives, he tries unsuccessfully to jest: *"Ladies and gentlemen, point your ears, so to speak, to the center of attention"* (p. 146). Only he laughs. Vanya cannot bear any humor at this moment and asks to be excused. Serebryakov responds: *"No, we need you here more than anyone"* (p. 146). Vanya insists: *"What is it you wish from me, sir?"* (p. 146). Serebryakov, who is usually offended by Vanya's irony, is willing to tolerate anything in order to prepare him for the fatal blow he is about to inflict. He asks: *"Why are you getting upset? (A pause). If I've done you wrong, please, forgive me"* (p. 146). Vanya does not believe that this apology is genuine. Serebryakov's hypocrisy infuriates him and he demands that Serebryakov end the charade: *"Drop that tone. Let us get down to the cause... What do you need?"* (p. 146). Luckily for Serebryakov, Marya Vasilyevna enters. He ignores Vanya, happily acknowledges her and begins his speech.

The speech has been well planned. In order to calm himself and his listeners, he opens with a quotation from Gogol's *The Government Inspector*: *"I've called you here, ladies and gentlemen, to tell you that the Inspector General is coming"* (p. 146). No one laughs but him. Serebryakov excuses his audience for the insult and continues. To the listeners' surprise, he tells them that he has called this meeting because he needs their assistance and their advice. He compliments them and says, *"...knowing your ever-*

present kindness, I hope to receive them" (p. 146).
Nobody has heard such flattery from him before.
They must be flabbergasted. Their surprise grows
when Serebryakov describes himself as an
impractical person. He says that although he may
be a scholar and a bookworm, he cannot
successfully manage his finances without the
knowledge and guidance of others - referring to
Vanya, Telegin and Marya Vasilyevna. His
transparent flattery begins to raise suspicions about
his motives and his hidden agendas. Their
suspicion increases when Serebryakov says: *"The
thing is that* manet omnes una nox ['night awaits us
all'] *... I'm old and ill... My life is finished..."* (p. 146).
This statement utterly contradicts his endless lust
for life and his determination to keep on writing,
publishing and most of all, to love. Do the listeners
hear the deceit in his words? Do they not fear that
these lies are meant to obscure a sinister intention
that will at any moment leap out at them? In truth,
Sonya and Yelena are too upset to listen to him.
Marina listens and knits, convinced that as long as
she can produce socks, she will survive any decree.
As he listens, Telegin becomes more and more
fearful of the impending blow, but feels he cannot
prevent it. Marya Vasilyevna is listening with
admiration, smiling at Serebryakov's humor,
impressed by his rich language and his quotations
in Latin. Vanya hears what has been said, but
dismisses it as nonsense, further proof of
Serebryakov's stupidity and self-importance. Then,
after the hypocritical statement that he is thinking
not of himself, but only of his young wife and

virgin daughter, Serebryakov details his plans, requesting authorization from the others:

> *"Our estate brings us, on average, no more than two percent. I propose we sell it. If we turn the proceeds into securities, then we'll receive anywhere from four to five percent, and I think we'll even have a few thousand left with which we would buy a summer house in Finland."* (p. 147)

Vanya is stunned. He wonders if his ears have deceived him and asks Serebryakov to repeat himself. Now Serebryakov cannot hide his desire for revenge and, like a matador following the stabbing of the bull, he toys with the bleeding animal. He feigns naiveté and repeats the less hurtful aspect of his plan: *"Turn the money into securities, and with whatever money is left over buy a summer house in Finland"* (p. 147). When Vanya says that he heard something else, Serebryakov happily twists the knife: *"I propose to sell the estate"* (p. 147). Now Vanya knows that his ears have not deceived him: *"fine, a brilliant idea... And where am I supposed to go, with my old mother and Sonya here?"* (p. 147). Serebryakov, drunk with revenge, responds mockingly: *"We'll talk about it in due time"* (p. 147). In other words, 'I could not care less. You should have thought about that before you attempted to steal my wife from me.' Vanya, not fully grasping Serebryakov's lust for revenge, attempts to make logical and moral claims:

*"Up until now, I was stupid enough to believe
that the estate belonged to Sonya. My late father
bought the estate as dowry for my sister. Up
until now I was naïve and understood the law
not the Turkish way, and thought that the estate
had passed from my sister to Sonya."* (p. 147)

Serebryakov is not shaken by Vanya's claims and
still intending to hurt him, responds: *"Yes, the estate
belongs to Sonya... I propose to sell it for Sonya's sake"*
(p. 147). He thus strongly implies that he does not
have Vanya's best interests at heart and that as far
as he is concerned, Vanya should take care of
himself. Vanya is shocked. He cannot see the logic
in the plan and says: *"Either I've lost my mind, or...
or..."* (p. 147). Unable to finish his sentence, he falls
silent. Why does he fail to complete his thought?
Surely, it is not because of Marya Vasilyevna's
open support of Serebryakov. He falls silent
because the thought is too threatening to utter.
Even later in the act, Chekhov will not expose what
Vanya is not yet ready to express verbally here. In
Act 4, which occurs only a few hours later, there is
a hint: in the hours between the acts, Vanya has
continued to contemplate the catastrophe that has
befallen him. In his scene with Astrov, after
describing the lack of logic with which the world
functions, he explicitly expresses a very frightening
idea: *"crazy is the earth that still supports you"* (p.
153). This thought may have entered his mind
earlier, during the meeting, and the full sentence
that he intended to say was: "Either I've lost my
mind or the world runs according to insane laws

that define injustice as justice." However, during the meeting, Vanya is not yet ready to surrender the convenient and secure notion that the world runs according to the laws of logic, morals and justice, so he stops speaking and takes a glass of water. Then he says: *"Say whatever you want, whatever you want…"* (p. 147), and again he fails to complete his thought: 'I cannot understand your logic at all'.

It seems quite odd that Vanya is not aware that the sale of the estate is intended as vengeance against him, even though Yelena, herself, has warned him about Serebryakov's jealousy. At this moment, he is still consumed by his failure to win Yelena. From his point of view, since he has been unsuccessful in stealing Yelena from her husband, Serebryakov would have no motive for revenge.

Vanya's harsh response is extremely surprising to the other members of the household. Ordinarily, he would respond with his characteristic mockery. He is certainly confident enough in himself to realize that his rights to the estate are valid and cannot be annulled unilaterally. But Vanya is in crisis today. Not only has he been decisively rejected by Yelena, but he has also just witnessed her in Astrov's arms. This is a severe blow, the likes of which he has never known. And so his reaction rises not from reason or logic, but from pain, frustration and despair.

How does Serebryakov react to Vanya's emotional outburst? He seems to be more surprised than anyone. He doesn't know that Yelena has rejected Vanya and was then seen by him in Astrov's arms, so he cannot understand this terrible rage. Surely he was expecting some shouting, arguing, even threats, for which he was prepared. But Vanya's pain is so great that even Serebryakov, who hates him, cannot refrain from reconsidering his plan: *"I don't understand why you are so upset. I'm not saying that what I propose is ideal, and if everyone finds it unsuitable, I'm not going to insist"* (p. 148). This is the very moment that Telegin has been waiting for. As soon as Serebryakov says he is willing to consider the opinions of the members of the household, Telegin, the sycophant, quickly intervenes and expresses his great admiration for scholars, not only because they deserve respect for their own sake, but because a distant relative of his earned a master's degree! Vanya cannot stand this chattering and continues to attack the plan. At this point, he still hopes that logic and justice still maintain some validity in the world:

> *"The estate was bought in those days for ninety-five thousand rubles. Father paid only seventy, leaving a debt of twenty-five. Now listen… The estate would not have been bought at all, had I not given up my share of the inheritance in favor of my sister, whom I loved dearly. And not only that, but for ten years, I worked like an ox and paid off the entire debt…"* (p. 148)

When Vanya presents these facts, Serebryakov understands that he must retreat and says: *"I regret having started this conversation"* (p. 148). However, even though the threat has been removed, Vanya cannot stop the flood of anger and bitterness. But he does not attack Serebryakov for his ridiculous plan to expel him from the estate. Rather, he judges himself for being so naïve, weak and defeatist his whole life:

> *"Twenty-five years I managed this estate; I worked, sent you money like the most diligent of clerks, and during this whole time, you have not once thanked me for my work. This whole time – when I was young and now – you paid me a salary of five hundred rubles a year – a beggarly amount! – and it has never occurred to you to raise it even one ruble!"* (p. 148)

Serebryakov sees that the discussion is going in a direction he does not desire. He did not foresee Vanya's harsh reaction and never thought that he would raise such unforgiving accusations against him. After retreating from his original decision to sell the estate, he apologizes for failing to increase Vanya's salary, explaining that he has never been a practical person. From his point of view, Vanya could have raised his own salary as much as he saw fit. However, it is too late to appease Vanya, who interprets Serebryakov's words as an insinuation that he should have stolen the money. Serebryakov meant nothing of the sort, of course.

Marya Vasilyevna and Telegin are also taken aback
by Vanya's extreme response. As far as they are
concerned, after Serebryakov's retreat the meeting
should have been over and the issue forgotten.
They attempt to calm Vanya. Telegin kisses him
and urges him not to spoil the good relations
between the inhabitants of the estate. But Vanya's
frustration is so great that he cannot stop his attack:

> *"Twenty-five years, cooped up with this mother,*
> *like a mole, in these four walls... All our*
> *thoughts and feelings were about you alone.*
> *During the day we talked about you, about your*
> *work, we were proud of you, uttered your name*
> *in awe; we wasted nights reading journals and*
> *books all of which I now despise!"* (p. 149)

Now it is Serebryakov's turn to become angry. He
does not understand what Vanya wants from him.
After all, he has decided against his plan and has
even apologized for failing to raise Vanya's salary.
Even so, Vanya continues to accuse him, calling his
scholarly achievements worthless:

> *"You write about art, but you understand*
> *nothing about art! All your work that I used to*
> *love is not worth a pin. You've been pulling the*
> *wool over our eyes!"* (p. 149)

Serebryakov sees that he cannot silence him and
asks the others to help. However, no one comes
forward. He decides to end the meeting and to
leave the room. Then Yelena comes to his aid and

demands that Vanya be silent. She acts not because she feels for her husband, but very likely she fears that Vanya, in his anger, might condemn Serebryakov for having married her, used and ensnared her with no means of escape. Vanya has spoken about these things on many occasions and she does not wish to discuss them publicly. Vanya, however, is only interested in his own concerns, not hers. He blocks Serebryakov's way and accuses him of ruining his life:

> *"You ruined my life! I have not lived! I have not lived! Thanks to you, I destroyed and wasted the best years of my life! You are my worst enemy!"*
> (p. 149)

Vanya's words echo in the hearts of everyone in the living room. His admission of his own failings, his missed opportunities and his profound sense of unworthiness forces them to confront their own failures. Telegin is the first to realize this and he exits the room. Serebryakov, incapable of examining his successes and failures and needing to silence Vanya, is prepared to surrender ownership of the estate to him. Yelena, too, more afraid than anyone of self-examination, wishes to escape this hell immediately. Painfully aware of what she would see were she to examine her life as courageously as Vanya has, she screams: *"I can't endure it anymore!"* (p. 149)

Vanya sees the way his life has been lost. He is sure that he is *"talented, clever and brave"* (p. 149). In his youth, he dreamed of being a writer or a philosopher: *"If I lived a normal life, I could become another Schopenhauer or Dostoyevsky"* (p. 149), but instead, he has become a chattering fool. Of course, Vanya's dreams are merely self-aggrandizing hallucinations. Although Chekhov does not endow Vanya with such well-developed skills, his yearning to understand the world and humanity through philosophy and literature is heartbreaking. Now, the pain of his lost life is so great that he feels that he may be losing his mind: *"I'm talking nonsense! I'm losing my mind"* (p. 149). In desperation, he turns to his mother for the first time in many years and begs for help: *"Mama, I'm so miserable! Oh, Matushka!"* (p. 149). Marya Vasilyevna sees her son's desperation. She has felt his frustration in recent years and knows that he has tried to escape through his love for Yelena. However, her only advice to him at this time is to accept his fate and listen to Serebryakov. Unaware of the inappropriateness of this advice, Marya Vasilyevna only adds fuel to an already raging fire.

Until now, Sonya, preoccupied with her own misery, has not spoken a word. But at this moment, it is her own suffering that enables her to see Vanya's. She, too, needs a mother to protect her. She falls to her knees in front of Marina and clings to the nurse, who has been like a mother to her since she was orphaned. Meanwhile, Vanya continues to beg for his mother's help despite the fact that she is helpless herself. Suddenly, a new thought enters his mind. He does not need any help from anyone. He knows exactly what to do. A formidable urge takes him over. He utters a threatening warning to Serebryakov, *"You will remember me!"* (p. 149), and exits.

The following events will clearly show that the formidable urge that overcomes Vanya is a desire to kill Serebryakov. Where does he go following his stormy exit? He goes to his room to look for his gun. Why does he have a gun? Owning a gun was customary among estate owners in those days, and in Russian literature, guns are a common symbol of status, a means of self-defense, dueling and sometimes of committing suicide. In Chekhov's *The Seagull*, there is a gun on Sorin's estate and Treplev uses it both in his suicide attempt and his actual suicide. In Act 4 of *Three Sisters*, there is a duel between Tuzenbach[50] and Solyony, leading to the death of Tuzenbach. Many other Russian writers and playwrights of the same period incorporated guns and the possession of guns into their works. Chekhov must have been familiar with the biography of poet Alexander Pushkin, who was killed in a duel he initiated in 1837, in order to defend his honor following the advances made toward his wife by a French aristocrat.

Vanya's gun was probably always in his room, which also served as his office. It is difficult to tell

---

[50] Tuzenbach was an army officer. During the play, he resigns from the army and in Act 4, he is a civilian holding a civilian's gun.

when he last used it. He probably did not practice shooting often, which is clear from the fact that he missed twice in his attempts to kill Serebryakov at close range. We can also assume that the gun was not loaded and that the bullets lay beside it, giving Vanya a few moments to reconsider his actions. Had the thought of killing Serebryakov ever crossed his mind before then? Unlikely. There is no indication in the play that Vanya is a violent person. Then how does he so quickly succumb to the uncontrollable urge to rush to his room, pick up the gun, load it and shoot Serebryakov, who has come to appease him? To help understand Vanya's actions and Chekhov's intentions at this moment, let us examine a principle in Aristotle's *Poetics:*

"But again, Tragedy is an imitation not only of a complete action, but of events inspiring fear or pity. Such an effect is best produced when the events come on us by surprise; and the effect is heightened when, at the same time, they follows as cause and effect...[1]"

In other words, the plot includes actions that induce both pity and fear, which surprise the spectator, yet spring naturally from the preceding series of causal events. The attempt to kill Serebryakov induces both pity and fear and can be understood as the cumulative effect of Vanya's acute despair and his humiliating defeat. He has missed every opportunity to own property or enjoy

---

[1] *Poetics* by Aristotle, translated by S.H Butcher Chapter 9, 1452 a1

a loving relationship or raise a family. And now, in his later years, when he finally has found a woman to love, the man who has sorely mistreated him all his life takes this woman away from him. And yet, despite all this, Vanya's action still seems surprising and 'out of character' because we do not expect a normal, decent, generous, good-hearted and non-violent man to do such a thing. Moreover, though Vanya's grudge against Serebryakov seems 'logical' from his and perhaps our perspective, no logic on earth could consider the old man's actions a crime.

For Chekhov, however, this is not enough. For him, the actions of an enraged, jealous man who sets out to kill the husband of the woman who has been stolen from him amount to not much more than a sentimental melodrama suited to a popular novel. Chekhov is after something more profound and disturbing. Therefore, he builds into Vanya a deeper, more surprising recognition, which triggers his urge to kill. But for the time being he leaves it vague and hidden until it is revealed in Act 4:

> *"This is strange! I attempted murder but no one's arresting me, no one is taking me to court. Therefore, they must think that I'm crazy. (With a bitter laugh) I'm crazy, but those who, in the guise of professor, learned conjurer, hide their mediocrity, stupidity, and their blatant callousness – are not! Not crazy are those who marry old men and then deceive them in front of everybody."* (P. 153)

230

Vanya describes the unbearable disparity between his understanding of madness and that of society: society sees *him* as insane, while Serebryakov and Yelena are considered sane. If society deems Serebryakov's injustice as just, sane and appropriate, then its ethical principles and moral criteria are utterly distorted. We can now re-visit Vanya's truncated line, which was discussed earlier: *"Either I've lost my mind, or... or..."* (p. 147). The full meaning would be something like: *"Either I have lost my mind ...* or the world, itself, is chaotic and governed by insane laws where injustice is justifiable". Vanya failed to complete that sentence because the idea was too overwhelming, too frightening to bear. Now, however, he realizes that he is not wrong and that the world does indeed run according to unreasonable and unjust laws. The professor, who by Vanya's standards is a mediocre fool, has not only been rewarded with fame and acclaim, but worse, with a beautiful, young wife. Vanya, on the other hand, a self-proclaimed man of talent, wisdom and bravery, has failed at everything. The professor, who received an estate without having to work for it, banishes him, even though he has devoted his entire life there. The woman whom he loves with all of his heart and soul does not reciprocate his love and his only friend and confidante for many years, steals that woman from him. His mother, who should support him during times of overwhelming crisis, upholds his enemy. And his impending old age reminds him that he has failed to achieve his dreams. Vanya now sees how naïve he has been in his lifelong adherence to a false view of the world around him. He feels that in order to survive in this world, he must now act, surrender his naiveté and proceed according to the rules of unreason where everything is allowed, including killing the man who has cheated and abused him his whole life. Begging in vain for his mother's help, he is struck by all of this and says: *"No, don't, don't tell me! I know what to do!"* (p. 149). He rushes to his room without explanation, picks up the gun and loads it.

In Acts 1 and 2, Vanya seeks to justify his pursuit of Yelena with the argument that he is acting justly toward both Yelena and himself. Now in Act 3, he abandons the need to justify. The realization that justice is useless and meaningless in our world allows him to take justice into his own hands.

Vanya exits. His worried mother follows. She sees his misery and now wishes to help. We do not see Vanya enter his room. We do not see Marya Vasilyevna follow him, watching as he loads the gun. We do not know what happens between them. Do they talk? Does Marya Vasilyevna realize his intentions? Perhaps she thinks that he is going to attempt suicide and tries to stop him. However, since she doesn't know that he is intending to shoot Serebryakov, her arguments would not be effective and she would not be able to convince him to put down the gun. Had she known, she would still not have been able to change his mind. From the moment that Vanya realizes what kind of world he lives in, nothing can stop him.

Serebryakov, Sonya, Yelena and Marina remain in the living room. Like her grandmother, Sonya is worried that Vanya might attempt suicide. She sees his misery and his depression, and his determination as he leaves the room points to some drastic action. Serebryakov angrily demands that Vanya be removed from his presence: *"Make him move to the village or into the wing, or I'll move out, but I can't stay in the same house with him"* (p. 150). Yelena agrees and demands further that they both leave the estate that very day. Sonya turns to her father in tears and begs for mercy: *"You have to show mercy, Papa! Uncle Vanya and I are so unhappy! (Controlling her despair) You have to show mercy!"* (p. 15)

She reminds her father of Vanya's dedication throughout the years, how he used to sit up all night with Marya Vasilyevna translating books for him and copying his manuscripts. How they worked hard for him, spending nothing on themselves. How their hard work kept the estate afloat. She does not claim that Vanya's accusations are correct, only for Serebryakov to understand them both and show some compassion. Yelena is touched by Sonya's words. She, too, sees Vanya's distress and worries that he may attempt suicide. Knowing her part in his misery, she turns to Serebryakov with great emotion: *"Alexander, for God's sake, talk to him... I entreat you"* (p. 150).

Serebryakov, who feels guilty for attempting to take revenge on Vanya in a most painful way, is swayed by these entreaties and decides to talk to him. In order to clear his name, he emphasizes: *"I'm not blaming him for anything, I'm not upset"* (p. 150). Yelena leaves with him and advises: *"Be gentle with him; calm him down"* (p. 150). In fact, she is advising herself, as well. She is well aware of her influence on Vanya, whose heart she has broken.

Still worried about her uncle, Sonya remains in the living room with Marina. Her painful separation from Astrov weighs on her, as well. She embraces Marina, yearning for comfort. Marina calms her: *"It's all right, my child. The ganders will cackle awhile and then they'll stop… Cackle and stop"* (p. 150). However, relegating the fight between her father and her uncle to the cackling of geese does not calm Sonya; she sobs and shakes. Marina strokes her head, offering two other homespun remedies: Trust in God because He is gracious and merciful. And I will also make you linden tea or raspberry jam and everything will be all right. None of this is really helpful, but Marina's empathy for Sonya is so great that for a moment it seems as that she manages to calm her. Suddenly, loud voices are heard behind the door. Marina is startled: *"How the ganders go at each other; damn them all"* (p. 150). Then a shot is heard and Yelena screams. Marina curses: *"Oh, damn you"* (p. 150), referring to everyone involved in the ruckus in the hallway.

We are not told exactly what occurred in Vanya's room. Like other great playwrights[51], Chekhov prefers to leave death, suicide or attempted suicide off stage. He does so in *The Seagull*, with both Treplev's attempted suicide and his successful attempt, and also in *Three Sisters*, with the duel between Tusenbach and Solyony. Wary of excessive emotionality in all of his plays, Chekhov was very likely concerned that Vanya's double attempt on Serebryakov's life might seem too pathetic, and so chose to leave the first attempt off stage.

Let us thus imagine the events that occurred in Vanya's room: he probably managed to find his gun and load it. Marina Vasilyevna, convinced that he is planning to shoot himself, tries to the best of her abilities to calm him down. In light of her support for Serebryakov in the living room, she probably continued to praise him, thereby infuriating Vanya even further, driving him to rush out into the hallway adjoining the living room. Marya Vasilyevna follows him. Vanya meets Serebryakov and Yelena, who have left the living room. They see the gun, panic and try to mollify

---

[51] Sophocles left Jocasta's death and the plucking out of Oedipus's eyes off stage in *Oedipus Rex*, as well as Antigone and Haemon's suicide in *Antigone*. Ibsen's Hedda Gabler commits suicide offstage and so does Joe Keller in Arthur Miller's *All My Sons*. Shakespeare, on the other hand, portrayed death on stage in many of his plays: *Hamlet, Othello, King Lear*, etc. Lorca too portrayed Yerma's strangulation of Juan on stage in *Yerma*.

Vanya, who does not co-operate. He points the gun at Serebryakov, fires and misses. Did he shoot to kill? Later in the play, he makes it perfectly clear that that was his intention. However, it is also possible that his misfire was 'Freudian' (i.e., a subconscious defense mechanism that prevented him from killing Serebryakov). Either way, Yelena screams. Marya Vasilyevna faints and is left on the hallway floor. Serebryakov escapes to the living room, with Vanya in pursuit. Yelena struggles to stop him at the doorway.

Serebryakov enters, running, shaking with fear: *"Stop him! Stop him! He's lost his mind!"* (p. 150). In the meanwhile, Yelena shows surprising determination as she tries to pry the gun out of Vanya's hands. Vanya manages to escape her grasp, enters the living room, discovers Serebryakov, who is trying to hide, and fires again. Again he misses and utters a curse, *"Oh, damn it, damn it… God damn it"* (p. 151). At this point he comes to his senses and realizes what he has done. Shocked and disgusted with himself, he throws the gun to the floor and sits. Yelena leans against the wall to keep herself from falling and begs: *"Take me away from here! Take me away; for the life of me, I can't stay here, I can't!"* (p. 151). Vanya sees the depth of the hole that he has dug for himself and knows that he has no more energy to climb the slippery walls and escape: *"Oh, what am I doing! What am I doing"* (p. 151). Sonya, still shivering, is powerless in the face of the storm raging before her. She clings to old Marina and murmurs, *"Nanny! Dear Nanny"* (p.

151). In despair, Vanya sits paralyzed. Slowly, the terrible thought that there is only one way out seeps into his mind.

Chapter 4 – Act 4

The same day. Vanya's room, which also serves as the office of the estate. *"It is an autumn evening. It is quiet. Telegin and Marina sit facing one another, winding the wool for her stocking knitting"* (p. 151). In describing the contents of the room, Chekhov tells us a great deal about the man who lives there. Vanya has turned his private area into a public one. Chekhov writes, *"next to the door on the right is a doormat for the peasants to wipe off their muddy boots"* (p. 151). Clearly, Vanya chooses to meet the farmers in his room. According to Serebryakov, there are twenty-six very large rooms in the house (p. 145). It is difficult to believe that Vanya could not find an alternative room to use as an office. Why, then, has he chosen to surrender his privacy? In his eyes, his own privacy is no longer important; he has simply given it up along with all his other needs -- family, love, possessions, real achievements, success. Opposite Vanya's work desk, strewn with ledgers and stationery, is Astrov's desk, brought into the room by virtue of their friendship. Vanya also shares his room with a caged starling. One can only imagine Vanya's empathy for the bird. A map of Africa hangs on the wall, *"most likely of no use to anybody here"* (p. 151). However, this map reveals that Vanya may at one time have planned a trip to Africa[52], which, as could be expected, did not

---

[52] In 1898, just before writing "Uncle Vanya", Chekhov himself planned a trip to North Africa. See *Chekhov*, by Henri Troyat.

materialize. Why did Vanya want to travel to Africa? Perhaps he was attracted to the exotic images of this far-away land created by the explorers Livingstone and Stanley at the end of the 19th Century. Among other things, they discovered Victoria Falls and the sources of the River Nile, greatly impressing Europe with their discoveries. This may well be one of Vanya's forgotten dreams, as well.

Chekhov's decision to set Act 4 in Vanya's room probably stems from his intention to focus on the culmination of his protagonist's journey over the course of the play. This is not a simple decision for the playwright, since he must find a way to include in this private space events which would ordinarily take place in a more public area. On the other hand, this challenge creates some interesting situations. For example, what are Marina and Telegin doing in Vanya's room at this late hour? According to the stage directions, they are winding wool for Marina's knitting. Why does this happen in Vanaya's room? Why not in the dining room, for example? The real reason will soon become evident; Vanya is under surveillance. Telegin says that Sonya is walking around the garden, *"looking for Ivan Petrovich. Afraid he might lay hands on himself"* (p. 152). Vanya, upon returning, says, *"Get out of here, leave me alone at least for an hour! I can't stand guardians"* (p. 152). Clearly Marina and Telegin are there to ensure that he is not left alone to make another attempt on his life. As mentioned in the previous chapters, here, too, Chekhov explicitly chooses a space that clarifies and strengthens the convergence of the act.

Based on the partial information given by the playwright, let us imagine the events that took place on the estate between noontime at the end of Act 3, and evening at the beginning of Act 4.

Yelena was adamant that she and Serebryakov leave the estate for good, and Serebryakov agreed. She was not prepared to stay there for another hour. According to Astrov (p. 156), they deliberated whether they should travel to Kursk in southern Russia, or to Kharkov, in the northeastern Ukraine. For reasons unknown, they decided to leave immediately for Kharkov and stay there until they decided where to settle. Yelena's decision to leave was made at noon after she had admitted that she loved Astrov but was terrified of realizing the relationship. Vanya's attempt on Serebryakov's life deeply disturbed her and strengthened her resolve to leave as soon as possible.

Serebryakov was also happy to leave, despite the difficulties traveling with his ill health and the crisis in his marriage. He was quite content with the results of the meeting. Although he did not intend to risk his life in the confrontation with Vanya, his plan was ultimately a success. He defeated his wife's suitors and she would remain with him. In order to distance her from the two men, he is prepared to leave the estate in the evening and to embark on a few days' journey to

Kharkov, even without knowing where he would live or what he would do.

Vanya has not recovered from the afternoon's events. Sitting in the chair, hopeless and exhausted after his second failed gunshot at Serebryakov, Vanya slowly realized that only suicide could end his suffering. Chekhov does not detail what happened next, but we can assume that as Vanya returned to his senses, he noticed the gun on the floor, picked it up and started walking to his room with the intention of locking himself in and shooting himself. While the others were too self-absorbed, Sonya very likely noticed Vanya's actions and attempted to take the gun from him. Astrov, having heard the gunshots probably quit his solitary walk in the garden and hurried to the living room. He saw Sonya grappling with Vanya and tried to assist her. Vanya lost hold of the gun but he managed to escape and run out of the house. Sonya and Astrov went looking for him throughout the estate. Meanwhile, Telegin picked up the gun and hid it in the cellar. A while later, Vanya managed to return to his room, open Astrov's medicine chest and take out a bottle of morphine. Astrov discovered this and refused to leave the estate until Vanya returned the bottle. This progression of events is based on Chekhov's partial description and may have happened otherwise, of course.

Sonya senses that Vanya's crisis is more acute than her own, and summons all her strength to save him from himself. Her efforts on Vanya's behalf also serve as a distraction from her distress about Astrov's rejection. Despite the fact that the two of them are looking for Vanya together, there is no hint of any discussion about their relationship. However, it is important to note that Sonya's wound has not healed. Although she seems able to function, her misery has not subsided, as shown in her first words to Vanya: *"I may be just as unhappy as you, but I'm not giving in to despair. I endure and will endure until my life ends by itself"* (pp. 154-155). She struggles to conceal her emotions and when she does burst into tears (p. 155), she is not only crying for her uncle, but for her own pain. Her decision to return to work immediately, even before Serebryakov and Yelena's departure, also denotes her internal turmoil – Chekhov tells us that she is nervously organizing the papers on the table (p. 155).

Astrov was probably in the garden during the meeting, heard the gunshots and rushed to the living room. Fortunately, he did not have to treat anybody. Since he did not personally experience the traumatic event, he was able to piece together the recent events and understand that Vanya wanted to end his life, and so he leaves with Sonya in search of her uncle. There was likely very little conversation between them during the search. When he discovered that Vanya took the morphine from his medicine bag, Astrov did not reveal this to Sonya for fear of worrying her and worsening her distress. He recognizes his responsibility for her feelings. He tells her about this only after she has entered Vanya's room. Astrov also worries that Yelena's decision to leave the estate with her husband is final. They have already decided to go to Kharkov and will soon be finished packing. He struggles to come to terms with this and hopes for a miracle that would allow him to meet with Yelena and convince her to change her mind. His pursuit of Vanya, who stole the bottle of morphine, also serves as an excuse for him to remain on the estate. His decision to return to his own estate is difficult for him because it signals defeat in his struggle for happiness, and also because he would be subjecting himself to a long, cold, lonely winter.

Marya Vassilyevna, who endured a difficult experience in Act 3, pretends that life has returned to normal. After the gunfire and her recovery from her altercation with Vanya, she returns to her room and seeks comfort in her books. In her first entrance, Chekhov stipulates that she is holding a book. Reading is very likely difficult for her on a day like this, when her son wishes to commit suicide and she cannot prevent him from doing so. She also realizes that Serebryakov, whom she so admires, is leaving and that she will never see him again. This means that she will probably spend the rest of her life alone. However, she gathers her strength and pretends to be interested in the book, all in order to ease her distress.

Marina and Telegin seem happy. The scandal has ended with no bloodshed. The risk of their unemployment has passed. They hope that everything will return to normal: tea at eight, lunch at noon, and dinner in the evening. However, it is difficult to believe that the two of them, having lived on the estate for so long, and being so close to their masters, feel no empathy for their crisis. They have seen how fragile Vanya and Sonya's lives are and their confidence in them has been shaken. What would become of them if Vanya committed suicide and Sonya became a nun? Due to their complete dependence, Marina and Telegin fear another disastrous crisis in the near future. We should therefore view their desire to return to 'normal' as a means of staving off another crisis, a cure for all of their ills. There is, of course, a contrasting interpretation, according to which Marina and Telegin take pleasure in the crisis of their landlords and are pleased that they have avoided unemployment. This interpretation carries an additional implication of class differences and conflict. However, it is difficult to accept this interpretation because of Chekhov's general approach toward his characters – they are human, their emotional mechanisms are functional, and despite their weaknesses and flaws, their responses to the events around them stem from their emotions rather than their ideological or social perspectives.

Why Is Act 4 Necessary?
The beginning of Act 4 raises a fundamental question. As we saw in Act 3, all the characters arrive at a relatively full awareness of their

existential condition: Vanya wishes to commit suicide, Astrov plans to return to his estate, Sonya has given up on the idea of marrying him, Yelena is fleeing her love for Astrov, Serebryakov is victorious, and even Marya Vassilyevna, Telegin and Marina return to their routine. Then why is Act 4 necessary? Why does Chekhov continue to tell the story of these characters, in apparent contradiction to Aristotle's rule in *Poetics*: "*An end is that which itself naturally follows some other thing, either by necessity, or as a rule, but has nothing following it*"(Chapter 7, line 29). In other words, the end of the tragedy is the moment following which the events are no longer relevant to the plot. Chekhov, who was aware of this logic, would not have written Act 4 without knowing that it would contain events that would further the plot, and that the decisions in Act 3 could still be reversible. This means that at the start of Act 4, Astrov and Yelena have not yet given up on each other, that Sonya and Astrov might possibly have a future together, and that even Vanya wishes for a miracle that would keep him from killing himself. All of these must still be possible, with only the plot developments in the last act preventing their occurrence.

The External and Internal Processes in the Scene
Telegin and Marina sit facing each other winding wool. Telegin is impatient. He hurries Marina because the carriage is ready for the journey to Kharkov and they must say goodbye to Serebryakov and Yelena. Telegin's impatience

seems somewhat strange since he remains seated waiting for Serebryakov and Yelena to complete their preparations for the trip. Then why does he hurry her? He is lazy and he wants to be free of winding wool just as he has managed to avoid every other task that has been assigned to him (p. 145). It is no coincidence that he is called a freeloader (p. 152). However, this is only a partial explanation. Chekhov would never choose an action that reflects a character's usual routine or traits. Telegin may also be impatient because he is wary of being in Vanya's room because Vanya might return and attempt suicide again. Telegin would have to stop him. This task is greater than he can handle and he is fearful of failure. Thus, he tries to avoid it. Chekhov offers proof for this: when Vanya enters the room, Telegin quickly exits (p. 152). Why does Marina insist on staying in the room? This has nothing to do with her wool winding, of course. She, unlike Telegin, is determined to stand guard, ready for the moment when Vanya might enter and she could save him from himself. And so, she delays Telegin's exit as well.

Telegin gives in to Marina and stays. Why does he tell her that Serebryakov and Yelena are going to Kharkov? Does she not know this already? Later, he will also tell her how the two of them decided to leave (pp. 151-152). Then she asks, *"Where is Sonya?"* (p. 152) and also, *"Where's his pistol?"* (p. 152). How is it that Telegin knows more than she does? He must have heard Serebryakov and

Yelena's conversation, and only later was sent by Astrov and Sonya to stand guard in Vanya's room with Marina. This scenario is useful because it enables the act to start with both Marina and Telegin in Vanya's room. However, its main function lies in the clarification for both actors that Marina is there determined to prevent Vanya from committing suicide, and panic-stricken Telegin enters the room only later, hoping to escape his assigned duty.

At face value, Telegin's external action is to report to Marina what he overheard from Serebryakov and Yelena. However, a hint of a more meaningful action appears later, when Telegin describes the day's events as *"a scene worthy of Aivazovsky's brush"* (p. 152). Aivazovsky was a Russian artist, famous for his stormy seascapes, portrayals of tempests, waves etc.[1] Telegin's unexpected reference shows that he is well aware of the tempestuous emotions that have overcome Vanya and that he does not make light of them. Rather, he is in awe of their intensity. And so, his report of the conversation is marked by that same feeling of awe. It is therefore possible that Telegin is not so much explaining the afternoon's events to Marina, as to himself, in an attempt to understand them. He is trying to sort out the havoc that he himself is feeling, and ends with the statement: *"...It wasn't in the cards for them to stay here. Wasn't in the cards..."*

---

[53] As described by Abraham Shlonski in his notes to the Hebrew translation of the play

(p. 152). But having failed to understand the day's events, he attributes them to a higher power, i.e. fate. Marina is satisfied with the couple's departure, since she holds them responsible for the afternoon's shameful events. She says, *"Raising a row like that just now, shooting – shame on them!"* (p. 152). Marina's interpretation of the events is hardly surprising. At the opening of the play, she had already sensed that the interruption to the routine of the estate was a bad sign (p. 117). She holds the professor and his wife responsible not only for that disruption, but also for the disruptions to both Astrov and Vanya's common sense and foiling Astrov's marriage to Sonya, whom she so loves. Now, her routine can be reinstated:

> *"And we will go back to living like before: tea a little past seven, lunch at noon, and in the evening – we sit down to supper; everything same as before, like good Christians…"* (p. 152)

Marina's reference to 'good Christians' illustrates the fact that she sees these disruptions not minor moral transgressions, but as real religious sins, disruptions to a world order. She sighs and immediately adds, *"it's been a long time since I, oh, sinner that I am, had noodles"* (p. 152). What do noodles have to do with disruptions to a world order? In the same way that Astrov in Act 1 (p. 116), seeing his pathetic efforts at self-examination, turns to the topic of his foolish moustache, so Marina, too, fearing that her criticism of the sins of her landlords might bring her to the awful conclusion that the entire household, herself included, is doomed to hell, changes the subject. She speaks of her longing for noodles in order to alleviate her anxiety. Telegin can certainly relate to Marina's desire for comfort food, and may also shudder with the thought that the turmoil on the estate is the result of the sins of its inhabitants - and very likely his own, the most egregious of which is sloth. He tells Marina that that very morning, a shopkeeper in the village shouted at him, *"Hey, you, freeloader!"* (p. 152). That shopkeeper must have seen his sins. Marina comforts him, saying, *"We are all freeloaders under God. Same as you, as Sonya, as Ivan Petrovich. No one sits around doing nothing, everybody's working hard! Everybody..."* (p. 152). She is, of course, referring mainly to herself.

After her fears of being destined for hell subside, Marina asks, *"Where is Sonya?"* (p. 152). Her question should be seen less as an enquiry as to Sonya's whereabouts, but more as an expression of concern for Sonya, a concern which increases as time wears on. Telegin informs her that Sonya is *"in the garden. Still walking with the doctor, looking for Ivan Petrovich. Afraid he might lay hands on himself"* (p. 152). This is not just information. Telegin, too, is worried, not only about Vanya, but also about himself. He knows the consequences he will suffer should Vanya be successful in his attempts to commit suicide. Marina takes up Telegin's concern. If Vanya is wandering around the estate with gun in hand, nobody can prevent him from shooting himself. Alarmed, she asks, *"Where's his pistol?"* (p.

152). Now it is Telegin's turn to calm her: *"I hid it in the cellar!"* (p. 152). Relieved, Marina dismisses him and laughs at her own concern: *"Oh, the sin!"* (p. 152). In other words, 'what sins we must commit because of them!'

The Entrance of Vanya and Astrov

Vanya enters from the garden, followed by Astrov. What have they been doing? According to Telegin, the chase after Vanya occurred in the garden. Astrov and Sonya both know that Vanya does not have his gun, but they fear that he may find another way to hurt himself; hence, they will not leave him alone. During their pursuit, Vanya may have asked that they leave him be. They in turn may have demanded that he return to the house and he refused. Finally catching up with him, Astrov may have asked Sonya to leave him alone with Vanya. Unlike Sonya, the doctor knows that Vanya has taken the bottle of morphine and he is worried that the bottle may be in his pocket.

Why does Vanya return to his room? Here, a clear, profound and plot-advancing decision is necessary, a decision that is not simply a variation of the chase that just took place in the garden. Vanya knows that the morphine bottle is in his desk drawer. He has hidden it there so that he could lock himself in his room, turn off the desk lamp, lie down on his bed and consume the contents of the bottle. However, during the chase, he felt that he had had enough and finally decided to end his life. As he enters his room, Vanya immediately asks Astrov to

250

leave him alone and orders Telegin and Marina out of the room. His request sounds rather reasonable: *"leave me alone at least for an hour!"* (p. 152). He is sure that will be enough time to carry out his plan. This means that his suicide plan is real and that he intends to carry it out as soon as possible. It is not a provocation or a cry for help. In despair, Vanya is convinced that there is no purpose to his life and that he must put an end to it.

Telegin, the coward, is quick to leave. Marina also gathers up her yarn and exits, but first she taunts Vanya: *"The gander: cackle, cackle!"* (p. 152). Repeating the barnyard imagery she used at the end of Act 3 (p. 150), she hopes to relieve his distress: 'Don't forget that your argument with Serebryakov was nothing but the cackling of geese. Nothing will come of it!'

After Marina's exit, Vanya notices that Astrov is standing very close to him. He worries that the moment he opens the drawer, the doctor will snatch the bottle from him, so he asks him to leave. Astrov replies that he would love to leave him and to return home, but that he will not do so until Vanya returns what he has taken from him. Vanya denies having taken anything. Astrov insists and demands that Vanya does not delay his urgent departure. Again, Vanya denies having taken anything. Thus far, neither of them has mentioned the word 'morphine'. Although we can sense that the subject is important, we do not know what the two men are talking about. Chekhov prefers not to name the stolen object in order to create mystery and curiosity, but why does Astrov not say the word? Perhaps to allow Vanya to abandon his plan more easily: 'Let us resolve this issue among ourselves. Give me what you have taken and I will not tell anyone'. However, Vanya does not give up so easily and Astrov has to threaten him: *"Really? All right, I'll wait a little longer, but then, sorry, I'll have to resort to force. We'll tie you up and search you"* (p. 153).

Vanya is not frightened by the threat. However, a major change occurs in his external action. Until now, he has made every effort to distance himself from his pursuers in order to carry out his plan. Now he confesses his failures, his thoughts and feelings to Astrov. What has caused this change? Let us examine his internal action, which has intensified since his failed attempts to kill Serebryakov. The internal action stemmed from Vanya's terribly painful feelings regarding his life's failures, Yelena's rejection, and the difficult realization that the world is not a place fit for him to live. He can no longer contain the pain. Now his internal action is his desire to alleviate his pain. And so, he tries to commit suicide. This is his first external action. He proceeds with this action until he enters his room, still determined to end his life. But the moment Astrov makes it clear that he will not allow it, Vanya realizes that he must employ a different strategy to relieve his pain. Thus, a new external action is born; he bares his heart to the doctor.

The first part of Vanya's confession is very puzzling: *"Oh, what a fool I made of myself: to shoot at him twice and miss both times! I'll never forgive myself for this!"* (p. 153). Is Vanya is really sorry that he missed? His actions over the last few hours indicate that he is no longer trying to kill the professor. Despite his emotional turmoil, he is not suffering "temporary insanity", and he is well aware that his poor aim saved Serebryakov's life. He also knows that Serebryakov does not deserve to die, despite his unreasonable actions. Later, we will see that he also understands the legal consequences of his attempted murder, and even though he is fed up with life, he certainly does not want to spend it behind bars. Then what does Vanya mean by the sentence, *"I'll never forgive myself for this"* (p. 153). He grasps that his failure to kill Serebryakov is yet another missed opportunity, and vows with painful sarcasm that he will never forgive himself for his lifelong chain of failures.

Astrov's reply is also puzzling: *"If you feel like shooting, shoot yourself in the head"* (p. 153). Is this the way one calms a suicidal person? Why does Astrov seem so impatient and crass? Surely he does not want Vanya to commit suicide so he can hurry back to his own estate (p. 152), nor is he concerned that he would be blamed if Vanya drank the morphine from his medicine bag. And Astrov would hardly be joking at such a delicate moment. In order to understand Astrov's inner process, let us examine how the events of the day have affected him. His meeting with Yelena at the end of Act 3 may have ended in disappointment, but the fact that she succumbed to him for a moment (p. 144) gives him some hope; later he even suggests again that she meet with him (p. 155). Vanya's attempt on the life of Serebryakov is not a traumatic event for him and, although he does not explicitly say so, he very likely views the debacle as pathetic and ridiculous. However, Vanya's attempted suicide is another matter. His friend's desire to end his life certainly upsets and frightens him. After all, he, too, has not achieved any of his dreams and sees himself as a failure. He, too, is caught in a trap that he cannot escape. Might Vanya's solution be right for him, too? This question has been weighing on him for hours, and terrifying him. This terror is very likely the cause of his callous challenge to Vanya. This observation reveals Astrov's internal action at the opening of Act 4. Since early afternoon when he became aware of Vanya's intentions, he has been plagued by his own desire to do the same, and he has been fending it off with all his might. The best tactic in such a battle is to avoid any empathy for his miserable friend. Thus, when he says, *"If you feel like shooting, shoot yourself in the head"* (p. 153), he is really saying: "Kill yourself whenever you like, but I am not a pathetic, emotional self-pitying wreck like you, and unlike you, I will not attempt suicide."

Unaware of Astrov's tumultuous emotional state, Vanya, self absorbed as ever, continues to explain, mainly to himself, his reasons for wanting to kill Serebryakov:

*"I attempted murder but no one's arresting me,
no one is taking me to court. Therefore, they
must think that I'm crazy. (With a bitter laugh)
I'm crazy, but those who, in the guise of
professor, learned conjurer, hide their
mediocrity, stupidity, and their blatant
callousness — are not! Not crazy are those who
marry old men and then deceive them in front of
everybody."* (p. 153)

At the end of Chapter 3, Vanya concluded that the
world is run by unreasonable rules that allow
unjust actions to be defined as just, and that if he
wants to survive this world, he must act
unreasonably. Therefore, it is reasonable to do
away with the person who ruined his life.
However, which of Vanya's actions reflect this
realization? We have seen that he admits his
failures, thoughts and feelings to Astrov. What
does Vanya hope to gain from this confession? It is
difficult to believe that he is trying to justify his
attempt to kill Serebryakov, especially when he
himself already regrets it. Cunningly, Chekhov
only reveals the answer to this question later in the
act. Soon Vanya will say, *"I'm so ashamed! If you
only knew how ashamed I am"* (p. 153). He does give
reasons for feeling ashamed, but there is no doubt
that, aside from his many failures, the attempted
murder of Serebryakov would certainly be one of
them. Therefore, his external action can be
understood as an attempt to convince himself that
the shooting was just – not to try it again, but to

alleviate his shame for doing it. As we have seen, Vanya is certainly embarrassed by his failure to kill Serebryakov, but now we see he is deeply ashamed for trying to do so. This external action also reveals Vanya's internal action: he yearns to alleviate the shame of his many past failures, and, most of all, today's failure to maintain his sanity in a moment of rage.

At this point, despite their friendship, Vanya is ready to blame Astrov not only for accepting the madness and injustice of the world, but also for attempting to steal the woman he loves. He says angrily, *"I saw it, I saw when you were embracing her"* (p. 153). Avoiding any empathy for Vanya, Astrov provokes him: *"Yes, sir, I was embracing her, and you get this. (He thumbs his nose)"* (p. 153). It is as though he is saying, "I have no pity for you and you would do well to stop pitying yourself."

Vanya is surely shocked. Has his one-time friend gone mad? Chekhov states that Vanya looks toward the door. Perhaps he is thinking of snatching the morphine bottle from the desk drawer and making off with it. However, he knows that Astrov would not permit him to do so, so he lashes out at him again, *"No, crazy is the earth that still supports you"* (p. 153). In Chapter 3, we saw that the madness of the world is Vanya's main reason for suicide. Astrov certainly understands this and tends to agree. He himself says similar things about mankind during his conversation with Yelena, particularly with reference to man-made environmental damage (pp. 142-143; pp. 123-124) and in his conversation with Sonya (p. 134). However, at this moment, he certainly avoids agreeing with Vanya because he might well draw the same conclusions. Therefore, he dismisses him: *"Well, that's stupid"* (p. 153). His ridicule of Vanya is not arbitrary. It is the external action through which Astrov carries out his internal action -- his yearning to suppress the death wish that resides in him.

Vanya's response is surprising. A moment ago, he confronted Astrov with a painful philosophical existential comment confirming the existential madness of the earth and its irrational inhabitants. Now, he replies with irony: *"Well then, I'm crazy, I'm beside myself, and I have a right to say stupid things"* (p. 153). This completely contradicts his previous statement, dismissing it as stupidity. It is difficult to assume that Astrov's ridicule, *"well, that's stupid"* (p. 153) was enough to cause such a profound change. This shift takes place because Vanya realizes the degree of pathos inherent in his statement once it was formulated and spoken aloud, and now he himself rejects it. Astrov's disparaging response helps him off his high horse and now their conversation undergoes a change, which we will later discuss.

The Test of Containment

The above interpretation illustrates the enormous challenge that Chekhov places before his actors – to interpret and carry out enormous emotional dynamics with minimal text in a relatively short length of time. Can such a challenge be met? Evidently, Chekhov thought so, since many such moments, brimming with emotional upheaval, can be found in all of his plays. What did Chekhov expect from the actors portraying his characters undergoing such an emotional rollercoaster? Firstly, he certainly expected the actors to understand precisely the most minute details of their character's emotional dynamics. These dynamics cannot be carried out "more or less" or "generally". He expects the actors and the director to break down each moment into precise actions, both external and internal, and to contain these actions – the internal actions in their hearts and the external actions in their minds and bodies – exactly as he does while he is sitting and writing. In fact, the writing would be impossible without it. Moreover, Chekhov also seems to expect every process that he himself contains in his heart and body to be successfully contained by the actor. This seems to be the main criteria in his writing process and as such, it must be highly exact, and he himself needs to be able to trust it completely. In other words, Chekhov needs to be sure that he is not cheating or deluding himself while writing an action. He must be certain that his feeling of "containment" of the action at hand is full, clear, honest and lacking in any pretense. This is the definition of the common term *"the playwright's artistic integrity"*: he must put each process that he writes to the "test of containment". A process that fails this test must be excluded from the play. This rule applies to the actor as well: each process that he enacts must also be put to the same test. The actor must not act out a process that he cannot completely contain.

Let us return to the events of the scene at hand. As mentioned above, Vanya has realized the pathos of his actions and has "dismounted his high horse". Now he takes a more ironic, detached stance from himself and can therefore genuinely listen to Astrov without the burden of his vulnerability and pain. Astrov senses this and can now address Vanya rationally:

> *"You are not crazy; you're just an oddball. A buffoon. Before, I used to think that all oddballs were either sick or crazy, but now I think that being an oddball is a normal state of being. You're quite normal."* (p. 153).

Astrov does not see Vanya as crazy, but as an oddball and a buffoon.[54] According to him, all people are that way. It is their normal state, and therefore, Vanya is normal too. What is Astrov's external action by these words? As previously determined, his internal action is his desire to

---

[54] Professor Golomb suggests substituting "buffoon" with "a ridiculous fool".

overcome his inner death wish. And so, his external action is to convince Vanya that he is normal, that he suffers from the exact same madness and foolishness as everyone else, and that he can therefore go on living, as everybody else does. Astrov assumes that by assisting Vanya in overcoming *his* death wish, he could overcome his own.

By this external action, Astrov manages to cause yet another great change in Vanya. Vanya is now prepared to consider options other than suicide. He has already admitted his great shame at his many failures and his pathetic attempt to murder Serebryakov. Now, the desire to kill himself, a desire that he is slowly surrendering, can also be added to the list of causes for his shame. Therefore, he asks painfully: *"What should I do? What should I do?"* (p. 153). The meaning of his question is clear: "I do not want to commit suicide, but what else can I do in order to ease this terrible pain? Astrov, in line with his abovementioned internal action, replies cruelly: *"Nothing"* (p. 153). In other words: "You must come to terms with your disappointment and your despair like everybody on the face of the earth". In truth, his response is directed at himself, as well. It is difficult to avoid amazement at Astrov's honesty and directness. He offers Vanya no consolation, no magical cure or illusion; rather he attempts to distance him from suicide by acknowledging the clear but painful existential truth. At this point, Astrov does not seem able to mislead himself.

At the very moment when Vanya openly regrets his decision to commit suicide, the most profound plot change occurs in the scene, that, as we well remember, began with his attempt to swallow the morphine. How does this change take place? It cannot be explained by an autonomous internal process in Vanya. If such a process were possible, the scene with Astrov would be superfluous. Astrov's pursuit in the garden certainly demonstrated that he cares about Vanya and values his friendship. However, the pursuit began before the two men entered Vanya's room without resulting in this dramatic change. Therefore, Vanya's change is brought about by Astrov's actions *during* their meeting. How does Astrov influence Vanya's decision to refrain from suicide?

Astrov's external actions are as follows: he initially tells Vanya that he will not allow him to attempt suicide, even if it means using force. Then, he is crude and disparaging about Vanya's desire to commit suicide. Later he mocks and deflates Vanya's self-pity, stating that everyone suffers as much as he does but most do not attempt suicide. And so, neither does Vanya. The accumulation of these external actions is important, but not as important as Astrov's internal action which is to battle his own death wish. Vanya senses this internal action even though it is not put into words. He senses it through the empathy between himself and Astrov, the same kind of empathy the spectator is developing for the doctor. Vanya senses that his good friend is fighting for his life, and this feeling urges him to fight against his own death wish as well, and for a moment even overcome it.

Now Vanya, having overcome his death wish, speaks very differently:

> *"Oh, my God… I'm forty-seven years old; suppose I make it till sixty, then I have another thirteen years left. Such a long time! How will I survive thirteen more years? What will I do, what will I fill them with? Oh, you see (fitfully squeezing Astrov's hand) … you see, if you could only spend the rest of your life in a new way. To wake up on a clear, quiet morning feeling that you have begun a new life, and that the past is all forgotten, diffused like smoke. (Crying) To begin a new life… Tell me how to begin… what to begin it with…"* (p. 153).

This monolog is unusual in its honesty and clarity. No more masks, no more hidden intentions. Vanya stands before us naked and exposed, and his external action is clear: he is begging Astrov to help him fulfill the inner action that he formulates so simply and directly – he wishes to start living. This monolog illustrates Vanya's process of peeling away his defense mechanisms[55], and for a moment, we can see the root of the primary internal action

---

[55] We will discuss this process in detail in chapter 5.

he has struggled to realize throughout the play. This moment of total transparency will pass quickly and we will soon see him seal the cracks that have appeared in his defenses, and put on new masks.

Astrov stands in front of Vanya, in shock. In the stage directions, Chekhov stipulates that Astrov is annoyed (p. 154). Vanya's desire for a full and profound life threatens to awaken his own immense desire for the same thing, a desire that he gave up when he decided to return to his estate. He knows that to acknowledge such a concession is very painful, so he is still unwilling to show any empathy toward his friend and bluntly interrupts him again: *"Oh, come on, please! New life! Our situation, yours and mine, is hopeless"* (p. 154). The cat is now out of the bag. Astrov admits that his situation is just as hopeless as Vanya's. However, unlike Vanya, he has come to terms with this hopelessness. He does not question or fight it.

Vanya asks, *"Is it?"* (p. 154), hoping to find out if Astrov's claim that neither of them stand a chance at a new life is final. Astrov replies that he is sure it is. This is a critical moment for Vanya. A moment earlier, he entertained some hope for salvation. Now, however, infected with Astrov's dark assessment, there is only disillusion. Does Vanya fully accept Astrov's statement? Does his death wish return? It seems that his fear of it does. He asks for a pill to allay his anxiety. Astrov refuses. A pill to remedy existential pain is nothing but an illusion. There will be no relief. Vanya must continue to bear the pain for the rest of his life. With the cold, cutting precision of a surgeon, Astrov describes the reality that he must accept:

> *"Those who will live a hundred or two hundred years after us, and who will despise us for having lived our lives so stupidly and tastelessly – they may find a way to be happy, but you and me… We have but one hope. The hope that when we're sleeping in our coffins, visions, maybe even pleasant ones, will visit us." (P. 154)*

There is no hope now and none in the future. There is, however, a slight consolation:

> *"Oh, well, my friend. In the whole district there used to be only two decent intelligent people: you and me. But in a mere ten years, this narrow-minded, despicable life has sucked us in; it has poisoned our blood with its rotten fumes, and we've become vulgarians like everybody else." (P. 154)*

Neither he nor Vanya are to blame for the deterioration of their lives. They have been poisoned by miserable social circumstances beyond their control. They must not blame or punish themselves. However, as mentioned before, Astrov's real external action is his own attempt to convince himself of his own arguments. He must remind himself that this is the reality that he, too, must accept. He, too, must not blame himself for his failures. Astrov's words echo Andrey's speech to deaf Ferepont in Act 4 of *Three Sisters*:

> *Oh, where is it, where did my past go – when I was young, cheerful, intelligent, when I dreamed and thought beautiful thoughts, when my present and future were full of hope? Why is it that the moment we begin to live, we become boring, drab, tedious, lazy, indifferent, useless, and unhappy...* (p. 217)

Vanya tries to grasp Astrov's harsh words, to digest his crushing claim that happiness is a mere illusion and that, in reality, life will be forever meaningless, useless and hopeless. On the other hand, for Astrov this as a positive sign, a calm acceptance that allows him to return to his role as a goal-oriented doctor: *"But don't try to smooth talk me, however. Give me back what you took from me"* (p. 154). Vanya denies having taken anything. Now, however, after their brutally open conversation, there is no place for niceties. Astrov clearly says, *"You took a jar of morphine from my medicine case"* (p. 154). Vanya does not respond. Astrov loses his patience and returns to the coarse tone of the opening of the scene:

> *"Listen, if you're so eager to kill yourself, then go off in the woods and shoot yourself there. But morphine, give it back to me; or people will start talking, speculating, and might think that I gave it to you... For me, it's enough that I'll be the*

one to do your autopsy... Do you think it's interesting?" (p. 154)

Why does Vanya not return the bottle to Astrov? Clearly, he has not yet completely given up the idea. He is concerned that he might still need the morphine, and he is correct. His death wish does not go away. And just at this crucial moment, Sonya enters.

Sonya's Entrance
We do not know where Sonya has come from, but we might assume the following: at the opening of the act, Telegin says that she is *"in the garden. Still walking with the doctor, looking, looking for Ivan Petrovich"* (p. 152). Sonya was surely worried about Vanya, but is also still lamenting Astrov's rejection, which she heard from Yelena a short while before. Since she knows that Astrov is now with Vanya in his room, she is certain that the risk of suicide is over. And now, for the first time since receiving news of Astrov's rejection, she has gone to her room to mourn and to be alone.

Other scenarios are possible but what *is* clear is that when she enters Vanya's room, her actions tell us that in the time that elapsed between leaving Astrov in the garden and her entrance into Vanya's room, she has been alone, has used the time to regain her strength and has come to a definite conclusion: *"I may be...unhappy... but I'm not giving in to despair. I endure and will endure until my life ends by itself"* (pp. 154-155).

We already know how important pride and self-control are to Sonya by her behavior at the beginning of Act 3 (p. 139). Indeed, she enters determined to revivify and maintain these qualities, and to assume responsibility for the management of the estate once again. As manager, her first task is to ensure Vanya's recovery and his intention to continue living. She also hopes that Astrov is still in Vanya's room and that he will see that she is not shattered.

But before Sonya can say a word, Astrov makes it clear that the crisis is in full force:

> "Sofia Alexandrovna, your uncle has made off with a little jar top morphine from my medicine case, and won't give it back. Tell him that it's… not smart after all. I've no time. I have to go" (p. 154).

Sonya immediately grasps the gravity of the situation and asks Vanya whether he has indeed taken the morphine. Vanya fails to answer. Astrov reconfirms that Vanya has taken it. Pretending to be unfazed and back to normal, Sonya addresses him with restraint: *"Give it back. Why do you frighten us?"* (p. 154). But Vanya is adamant. She continues to urge him gently, saying, *"Give it back, Uncle Vanya"* (p. 154). He does not answer. Maintaining her self-control, she suggests that he take example and draw power from her, for she has found the way to overcome her misery: *"I may be just as unhappy as you, but I'm not giving in to despair. I endure and will endure until my life ends by itself. You, too, must endure it"* (pp. 154-155).

Sonya says these things to Vanya, but she directs them to Astrov as well, and most of all, to herself, so that she may continue to be strong despite her pain and misery, so that she may act bravely, and so that she will not resort to desperate means. She begs Vanya again, *"Give it back! (Kisses his hands) My dear, good Uncle Vanya, give it back"* (p. 155). Vanya remains silent and she can no longer control herself. She breaks down and cries, *"You're so kind-hearted, you'll have pity on us and give it back. You have to endure it, Uncle! Endure!"* (p. 155). Vanya's kind heart cannot bear to cause her pain; he cannot remain aloof from her misery. Finally, he surrenders and returns the morphine to Astrov, but at the same time he clings to the habitual routine that has caused him to despise his life: *"But I must get to work quickly, do something quickly, otherwise, I can't... I just can't"* (p. 155). Had he completed that sentence, he would have added, 'I can't... promise you that I will be able to go on living.' Sonya is quick to encourage him and herself even more so: *"Yes, yes, to work! As soon as we see our folks off, we'll sit down to work"* (p. 155). They are both trying to gain control over their inner chaos through their familiar routine of work. Sonya turns to the desk, *"nervously straightening the papers"* (p. 155), exposing her difficulty in controlling herself. She doesn't read what is written on the papers as she shuffles through them; there is no need. She has known for a while that they have *"neglected everything"* (p. 155).

Sonya says nothing to Astrov, but all of her actions are directed toward him. He picks up on this fact and says, *"Now I can go"* (p. 155). We will soon discover how precise his choice of words is: he can go now, but once again he wishes to stay. Leaving now means final and complete surrender of his last chance for happiness. As we observed at the beginning of this chapter, despite what he says to Vanya, Astrov still sees happiness as a real possibility. Fortunately for him, Yelena enters.

Yelena's Entrance
Following the events of Act 3, Yelena has easily convinced Serebryakov that they should leave the estate for good. As previously mentioned, her reason for insisting on their departure is in part due to the attempted murder of Serebryakov, but it is primarily a desperate response to the panic she felt when she realized her love for Astrov. She is probably aware of Vanya's suicide attempt and cannot avoid acknowledging her part in his anguish. Yet, why does she make no effort to save him, like the others? Various reasons can be provided for this: her selfishness, her guilt, and the fact that Astrov and Sonya are already tending to him. Another reason might be that she continues to see herself as a minor character, as she mentioned to Sonya (p.137), and thus is unable to play a significant role in the unfolding drama. However, the main reason seems to be that were she to join in

the attempt to save Vanya, she and Astrov might come into close contact and thus jeopardize her decision to leave. Her external actions at the end of Act 3 were focused on deciding where to go and on preparing for the journey. But her internal action is far more complex. As mentioned earlier, Chekhov's strategy in planning Act 4 was based on the assumption that the events initiated in Act 3 had not yet come to fruition, particularly the development of the relationship between Astrov and Yelena. This means that the two characters have not yet completely given up on their love. In the hours following Act 3, while packing her things, Yelena did not stop thinking about her relationship with Astrov and even the possibility of running away with him. Similarly, Astrov was thinking about her during his pursuit of Vanya, waiting for an opportunity to ask her once again to live with him on his estate. And now, the desired opportunity has arisen. The packed suitcases and the waiting carriage prove to the suspicious household that Yelena does indeed plan to leave with her husband, thus dispelling any ideas about her hidden intentions concerning Astrov. She herself will soon tell him, "...*I can look at you bravely now because we're leaving...*" (p. 155). But in truth, her goodbye is nothing but an excuse to meet him again, and her entrance into Vanya's room is one last attempt to realize the possibility of spreading her wings and *"flying as a free bird"* (p. 141), as she described at the beginning of Act 3. Her internal action is still the desire to escape the emotional trap

that she is in. The power of her final meeting with
Astrov lies in the possibility of realizing this action.

Thus, Yelena enters Vanya's room determined to be
alone with Astrov. She knows that Vanya is in the
room and has therefore convinced Serebryakov
ahead of time to make peace with him. She
completely ignores Vanya's crisis and asks him to
go and speak to her husband. Vanya does not take
her cue. He knows that Yelena wishes to stay with
Astrov and can probably guess her reasons.
Sonya's intervention is surprising. She is no longer
naïve; she knows that Astrov is in love with Yelena
and intuits immediately that Yelena wishes to be
alone with him. Why is she so generous with
Yelena and Astrov? Why does she convince Vanya
to leave the room, and then follow after him? As
we have already established, Sonya's internal
action is to rehabilitate her dignity and regain her
self-control following Astrov's rejection. Indeed,
her external action – leaving Yelena and Astrov
alone in the room – proves both to her and to the
others that she is no longer hurt, nor is she
threatened by their meeting. It is useful to note that
her actions are gradual. At first, she says, *"go, Uncle
Vanya"* (p. 155). She probably did not intend to join
his meeting with Serebryakov, but rather to busy
herself with goal-oriented work that would allow
her some control over her emotions. However,
when Vanya refuses, she takes him by the arm and
says: *"Let's go. You and papa have to make peace. It's
important"* (p. 155). It is impossible to remain
untouched by her maturity. She takes responsibility

for the actions of her uncle, who is more than twice her age. We will later see that she must bear the responsibility for his life, as well. When Vanya and Sonya exit, Yelena and Astrov are alone in the room.

Yelena and Astrov's Scene

Despite Yelena's powerful internal action and her knowledge that this is her last chance to realize it, she continues to act cautiously and to conceal her true intentions. She is desperate to escape the trap in which she lives, but she is also terrified of spreading her wings. And so instead of falling into Astrov's arms and saying, "I want to escape with you to your house", she says, *"I'm leaving"* (p. 155). She hopes that he will hold onto her, take her to his carriage and drive his horses home. Astrov is shocked. When she entered the room, he was sure that she had come to tell him that she loves him. Otherwise why would she have chased Vanya from the room. He looks at her hesitantly, wondering what she is feeling. She notices this and interprets his hesitation as reservation and her concern grows. She gives him her hand and says, *"Good-bye"* (p. 155).

Astrov answers carefully: *"Already?"* (p. 155), hinting that she should not be so quick to leave or they will miss their last chance. She again answers cautiously, *"The horses are here"* (p. 155). For a moment, Astrov thinks that he may have misunderstood her intentions and that she really wants to leave, so he says, *"Good-bye"* (p. 155).

Yelena then finds a way to continue the conversation, which, at face value, has ended. She gives him the following reminder: *"You promised me today that you would leave"* (p. 155). She does not add, 'Take me with you'. Astrov interprets her words simply and he answers, *"I remember. I'm leaving"* (p. 155). At this point, Chekhov characteristically calls for a pause, without stating what occurs in the silence. Astrov clearly does not want or intend to leave. During the pause, he realizes that he must be more daring, so he finally addresses Yelena more personally: *"Did I frighten you?"* (p. 155). He is probably referring to the moment when he declared his love and she was perhaps frightened by her acquiescence. She does not seem quick to answer. He takes her hand and asks, *"Is it so scary?"* (p. 155). Now, it is clear that he is asking her whether her desire for him is really so terrifying in her eyes. She understands his meaning perfectly and answers 'yes'. Now with his hands grasping hers in a moment of intimacy, he asks openly: *"Stay, why don't you! Well? In the forest preserve"* (p. 155). On hearing this, Yelena pales with disappointment, thinking, "Is that all? Just a meeting in the forest? I want much more than that. I will not be satisfied with a fleeting flirtation. I do not want to steal a crumb of enjoyment; I want to be happy forever!" Suddenly she is shocked: "What am I to him? Maybe he thinks that I am a woman of questionable moral character, easily seduced by him!" She controls herself and responds:

273

"No... It's done... And why I can look at you bravely now is because we're leaving... I ask you one thing: think better of me. I'd like you to respect me." (p. 155)

Despite Yelena's self-control, her anxiety does not allow her to reveal her true desire. She says that she wants him to respect her, but she does not elaborate. Does she expect him to respect her despite the fact that she is running away from him and from herself? It seems she does. However, she may also be hinting that the respect she desires would be for him to save her from the trap that she is in, rather than an offer of a brief flirtation in the woods. Astrov, who would like very much to save her from her husband, fails to receive her message. He thinks that she is using the commonplace term 'respect' to keep herself from surrendering to him. He responds impatiently: *"Ah!"* (p. 155) It is as though he is saying, "You are not listening to me. I am not talking about your petit bourgeois pride, but about your real life." At this point, he removes his mask and speaks frankly:

"Please stay! Admit it, there's nothing for you to do in this world; no goal in life, nothing to occupy your mind, and sooner or later you'll give in to feelings – it's inevitable. Then isn't it better if it doesn't happen somewhere in Kharkov or Kursk, but here, out in the country... At least it's poetic, even the autumn is beautiful... Here you have a forest preserve and rundown estates in the style of Turgenev..." (pp. 155-156)

Astrov begs her to stay. He is no longer talking about a brief encounter in the woods. In fact, he upgrades his offer and presents her with the opportunity that she truly, adamantly wishes for – to surrender to her passion and find purpose in her life. He adds ironically that the natural country scenery is much better suited to such pursuits than the streets of Kharkov or Kursk, mocking her intention to live in these cities with her husband. He seems to have said almost everything that Yelena has wanted to hear. He stands and looks at her, expecting her to fall into his arms and say, "take me with you". However, to his surprise, she responds with utter resistance:

> "How funny you are... I'm a little upset at you and yet... I'll always remember you with fondness. You're interesting and unique. We'll never meet again, and so – why hide it? I was taken with you a little. Well, let's shake hands and part as friends. Don't think badly of me."
> (P. 156)

Why doesn't she finally give in? He has been completely truthful with her. His observations are sharp and accurate. Why doesn't she take the hand he is offering to help her out of her trap? This is one of the most fascinating questions in the play. In order to answer it, we must begin by returning to Yelena's description of herself in Act 2: *"I'm a tedious, minor character... In music, in my husband's house, in love – everywhere, I was always only a minor character"* (p. 137).

A minor character does not determine the progress of the play but leaves it to the main characters. Yelena desperately wants to determine the course of her life. She entered Vanya's room in order to make the fateful move that would allow her a new life; she was even prepared to leave behind her entire past. Her weakness in seeing herself as a minor character is, no doubt, the reason for her paralysis here, too. However, as we have seen throughout the play, Chekhov never justifies the actions of his characters by their habitual, familiar characteristics. Here too, he is not content with Yelena's weakness as the entire justification for her rejection of Astrov. As a supremely methodical playwright, he always offers a specific action *in the present,* to justify an action. Thus, Yelena's weakness serves only as a background for her refusal. What, then, is the specific action in that moment that causes Yelena to reject what she has wanted so badly? It is found in Astrov's speech: *"Admit it, there's nothing for you to do in this world; no goal in life, nothing to occupy your mind…"* (p. 155).

Astrov's external action with these words is to reflect Yelena's real situation back at her, so that she may see it. Looking at this reflection of herself, Yelena sees the boring, weak, helpless character that she despises. She is frightened by this reflection. Her weakness takes over and she is certain that she will never be able to carry out her

276

desires. She will never be able to decide her own fate.

At this point, she quickly averts her gaze from the mirror and, with a joke avoids dealing with his painful honesty. She laughs and says, *"How funny you are"* (p. 156), adding, *"I'm a little upset at you"* (p. 156). She is probably referring to the fact that his cruel observations have angered her. However, she is still hesitant: *"...and yet..."* (p. 156). She might have continued, "...and yet, I am still willing to come with you", but a great weakness overcomes her again and she clings to the lie she told when she entered the room: *"I have come to say goodbye"*. And the lie continues: *"I'll always remember you with fondness"* (p. 156). More likely she will remember him with a sense of panic and fear. Then she defends herself once more: *"We'll never meet again"* (p. 156). This thought strengthens her resolve and allows her to admit the following: *"...and so – why hide it? I was taken with you a little"* (p. 156). In this moment of strength, she hopes, again, to hear him say, "I love you too. Come with me," but he does not, and she gives up: *"Well, let's shake hands and part as friends. Don't think badly of me"* (p. 156).

Why does Astrov hear her words as a final, absolute rejection? Why doesn't he take encouragement from her confession of love and continue his fight for her? Here, too, the answer should not relate to Astrov's habitual character traits, but in Yelena's present action. Let us recall that Astrov's primary internal action throughout

277

the play is to achieve a long-desired salvation. Therefore, he desperately clings to Yelena, whose love could bestow upon him the salvation he yearns for. Now, however, he perceives things differently. Yelena has revealed a deep-seated weakness; she is unsure, hesitant, unable to come to the decision to save herself. If she is unable to save herself, how could she possibly save him? He finds it difficult to ignore what he has just said to her: *"...there's nothing for you to do in this world; no goal in life, nothing to occupy your mind..."* (p. 155). He suddenly realizes that he has misled himself and mistakenly put his hopes in her. He now understands that not only have his chances run out, but that he has never really stood a chance. He, too, confronts the fact that he is just as weak as Yelena and that, like her, he will never achieve salvation.

Astrov gives up. This renunciation must entail enormous pain and despair. Despite the fact that he does not break easily, he knows that he must relieve his pain before his heart cracks in two. And so he struggles to convince himself that he is fortunate that Yelena did not surrender to him, and that he has, happily, been saved from disaster. Right from his first words, he accuses her of selfishness and of laziness:

> *"You came here with your husband, and everyone who was working and pottering around here, who was creating something, suddenly had to drop whatever they were doing*

and spend the entire summer attending to your husband's gout and you" (p. 156).

He has also been damaged:

> *"I was taken with you, I didn't do anything the whole month; and during this time people were ill, and the peasants were bringing their cattle to graze on the seedlings that I am planting" (p. 156).*

Ironically, he accuses her of the very things that she has accused all men of in Act 1: *"...no matter where you and your husband set foot, you bring destruction everywhere"* (p. 156). Despite claiming to jest, he certainly means every word that he says, and adds, *"...I'm convinced that if you stayed, the devastation would be enormous. I would perish, and you... wouldn't come out unscathed"* (p. 156). Thus, Astrov now attempts to convince himself that he will only be saved by her departure and that the enormous pain he is experiencing right now not will, in fact, redeem him from total ruin in the future. *"So leave! Finita la commedia"* (p. 156). Why does he speak in Italian? He does this in order to create a distance between his words and his true feelings. And why does he call the events of the past month "a show"[57]? He does this in order to convince himself that they were not "real"; that they occurred only in the minds of the participants, and now that the

---

[57] In this Italian term, the word "commedia" means "a show"; not necessarily "a comedy".

curtain is coming down, they may return to their normal lives as though nothing had happened. Astrov refuses to admit the painful truth of his life's failure, which was revealed during this little "*commedia*".

Does Yelena hear his words? Does she register them? She seems to register them and feel their sting. She knows that he is right. She cannot deal with his accusations. Thus far, she has not even begun to imagine how much unintentional damage she has caused to those around her. Is she really to blame to the degree that Astrov expresses? Are there no other guilty parties? Should she apologize? Would an apology do any good? Is there a way of repairing the damage she has done to her husband, to Vanya, to Sonya and to Astrov? Once again Yelena feels completely helpless in the face of these difficult questions. She can do nothing but take a pencil from the desk and say, "*I'm taking this pencil as a keepsake*" (p. 156). It is as though she has said, "I have heard and understood you. I do not know how to respond right now, but I will remember these questions and ponder them for the rest of my life".

Astrov, still trying to ease the pain of Yelena's rejection, attempts to build a philosophical claim that their frustrating relationship is just one of many random events in the world, events that cannot be explained and which occur through no fault of either of them. This philosophical claim, however, masks his enormous desire to hold her, kiss her and know that, despite everything that has been said and done, she loves him after all. Like a child, he believes that his illusion will ease his pain. And so, he requests a goodbye kiss, a kiss that he hopes will turn back time and bring them both salvation after all.

He kisses her cheek cautiously, anxiously. She is disappointed. She, too, was expecting a completely different kind of kiss, and she responds, *"I wish you all the best"* (p. 156). Then she momentarily and unexpectedly decides to take the initiative, perhaps for the first time in her life, and she embraces and kisses him passionately. Will they now finally be able to admit their love and be saved? No, says Chekhov: *"…the two quickly move away from each other"* (p. 156). Yelena is the first to admit that their attempt has failed. *"I must go,"* she says. He gives in as well: *"Go, go quickly. If the horses are ready…"* (p. 156). She lingers. He urges her, *"…just go"* (p. 156). At this point, voices are heard outside the room. Now Astrov knows for certain that the end has come. He says, *"Finita"* (p. 156).

In light of this discussion, it is interesting to follow the written correspondence of Chekhov himself with his wife, actress Olga Knipper, who portrayed Yelena in the first production. Staged at the Moscow Art Theatre in 1899, the play was directed by Stanislavski, who also played Astrov. Knipper wrote to Chekhov, who was at Yalta, Crimea:

*"Alexeiev (Stanislavski)'s comment regarding
Astrov's last scene with Yelena embarrasses me:
In his interpretation, Astrov addresses Yelena as
an enthusiastic man in love, clinging to his
emotion for dear life. In my opinion, if this were
the case, Yelena would follow him. She wouldn't
reply: 'how funny you are...'. Moreover, he is
very cynical with her, and even makes fun of his
own cynicism. Isn't that so?"*

Chekhov responded:

*"This is not right. Absolutely not right! Astrov
is taken with Yelena. Her beauty attracts his
heart. However, in the last act, he is already
aware of the fact that nothing will come of it and
that Yelena will disappear from his life forever.
At this point, he talks to her in the same way
that he discusses the African heat, and kisses her
meaninglessly, out of boredom. Should Astrov
carry this scene out tumultuously, Act 4's quiet,
limp atmosphere would be lost.*

Chekhov's stresses that Astrov is not at all cynical.
He is still taken with Yelena's beauty, but in the
final act, he is aware that nothing will come of it
and that Yelena will be gone forever. However,
why does Chekhov emphasize that Astrov speaks
to her in the same way that he speaks of an African
heat wave? Had Astrov relinquished all hope, he
would not have suggested that they meet in the
woods on the following day. Dismissing Astrov's
cynicism and knowing that he is still greatly

interested in Yelena, Chekhov is concerned that Stanislavski will express this hope too enthusiastically. Chekhov sees Stanislavski's enthusiasm as unnecessary sentimentality[58] and makes clear that the acting should be restrained and that Astrov should kiss Yelena seemingly out of idleness, rather than passion.

The Entrance of Serebryakov, Vanya, Marya Vasilyevna, Telegin and Sonya

Where have all these characters come from and why do they all gather in Vanya's room? Prior to this they were in the living room or the dining room, where Sonya led Vanya in order to make peace with Serebryakov. The peace-making process appears to have gone well. Vanya apologized and Serebryakov forgave him, and even asked for Vanya's forgiveness. Vanya states that he will continue to pay him the same amount that he has always received. Everything has returned to normal between them.

Serebryakov has led the group into Vanya's room, claiming that he must say a festive goodbye to Astrov. However, the real reason for his entrance is his fear of what might be going between Astrov and Yelena. They have been together in the room

---

[58] Chekhov was sometimes critical of Stanislavski's interpretations of his plays. In her essay, "Chekhov's Comedy", Leah Goldberg even raises the assumption that Chekhov subtitled *The Cherry Orchard* as a comedy in order to prevent Stanislavski from employing unnecessary pathos.

for a long time and as their conversation grows, so does his fear. Vanya and Sonya, also concerned about the length of the conversation, join him. Telegin and Marya Vasilyevna are there to take part in the festive parting celebration that Serebryakov has promised, and, more to the point, to ensure that the departure takes place and that Serebryakov and Yelena leave as soon as possible.

Serebryakov is the active character in this brief parting scene. As noted, his external action is to put an end to the conversation. He does this by affecting an obsessive and haughty demeanor:

> "Let bygones be bygones. After what happened, in the last few hours I've thought so much about it that I could probably write a whole treatise for the edification of future generations on how to live one's life." (p. 157)

His strong desire to talk attests to the depth of his worries. Will Yelena really join him? Will they arrive safely at Kharkov? Will she continue to live with him there? By his chattering, he wishes to prove to himself and the others that his authority has not been undermined. He has much to say and they would do well to listen to him. He is attempting to clarify to them and to himself that, despite their panic-stricken departure, he has not broken down. On the contrary, everything is back to normal. What happened is in the past and Yelena will be his forever. To emphasize that all of the disagreements, claims, grievances, anger and

284

hatred have ended, he turns to Marya Vasilyevna, whom he once called *"that old idiot"* (p. 127), kisses her hand and affectionately calls her *maman*. Marya Vasilyevna kisses his hand in return and requests him to send her a photograph so he would know that her admiration for him has not waned. Telegin too, relieved that the threat that has plagued him is now gone, wishes Serebryakov a safe journey. Serebryakov kisses Sonya and wishes her well, and then makes a parting speech to Astrov. His words seem to express warmth and friendship, appreciation and respect, but, in truth, they are mocking and hurtful. They emphasize that despite his old age, he has succeeded in keeping Yelena for himself, unlike the younger men who did nothing but talk.

We must exercise care in interpreting Serebryakov's actions and not judge him too harshly. He knows better than anyone that his insistence on seeing himself as victorious barely covers a gnawing fear that his defeat will soon draw near, either because of his age or worse, Yelena's escape while he is still living. He bows to everybody and exits, well aware of the uncertainties ahead. Marya Vasilyevna and Sonya escort him to the carriage.

Astrov, Vanya, Yelena and Telegin remain. Vanya must now part from Yelena. Chekhov does not grant Vanya a private farewell meeting with Yelena, as he did for Astrov. The reason for this is clear. Their parting actually took place during Act

3. They both know that there will be no rekindling of their relationship. He simply kisses her hand affectionately. Chekhov stresses this because the kiss is not a gesture of polite goodbye, but rather an act of pain, sadness, regret and despair. Yelena senses this and Chekhov tells us that she is moved. She knows that she will miss his friendship. Overwhelmed with emotion, she kisses Vanya's head and hurries out, without a last goodbye to Astrov.

Astrov does not follow after her. He knows that she is lost and that any words would be superfluous. He looks at Vanya and sees all too clearly that their friendship has died. Indeed, from this moment he will only receive short, cold responses from his one-time friend. Vanya will turn away from him and busy himself with the papers on his desk. Astrov is keenly aware of the deep pain he has caused him. And though he does not want to leave, he asks Telegin to prepare his carriage.

What caused this deep change in Vanya's attitude toward Astrov? When Vanya returned to his room at the beginning of the act (p. 152) with Astrov following, they engaged in a very meaningful conversation, a dialogue between close friends. What has happened since? Astrov's most recent callousness hurt Vanya gravely and dampened any interest in further conversation. Moreover, Vanya does not know what Astrov and Yelena spoke about after he left his room, but that very fact indicates Astrov's insensitivity to his misery. But perhaps the most important reason for this is that Vanya has become increasingly self-absorbed in his thoughts that the life he had hoped for has ended.

Telegin exits. Astrov collects his paints from the desk and packs them away. These are the paints that he used to create his maps during the many hours that he spent in Vanya's room. Will he continue this work back home? The thought of his future loneliness is beginning to weigh on him. He tries to engage Vanya: *"Why aren't you going to see them off?"* (p. 157). He knows the answer to this question all too well, but hopes that Vanya will in some way rekindle their friendship. Vanya offers a banal response: *"Let them leave, but I... I can't. It's hard for me. I need to occupy myself with something quick... Work, work!"* (p. 157). Astrov can fill in the missing words in Vanya's speech: "Let them leave, but I [will stay here and rot]... I can't [talk to you]. It's hard for me. I need to occupy myself with something quick... [Don't bother me. Let me] work, work!"

They fall silent. The harness bells jangle harshly as the carriage sets on its way. Astrov addresses Vanya again: *"They're gone. The professor is glad, I bet! Wild horses won't drag him here again"* (p. 158). He may be talking about Serebryakov, but his external action belies a deeper need: "Now, only you and I are left, and we must rebuild our friendship." Vanya does not respond.

Marina enters and says, *"they're gone"* (p. 158). She sits and takes up her knitting. She returns to her previous life, her work - to knit, to offer tea and vodka, to remind everybody when it is time for bed. However, we will soon see that she has returned to fulfill another equally important purpose.

Sonya enters wiping tears from her eyes, saying, *"They're gone"* (p. 158). She may be crying because her father, who has never truly been a father to her, is gone, never to return. She is also crying because of her situation. When she says, *"hope to God they get there safely"* (p. 158), she is really praying for herself. But Astrov's presence does not allow her to sink into self-pity. She gathers her strength and addresses Vanya: *"Well, Uncle Vanya, let's do something"* (p. 158). He immediately agrees: *"Work, work"* (p. 158). In his heart, he is saying, "anything to avoid thinking about myself and my despair." Surprisingly, Sonya does not speak to Astrov, who is nearly packed. Not even polite small talk. However, what she says to Vanya is also directed at Astrov. Her insistence on getting back to work - turning on the desk lamp, filling the inkwell, attending to the accounts of the estate that have been neglected – all this is a clear statement pointed at Astrov: "I am returning to my normal life. I will do anything in order to ease the pain you have caused me. If you do not plan on marrying me, you are no longer welcome here". Then she adds surprisingly, *"I'm sad that they're gone"* (p. 158), making it clear to him that her sadness is not due to his departure. But we know that she is also mourning the end of their relationship.

Marya Vasilyevna enters, and even she says, *"they're gone"* (p. 158). She sits down and picks up a book. Is she really reading? We have already surmised that she is probably unable to read. Why has she entered? She cannot return to her room. The sense of mourning enveloping the estate weighs upon her, as well. Like all of the inhabitants of the estate, including Telegin, who will soon arrive, she must participate in the ceremony of mourning in Vanya's room. Chekhov makes each character enter with the ritual repetition, "they're gone". Each in his own way joins the other mourners, and together they pretend to return to life as it was. Vanya and Sonya lead the sad ceremony, discussing banal concerns about bills that have not been paid. They are not mourning the departure of Serebryakov and Yelena; they all are grieving the death of hope – hope for some semblance of happiness that would grant meaning to their lives.

Though he, too, grieves, Astrov feels disconnected from the ceremony. The depth of the rift between him and Sonya and between him and Vanya is now painfully clear. He knows he must leave, but longs to be part of the warm atmosphere created by the family gathering. He says: *"I don't want to leave"* (p. 158). His horses can be heard outside and he knows that his carriage is ready. He secretly wishes that Vanya would ask him to stay. Vanya is silent.

Astrov repeats that he must leave, hoping that Sonya will stop him. She too is silent, so he packs his maps away.

Now Marina intervenes: *"What's all the fuss? Stay awhile"* (p. 158). She, of course, is still trying to heal the rift between Astrov and Sonya. However, Astrov would prefer that Vanya or Sonya ask him to stay. But Vanya continues to ignore him and reads aloud from a bill that he is examining: *"'From the old debt, two seventy-five remaining...'"* (p. 158).

A workman enters and informs Astrov that the carriage is ready. Astrov realizes that there is no other choice. He hands his medicine case, suitcase and folder to the workman, who then exits. Astrov lingers a moment longer. Nobody says goodbye. He turns to Sonya: *"Well, then..."* (p. 158), as though he were asking, "do you really want me to go?" Sonya replies: *"When will we see each other?"* (p. 158). Her subtext is: "Yes. If you do not propose marriage this very second, I want you to go." Astrov understands and answers, *"Probably not before summer"* (p. 159). Then he adds with a glimmer of hope that their relationship could be resumed: *"Needless to say, should anything happen, just let me know – and I'll come"* (p. 159). His meaning is clear: "If you should want me, let me know and I will come immediately." Sonya appears to grasp the hint, but ignores it. At this point, she wants him to declare his desire for her first. Astrov shakes hands with the others and thanks them for their hospitality. When he kisses old Marina on her head, she makes another attempt at reconciliation: *"Leaving before tea?"* (p. 159). He does not want any tea. Then, as in the beginning, she offers him vodka, which he cannot refuse. Marina leaves to fetch the vodka. Astrov quickly seizes the opportunity to engage Vanya in conversation. He suddenly remembers that one of his horses is limping, which he noticed earlier when the horse was led to drink. Vanya replies bluntly: *"You have to reshoe"* (p. 159). Astrov clutches at the loose horseshoe as an excuse to carry on the conversation: *"I'll have to stop by at the blacksmith's in Rozhdestveny. No getting around it"* (p. 159). Vanya does not respond and Astrov realizes that for Vanya, the friendship is over. He is overcome with sorrow. He thinks with dread about the long, lonely winter ahead of him. He notices the map of Africa on the wall and says, *"It must be baking hot in this Africa now – something terrible"* (p. 159). He longs to be in warm exotic Africa, where, as Sonya said, *"the people are beautiful, adaptable, passionate, their speech is elegant and their gestures are graceful"* (p. 123). This fantasy warms his heart, but Vanya answers coldly, *"It probably is"* (p. 159). Astrov feels the indifference of the reply and is filled with sorrow, yet again.

Marina enters with a tray of vodka and bread. Astrov drinks. Marina, still hoping to delay his departure, says, *"You should have some bread with it"* (p. 159), but Astrov knows the time has come. He wishes the others well, asks Marina not to escort him out, and leaves.

Sonya picks up a candle and follows him. Chekhov indicates that she escorts him, but we the spectators do not know this. We are still expecting something to happen between them - for Astrov to come to his senses, fall to his knees, beg Sonya's forgiveness and propose to her; or for Sonya to cling to his coat and ask him to reconsider. But to our dismay, the sound of the horses echoes through the estate. Marina says, *"he's gone"* (p. 159). A moment later, Sonya returns, sets the candle down on the table and also says, *"he's gone"* (p. 159). The miracle has not happened and the mourning ritual continues. Vanya continues to mourn his life while tending to the accounts. Telegin enters, tunes his guitar and accompanies the grim ceremony.

Vanya can no longer keep up the pretense. The mourning ceremony, which was intended in some way to strengthen the living, cannot keep his death wish at bay. However, his determination to commit suicide has dwindled. His courage has gone. He thus strokes Sonya's hair, begging for guidance, *"I'm so miserable! If you only knew how miserable I am"* (p. 160). No details are needed. She knows exactly how difficult it is to pretend that life has returned to normal, that they can go on living as before. She looks at him and knows that he is begging her to encourage him to end his life. Twenty-year-old Sonya, whose strong religious convictions we have seen, recoils at the very thought. She gathers all her strength and responds with a long monologue, much like a sermon she might have heard in church, in which she tries to convince him, and probably herself too, to choose life.

She repeats the word "life" in its various forms six times in order to convince herself that life is, indeed, worthwhile, and that when their time comes, God will repay them for their continual suffering with *"a bright, beautiful and fine life"* (p. 160). Then, they will be able to look back and laugh and finally be at peace. She emphasizes, *"Uncle, I believe, believe passionately, fervently"* (p. 160). Does Sonya really believe her own words? It does not seem so. Rather it seems that she desperately longs to believe. She looks at Vanya and sees that her words have only increased his despair. She feels that her sermon sounds empty and meaningless and she becomes frightened. However, she refuses to accept the logical conclusion that there is no use in continuing with the life of misery that they have been destined for. She gathers her energy again, and clings to her Sunday sermon: *"We will rest! We'll hear angels, we'll see the sky studded with diamonds, we'll see all earthly evil and all our suffering drown in mercy that will fill the world"* (p. 160). She remains unconvinced, however, by these grandiose promises of "angels" and "diamonds" and replaces them with more modest, earthly expressions: *"...our life will become quiet, tender, and sweet as a caress"* (p. 160). Another moment goes by and her faith falters further. She says that she just believes, or hopes that this will be the case, but when she wipes the tears from Vanya's eyes and sees his suffering at such close proximity, she knows that even her hope is probably an illusion. Finally, she cannot go on with nothing, so she promises him just the simple feeling of relief, like that at the end of a long day in the field: *"We will rest… (Embraces him) We will"* (p. 160). Just this and nothing more.

The watchman taps somewhere outside. Telegin strums softly. Marya Vasilyevna writes something in the margin of one of her journals. Marina knits. Vanya is silent. Has his death wish overcome him? Has he decided to end his life? Perhaps Sonya senses this and her heart is filled with fear. She realizes that from now on, she will be responsible for his life. She repeats her promise: *"We will rest"* (p. 160). Yet, she seems somehow to know that this promise will probably not be kept either. The curtain falls slowly.

Chapter 5 - An Analysis of the Play's Structure

Uncle Vanya. Habimah Theatre, Tel Aviv, 1986. The stage lights have faded, the applause has subsided, and house lights illumine the crowd once more. They make their way to the exits of the theatre with the voice of the actress playing Sonya still reverberating in their minds: *"...just wait, Uncle Vanya, wait... We will rest... We will"* (p. 160). They can still see the pain on the face of the actor portraying Vanya. One spectator remains seated in the back row, attempting to assimilate his impressions of this unforgettable production. That spectator is me! In that liminal moment, caught between dark and light, I linger in my seat, surprised by the realization that despite the sorrow and pain at Vanya's defeat, I feel no despair or disappointment at all. On the contrary, Vanya's painful fall inspires in me feelings of clarity, determination and hope. I did not know at the time how to define that hope or what precisely had become clear to me, or what I was determined to do as I headed out into the street. But the feeling was so real that I could not help but wonder about this powerful paradox. In the face of Vanya's catastrophic failure, I was inspired and empowered by his struggle to correct the mistakes of the past and to live an emotional life filled with the yearning *"to wake up on a clear, quiet morning, feeling that you have begun a new life, and that the past is all forgotten, diffused like smoke"* (p. 153).

The Dramatic Paradox

An examination of the viewing experience of other plays yields similar results. In Shakespeare's *Romeo and Juliet*, the young lovers fight for the right to realize their love, which was forbidden by their families. A catastrophe occurs at the end of the play as the two characters kill themselves. Yet, the audience, young and old, do not leave the theater thinking, "forbidden love is a dangerous adventure. We must avoid it at any cost." Most people feel the opposite: forbidden love is a profound experience that expresses our right to follow our hearts. We would never give up a love like this, even if it were forbidden. Rather we would strive to realize this love in every possible way. In other words we do not see the 'failure' of Romeo and Juliet as a danger signal to eschew the realization of forbidden love – which is the characters' primary internal action. On the contrary, their failure strengthens our desire to realize that very same internal action in our own lives.

An examination of Sophocles' *Oedipus the King* yields a similar conclusion. Oedipus' primary internal action is to gain sovereignty over his life despite the gods' decree. He struggles with this from the moment the Oracle proclaims that he will kill his father and marry his mother. Thinking that Polybus and Merope of Corinth are his parents, he flees and enters Thebes, unaware that his real parents are Laius and Jocasta, who rule the city. Oedipus kills Laius and marries Jocasta, just as the oracle prophesied. When he realizes his failure, he plucks out his eyes. After seeing this play do we say to ourselves, "to fight against the gods' decree is dangerous to mortals and therefore I must surrender and accept it"? Or do we think, *"The struggle for sovereignty over one's life and for freedom from the gods' decree is a heroic struggle that gives meaning to life"*? Most spectators would follow the second option. This is borne out by our great sense of compassion for the tortured Oedipus and a feeling that he does not deserve such harsh punishment. Thus we arrive at a surprising conclusion: if our yearning for sovereignty over our lives increases while watching the play, then the play undermines the gods' authority. In practice, then, *Oedipus the King*, which was staged in Athens to worship the gods, subverts their authority and that of the existing social order.

Scholars have noted this phenomenon in which the tragic play offers the spectator an empowering, corrective experience. Lascelles Abercrombie, for example, writes the following in his book *Principles of Literary Criticism* (1960):

> *"Tragedy shows the divine punishment in life. However, due to the unity inherent in the tragic drama, even the divine punishment in life becomes an example of the world that we long for so deeply (…) Things that would only sadden us in real life become those things that, in the tragic work, so lift our spirits."*

In her outstanding book *Elements of Tragedy*,
Dorothea Krook writes:

> *"Having been exposed to a spectacle of suffering*
> *as terrible as any we have ever witnessed, we*
> *would expect to feel – as in such a situation we*
> *would feel in life – intolerably depressed and*
> *oppressed; heavy with the sense of the*
> *helplessness of man and the hopelessness of the*
> *human condition; bitter, angry, and in despair*
> *about the seemingly wanton cruelty of it all. In*
> *fact, what we feel is something quite different.*
> *We feel, extraordinarily, liberated from pain and*
> *fear (Aristotle's "purgation" of the emotions of*
> *pity and terror); not depressed or oppressed, but*
> *in a curious way exhilarated; not angry and*
> *bitter but somehow reconciled; our faith in man*
> *and the human condition not destroyed or*
> *undermined but restored, fortified, reaffirmed."*
> *(p. 14)*

Krook calls this experience *"the affirmation or
reaffirmation"* (p. 14). Her conclusion is that tragedy
reaffirms "the dignity of man and the value of
human life" (p. 14). However, she emphasizes that:

> *"the final 'affirmation' of tragedy springs from*
> *our reconciliation to, or acceptance of, the*
> *necessity of the suffering rendered intelligible by*
> *the knowledge: by illuminating the necessity of*
> *the suffering, the knowledge reconciles us to it;*
> *by being reconciled to ('accepting') the suffering*

as necessary, we reaffirm the supremacy of the
universal moral order" (p. 17).

Krook does not define her "the universal moral order" (p. 17). If she means by this the traditional cosmic hierarchy with God and His messengers at the top, followed by kings and governments, and man, subject to the decrees of divine right, at the bottom, it is impossible to avoid disagreeing with her. Not only does tragedy refuse to affirm the supremacy of this 'universal moral order', it challenges and undermines it.

After seeing *Uncle Vanya*, the spectator leaves the theater with the feeling that his desire to turn over a new leaf in life, in contrast to the social order surrounding him, is legitimate. He leaves *Romeo and Juliet* empowered with the feeling that his heart's aspirations take precedence over those of his society. Oedipus, reaffirms that he, rather than the gods, determines his own fate, and Antigone strengthens his hope that the king is not an absolute ruler and that a citizen can struggle to follow her heart. [59]

---

[59] I assume that the educated reader could argue that in Sophocles' play, Antigone fights for the idea that God's authority is greater than that of the king, rather than fighting for the right of the citizen to disobey the king's orders when they are unacceptable to him. In my humble opinion, Sophocles, well aware of the censorship in Athens, could not stage a play that would clearly state this so boldly. Therefore, he replaced the heart's decree with that of God, in hopes that the spectators would understand his true intention. The words of the chorus leader at the end of the play, *"reverence towards the gods must be inviolate"* sound to me like lip service,

In light of this discussion, I prefer to replace Krooks' *'affirmation or reaffirmation'* (p. 14) with the term **dramatic paradox**.[60] Using the terms we have defined thus far, the dramatic paradox is the contrast between the protagonist's failure to realize his primary internal action and the empowerment of the spectator to realize the same internal action in his own life. Aristotle does not define this term in *Poetics*, but clearly indicates the tragic preference:

> *"A well-constructed plot should, therefore, be single in its issue. The change of fortune should be not from bad to good, but, reversely, from good to bad. It should come about as the result not of vice, but of some great error or frailty in a character..."* (Chapter 13).

Aristotle even argues that because of this reversal of fortune, the spectator is inspired to greater compassion for the protagonist.[61] He knew, of course, that compassion for the protagonist means empathy for his actions, despite or *because of* the fact that he challenges the social, religious and political order in which he lives. I tend to suspect

---

indicating that Sophocles had to mask his true intentions in order to allow the play to be staged.

[60]Alternatively, this term could have been called "the tragic paradox", but since it applies to any serious modern drama, even if it is not considered a tragedy, I prefer to use "the dramatic paradox".

[61] See the discussion at the beginning of Chapter 13 in *Poetics*.

that Aristotle clearly understood the subversive impact of the tragedy on the spectator, but chose not to describe it explicitly, fearing the same persecution his teacher, Socrates, met before him.

Though Chekhov did not use the term "dramatic paradox" in his writings, its presence suffuses his plays. In each of his three other great plays, he gives us a protagonist whose struggle and failure evokes the empathy of the spectator. In *The Seagull*, Konstantin Treplev fails to realize his love for Nina Zarechnaya and then commits suicide. In *Three Sisters*, Olga, Masha and Irina fail to rescue themselves from the country province and their dream of living in Moscow shatters. In *The Cherry Orchard*, Liubov Andreyevna returns from Paris to rebuild her life in her childhood home. After failing to do so, she returns to Paris as the axe falls on the trees of her beloved orchard.

How Does the Failure of the Protagonist Empower the Spectator?

It is important to remember that during the play, the spectator experiences a strong sense of empathy for the protagonist. The spectator resonates with the protagonist's primary internal action.[62] However, the resonance not only reflects the protagonist's action, but also an independent action in the spectator, himself. For example, a person watching *Uncle Vanya* feels Vanya's yearning to

---

[62] We will define empathy in more detail later.

redeem his past failures and to start a new,
meaningful life, which in turn inspires in the
spectator an autonomous desire to save himself
from his own failures and to embark upon a new
and meaningful life in the reality he inhabits.

Why does the protagonist's failure *empower* the
spectator rather than dishearten or frighten him? In
order to answer this question, let us examine a
mechanism familiar to most of us, the nightmare,
and see how it may be compared to the experience
of viewing a tragedy. A man may dream of getting
lost in a dense forest. He uses all his power to run
through the undergrowth and escape the many
threatening dangers on the way; but before
reaching a safe haven, he falls into a dark abyss. At
this point, the dreamer usually wakes and after a
while, manages to calm himself. It may well be that
the evolutionary process has created the nightmare
mechanism in us in order to strengthen our
determination to escape the dangers lurking in the
"jungles" of our lives. Despite the fact that at the
end of the nightmare we are plunged into a dark
abyss, upon awakening we find ourselves safe and
sound. We have passed through a threatening
experience, but have re-emerged alive, having
gained strength and wisdom. Thus, when we
encounter similar threats in reality, we are
equipped to deal with them with greater
determination and courage, as Freud (1988,
Hebrew edition) himself writes in *Beyond the
Pleasure Principl*e: *"These dreams, while developing
signs of anxiety... intend to fulfill what has been harmed*

by overcoming the stimulus."(p. 113) and as Rolnick (2004) explains in the preface to *The Interpretation of Dreams* by Sigmund Freud: *"The purpose of the nightmare is to expose and re-expose the dreamer to trauma, exercising the self-preservation urges of his self"* (p. 26).

The structural comparison between the nightmare and the process of viewing a tragedy is clear: seated in the theater, we join the protagonist on his journey fraught with lurking dangers, *en route* to his destruction, at the end of which he plunges into a dark abyss. However, when the curtain descends, we find ourselves safe and sound in our seats just as when we wake from a nightmare - safe in our beds. And just as the nightmare can prepare us to face the terrors of reality, so the tragedy can prepare us for the challenges that we will endure outside the theater as we struggle to realize our main desires. In *The Theatrical Experience*, Zmira Heisner and Karine Hizkiya describe this very clearly: *"Theater in general and the tragedy specifically, allow us to experience existential fear in a controlled fashion, without threatening our sense of self, but on the contrary: In a way that empowers and reaffirms the human self"* (p.121).

The Structural Elements that create the Dramatic Paradox

The presence of dramatic paradox in each of Chekhov's full-length plays indicates that the playwright intended his work to inspire and strengthen the spectator's struggle to realize in his own life the internal action that the protagonist wishes to realize on stage. This observation also attests to the fact that the reform of the world and of mankind by empowering sublime internal actions in the spectator ranked high among Chekhov's priorities.[63] Therefore, let us attempt to examine the dramatic structures by which the playwright ensured the efficacy of the dramatic paradox. In this discussion, we will attempt to identify and decode the primary structural elements he employed in *Uncle Vanya* - the exposition, the protagonist, the plot and the catharsis.

The Exposition

The exposition is the first part of the play where we learn about the setting, the characters, their pasts and the relationships between them. The exposition often reveals the primary external and internal actions of the lead characters. We will now examine the means Chekhov employs to create an effective exposition.

a) Strong Compression

As discussed in Chapter 1, each of the main characters begins the play with very powerful and compressed internal actions. Vanya enters with a strong desire to deliver himself from his past failures and start a new emotional life. Astrov yearns to be free of his failures as a doctor and

---

[63] We will discuss this in further detail later.

from the loneliness and emptiness he feels in his life. Serebryakov fights with all his might to remain a virile, productive and beloved person. Yelena yearns to escape the emotional trap that she has forced upon herself from the day she married Serebryakov. And Sonya longs to be a wife worthy of Astrov. Chekhov painstakingly creates strong compression in the exposition because only highly motivated characters can actively move the plot forward. Without this compression the characters would abandon their actions the moment they encountered an obstacle. To this end Chekhov meticulously constructs detailed dramatic biographies that clarify both the source of the compression and the phase of compression each character occupies at the opening of the play. The dramatic biographies of the characters in *Uncle Vanya* are detailed in Chapter 1.

b) An Effective Generating Event

In Chapter 3, we defined the term '**generating event of the act**'. We will now explore the '**generating event of the play**', i.e., an event that sets in motion the plot of the entire play. We have already seen that the characters contain a primary internal action that has been compressed within them long before the start of the play. This internal action sometimes forces them to act with little intensity before the beginning of the play, and, at other times, it does not force them to act at all. In spite of Vanya's conscious attraction for Yelena, we have no knowledge that he has pursued her or clashed with Serebryakov over her during their previous visits to the estate. However, Vanya's internal action has gradually ripened and now, with both of them having come to live on the estate shortly before the start of the play, he can no longer avoid active pursuit. His internal action has reached an advanced stage by this time and Yelena's presence affects him all the more. Thus, the arrival of Serebryakov and Yelena to live on the estate can be seen as the generating event of the play.[65] This event is so powerful that it not only drives Vanya and Astrov to desperate pursuit of Yelena, it also causes Yelena, for the first time in her marriage, to respond to the advances of a man other than her husband. Moreover, it motivates Sonya to demand that Astrov accept her love for him, and Serebryakov to fight back against Vanya and Astrov, as detailed in Act 3. According to Chekhov, the key to the construction of an effective exposition lies in the combination of an optimal state of compression in the characters and an effective generating event that forces them into action. In *Uncle Vanya*, the generating event occurs before the start of the play. This is also the case in *The Seagull*, where the generating event is the arrival of Arkadina and Trigorin to Sorin's estate; in *Three Sisters*, the generating event is Vershinin's assignment as commanding officer of the artillery

---

[65] The generating event of Act 1 is not necessarily that of the whole play. As previously mentioned in the discussion in Chapter 3, the generating event of Act 1 is the morning argument between Vanya and Serebriakov. On the other hand, Yelena and Serebriakov's settling down on the estate is the generating event of the whole play.

unit on the neighboring base; and in *The Cherry Orchard*, it is the return of Liubov Andreyevna and her entourage to her estate. The generating event is a prerequisite for an effective exposition. Without it, the characters would remain passive despite the ripening of their internal action and therefore the plot would not develop. Chekhov rejects the possibility that the characters would decide to take action only as a result of their compression, which is a given general factor that exists over time. Chekhov demands precise reasoning for their decision and its timing, which is, as previously explained, provided by the generating event.

c) The Outsider's Visit

In all four of his great plays, Chekhov initiates the exposition based on a dramatic principle used by many other playwrights - *the outsider's visit*. This principle enhances the playwright's ability to create an effective exposition because, as the outsider receives necessary information from the other characters about the goings on in his new location, so does the audience. Actually the outsider onstage represents the spectators in the audience because his level of knowledge is similar to theirs. However, the mere bridging of the information gaps is not an effective enough dramatic process in Chekhov's eyes, and so he meticulously bases this bridging on powerful external and internal actions. Let us look, for example, at the scene with Astrov (the outsider visitor) and Marina, at the beginning of Act 1:

307

"Well… In ten years I've become a different person. And why is that? I'm overworked, Nanny. On my feet from morning till night, never resting; at night, I lie in bed afraid that they might drag me out to see a patient. The entire time we've known each other, I haven't had a single day off. How could I not grow old? But then, life itself is boring, stupid, and filthy…" (p. 116)

Astrov's words reveal that he is a doctor who has been living in the county for about ten years, and that his life is so difficult that he calls it *"boring, stupid, filthy"* (p. 116). Astrov's description of his life is, of course, an external action. However, a more meaningful external action is his self-examination in the presence of Marina. In the same scene, Marina's words to Astrov and Vanya also teach us a great deal:

"Some customs! The professor gets up at noon, and the samovar's been boiling all morning, just waiting for him. Before they got here, we used to sit down to eat at noon, like everybody, but now it's after six. At night, the professor reads and writes, and then, around one in the morning, out of the blue, there goes the bell… Heavens, what is it? Tea! Wake everyone up for him, start the samovar… Some customs!" (P. 117)

Marina may be telling Astrov about the occurrences on the estate since the arrival of Serebryakov and Yelena, but her more pointed external action is to demand that Vanya, the estate manager, restore order on the estate.

Now let us examine Vanya's actions in this scene. After Serebryakov returns from his walk, he passes Vanya and Astrov by. Vanya, surprised, turns to Astrov, the outsider, and recites:

> *"The professor still sits in his study from*
> *morning till night writing.*
> *With straining brain and furrowed brow,*
> *We write heroic odes nights and days,*
> *But neither we nor they receive the praise."* [66](p. 119)

Later, Vanya details Serebryakov's life story from his birthday until the present moment. The bridging of information gaps is necessary since Astrov may not know the details of Serebryakov's biography. But while these biographical facts are important, Chekhov provides a stronger and much more meaningful external action for Vanya: his attempt to prove to himself that Serebryakov is not worthy of Yelena.

Moreover, these *external* actions are still not enough for Chekhov. As we saw in Chapter 1, he insistently assigns powerful internal actions for the two characters: Astrov yearns to alleviate his

---

[66] This is a quote from a well-known satiric poem by Ivan Dmitriev (1794) about a talentless poet and his fruitless attempt to write a lyrical poem.

disappointment in himself and in his life, and Vanya yearns to justify to himself his open pursuit of Yelena, the wife of his brother-in-law.

The outsider's visit is key to the exposition of Chekhov's other plays, as well. Arkadina and Trigorin arrive for a visit to Sorin's estate in *The Seagull*. In the exposition of *Three Sisters*, Lieutenant Colonel Vershinin attends Irina's birthday party at the Prozorovs' house, and in *The Cherry Orchard*, Liubov Andreyevna and her party return to the estate after many years' absence. A close examination of the exposition in each of these plays shows that, for Chekhov, the exchange of information between the outsider and the other characters serves primarily as a platform for the revelation of powerful external and internal actions.

d) The Apparent Status Quo

In addition to the clarification of the past, which creates the characters' dramatic actions, Chekhov's expositions provide a detailed description of the present moment in each of his plays. On the surface, we see a routine free of conflicts. However, upon closer observation, we see that this apparent status quo is but the tip of an iceberg protruding from the routine life and threatening to destroy it. Most of the characters are generally unaware of this threat and those who *are* aware of it, deny its existence.

In *Uncle Vanya*, the apparent status quo is as follows: Vanya, his mother and Sonya, his niece, are living in retired Professor Serebryakov's provincial estate. Astrov, a single doctor, who is also Vanya's friend, resides on a neighboring estate and struggles to decide whether he should marry Sonya. At the beginning of the summer, Serebryakov and his wife arrive to settle on the estate, and avoid the high cost of living in the big city. However, in Act 1, Chekhov provides an important clue as to how this status quo is going to shatter – Vanya openly pursues Serebryakov's young, beautiful wife. This duality creates, on one hand, the illusion of calm, country life, but on the other hand it contains the seed of destruction: the protagonist refuses to accept the apparent status quo and will fight to the end in order to change it.

In the first act of *The Seagull,* the apparent status quo is as follows: Treplev, who is in love with Nina, lives on his uncle Sorin's large estate. His mother, the famous actress, Arkadina, has arrived for one of her occasional visits to her brother's estate with her lover, the famous writer Trigorin. At the beginning of the act, we witness Treplev's tortured "rebellion" against his mother and at the end, Nina's attraction for Trigorin.

Three Sisters opens with Irina's birthday party. The whole family celebrates the occasion with officers invited from the neighboring artillery unit. Near the end of the act, several cracks can be seen in this calm setting: Irina is unable to acquiesce to

Tuzenbach's advances, Masha's relationship with Kulygin, her husband, is on the verge of a breakdown and Lieutenant Colonel Vershinin, whose wife is mentally ill, has shown an interest in Masha.

In *The Cherry Orchard*, the inhabitants of the estate await the return of owner, Liubov Andreyevna and her daughter Anya after a long absence. They are certain that Liubov Andreyevna will solve the estate's financial problems. However, it quickly becomes clear that Liubov Andreyevna, having endured the accidental drowning of her son and a suicide attempt in Paris after a failed relationship, is completely unable to cope with impending loss of the estate.

Most of Chekhov's characters cling to this fictitious status quo as though it were a lifebuoy. Only the protagonist, who is unable to accept it, initiates actions that expose the iceberg in all its depth, revealing the lies and denials that the characters hide behind, until, by the end of the play, they are left completely helpless even in their own eyes.[67] The apparent status quo often also contains a social-religious-moral order that is valid at the start of the play. As we have seen in the examples of classical tragedy above, *Romeo and Juliet*, *Oedipus the King* and *Antigone*, this order is always

---

[67] This statement is true, of course, only in reference to plays that contain a clear protagonist, such as *Uncle Vanya* and *The Seagull*.

undermined by the protagonist. In modern drama, as well, the protagonist adopts an oppositional stance against the status quo, fighting to change the social-religious-moral order in which he lives. Nora in *A Doll's House*, Hedda *in Hedda Gabler*, Miss Julie in *Miss Julie*, and Chris in *All My Sons*, are but a few of many examples. [68]

The Protagonist

The protagonist is the main character in both classical tragedy and modern drama. His primary internal action is very powerful and thus, he is most responsible for the creation of the plot. The protagonist's failure at the end of the play is the most painful experience and creates the deepest empathy in the spectator's heart. He usually suffers a terrible catastrophe: he dies, by his own hand or another's, plucks out his own eyes, loses his mind, or, perhaps worst of all, suffers an internal or spiritual death. In many plays (*Hamlet, Macbeth, Othello, King Lear, A Doll's House, Hedda Gabler, A Streetcar Named Desire, Death of a Salesman, Mother Courage and her Children*, etc.) the protagonist can be easily identified. In Chekhov's plays, however, this is not always so.

In *The Seagull*, it is obvious that Treplev is the protagonist for two reasons: he drives the play forward with his revolt against his mother and

---

[68] After a brief overview of international drama, I have not found a single protagonist who defends the social-religious-moral order in which he lives.

Trigorin, and having lost the desperate struggle for Nina's heart, he commits suicide at the end of the play. In *Three Sisters*, however, it is difficult to decide. Is it one of the three sisters? Or could it be their sister-in-law, Natalia Ivanovna? In *The Cherry Orchard*, Liubov Andreyevna is certainly the defeated character at the end of the play, but Lopahin also creates important elements in the plot. In *Uncle Vanya*, it is quite clear that Vanya is the protagonist. Much can be learned from this play regarding Chekhov's treatment of the status and characteristics of the protagonist.

a) The Protagonist's Strong Compression
We have discussed the protagonist's compressed primary internal action and we have also seen how this compression developed over a long period before the start of the play. In Chapter 1 we detailed the genesis of Vanya's compression following the death of his sister, Vera Petrovna, as his feelings of loss revealed the emptiness of his life.

b) The Protagonist's Fatal Mistake
In *Poetics*, Aristotle emphasizes the following:

> *"It follows plainly, in the first place, that the change of fortune presented must not be the spectacle of a virtuous man brought from prosperity to adversity [...] Nor, again, that of a bad man passing from adversity to prosperity [...] but that of a man who is not eminently good and just, yet whose misfortune is brought*

about not by vice or depravity, but by some error or frailty." (Chapter 13)

Aristotle uses the term *"hamartia"*, which means "mistake, error, missing the goal" (Halperin, *On the Poetics,* p. 92). He later stresses that the mistake should be substantial, i.e. fatal and final, leading to the total failure of the protagonist at the end of the play. What is Vanya's fatal mistake? Could it be his years of self-sacrifice and the surrender of all of his personal aspirations, at first for the good of his sister and then for the benefit of Serebryakov? This is certainly a mistake and it began long before the beginning of the play. However, had Vanya continued to live a life of self-sacrifice and surrender, the play would not have occurred at all, and he would not have attempted to kill Serebryakov and then himself. The play happens because Vanya decides to put a stop to his self-sacrifice and *"wake up on a clear, quiet morning feeling that you have begun a new life, and that the past is all forgotten, diffused like smoke"* (p. 153). In other words, even before the play began, he had decided to realize the primary internal action that had been gestating in him since the death of his sister. His determination leads him to pursue Yelena. His pursuit of Yelena leads him to attempt to kill Serebryakov and then, his failure to satisfy his desires leads him to attempt suicide. What then is Vanya's mistake? Despite the familial, social and moral conditions in which he lives, and despite his age and past failures, he assumes that *this time* he could successfully realize his primary internal action and be happy. Throughout the entire play, Vanya's main actions stem from this mistaken assumption. It is only in Act 4, when he begs Astrov to teach him *"to begin a new life... Tell me how to begin... what to begin with"* (p. 153), and Astrov responds, *"we have but one hope. The hope that when we're sleeping in our coffins, visions, maybe even pleasant ones, will visit us"* (p. 154), that Vanya finally recognizes his mistake and comes to terms with the fact that he is destined to a life of frustration, disappointment and suffering until he dies.

c) The *Hubris*[70] of the Protagonist

As we have observed, the primary internal action of the protagonist must be powerful enough to drive the play forward. In addition, we already know that the realization of this action is doomed to fail, despite huge efforts by the protagonist. This indicates that the primary internal action of the protagonist is, by nature, impossible to realize. In classic tragedy, it is always beyond the powers of mortals. Such is Oedipus' attempt to gain sovereignty over his life against the gods' decree, or Antigone's attempt to realize the dictates of her heart, which Sophocles calls *"the god's decree"*,

---

[70] Aristotle's definition of hubris in *Rhetoric* (1379b) is as follows: *"Hubris consists in doing and saying things that cause shame to the victim...simply for the pleasure of it"*. However, this definition is no longer accepted by theatre scholars. Nowadays, hubris is understood to mean "excessive pride or self-confidence" (Random House Dictionary, Oxford Dictionary).

despite Creon's commands. The *hubris* of the protagonist, then, lies in his excessive confidence that he will be able to realize an impossible primary internal action.

Does Vanya, too, suffer from hubris? Is his yearning to turn over a new leaf and free himself from his sense of failure and self-accusation also impossible for a mortal to realize?

Let us try to imagine Chekhov's perspective regarding the primary internal action of his protagonist. *Uncle Vanya* was first staged on October 25, 1899 at the Moscow Art Theater. Chekhov was thirty-nine, single and living in Yalta due to his illness. In a letter to his sister, Marya, approximately two weeks after the opening, he complained:

> "...how boring and silly to go to sleep at nine
> p.m., despondent and angry in the knowledge
> that there is nowhere to go, no one to talk to and
> nothing to work for, since you will never see the
> fruits of your labor anyway! The piano and I –
> two objects that silently exist here in the house,
> wonder why we have been set here, with nobody
> to play us" (Henri Troyat, 1984).

Chekhov was eight years younger than Vanya but was subject to deep feelings of despair and emptiness quite similar to those of Vanya. The passage from his letter indicates that he accepted his fate without a hint of hope. That is to say,

317

despite the great success of the play, he felt as though he had no chance of living a meaningful emotional life. Astrov also seems to reflect the feelings of the playwright:

> *"Those who will live a hundred or two hundred years after us, and who will despise us for having lived our lives so stupidly and tastelessly – they may find a way to be happy"* (p. 154).

Not only did Chekhov feel that happiness was beyond his own reach, but that it was beyond the reach of all human beings in the world, including Vanya.

Thus, Vanya's hubris is rooted in his confidence that he can change his life and spend his remaining years happily and meaningfully, despite his age and despite the fact that he has missed all of his past opportunities. This primary internal action is, in Chekhov's view, beyond the capabilities of a mortal.

Fortunately for Chekhov, writing the play affected him in much the same way as it impacts the spectator. Just as the spectator feels empowered by witnessing Vanya's failure, so was Chekhov empowered by the writing process. A year and a half after the production, he married actress Olga Knipper, who had played Yelena, thereby fulfilling in reality the dream that Vanya never achieved on stage.

Chekhov probably knew that the hubris of the protagonist must be present in every play and that his primary internal action must be impossible to realize.[71] The reason for this may be that the protagonist's primary internal action is also the playwright's, who also struggles unsuccessfully to realize his own deepest impossible yearnings. However, there are also other reasons for this. **A structural reason:** We have seen from the start of the play that the protagonist struggles to alter the apparent status quo, thereby finding himself in conflict with the other characters who wish to maintain that status quo. Without hubris, the protagonist would not dare engage in this battle, nor would he drive the plot of the play. **An existential reason:** Because of the empathy the spectator develops for the protagonist over the course of the play, he himself experiences the primary internal action of the protagonist, which is impossible to realize. Thus, an independent internal action is created in the spectator, which is very similar to that of the protagonist and that, similarly, cannot be realized in his own personal-social context. And so the spectator struggles to realize seemingly unrealizable desires in his own life. Thus, the tragedy offers a higher challenge to the spectator, encouraging him to fight the prohibitions placed on him and contributing to his development as an independent human being who

---

[71] Chekhov saw this clearly in the classic tragedy and also in many modern dramas: Ibsen's *A Doll's House,* and *Hedda Gabler,* and Strindberg's *Miss Julie,* etc.

follows the decrees of his heart. Being so familiar with the weakness and wretchedness of man, Chekhov refused to accept the sentence imposed on him by nature. All of his plays contain this existential mechanism that is meant to exalt and redeem human beings by strengthening their desire to fulfill their dreams.

d) <u>The Cruelty of the Protagonist</u>
Vanya's biography shows that among his main characteristics are his sensitivity and generosity. Even before the play begins, these qualities are manifest in the surrender of his inheritance for his sister's sake, his dedication to Serebryakov's career, his love for Sonya and the close relationships he forms both with Astrov and with Yelena. At the start of the play, before Vanya disrupts the status quo, these noble qualities are still apparent. However, traces of the selfishness that will later hurt Serebryakov are already emerging, most evident in his relentless pursuit of Yelena. In Act 2, Yelena still considers Vanya an empathetic, sensitive person:

> *"Ivan Petrovich, you're intelligent and educated, and it seems you should understand that the world is perishing not because of some thieves or fires but because of hate, rivalry, and all these petty squabbles"* (p. 129).

She even expects him to help make peace among the inhabitants of the estate: *"instead of grumbling, you ought to help everyone make peace"* (p. 129).

320

However, due to his determination to fulfill his primary internal action through his unwavering pursuit of Yelena, Vanya behaves more and more cruelly, mercilessly inflicting pain on others with no consideration of their emotions.

At first, Vanya directs his cruelty toward Yelena herself, saying:

> *"the blood of a water nymph flows in your veins, so then be a nymph! Let yourself go at least once in your life; quickly fall head over heels in love with a water sprite, and plunge head-first straight into a deep, still water..."* (p. 139).

She is aware of his cruelty and responds angrily, *"leave me alone! This is so cruel"* (p. 139). His cruelty increases until the climax of Act 3 when he shoots at Serebryakov intending to kill him. Failing that, he directs his cruelty towards himself and attempts suicide.[72]

Aristotle was, of course, aware of the flaws in the character of the protagonist. He even stipulated

---

[72] The cruelty of the protagonist is ubiquitous in both classic and modern drama: Oedipus plucks out his eyes; Macbeth kills anyone who threatens the crown; Hamlet kills Polonius, drives Ophelia into madness and eventually kills Laertes and Claudius. Hedda Gabler burns Lovborg's book and then commits suicide; Yerma kills her husband, Juan; in *A Doll's House* Nora abandons her children; In *All My Sons*, Chris forces his father to commit suicide, etc.

that the protagonist should be an imperfect person, incomplete and unjust, and that the transition from success to failure should occur not as a result of incompetence and malice, but as a result of a mistake of some sort (*Poetics*, Chapter 13). However, he also explained that the protagonist's own cruelty causes his suffering, which, in turn, arouses the spectator's empathy. The terms that we have defined so far enable us to provide a more exact explanation: the protagonist's cruelty is driven by his need to realize the primary internal action compressed within him. He cannot eradicate this need because its realization is more important to him than anything else, sometimes even more than his own life. It is also important to stress that the protagonist is always aware of the pain he causes others. Vanya, too, is aware of the anguish he causes Yelena and of the panic that he instills in Serebryakov when he fires at him. However, he is driven to fight for the realization of his internal action despite his awareness. If Vanya were unaware of his actions, the pain that he inflicts would not be intentional and thus, he would not be responsible for it. The cruelty of the protagonist is so acute precisely because he is fully aware of it, although, as we are about to see, he acts out of impaired judgment.

What causes the protagonist to lose judgment in relation to both himself and others? Why does he continue to fight even when the extent of the destruction and the pain it has caused are clear to him? In *Elements of Tragedy*, Dorothea Krook cites a passage from Northrop Frye's *The Anatomy of Criticism*:

> *"Something of Nietzche's mountain-top air of transvaluation clings to the tragic hero, his thoughts are not ours any more than his deeds, even if, like Faustus, he is dragged off to hell for having them"* (p. 38).

Frye is saying that in his battle to realize his primary internal action, the protagonist becomes intoxicated by the idea of his salvation. This intoxication causes him to abandon rational judgment and detach his actions from common moral values, consideration, sensitivity, benefit or loss. An infamous example of this is Macbeth, who is so besotted by his desire to achieve sovereignty over his fate[73] that he chooses to embark on an uninhibited killing spree.

The reaction of the spectator to the protagonist's abandonment of moral judgment is rather surprising. The spectator generally continues to feel empathy toward him despite his cruelty. Neither outraged nor protesting, the spectator acknowledges the protagonist's cruelty and even accepts it. This fact clearly proves that the spectator

---

[73] This is an interpretation of the primary internal action of Macbeth, who was told by the three witches that he would become king but not his children, whereas Banquo's children would rise to the throne. From that moment on, Macbeth was filled with an intense desire to determine his destiny independently, killing anyone who threatened his crown.

also abandons his moral judgment, holding fast to the powerful action that has permeated him through his empathy for the protagonist, as if that action were superior to the moral codes of the society in which he lives. Is tragedy, then, designed to subvert the sound, moral and logical conduct of life? The answer seems to be yes. And in so doing, tragedy plays an important role in creating the necessary balance between the moral codes, integrity and logic imposed by society, and the disorderly, lawless and passionate urges that rise within us, demanding satisfaction.

e) The Protagonist's Awareness
To what extent is Vanya aware of himself, his motives and the meaning of his actions? At the start of the play, he is certainly aware of his past failures, his feelings of missed opportunity and despair. In Act 1, he says the following to his mother:

> "I'm forty-seven years old now. Until last year, I tried deliberately, just like you, to obscure my vision with all this pedantry of yours, so as not to see real life – and I thought I was doing the right thing. But now, if you only knew! I lie awake at night, frustrated and angry that I've so stupidly wasted the chance to enjoy all those things that my old age denies me now!" (pp. 121-122)

His words express a sharp, vivid awareness, but he does not admit full responsibility for his state at this point. Later in Act 2, he places the responsibility on Serebryakov:

> *"Oh, how I've been deceived! I worshipped the professor, this pathetic, gouty man, worked like an ox for him! (...) and now? He's retired, and his life's work is now for all to see: not a single page of his labor will survive him, he's completely unknown, he's a nonentity! A soap bubble! And I've been deceived... I see... stupidly deceived..."* (pp. 130-131)

Placing responsibility on others, Vanya enters a state of denial. He is aware of his own responsibility, but at this moment is unable to admit it. Later in Act 3, the denial is in full force. He shouts at Serebryakov, *"you ruined my life! I have not lived! I have not lived! Thanks to you, I destroyed and wasted the best years of my life! You are my worst enemy"* (p. 149). Only in Act 4, after attempting to murder Serebryakov and take his own life, does he admit to Astrov:

> *"...if you could only spend the rest of your life in a new way. To wake up on a clear, quiet morning feeling that you have begun a new life, and that the past is all forgotten, diffused like smoke. (Crying) To begin a new life... Tell me how to begin... what to begin with..."* (p. 153)

Vanya does not overtly admit his mistakes but this speech shows that he wishes to begin a new life. This means that he acknowledges responsibility for his failures and asks for another chance to start over and not repeat the same mistakes. In sum, Vanya's awareness of his situation is sharp and clear at the start of the play, but he is in denial as to his responsibility for his acts. Through the course of the play, his awareness grows and by the end of Act 4, he fully acknowledges his part in his own suffering and that of others.

Vanya also becomes increasingly aware of his effect on others. For example, throughout the play, he disparages Serebryakov, his career and his illnesses; he is enraged at the old man's exploitation and, as we have just seen, blames him for ruining his life. At the end of the play, accepting responsibility for his own failures, he acknowledges the pain he has caused Serebryakov and even promises him the following: *"You'll be receiving regularly the same amount as before. Everything will be the same as before"* (p. 157). Although this compromise does not contain an acknowledgement of Serebryakov's positive qualities, at the very least, Vanya has accepted the reality that Yelena will continue to be his wife. Vanya also becomes increasingly aware of Yelena's feelings throughout the play. At the beginning of Act 3, he is aware of what she is trying to hide and says to her cruelly, *"the blood of a water nymph flows in your veins, (...) Let yourself go at least once in your life..."* (p. 139). At the end of the play, however, he admits that he has done her a grave injustice and asks her forgiveness: *"Farewell... Forgive me... We'll never see each other again"* (p. 157). Vanya's awareness of his relationship with Astrov is especially interesting. At the beginning of the play, we witness the great closeness between them. Vanya invites Astrov into his room in complete trust. Till the end of Act 2, he does not even entertain the idea that Astrov has fallen in love with Yelena. However, between Acts 2 and 3 he becomes aware of it, and, at the beginning of Act 3, he sees Astrov embrace Yelena. Yet, through most of Act 4, Vanya feels close to Astrov because of the doctor's efforts to prevent his suicide. But by the end of the act, he knows that his relationship with Astrov will never be mended, and when Astrov begs for an invitation to let him stay at the estate, Vanya does not respond.

Plot

What methods did Chekhov use to develop the plot of his plays? This is a particularly difficult question to answer because Chekhov's four great plays differ in their plot structures and these differences must indicate different writing methods as well. *Uncle Vanya* stands out from the four in the clarity of its plot structure, which is based on a single protagonist who is compressed with an extremely deep, exceptionally powerful internal action. Thus, it is he who carries most of the responsibility for advancing the plot. In *The Seagull, Three Sisters* and *The Cherry Orchard*, the responsibility for the progress of the plot is divided among various characters and the hierarchy of action determined mainly by the intensity of their primary internal actions. Let us now attempt to discover a few basic principles.

a. Preplanning the Plot
Before setting pen to paper, did Chekhov's preparation include a detailed plot structure? Chekhov described the writing process of *The Cherry Orchard* in a number of letters to his colleagues. On January 20th 1902, he wrote the following to Olga Knipper:

> "I have not written to you about the next play not because I have no belief in you, but because I do not yet have any belief in the play. It has shown a certain glimmer in my mind, like the breaking dawn, and still I myself do not understand what it is or what shall come of it, and it changes daily"

About nine months afterward, on October 1st, Chekhov wrote to Stanislavski saying that his deliberations have not yet ended and that he was still in the planning stage:

> "On the 15th of October I will be in Moscow and I will explain to you why my play is not yet ready. The skeleton exists, but I do not yet have enough energy"

Only on March 1st 1903 did he write the following to Olga Knipper:

"For the writing of the play, I have already laid sheets of paper on my desk and written the title" (quoted from notes to the Hebrew edition of Chekhov's four great plays by A. Schlonski, 1998)

This means that Chekhov planned the play at least a year and three months before writing a single word; whereas the writing itself took about seven months. In mid-October 1903, the play was sent to Stanislavski, but Chekhov continued to make changes during rehearsals in December of that year. What took place during the fifteen months of preparation? In Chapter 1, we discussed how Chekhov devised his characters' dramatic biographies prior to beginning the writing process. We also concluded that without these biographies, he would not have discovered the primary internal actions of the characters, so essential to the writing of Act 1. Chekhov's letter to Stanislavski shows that he had also planned the major events of the play and that prior to writing, he already possessed a complete skeleton of the plot. This skeletal structure was created out of the exploration of the *actions* of the characters and not through general descriptions of their personalities and qualities. Echoes of this can be heard in Trigorin's description of his writing process in *The Seagull*. After meeting Masha, who is in love with Treplev, he makes the following note: *"Takes snuff and drinks vodka... Always in black. A schoolteacher loves her'* (p. 84). Later, in his conversation with Nina, as the dead seagull lies at her feet, he says to Nina:

*"I had an idea... An idea for a short story: a
young girl, like you, has lived by the lake since
childhood; she loves the lake like a seagull, and is
happy and free like a seagull. But a man
happened to come by, saw her and, for lack of
anything better to do, destroyed her, like this
seagull here."* (p. 88)

Just as Trigorin took notes on the actions of his
characters, so did Chekhov, thereby preparing the
plot even before he began writing the scenes.
Chekhov was very likely aware of Aristotle's
suggestion to the playwright:

*"As for the story, whether the poet takes it ready-
made or constructs it for himself, he should first
sketch its general outline, and then fill in the
episodes and amplify in detail ..."* (*Poetics*,
chapter 17)

The Planned and the Spontaneous

The fact that the planning process of *The Cherry
Orchard* lasted a year and three months, while the
writing process took about seven months, attests to
the degree of care that Chekhov took in planning
the play. Clearly the planning process was his main
source of inspiration. However, despite the
meticulous planning, it also seems that Chekhov
allowed himself the freedom to make spontaneous
plot-related decisions as he went along. The writing
process of *Uncle Vanya* is different from that of his
other plays, since it is an adaptation of his earlier

play, *The Wood Demon*. Therefore, the balance between the planned and the spontaneous that characterized the writing of his other plays is not quite evident here. However, since Act 4 of *Uncle Vanya* is fundamentally different from the final act of *The Wood Demon*, it can be regarded as a new creation where this balance can be discovered. An example of a spontaneous plot-related decision can be seen in Astrov's final goodbye scene with Vanya and Sonya, near the end of the act. We have already seen that even before the start of Act 4, Astrov had decided to leave the estate, the disappearance of the morphine bottle being the only factor hindering his departure. Yet, even after the bottle is recovered and he and Yelena have said goodbye, and the servants have brought his carriage to the door, Astrov still does not leave the house. Ever careful and attentive in his extensive preplanning, Chekhov knows that Astrov must leave. But because of his deep sense of empathy for the character, which allows him to feel Astrov's loneliness, he realizes how difficult it is for Astrov to leave Vanya and Sonya, despite the awful pain he has caused them, and, therefore, he delays Astrov's departure. Astrov himself is surprised by the depth of his loneliness -- and Chekhov seems to be surprised too. And even though this discovery occurs at the end of the play, and it certainly slows the pace at a critical moment, Chekhov does not hesitate to include it in the plot, thereby exposing another facet of Astrov's personality hitherto unknown to us.

<u>c) Development of the Plot through the Characters</u>
The above example confirms the importance of the
role of the characters in Chekhov's process of plot
development. In Chapter 1, we defined the plot as
the series of the characters' external actions. We
also made clear that the external actions are the
means by which the characters attempt to realize
their internal actions. This means that in order to
choose the appropriate external action, the
playwright must himself feel the character's
internal actions. Stanislavski was adamant in
stressing the importance of internal actions in
Chekhov's writing:

> *"Chekhov, like no one else, was able to create*
> *inward and outward artistic truth. This is why*
> *he was able to say the truth about men. This*
> *could not be said if they were surrounded on*
> *stage by falsehoods. Chekhov gave the inner*
> *truth to the art of the stage as the foundation for*
> *what was later called the Stanislavsky System"*
> (Stanislavsky, 1956, 350-351)

Observing the examples in the previous paragraph,
it seems that Chekhov developed his plot using the
following mechanism: at every moment in the
scene, he tries to feel the internal action of each
character and asks himself what the character will
do to realize it, i.e., which external action will
enable the character to achieve his goal. We
explored this mechanism in Chapter 3, in the
analysis of the scene between Astrov and Yelena
and we saw that Chekhov did not choose the next

332

external action for the character, but allowed the character to choose his or her own action. This means that Chekhov saw his characters as autonomous entities, each with his or her own inner world and internal actions, and each knowing better than the playwright the appropriate external action at any given moment. At the end of the analysis of the scene, we even reached the conclusion that Chekhov's writing process was dialectical in nature: on one hand, the autonomy of action he affords his characters, and on the other, the basic data of the scene - the convergence and the compression - which he determined ahead of time. In this way, we observed the similarity between Chekhov's writing process and the improvisational process of the actor. In this process, the director determines the basic data for the actors, who internalize the internal actions, and then spontaneously carry out their external actions through the text or physical action. In his writing process Chekhov does the same: sitting at his desk, he determines the basic data for his characters and then carries out their actions spontaneously in his imagination. In this context, it is interesting to cite Aristotle's directions to the writer:

> *"In constructing the plot and working it out with the proper diction, the poet should place the scene, as far as possible, before his eyes. In this way, seeing everything with the utmost vividness, as if he were a spectator of the action, he will discover what is in keeping with it, and*

be most unlikely to overlook inconsistencies."
(Poetics, Chapter 17)

d. The Special Role of the Protagonist

We noted above that since the protagonist's internal action is more powerful than that of the other characters, his part in the creation of the plot is most essential. In fact, the protagonist is the playwright's primary agent in the development of the plot and at each moment, he "consults" him regarding the next step. How does this consultation manifest in Chekhov's writing process? In this play, we detect a great closeness between the playwright and his protagonist. In the letter to his sister Marya, written about two weeks after the premiere of *Uncle Vanya* and cited at the beginning of this chapter, Chekhov admits the following:

> *"How boring and silly to go to sleep at nine p.m., despondent and angry in the knowledge that there is nowhere to go, no one to talk to and nothing to work for…The piano and I – two objects that silently exist here in the house, wonder why we have been set here, with nobody to play us"* (Troyat, 1989, 229-230)

This letter reveals a deep, intimate bond between Chekhov and Vanya. This intimacy allows, Chekhov to "consult" with Vanya continuously about his next choice of action. This 'consultation' occurs throughout the play – whether Vanya is on stage, offstage or between the acts. Of course, we,

334

the spectators, only learn about these consultations through the actions we see onstage.

For example, let us observe the events that occur between Acts 3 and 4. Following the second shot at Serebryakov, Vanya sits, exhausted, and says in despair, *"Oh, what am I doing! What am I doing?"* (p. 151). This is, without a doubt, a very difficult moment for Vanya, as he realizes the severity of his actions and understands that his only way out is suicide. We must surmise that Chekhov feels great empathy for the character he created, who is seized by an overwhelming terror that clutches at the throat of playwright himself and refuses to let go. Even after the act is over, Chekhov continues to see Vanya, sitting in his chair, his heart pounding. He sees Vanya bend over to pick up the gun he had dropped earlier in the scene and place it in his pocket. He hears Vanya say to himself, 'I will go to my room and put a bullet through my head". In his mind's eye, Chekhov sees the other characters in the living room: Serebryakov stunned to silence, Yelena, fainted, in a heap on the floor, and Sonya, kneeling next to Marina. He asks himself: who saw Vanya's actions and who could take the gun from him? The most logical answer is Sonya. He sees her approach Vanya and demand that he give her the gun. Vanya refuses; she is adamant and perhaps even takes the gun from him by force.

These images run through Chekhov's mind again and again. He examines Vanya closely. He sees his determination to put an end to his life and, after a while, he sees him leave the living room, telling Sonya to leave him alone. Where does Vanya go? Chekhov knows that Vanya wants to be alone in order to carry out his plan; he sees him go toward his room. Then he sees the panic-stricken Sonya, who will not let him go alone. She hurries after him. After hearing the gun shots, Astrov enters. Sonya asks his help and both of them run after Vanya. Again, Chekhov follows the protagonist as he enters his room. Vanya sees the medicine bag in the corner and hurriedly takes a bottle of morphine. He lingers for a moment of final self-examination before drinking the draught. Chekhov hears the footsteps of Sonya and Astrov in his own ears. He sees Vanya quickly put the bottle in his drawer and shut it. When Sonya and Astrov enter, Chekhov hears Vanya scream at the top of his lungs, demanding that they leave him alone. The two insist that they know his intentions and they will not allow him to injure himself. Enraged, Vanya leaves the room; the doctor and Sonya follow.

The critical reader can, of course, claim that this description of Chekhov's thoughts and feelings is imaginary and lacks textual evidence. True, there is no proof of these things in the play itself. Even so, just as we the audience are moved by Vanya's plight, there can be no doubt that Chekhov experiences profound empathy for his protagonist and that Vanya's thoughts and emotions permeate his heart and mind. Even if my description lacks factual accuracy, its essence is not far from the truth.

e. The Time-frame of the Plot

Chekhov often extends the plots of his plays over long periods of time. In *The Seagull*, the first, second and third acts occur within a few weeks of each other, but two years pass between acts three and four. In *Three Sisters*, a year and eight months elapse between the first and second acts, and two and a half years between acts two and three. On the other hand, *The Cherry Orchard* opens in May and ends in October of the same year. *Uncle Vanya* begins in the middle of summer and ends in the autumn, less than three month's time. [74]

Chekhov is aware that allowing for a long time span between acts does not afford him the option to develop the events of one act directly into the next. The passage of time blurs the impact of the events of the previous act; some events are forgotten and new events occur that affect the characters with more immediacy. The result is that the accumulation of external actions from one act to the next is weakened. Unlike Chekhov, Ibsen and Strindberg made use of the proximity in time from act to act in most of their plays, allowing the escalation of external action to gather strength and unify the development of the plot. Chekhov's task,

---

[74] Ibsen spreads his plays over the course of only a few days. Strindberg's *Creditors* occurs in one evening and *Miss Julie*, in one night.

therefore, was to create a unified plot despite the extended passages of time between acts. How did he create this necessary unity?

In their plays, both Ibsen and Strindberg created events that are linked to each other through dramatic logic[75], through both external and internal actions. Their meticulous attention to the logical continuity of external actions from act to act compelled them to limit the time frame of their plays. Chekhov assumed that he could maintain the unity of his plots even if he were not to create continuity of the external actions. He accomplished this through sustaining the continuity and strength of the internal actions.

For example, let us observe the transition from Act 2 to Act 3 in *Uncle Vanya*. As noted, two months elapse between the acts and Chekhov knows that the continuity of external actions cannot be sustained over this time. Therefore, he makes no reference to the events of Act 2 when Act 3 opens. He does, however, ensure accurate continuity in his characters' internal actions: both Vanya and Astrov deepen their yearning for salvation through Yelena; Sonya strengthens her desire to be worthy of Astrov's love; Yelena continues her longing to escape her internal trap; and Serebryakov is even more determined to maintain his self-image of a

---

[75] As Aristotle (*Poetics*, chapter 15) defines it, "A given character should speak or act in a given way, by the rule either of necessity or of probability".

man at the height of his masculinity.[76] It is not
surprising that Chekhov prefers to unify the plot of
Uncle Vanya through the continuity of internal
actions. We have already seen that the internal
world of his characters is far more important to
him than their external existence.

Catharsis

Catharsis is one of the most difficult terms to define
in dramatic theory. Aristotle himself probably
offered a full definition of it in his *Poetics*, but
unfortunately, as Halperin points out in her *Poetics.
Translation, Introduction and Commentary* (73), the
definition has been lost, leaving us with only a
partial understanding:

*"Tragedy, then, is an imitation of an action that is
serious, complete, and of a certain magnitude; in
language embellished with each kind of artistic
ornament, the several kinds being found in separate
parts of the play; in the form of action, not of narrative;
through pity and fear effecting the proper purgation
(Catharsis) of these emotions."* (*Poetics*, chapter 6).

Over time, scholars have offered various conflicting
views. Does catharsis take place in the spectator or
the protagonist?[77] Halperin claims that catharsis is a

---

[76] These internal actions are described in much detail in the
beginning of Chapter 3.

[77] An informative review of the different approaches to
catharsis can be found in "On Aristotle's Philosophical
Poetics" by Yoav Rinon (2003, 78-87)

process that the spectator undergoes: *"In my opinion, this term indicates a process of mental and spiritual catharsis that occurs in the spectator of the tragedy as an aesthetic experience"* (74).

Zmira Heisner and Karin Hizkiya adopt a similar definition, inspired by Jonathan Lear (2001): *"An emotional relief from the burdensome feelings experienced by the audience from the outset, as a result of the possibility of the tragic events becoming a part of its life"* (2006, 121).

Another perspective is offered by, Gerald Else:

> *"The catharsis is not a change or end-product in the spectator's soul [...] but a process carried forward in the emotional material of the play by its structural elements, above all by the recognition. The tragic protagonist is the one who needs to undergo a purgation process. The recipients of the play must recognize that while the action that the protagonist has carried out is indeed terrible, he is not rendered impure since his intent was not malicious."* (1957, p. 439)

Despite this dispute, it is important to recognize that these two processes – one experienced by the spectator and one by the protagonist - are essential to the tragic experience. Therefore we will define two[78] separate terms: **The spectator's catharsis is** a

---

[78] In the comparison we made between the process that Vanya undergoes and that which Chekhov himself experiences, we

mental and spiritual cleansing process that occurs inside the spectator during the play. **The protagonist's catharsis is** a mental and spiritual cleansing process that occurs in the protagonist as a result of his actions during the play.

What is the relationship between these two terms? To understand how they relate to one another, we will use a term familiar in our daily discourse - empathy. Merriam-Webster defines empathy as

> "the action of understanding, being aware of, being sensitive to, and vicariously experiencing the feelings, thoughts, and experience of another of either the past or present without having the feelings, thoughts, and experience fully communicated in an objectively explicit manner".

In the world of drama, where the relationship between spectator and character is an important structural element, a more precise definition is called for: empathy is a communicative process that occurs between the spectator and the character, which allows the spectator to experience the character's emotions. When an actor portrays a character accurately and authentically, the

---

suggested the possibility of the existence of a third catharsis: A mental and spiritual cleansing process that the playwright undergoes while writing the play. Aristotle did not discourse on this process, although Plato mentions it. *Viz.* Spiegel (1971, 105).

spectator undergoes a spontaneous process of deciphering the character's feelings – not necessarily on a cognitive or conscious level - as if they were his own. This differs from 'identification' which in general conversation refers to an agreement with or support for an idea, or a person who fights for it. Thus, whereas identification occurs on a cognitive level, empathy is an emotional response.

If the playwright's purpose is to generate a catharsis in the spectator, then he must create a catharsis for the protagonist, which will in turn generate through empathy the intended catharsis in the spectator. In other words, the protagonist's catharsis is always the cause of the spectator's catharsis.

Vanya's Catharsis

What, then, is the catharsis, the mental and spiritual cleansing, that occurs in Vanya throughout the play and particularly in the final act? The terms that we have defined thus far allow us to provide a clear answer: the catharsis that Vanya undergoes at the end of the play is his final and absolute surrender of the realization of his primary internal action. This surrender is cleansing because it allows Vanya to liberate himself from his hubris and his obsession to achieve his primary internal action at any cost, and of his cruelty toward himself and others.

Vanya's surrender is the final step in his emotional process. Until almost the middle of Act 4, he is still fighting tenaciously to realize this primary internal action. At the end of his last openhearted conversation with Astrov, he still hopes:

> *"(…) if you could only spend the rest of your life in a new way. To wake up on a clear, quiet morning feeling that you have begun a new life, and that the past is all forgotten, diffused like smoke. (Crying) To begin a new life… Tell me how to begin… what to begin with…"* (p. 153)

At this point, he still believes that a new life is possible. He continues to seek a way to begin again. Only at the end of the act does he recognize his utter defeat. He completely gives up any hope of a new life and returns to his customary duties, with the clear knowledge that he will continue to live his old life in frustration, despair and suffering.

The process of surrender, however, does not occur all at once. Chekhov hints at it earlier in the play. In Act 1 Vanya says, with slip of his tongue, *"It's good weather to hang yourself"* (p. 122). Clearly at that moment, it has crossed his mind that one day he may have to give up hope for a new life. However, a real acceleration in the process of his surrender takes place at the end of Act 3. After missing his second shot at Serebryakov, Vanya sinks into a chair in despair and the gravity of his situation seeps into his consciousness. Even so, at the beginning of Act 4, he continues to battle with whatever power he has left. Only after Astrov adamantly says that all hope is gone, does he finally give up.

The Catharsis of the Spectator

In optimal conditions, when the actors portray the characters' actions fully and the spectator avails himself of the full viewing experience, he will very likely empathize with Vanya and experience with him the surrender of his primary internal action. The spectator may also experience a complete surrender of his own hopes for a new life, and an acceptance of the internal death to which he is sentenced. As mentioned at the beginning of this chapter, however, in comparing the nightmare experience with the experience of viewing a tragedy, the spectator's process of surrender ends, not with Vanya's despair, but with the strengthening of his own struggle to realize his autonomous desire to turn over a new leaf in his life. The spectator becomes more determined to forget the past with all its failures and mistakes and overcome his anxieties to realize his own primary internal action. Thus, the catharsis of the spectator engenders the affirmation or re-affirmation that fortifies his belief in the power of man and his sovereignty over his own life.

Vanya's Tragic Process

According to the definitions we have offered above, the catharsis of the protagonist brings about the catharsis of the spectator. The main question for the playwright, who wishes to create this double catharsis, is how to first create the catharsis of the protagonist. Let us examine the structure of Chekhov's plot to see how he brings Vanya to the catharsis – to the final surrender of his primary internal action.

It is not surprising to discover that Chekhov adheres to the five stages of the Aristotelian tragic plot.[80] At the same time it should be noted that Chekhov himself avoided calling the play a tragedy or even defining the genre of the play at all. He gave it the subtitle, *Scenes From Country Life.* Clearly he consciously structured the play after Aristotle, but his loathing of labels led him to eschew them. He preferred to discuss the meaning of his play, rather than its 'category'.

a) The Fatal Mistake (*Hamartia*)
In our discussion of the protagonist we saw that Vanya's fatal mistake was his obsessive struggle to realize his primary internal action. Owing to poor judgment and despite his age and string of past failures, Vanya assumes that he will be able to turn over a new leaf in his life and win happiness despite the familial-social-moral status quo in which he lives.

b) The Terrible Act (*Deina*)
According to Halperin, *"the terrible act is the second stage in the tragic action sequence. It is the mistaken*

---

[80] Aristotle's *Poetics* chapters 11-14.

action that causes the hamartia. Its unique quality is
that it results in a terrible, disastrous and irreversible
action" (1978, 95). This act is *"a terrible action that*
immediately and unavoidably creates suffering of the
character that it is done to" (Sternberg, 1973, 26), and
for the protagonist as well.

While Vanya's hamartia appears as his obsessive
struggle to realize his primary internal action, the
deina or the carrying out of the hamartia through
external action, is his dogged pursuit of Yelena. It is
clear throughout the play that this pursuit is
harmful to Yelena, threatens her and causes her
pain. It also causes much suffering for Vanya. This
pursuit is not a 'terrible act' as Aristotle describes
it: "terrifying, disastrous, irreparable and lethal.[81]
Rather Chekhov chooses a less lethal act for his
protagonist, more typical of modern drama.[82] In its
essence, however, it is equivalent to the act as
defined by Aristotle: *"...the tragic incident occurs*
between those who are near or dear to one another"
(*Poetics*, chapter 14). While Vanya and Yelena are
not blood relatives, they are very close to each
other. On this matter, Halperin writes:

> *"[...] despite this fact, it does not seem as*
> *though Aristotle limited the terrible act to blood*

---

[81] Among the 'terrible acts' listed Aristotle: Medea who kills
her children; Oedipus who kills his father and sleeps with his
mother.
[82] In *The Seagull*, Treplev compulsively pursues Nina
Zarechnaya; In *A Doll's House*, Nora hides the forgery of her
father's signature from her husband.

relatives only, and it should be assumed that had
he seen Shakespeare's tragic play "Julius
Caesar", he would have included in his examples
a terrible act committed among close friends,
whose relationship can be much stronger than
that of blood relatives" (1978, 100).

c) The Reversal of the Situation (*Peripeteia*)
The reversal of the situation is *"the third stage of the*
tragic action sequence [...] A border point in which the
direction of occurrences is reversed to its opposite"
(Halperin, 1977, 35). As Aristotle himself articulates
it: *"Reversal of the Situation is a change by which the*
action veers round to its opposite" (*Poetics*, chapter 11).
This definition is quite vague and makes it difficult
to discern whether the reversal occurs at the level
of the internal or external action.

> *"the exact meaning of the peripeteia has sparked*
> *a long debate among interpreters [...] This dual*
> *meaning lies in the question, 'is the reversal a*
> *reversal of action, of the sequence of events, or is*
> *it a reversal of the goal that the character aims to*
> *achieve?'"* (Halperin, 1978, 103).

To conclude her detailed and informed discussion,
Halperin writes:

> *"A reversal is a tragic change in the sequence of*
> *actions and events, which involves the tragic*
> *reversal in the intention of the person who*
> *carries out the actions. Until the reversal, this*
> *person acted to achieve a specific goal, but from*

the reversal that foiled this goal, the person acts to fulfill an opposing goal." (Halperin 1978,105)

Thus, Halperin states that the reversal must occur not only in the character's action, but also in his intention. In our terms, the reversal is a change of direction in the protagonist's primary internal action and in the series of external actions that follow.

The reason for the reversal that occurs after the deina – the terrible act - is the suffering that it causes both the protagonist and the affected characters. In order to understand the reversal in *Uncle Vanya*, let us look at Act 3. At the start, Vanya is still in stubborn pursuit of Yelena. Does the reversal begin when he returns to the living room with the bouquet of roses and sees her in Astrov's arms? (p. 144). Despite both his and Yelena's suffering, Vanya does not reverse his external action at this point, nor does he alienate himself from Yelena. His verbal response does not indicate a reversal in his internal action: *"Helene, I saw everything, everything…"* (p. 145). A moment later, Serebryakov and his entourage enter for the meeting. During the meeting, Vanya's battle with Serebryakov intensifies and, despite his new insights, he leaves the room in order to fetch his gun. He then shoots at Serebryakov who has followed after him and shoots at him again after the old man flees to the living room. These external actions are still part of Vanya's struggle against

Serebryakov and hence do not yet constitute a complete reversal. The reversal manifests only when Vanya sinks into a chair, exhausted, and in his despair, says, *"Oh, what am I doing! What am I doing"* (p. 151). As a result of the intense suffering Vanya has caused himself and those around him, he has undergone a dual change – both in his internal action and in the external actions that flow from it. His new, internal action is to free himself from the obsessive desire to begin a new life, and his external action, which is understood by the spectator only in retrospect, is his attempt to commit suicide. At this crucial moment, the meaningful reversal has occurred. However, at this point, the reversal is incomplete and still reversible as we can see in Act 4, when Vanya tries once again to turn over a new leaf after all. It is only after his openhearted conversation with Astrov (p. 153) that he arrives at the final surrender of his life, thereby completing the protagonist's necessary mental and spiritual cleansing process

d) The Recognition (*Anagnorisis*).

The term 'recognition' has also been interpreted in many ways, which Halperin details extensively (1978, 106-126). According to Aristotle, it is *"a change from ignorance to knowledge, producing love or hate between the persons destined by the poet for good or bad fortune* (*Poetics*, chapter 11). Many scholars posit that recognition is the discovery of "certain details" about a person or "certain circumstances"; others make a narrower claim that *"tragic recognition is the discovery of the identity of a dear blood relative"*

(Halperin, 1978, 107). Other perspectives widen the definition and state that recognition is the discovery of broad fields of circumstance, of whole situations that were not previously recognized, or previously mistaken (Halprin, 1978, 109). Aristotle himself ties recognition to reversal: *"The best form of recognition is coincident with a Reversal of the Situation"* (*Poetics*, chapter 11). Humphrey House states that *"the discovery of the reality of the matter is the fearful awakening from a state of unknowing, which is the essence of the [fatal] mistake"* (House, 1961, 98). In other words, *recognition is the sudden awareness of the fatal mistake*. This broad definition allows for a more inclusive understanding and in terms of our discussion of *Uncle Vanya*, we can say that anagnorisis is the protagonist's recognition of his failure to realize his primary internal action. And, as prescribed by Aristotle, it occurs at the same time as the reversal. Moreover, the reversal occurs *as a result of* the recognition. In other words, the reversal of the direction of the protagonist's external action is the result of his recognition of his fatal mistake, i.e., the recognition of his failure to realize his primary internal action.

Chekhov implements this process in *Uncle Vanya* most precisely, although, as previously mentioned, he extends the events from the end of Act 3 to the beginning of Act 4. We have already described Vanya's moment of recognition at the end of Act 3 when he misses his second shot at Serebryakov and sinks into a chair (p. 151). At this moment, Vanya recognizes his failure to achieve his primary internal action and that there will be no new beginning. Now, his new internal action becomes the desire to put an end to that obsession. The result is a new *external* action - to commit suicide. But as we assumed in Chapter 4, when he tries to pick up the gun, Sonya and Astrov intervene and Telegin hides it in the cellar. Ironically, Vanya fails even in committing suicide.

e) The Suffering (*Pathos*)

According to Aristotle, *pathos* "*...is a destructive or painful action, such as death on the stage, bodily agony, wounds, and the like*" (*Poetics*, chapter 11). He consistently uses the term 'action' in order to stress that this suffering must occur on stage and not 'in the wings'. The main sufferer is, of course, the protagonist, and his suffering is the very last stage in his tragic journey. This definition distinguishes the early anguish of the protagonist from his final pathos. In every tragedy, the protagonist carries out actions that involve suffering as detailed in our discussion of the terrible act. As early as Act 1, Vanya suffers as a result of Yelena's rejection. And the more he is rejected, the greater is his suffering. His misery increases in Act 3, first, when he sees Yelena in the arms of Astrov, then when Serebryakov announces his intention to sell the estate, and most poignantly, when he twice misses shooting Serebryakov. These painful actions do not yet constitute the pathos that Aristotle refers; they are important to the structure of the plot, building one upon the other culminating in Vanya's recognition and reversal. The Aristotelian pathos is the suffering which follows the recognition and the reversal, and is a result of them.

What, then, is the pathos in *Uncle Vanya*? After the recognition and the reversal at the end of Act 3. Vanya sits down, exhausted, and recognizes that his chances of starting a new life are nil. He experiences intense internal agony: he has lost Yelena, he knows that he will never marry or have a family or enjoy any intimate relationship. His helplessness forces him to decide to end his life and thereby end his pain. Then, at the start of Act 4, when he and Astrov engage in an honest conversation (p. 153), Vanya overcomes his suffering, changes his mind about ending his life and returns the morphine bottle. He even expresses a belief that he will be able to start anew after all and begs Astrov to teach him how to do this. The fact that for this brief moment Vanya overcomes his anguish indicates that he has not yet reached his last and final suffering - the Aristotelian pathos.

It is only in the last, openhearted conversation with Astrov that Vanya arrives at the final recognition of his failure. Only then does he finally surrender the idea of a new life and decide to return to his work and to his old meaningless life. In his final words, he turns to Sonya and says, *"Oh, my child, I'm so miserable! If you only knew how miserable I am"* (p. 160). Vanya knows that in his surrender he has sentenced himself to a fate worse than death. He will live in despair, frustration, pain, shame and self-hatred until his death. This resignation to a wretched life, so evident even before the curtain falls, is the pathos described by Aristotle. Although Chekhov does not strictly adhere to Aristotle's instruction that the final suffering must involve either death or severe physical injury, he sentences Vanya to a death far worse: internal death, the death of a man's spirit, a suffering far greater than physical death.[84]

Chekhov was ambivalent about the fundamental dilemma involved in ending a play. In a letter to his friend Aleksei Sergeyevich Sabourin he wrote: *"He who finds a new ending to a play will start a new age"* (Chekhov, 1964, 117). .

Plays in which the protagonist suffers an internal death were, of course, written before *Uncle Vanya* (Ibsen wrote *A Doll's House* in 1878/9), but it seems as though Chekhov saw this as a "new kind of play", differing from classic tragedy in which the protagonist undergoes physical death. In his early works (*Ivanov*, 1887; *The Wood Demon*, 1889; *The Seagull*, 1896) the protagonists die after committing suicide. When Chekhov wrote *Uncle Vanya*, however, a new version of *The Wood Demon*, he had discovered that internal death is far more effective

---

[84] The protagonist physically dies in all of Shakespeare's tragic plays. In the modern drama, on the other hand, many playwrights have employed a strategy similar to Chekhov's. Some examples of this are Ibsen in *A Doll's House*, Tennessee Williams in *A Streetcar Named Desire* and Brecht in *Mother Courage and Her Children*.

than the physical death. This holds true is the two plays that followed, *Three Sisters* and *The Cherry Orchard*.

As mentioned above, Aristotle defines Pathos as *"a destructive or painful action, such as death on the stage, bodily agony, wounds, and the like"* (*Poetics*, chapter 11). This definition conflicts with the intuitive interpretation that sees suffering as a sensation of pain, rather than as an action. What, then, does Aristotle mean? When King Oedipus plucks out his eyes, he carries out an external action that causes great pain. Internally, however, Oedipus' true pathos is his pain over his defeat by the gods, and his recognition of man's powerlessness over fate. One could say that the physical pain of plucking out his eyes is, in some way, intended to alleviate the internal pain of his defeat, in the way that the Antigone's suicide is intended to alleviate the pain of her defeat. Thus, it seems that Aristotle's pathos-related suffering refers to a deeper, inner pain, caused by the complete and final surrender of the primary internal action. So it is with Vanya as he completely and finally surrenders his hope for a new life. What then is Vanya's external action, which expresses this suffering? He busies himself with the accounts of the estate, which is a physical action. His external action is to commit "internal suicide" by returning to a deadly routine. His internal action, then, is his effort to accept the spiritual death sentence he has imposed upon himself.

The Reform

The above discussion illustrates the extent to which Chekhov adopted the Aristotelian tragic structure in his writing of *Uncle Vanya*. A detailed examination of the plot in his three other great plays leads to a similar conclusion, despite their structural differences. For Chekhov, the Aristotelian structure ensures the greatest effect on the audience. He recognizes that in an artistic creation, catharsis is by far the most powerful instrument to transform the lives of his spectators. Chekhov's desire for reform is no secondary matter. In all of his plays he has created characters who wish to change their lives. Treplev and Nina in *The Seagull*; Vanya and Astrov in *Uncle Vanya*; Olga, Masha and Irina in *Three Sisters*; Liubov Andreyevna and Trofimov in *The Cherry Orchard*. For the most part, the desire for change rests in the personal life of the character, but in some instances, there are intimations of social reform, as well.

It is interesting to note that the Russian censor made only two deletions in *The Cherry Orchard* before the play was staged in Moscow's Artistic Theater. In Act 2, Trofimov says the following (Censored words appear in bold lettering):

> *"They're all so serious, with stern faces, and talk only about important things, but while they go on philosophizing,* **right in front of our eyes, the workers are eating garbage, sleeping without pillows, thirty or forty to a room, and everywhere bedbugs, stench, dampness,**

moral squalor... " (Notes to the Hebrew edition p. 249)

Later, he continues:

> *"Anya, just think about it: Your grandfather, your great-grandfather, and all your ancestors owned serfs; they owned living souls (...)* **Owning lives has distorted all of you – those who lived before and those who are living now – to such an extent that your mother and you and your uncle don't notice anymore that you're living on credit, at the expense of others, at the expense of those whom you don't even let in past the entryway...** " (p. 252)

Astrov also expresses distinct social attitudes in *Uncle Vanya*:

> *"The third week of Lent, I went to Malitskoe where the epidemic was... spotted fever... In the huts, peasants are side-by-side, all in a row... The filth, the stench, the smoke, the calves are on the floor next to the sick... And the pigs are there, too..."* (p. 117)

Later, he speaks even more explicitly:

> *"I understand if the cut-down forests were being replaced by new roads, railways, plants, factories, and schools – the people would be healthier, richer, more intelligent – but there's*

nothing of the sort! The same swamps and
mosquitoes exist in the district, the same
impassable roads, abject poverty, typhus,
diphtheria, fires..." (p. 142)

Chekhov himself provides a clear, personal
example in his life of his social agenda:

> *"It happened near the end of 1889. After reading*
> *at random notes his brother Mikhail had made*
> *during a lecture on criminal law, Chekhov*
> *muttered, "all our attention is centered around*
> *the criminal until the moment he is sentenced,*
> *but when he is sent to prison, we forget him*
> *entirely. And then, what occurs in prison?"*
> *From that moment, he was restless. (...) He had*
> *to shake off the gossip chatter and the false*
> *glamour. To reach the ends of Syberia. (...) And*
> *to look at the real suffering in the face: The*
> *suffering of those sentenced to physical labor,*
> *jailed on Sakhalin Island in the Pacific Ocean."*
> (Troyat, 1989, pp.109-110)

Soon afterward, in April, 1890, despite ill-health,
Chekhov, traveled to research and document the
sufferings of the prisoners on Sakhalin Island for
seven months. On his return to Moscow, he
reported his findings with unprecedented and
compelling force. Though there are many
interpretations regarding this journey Chekhov's
main motive was, undoubtedly, his desire for
reform. However, it is not surprising that after his
journey, Chekhov discovered that his journalistic

efforts had little effect and that his most meaningful contribution would be through his writing. Despite this realization, he did not stop his extra-literary activity. In 1899 he instigated the establishment of a clinic for tuberculosis patients in Yalta. Troyat writes:

> "It took him two months to gather the forty-thousand rubles he needed for the erection (of the clinic). [...] During his generous activity, there was nothing that saddened him more than the indifference of a few, so-called "advanced" people, who would not help him, with the excuse that the task was too difficult to have a chance of success" (p. 230).

Chekhov learned from Aristotle that for the spectator, catharsis arises out of empathy for the suffering of the protagonist, and this empathy strengthens his own yearning for change and transformation. What is the transformation that Chekhov desires through Vanya's catharsis? Let us examine Halperin's conclusion of her analysis of the structure of the tragic play:

> "The recognition should arrive at the end, after the reversal, which opens the protagonist's eyes and shows him his mistake. Then the awful suffering comes, the tragic suffering of a man who stands in front of the wreck of his life with the knowledge not only that it cannot be rectified but that he himself is responsible for its damage. This crushing, heart-wrenching pain leaves the

sufferer helpless. All that he can do is suffer and
cry out – Not for help, since nothing can be
saved, but a terrible cry of horror, a shocking cry
of despair, which expresses the helplessness of a
man faced with the results of his actions."
(1978, 135)

This is also the cry that echoes in Vanya's silence as he sits broken-hearted next to Sonya, attempting to calculate the expenses of the estate that he has failed to manage. He recognizes his responsibility for his mistakes and he knows that he can never correct them. In order for the spectator to fully experience Vanya's surrender of the struggle to start anew, and to become fully aware of his recognition of his failures, he must pass through the five stages of the tragic process with Vanya: the fatal mistake, the terrible act, the reversal, the recognition and the suffering. Chekhov portrays these five stages precisely so that the spectator can experience them completely, in due succession. Chekhov knows that only in this way can he ensure that the spectator shares Vanya's catharsis, and that as he leaves the theater, the dramatic paradox described earlier would take place: that Vanya's surrender would redouble the spectator's determination to continue the battle that Vanya had lost. In this way, Chekhov empowers his audience and encourages them to create for themselves a life that is more emotionally full, more satisfying and more meaningful. He expects his audience to struggle for their right to be happy, whether their battle occurs internally, with people close to them, or in the society in which they live.

Glossary

This glossary is intended for the use of readers who wish to review the definitions of the terms included in this book. These are not Chekhov's terms, but those developed by the author for the purpose of discussion of Chekhov's plays and the process of playwriting in general.

Action:
Internal Action
The desire of a character to alleviate its emotional distress. This action occurs in the heart of the character, unlike the external action, which occurs in its mind and body. It is important to note that the internal action is **not** the character's emotional distress, but rather the character's yearning to alleviate this distress. In order to identify the internal action, we must first identify the emotional distress. The spectator also does not decode the character's internal action in his mind, rather feels the action through empathic response.

External Action
A deed carried out by a character's mind and body, which has meaningful cause and effect. The character is aware of this deed and of its reason, and is able to estimate its results. The character is aware of its external action: The character thinks about it; it is a part of the character's tactics and strategy. The character's will is a part of its external action, as well as being the reason for this action.

The spectator will, at times, figure out the character's external action while it is being carried out, and, at times, he will realize it only after it is completed. It is necessary to distinguish between a character's external action and its physical action, which is a means to accomplish the external action.

Primary Internal Action
The desire of a character to alleviate its primary emotional distress. It stems from the main, meaningful emotional distress in the character's life in the period prior to the beginning of the play. The character's primary internal action is the reason for most of the character's external actions over the course of the play.

Physical Action
An action carried out by the character's body.

Antagonist
A character in conflict with the protagonist (see definition below).

Catharsis of the Protagonist
A process of emotional and spiritual cleansing that the protagonist undergoes through his actions.

Catharsis Of the Spectator
A process of emotional and spiritual cleansing experienced by the spectator of the tragedy during the play.

Compression of a Scene
This is the combined collection of the characters' internal actions at the beginning of a scene. For the playwright it is essential to establish precisely the compression of a scene either before or during the writing process, in order to create the conflicts within the scene and to further the plot.

Conflict between Two Characters
Refers to the clash of the characters' **internal** actions, fundamentally differs from the clash in the characters' external actions.

Convergence of a Scene
The collection of the characters' external actions at the beginning of a scene. For the playwright it is essential to establish the convergence of the scene in order to develop its plot.

Dramatic Biography of a Character
The series of events in the life of a character, which creates its primary internal action. For the playwright, the construction of the protagonist's dramatic biography is an essential stage in the planning of a play since, without it, there is no rationale for the character's primary internal action, without which there is no justification for the plot.

Dramatic Irony
When the playwright or the director establishes dramatic situation in which the spectator knows more about the character than character knows about himself.

Dramatic Paradox
The contrast between the protagonist's failure to realize his primary internal action and the empowerment of the spectator to realize the same internal action in his own life.

Dramatic Yield
The deepening of a character or his/her relationship with other characters, or the strengthening of the plot, resulting from the dramatic choices of the playwright or the interpretation of his interpreters.

Empathy
The communicative process which enables the spectator to experience the feelings of a character on stage, or enables one character on stage to experience the feelings of another.

Generating Event of a Play
An event that motivates the characters of a play to begin to realize their primary internal actions. This event usually occurs before the beginning of the play, but it may occur once the play has begun.

Generating Event of an Act
An event that causes the characters to intensify the realization of their internal actions at the beginning of an act. It usually occurs before the act has begun, or immediately at its beginning.

Hubris of the Protagonist

The protagonist's hubris is his excessive confidence in his ability to realize an impossible primary internal action.

Ironic Text

A text that contains a contradictory, undermining, satiric or ridiculing subtext.

Plot

The sequence of external actions of the characters in a play.

Plot Gap in a Scene

The gap between the external actions of the characters at the beginning of a scene and their external actions at its end. This gap determines the development of the plot and its pace.

Protagonist

The main character in a play, possessing the most powerful primary internal action. The protagonist experiences conflicts with the other characters and by his actions thrusts the plot forward. The protagonist pays the heaviest price for his mistakes and eventually experiences catharsis.

Realization of an Internal Action

This is the process by which the internal action is realized by means of external actions.

Soliloquy

When a character turns toward the audience in order to speak his innermost thoughts and feelings. The other characters in the play cannot hear this text. A soliloquy is different from a monolog in that it is directed towards the audience with the other characters unable to hear it. A monolog is most often directed toward another character in the play.

Shift

A change in the external actions of a character in a scene. Such a change is essential in every scene. The more shifts the playwright provides, the larger the plot gap and the quicker the pace of the plot.

Sub-text

Subtext is the unspoken or underlying meaning that the character cannot or does not wish to express openly, hoping that the listener will understand it, nonetheless. Subtext is often mocking, hurtful, complimentary or in some way contradictory.

Bibliography

Abercrombie Lascelles (1979). *Principles of Literary Criticism*. Greenwood Press Reprint; New edition

Aristotle, *Poetics*. *Translation, Introduction and Commentary* by Sarah Halperin (1977). Bar-Ilan University, Israel

Aristotle, *Poetics*. Translated by S.H. Butcher (1961) Hill and Wang

Aristotle, *Poetics*. *Translated, with an introduction, notes and an essay by Yoav Rinon*
(2003). The Hebrew University Magnes Press, Jerusalem

Bentley, Eric (1964). *The Life of the drama*. New York: Atheneum.
--- (1987). *The Playwright as Thinker*. New York: HBJ Publishers.
--- (1987). *Thinking About the Playwright*. Northwestern University Press. Chicago

Buchanan, Scott (1975). *Poetry and Mathematics*. Chicago: University of Chicago

Chekhov, Anton; (2011). *Anton Chekhov, Five Plays*. Marina Brodskaya (trans.), Stanford University Press, 2011, Stanford, CA .

Chekhov, Anton (1964). *Letters on the Short Story, the Drama, and Other Literary Topics*, Selected and Edited by Louis S. Friedland. London: Vision Press.

Else, Gerald F. *Aristotle's Poetics: The Argument*. Harvard University Press.
Cambridge, MA, 1957)

Esslin, Martin (1977). *An Anatomy of the Drama*. New York: Hill and Wang.

Fergusson, Francis (1953). *The Idea of a Theater*. New York; Doubleday Anchor.

Freud, Sigmund (2010). *Beyond the Pleasure Principle*. CreateSpace Independent Publishing Platform

Freud, Sigmund (2005) On Dreams, with introduction by Eran Rolnick. Ressling, Tel Aviv

Frye, Northrop (1975). *The Anatomy of Criticism*. Princeton: Princeton University Press.

Golomb, Harai (2001). "Chekhovian Plays Viewed Through Implied Actors", *Russian Theatre Past and Present*. Idylwild, CA: Charles Schlacks Publisher.

Goldberg, Leah (1968). *The Russian Literature of the 19th Century*. Hapoalim Publishing House, Tel Aviv

Halperin, Sarah (1978). *On The Poetics by Aristotle*, Bar-Ilan University, Israel.

Heisner Zmira and Heskia Karin (2006) *Experiencing Theatre: Introduction to Drama and Theatre*. The Open University of Israel.

House, Humphry (1956). *Aristotle's Poetics: A Course in Eight Lectures*. London: Rupert Hart-Davis, 1958.

Krook, Dorothea (1970) *Elements of Tragedy*, Yale University Press.

Lear, Jonathan (2001). "*Katharsis*", *Aristotle's Poetics*. Amelie Oskenberg-Rorty ed. Princeton: Princeton University Press.

Magarshack, David (1972). *The Real Chekhov*. London: George Allen & Unwin Ltd.
--- (1980). *Chekhov the dramatist*. London : Eyre Methuen.

Megged M. (1976) *The Modern Drama*, Massada, Israel.

Styan J.L. (1971). *Chekhov in Performance*. Cambridge: Cambridge University Press.

Spiegel, Nathan (1971). *On Aristotle's Theory of Poetry*, Bialik Institute, Jerusalem.

Stanislavski, Constantin (1963). *Creating a Role*. Translated by Elizabeth Reynolds Hapgood. Geoffrey Bles. London.

Stanislavski, Constantin (1956). *My Life in Art.* Translated by J.J Robbins. Meridian Books. New York.

Troyat, Henri (1988) *Chekhov.* Ballantine Books

Wallis, Mick and Shepherd, Simon (1998). *Studying Plays.* London: Arnold Publishers.

Note: All books published in Israel are in Hebrew.